the CATCHER

by Gary Towers

&

Genevieve Frazier

Published by: Gary Towers & Genevieve Frazier

Acknowledgments and special thanks:

Cover art and design by Ted Burn tedsart@bellsouth.net

Edited by Kristopher A. Bryant kbryantpc@gmail.com

eBook formatting by Laura and Frank

TABLE OF CONTENTS

Chapter 1

An Elementary Abduction

On the day Lisa Collins disappeared the fifth-grader was walking the eight blocks from school to home. Once a week, Lisa's mother allowed the purchase of a smoothie, and today her treat was a blueberry-banana from Indigo, a Caribbean restaurant five minutes from home. The child was smiling as she anticipated a bonus to her allowance for the A she received on her history paper.

It was one of those flawless, warm and sunny March days that seemed to make up for all the preceding cold and rainy ones. As Lisa traversed the worn, concrete sidewalks, uneven from the nudging roots of century-old trees, birds chirped and squirrels scolded one another.

Although she was barely eleven years old, Lisa Collins resembled a budding thirteen. She was tall for her age, lean, blonde, blue-eyed and had high cheekbones. Someday she should be a very shapely and attractive woman. Her clean, good looks were complemented by an expression of high intelligence but naïveté. Lisa was a striking, beautiful child.

The girl wore navy culottes with a red hemp belt, knee socks, brown Sperry's, a starched white dress shirt and pale blue windbreaker with the sleeves rolled. Public schools had a mandatory dress code, which Lisa preferred. Her mother could never afford the designer clothes many of Lisa's classmates sported. Uniforms were an equalizer. On her shoulders was the school mandated, transparent backpack, which held books, a notepad, several binders, an assortment of pen and pencils and the essay marked A+ that she was to have her mother sign. The essay assignment: *Who Was Rome's Greatest Emperor, and Why?* Lisa chose Marcus Aurelius, a brilliant leader who ruled one hundred and fifty years after the birth of Christ. Marcus Aurelius had not believed in any of the gods widely accepted at that time, but permitted his people to worship them and patronize the numerous temples built in their honor. One Aurelius quote that struck Lisa as particularly sage advice was, "Thou wilt find rest from vain fancies if thou doest every act in life as though it were thy last." Lisa had closed her essay with that thought, and her teacher, Ms. Matthews, had written beside it, "Superb! If you practice this throughout life, you will be a happy person, and go far, indeed!" *I wonder how far I will go, and what will I become? I hope I do not need to struggle like my mother.*

Lisa missed her father, but never complained. Her mother worked long hours to provide for them. Sometimes Lisa would wake at night and hear her mother crying.

As Lisa continued along the winding sidewalk, she readjusted the backpack. Once at home she planned to

2

change into gym shorts for a quick jog through the neighborhood. She would be entering middle school next year and hoped to qualify for the track team. Sports, she thought, would provide the best opportunity to travel.

She turned off the sidewalk along North Highland onto Amsterdam Avenue, a quieter side street. Lisa glanced at her mobile phone. She was glad to have the phone, even if it were not the latest technology that most of her friends possessed. Not even a touch-screen! But for the child's safety, her mother deemed the additional monthly expense a necessity.

Fifty yards ahead, beside a small, half-acre park that had one set of swings and two weathered wooden benches, Lisa watched a white, four-door car slowly pull to a stop. The driver's door opened, and a policeman got out. No, a policewoman! The officer was quite tall and wore a dark uniform, sunglasses and black hair twisted up under the hat.

The policewoman had a clipboard in one hand. She looked around, saw Lisa, raised the other hand in greeting and began walking toward her. Lisa frowned slightly, wondering what was going on. She suddenly hoped that no house had been burglarized or, worse, no one she knew had been hurt. She was constantly reminded by her mother to keep doors locked and do not speak with strangers. When Lisa and the policewoman were ten feet apart, the officer smiled and in a pleasant voice asked, "Do you live around here?"

"Yes." Lisa decided a uniformed officer could not be included in her mom's category of individuals she should consider a stranger. Her mother was such a worrier.

"Do you know anything about a gray puppy?" The policewoman glanced at her clipboard. "A gray, sheepdog puppy named Rex who lives on this street?"

Lisa was surprised at the policewoman's beauty. She had not seen many officers up close, although they now had one posted at her school. But he was male. The lady looked strong and had a tan. Lisa wondered what was wrong. "Yes, that's the Anderson's dog. They live a block away."

"Hmmm," the policewoman answered, looking again at the clipboard. "We weren't aware of the family name. We had an anonymous call this morning reporting mistreatment of a puppy named Rex by neighborhood boys." Lisa knew Rex. She had been playing with him just yesterday, and he had torn her shoe. Her mother was displeased when she saw the hole but said it was about time to replace them anyway. The policewoman looked at Lisa and smiled again. "If you've got a minute, I'd like to ask you some more questions."

"Sure." She liked Rex and hoped he was unhurt.

"Great." The officer looked around. "Let's sit over here." She gestured to one of the wooden park benches set a few yards back from the sidewalk.

Following her to the bench, Lisa heard a thin screech of rubber and turned to see Timmy Taylor, the nine-year-old

4

neighborhood terror, flash by on his bright-green mountain bike. Timmy was, in her mother's words, "a continuous live wire," a wild child who always seemed to get into trouble. Her mother said Timmy just needed more structure than some kids.

As they sat on the bench, Lisa placed her backpack on the ground and set the smoothie between herself and the officer, who suggested, "If you have paper in your backpack, why don't you get it out? You may want to take some notes yourself."

"That's a good idea."

As the girl turned aside and dug into her backpack, the officer lifted Lisa's drink, shifted a bit to the left and dropped two colorless pills into the cup. She snapped back the lid and stirred the straw around a few times.

Having located her pad and pen, Lisa turned back to the lady and looked at her attentively. The officer smiled and gave the drink to Lisa, who innocently drank the now tainted beverage. Lisa wondered why this woman made her a bit nervous, but the smoothie was a comforting friend.

"How big is Rex?" the officer inquired.

"He's this high," Lisa said, holding her hand a foot above the ground. Lisa looked at the shiny badge on the chest and noticed the name: Sgt. Shaw.

"Have you ever played with Rex?"

"Yes." What was that smell on the policewoman?

"Is Rex nice? Does he bite?"

5

"No," said Lisa, "I mean yes, he's nice, and no, he doesn't bite. Is Rex OK? Is he hurt?" Lisa then identified the smell as coconut, plus something else. What was the other smell? And why was her head suddenly getting heavy? And what were those spots floating over her eyes?

"Young Rex will be fine," the policewoman replied, "he's at the vet's. Here—you can read his condition in the report."

The officer extended the clipboard to where Lisa could see a white-gloved finger pointing to the center of the page. Lisa began to read the document, but the words were blurring on the page. The policewoman glanced up and down the street. The boy on the bike had passed, and no one else was in sight. Only one house, directly across the street, had a view of this particular place in the park, and the front of the house was almost entirely blocked by overgrown shrubbery.

The drug now in Lisa's system was rohypnol, commonly known in street slang as "roofies." Tasteless and odorless, it takes effect quickly, robbing the victim of memory and control. Lisa yawned, closed her eyes and leaned back onto the bench, in a deep sleep the moment her head touched the wood. The officer reached and cradled the child gently in her arms. She smoothed Lisa's blonde hair. Among other things, the policewoman was an accomplished actor.

The woman glanced up and down the street, pulled her cap down tight and carried the girl into a lush stand of bushes six paces behind the park bench. She laid the unconscious girl on the ground next to a very large sailing carryall. She pulled open the long zipper and removed a heavy black body bag, one that resembled those used in combat for cadavers, but this bag had been custom-altered with dozens of two-inch square air vents covered with black mesh netting. Air could circulate into the bag, but light did not reflect out, shielding the bag's contents.

The policewoman carefully tucked the child in the body bag, zipped it shut and then removed her entire uniform.

The woman's body was spectacular: she was five feet eleven inches barefoot, with long muscular legs, firm round breasts, the buttocks of a sprinter and a flat, hard stomach. She whipped off the black wig to reveal a silky bun of lush, dark-red hair. She shook the hair loose, gathered it in a ponytail and secured the thick locks with a black cotton scrunchie.

She quickly changed into gray, sweat-stained jogging attire, stowed the police clothes and props in the sail bag and zipped it closed. The woman picked up both bags and peered out of the bushes. Another kid on a bicycle—no, it was the same boy from before—raced down the road again.

Now in the guise of a runner, she emerged from the bushes and walked to the white car. On her arm carrying the body bag, clearly-defined muscles bulged and bunched, but no effort showed in the woman's face, balance or gait. She might have been carrying an attaché case instead of a bag containing an eighty-pound body. She used the remote to pop open the trunk, swung both bags inside, shut it quietly, got inside the car and turned on the ignition. The woman checked her face in the rearview mirror, opened her Gucci purse, removed a peach colored Lancôme lipstick from its case and unhurriedly applied it to her mouth. She closed the lipstick case, replaced it in the purse, looked at her face once again in the mirror and whispered, "An elementary piece of cake."

The woman put the car into gear, drove slowly up the street and turned left onto North Highland Avenue. She smiled, knowing that her job would be complete in another seven hours. Sometimes the catches did not go this smoothly. But the pay was superb.

Off the coast of Georgia lies one of the world's great vacation secrets where people escape for secluded getaways. The four Golden Isles are St. Simons, Little St. Simons, Jekyll Island and Sea Island. The finest of the four, if wealth and exclusivity define such, is Sea Island. It is noted for Sea Island cotton and The Cloister hotel; the former is considered to be the world's finest cotton and the latter one of the world's finest hotels.

Originally opened in 1928, The Cloister is a world-class hospitality legend. A Five-Star, Five-Diamond hotel, it is an exceptional blend of luxury, discretion, style and Southern charm. The Cloister and Sea Island are a first choice for the quiet rich, making it one of the last places one would expect to encounter an abducted child, which is precisely why it was chosen as a rendezvous site.

At 9:18 p.m., one-half mile from The Cloister, the white Ford Crown Victoria cruised up the long curving driveway of the PalmAire Marina, a private boat facility. It was lined on both sides by massive live oak trees, so called because of their perennial greenery. Under the clear, star-filled sky, the trees formed a thick canopy that shaded the Ford from pale moonlight. The car slowly pulled into a visitor parking slot. As the engine turned off, the only prominent sounds were a chorus of tree frogs and scattered pockets of mild laughter from the pleasure vessels and yachts moored at the 150-slip marina.

The driver door opened, and the tall woman emerged, wearing her third and final costume of the day: white Bermuda shorts, sky-blue cotton tank top, gold snake belt, gold earrings, thin gold choker necklace, wedding band, platinum Ebel wristwatch and white, rope-soled sandals. As she walked around the car to the passenger side, a young Latino security guard casually observed her movements. The guard saw that the woman looked damn good, even in this half-light. Her shiny red hair was pulled back in a ponytail,

9

Ray-Bans on top of her head, not frou-frou sunglasses like he saw on a lot of the women here. She was tall, muscular and definitely an athlete. Maybe even professional.

As the woman opened the passenger door and leaned in, the guard stared appreciatively at her rear. She removed a sleeping child from the front seat, and he mumbled, "Shit, married." Still, some of the married ones like to play, too, he knew from experience.

The woman lifted the unconscious Lisa Collins, cradling her head on a bare, golden shoulder. Lisa wore new clothes: a London Hard Rock Cafe t-shirt, khaki shorts and her hair had been died jet black. The woman reached into the car, retrieved four colorful helium balloons, wrapped the strings around one of Lisa's wrists, reached in again, removed the large sail bag, kicked the door shut and walked toward dock number II. On each balloon was the logo of Six Flags Over Georgia, an amusement park west of Atlanta.

Through compact binoculars, the security guard studied the two. They've spent a day at Six Flags, and the kid is exhausted, but not the mother. She looks so strong as if she could go all night long. He'd give it fifteen minutes and then check out Dock II to see who was sleeping and who wasn't.

He watched the mother carry her child up the gangplank and enter the large yacht. On the top deck, a big person, outlined against the moonlit sky, took a long pull on

10

a cigar, its tip glowing bright orange. Then the figure went below.

The guard continued his rounds. Ten minutes later he returned and saw the woman, alone, emerge from the yacht. The engine turned over just when her foot touched the dock, as if on cue. The tall woman strode across the parking lot as the yacht slowly pulled away and began a gradual turn out to sea. A gentle swell lifted the 80-foot vessel and moonlight blazed briefly on the stern's yard-tall gold letters. *The Samaritan.* Powerful twin diesels engines gave a pleasant deep rhythm, slowly pushing the yacht toward the horizon.

The woman had observed the guard watching her and was displeased to see him reappear. She casually walked past the white car, pretending to examine the nails of one hand, as if to show that was her only concern. She approached a black Jaguar convertible, unlocked the trunk and placed a large aluminum case inside. She had confirmed its contents before leaving the yacht; two hundred fifty thousand in U.S. currency, alternating packs of fifties and hundreds. She removed a stack of fifties and placed it into her purse. As she closed the trunk, the security guard approached. The husky young man tipped his hat, smiled slightly and said, "Good evening."

"Hello." *That's right, Pedro, look me over.*

"I noticed you arrived in a different car."

"That's right. I was just dropping off our daughter." The woman cocked a thumb over her shoulder. "My ex got

11

to keep the boat and I got one house and this car. I use a rental in heavy traffic." *Ask me one more question, Pedro, and...*

"Will you be staying here tonight?"

The woman smiled and answered, "No. But I could stay another fifteen minutes."

The guard's eyes narrowed. "I do not understand."

The woman looked down at the man's groin. "Hop in the car," she cooed. "I don't bite. At least not very hard."

That was all the guard needed. He opened the door and got in, thinking this seemed too good to be true, but he was not about to pass up the opportunity. Amid the noise of settling in the seat, he unsnapped the pistol holster at his right hip, closing the car door as he popped the snap, to mask the noise. *Just in case...she may be loco.*

The woman started the car, put it in gear and slowly accelerated toward a position in the parking lot where one of the oak trees cast a large dark shadow on the asphalt. She was not concerned with the security camera. The car was not hers, and she had no intention of getting out.

As the Jaguar crept into the shadow, the guard buckled his seatbelt.

"Oh no, honey," the woman purred, "unbuckle that belt. And the two on your pants." She put the car in park and turned off the engine. "I don't know what your love life has been like lately, but it's been lonely for me. My lawyer kept telling me to act like a nun until the divorce was final.

And when I'm like this, I like the gentleman to go first. Then he's more relaxed with my turn."

She opened her purse, removed a small tube and squeezed K-Y jelly onto her palm. She rubbed the lubricant onto her hands, looked at the man's lap and said, "Let's see your friend salute."

The guard quickly unbuckled his holster and trouser belt. As he unzipped his fly and felt inside, the woman replaced the tube into her purse, reached up to his head, removed his cap and dropped it onto the backseat. She kept her right hand on the back of his neck, massaging it with thumb and forefinger. She put her left hand on his left thigh and slowly moved it upward. When the man looked down, she struck in a flash: she whipped the DuPont fishing line over his head and yanked the two small oak pegs that tightened the garrote.

As they all do, the man reached up to his neck with both hands, which made it easy for her to slip his pistol from the holster. While he struggled and bucked in the car, the woman used her right elbow to hammer his head until the man blacked out. She started the dashboard digital timer and placed two fingers on the base of his left carotid artery. When the digital readout hit 4:38, the pulse began to flutter. At 4:50 the weak vibration ceased.

She drove out of the lot and onto the roadway. Ten minutes later she spotted the familiar long bridge over one of the many marshes that connect Sea Island with the mainland.

13

It was a popular dumping ground for small refuse. No car lights were visible in each direction. She quickly braked to a stop, dragged the man from the car, tumbled him over the bridge rail and heard the heavy splash. The body slowly settled, partially submerged, face down. What looked like a log began to animate and move to the corpse. The drought in this part of the country had made the alligators a problem on golf courses during the day and many other places at night. The large reptile swam to the fresh meal, quickly snapped down on the carcass and pulled it under the black water. The woman trotted back to her car, settled in, retrieved the cap from the rear seat and flung it out the passenger window, Frisbee style. The woman instantly had the car moving again. She chuckled. A hungry alligator in a drought is almost as good as cremation.

The woman pressed buttons that undid the latches of the convertible roof and flipped the switch that made the soft-top accordion up and down. She opened a bottle of Herra Dura Silver tequila and poured a generous amount into a black yachting mug. From a small cooler, she removed a lime wedge and squeezed it over the Herra Dura, dropped the wedge in, picked up three ice cubes from the cooler, put them into the mug and slowly stirred the cocktail with a slim, tan, manicured forefinger. After a few revolutions, she removed the finger and licked off the tequila.

She dialed a pre-set number in her Bluetooth, and while the phone rang, took a long drink from the mug. The full moon, now almost directly overhead, shone down brighter, picking up the highlights of the car's interior and exterior chrome, the woman's gold jewelry and the ice cubes that sparkled in the moonlight. On the Jag's speakerphone, a woman's voice politely asked, "Ritz Carlton, Buckhead, how may I help you?"

"Room 2212, please."

As the operator rang the room, she turned up the volume on the speakerphone.

"Hello." A man's voice.

"Hi, lover, I'm on the way. I should be there in about five hours."

Two hundred and seventy miles away, a man in bikini underwear was performing dips on a chrome skeletal exercise rig in a corner of a large, luxury suite. The lights in the room were muted, the man's back was very broad, his waist and hips were trim, long black hair was in a ponytail, and as he slowly continued the dips, he talked into the phone piece cradled around his ear. "Take your time. We're not going anywhere." Over the man's shoulder, the lights and buildings of Atlanta could be seen through the suite's window, twenty-two stories above the street.

"Just don't start without me," the woman responded. "I want you both fresh."

"We'll wait." The man stopped exercising and dropped to the floor. An exquisite black woman brought the man a drink, draped a large white towel around his neck and softly kissed his free ear.

The kidnapper was Fionna Marceau, 35 years of age. She was French-Malaysian. She had one of the most unusual jobs imaginable and was paid extremely well for her professional efforts because of the great risks. But Fionna enjoyed taking risks.

Repeatedly expelled from schools, she ran away from home at fourteen, and for the next dozen years worked as a nude dancer in Amsterdam and a prostitute/call girl wherever and whenever the whim hit her. For several years, she had been the mistress of an older, well-to-do Spanish restaurant owner. At 29, just when she believed the thrill in life was over, she met Rafael Garcia. Rafael was a former bodybuilder who had drifted into organized crime. Over a fifteen-year career he had made a name for himself as an international freelance troubleshooter. One afternoon while traveling in Madrid he met Fionna at a sidewalk cafe. They had dinner and soon were inseparable. Within a few weeks, both had confided to each other about their respective pasts, and those revelations increased the mutual attraction.

Initially, Rafael Garcia was reluctant in taking his new girlfriend on assignments, but she relished helping him and worked like a tireless Cyborg. Her ruthlessness soon began to chill even Rafael Garcia. Unlike Fionna, he never did really develop a taste for blood as an alternate lubricant in bed. When he learned about a new organization that was looking for women with singular qualifications, he told Fionna, anticipating she might be interested. This might be the ruse he needed to smoothly extricate himself from the relationship. He was truly fond of Fionna, but after a year he had decided the only way to truly make a clean break would be to kill her. And he did not really want to do that. If nothing else, it might tarnish his professional status.

Rafael Garcia informed Fionna about the new group, De Blauwe Organisation. At first she was mildly interested, then intrigued, and ultimately, with Garcia's help, granted an audition. She was immediately hired.

De Blauwe Organisation was created to be a very special enterprise. It was founded, in short, to be a custom-ordered kidnapping service.

Several times a year, Fionna was hired to "Catch" various individuals, with her price rising with each success. She was a natural hunter and actress, a physical wonder and she loved her work. She took it very seriously, focusing upon the new profession with amazing passion. She was always in superb shape. Soloflex, pedaling a weighted bike, gymnastics and even boxing were parts of her physical regimen. In boxing, she preferred to spar with men. Worthy female sparring partners were difficult to meet. She was skilled with weapons and did not hesitate to use them.

Each abduction was planned with infinite care, and most were usually variations of just a few themes. She would stalk the target, working out a strategy along the way, frequently using a variety of costumes. She had, on occasion, impersonated a homeless person, park ranger, UPS driver, cripple, a Jehovah's Witness canvassing door-to-door and, on one truly well-orchestrated job, had posed as a stranded motorist, complete with a McDonald's counter girl uniform. After each job, she would develop an enormous sexual appetite, and she thoroughly enjoyed herself immediately following projects.

Now, with the wind whipping her crimson ponytail, the liquor heating her insides and the wonderful sensation building between her legs, Fionna Marceau was on her way to enjoy another mini-vacation of sex, drugs and alcohol. It helped clear her mind of any guilt that may invariably rise to a level of consciousness.

After only five years, Fionna Marceau was the top Catcher of De Blauwe Organisation, an illicit, totally immoral Dutch-based group whose name, roughly translated, meant The Blue Company.

Chapter 2

Safely Retired?

The two men had one illegal deer, and for a few seconds they debated whether to try for another. Emotion won over intelligence.

Their mediocre minds were greatly impaired, a result of alcohol and marijuana.

It was just after 4:00 a.m., temperate weather for March, and the moon made hunting easy in the remote north Georgia woods. Easy because a hard winter had the deer less shy in their search for food. Both men were in their twenties, both had served prison time and they did not seek venison—they collected antlers year round. A few racks were found on the ground, shed some months earlier, but they were more interested in harvesting the trophy antlers still attached to healthy bucks.

The nearest lake home was at least a mile away, but just to be safe, they left the guns in the truck and were using bow and arrows. The men only spoke when necessary and then in low whispers. They used sign language: one finger tap to the shoulder meant, "Stop and listen"; two taps meant, "I think I see a deer"; three taps meant, "There is a deer." If caught by the Department of Natural Resources, it meant confiscation of their possessions and truck, plus fines and maybe jail, since the two were on parole.

The poachers had been hunting since midnight; now they squatted and lit their fourth joint. As was the custom on their nocturnal poaching treks, the last stick was the largest— this one the size of a man's thumb. Forget the fact that deer can smell the smoke.

Tired but calmed by the new cannabis glow, they began the arc that would complete a large circle back to the truck. One man carried a red spotlight, which illuminated their way but was invisible to deer. The other man had a powerful halogen light. When they spotted a buck, the halogen would display the prey, and the "shined" animal would freeze. A sole deer staring at a sudden, surprising cold headlight.

Fifty yards ahead, the trees thinned into a slight clearing, and in the center of the clearing, glowing by silver shafts of moonlight, stood a grand prize buck that made both men stop and gawk. It was a gigantic beast with a 12-point rack that somehow had not yet been shed or lost in a fight. The first man drew back to shoot. The second man unsheathed his Bowie knife, flicked on the bright blaze of the halogen spotlight and pointed it at the animal. The buck turned its massive head with majestic horns. The archer let fly, a silent arrow flashed into the light beam, grazed the stag's rump, made a whip-thrash noise far beyond in the trees and the buck bolted and vanished in three bounds.

"Cock-sucking bastard," knife man hissed, "your aim's always for sh…" The first man quickly grabbed the angry partner. He straightened his arm to two o'clock, where he had redirected the white light, and the sidekick's jaw dropped.

The huge, looming house was unlike any structure either man had seen. It appeared to be made of wood, but one would have to touch it to be sure. It was three stories high, with a sharply angled roof. There were half a dozen dark windows on the back, lake side. The house had been painted with curving slashes of olive, dark green, brown and purple, each hue barely discernable in the shifting shadows from trees and moonlight. The man blinked to focus his impaired vision as he played the bright beam across the house. The men were transfixed. What kind of place is this? The house was camouflaged to blend in perfectly with the woods and both men were amazed they had come so close without seeing it sooner. It was enormous. No lights were on. There were no sounds or apparent movement in or around the building. Was it occupied?

They had the same thought. A home this magnificent outside should yield very fine things inside.

Archer man whispered, "Goddam! Fuck that buck! You do a loop around the house. I'll watch here."

The man withdrew a large hunting knife from its sheath, buttoned his black pea coat, swept the light back and forth ahead and began to slowly circle the residence.

Now another set of eyes focused sharply on the men, thinking there might possibly be trouble. For over an hour, the two antler poachers had been stalked by a curious local. The third stalker sat and patiently waited to see what the pair would do.

The surveying poacher completed his loop, whispered to his partner and the two walked up the steps of the deck, crossed the wide teak expanse, stopped at the large bank of sliding glass doors and the man with the flashlight pressed it against the glass.

The beam slowly played across the leather furniture, marble coffee table, oriental rugs, wood paneled walls and floor to ceiling bookshelves. The men marveled at the opulence in the soaring great room.

Knife man kicked the glass softly, then harder, to test its strength. As he stepped back to ponder how to break in, the flashlight beam reflected off the sliding glass door back into the third stalker's eyes. A pair of large, scarlet eyes the two poachers had never seen on a human.

Both men spun around, and the beam illuminated the stalker.

It was a huge, muscled Airedale, one on the largest that ever lived. The animal sat on its haunches, calm, motionless. Knife man extended his blade, started walking to the Airedale and hissed, "Git! Git, fuckin…" In an instant the dog bounded onto him.

Powerful vise-teeth mauled knife man's wrist, tore once and flung the blade loose, where it rang off a glass door. The men screamed in terror, knife man's wail an octave higher to reflect the pain, as he was jerked down onto the cold, hard deck. The Airedale found a fresh grip on knife man's bicep and began to violently thrash the entire body left and right. The arm was paralyzed by the clamped jaws, and the three functional limbs began to frantically scrabble on the decking. His partner dropped bow and flashlight, clopped across the deck, leapt the steps, hit the ground running and tore off through the woods.

The dog switched to the other arm of the terrified man, seized the left shoulder and used it as a fulcrum to horribly wrench the body to and fro with unbelievable speed. The man's soprano screams altered to a higher, siren pitch of utter lunacy. After several seconds of vigorous scything, the Airedale released the man and paused, briefly. Then the dog took off after the other man, who could be heard bumbling in the woods.

The Airedale's greater speed soon placed man and animal just forty yards apart. The dog slowed to an easy trot, following the panicked, doped poacher.

In a couple of minutes, the man reached the Ford F-150 and dug in his pocket for the keys. He whispered curses and began to soil his dirty jeans. He grasped the master key, rammed it into the lock and jerked open the door. But he was not allowed in.

The man's back was to the dog. The Airedale sprinted, did a strange leap with a half twist, landed on its thick-furred back, slid along the ground for eight feet and when the dog's head reached between the man's legs, the muzzle lunged upward and snapped onto the man's groin. The man was instantly jerked to the ground. His head whipped backward, the moon lit up the straining muscle cords of his neck, his mouth opened wider than it had ever been, though no sound came out, and his hands gripped both sides of the dogs thick neck and held on as the Airedale thrashed his body in a left-right ride.

The wrenching lasted half a minute. The dog released, flipped upright on all fours, walked backwards several feet, sat on its haunches and stared at the man. The poacher was on his side, in a semi-fetal curl, motionless, while the dog remained and began to lick the fur on its chest, waiting for the second poacher to reach the truck.

Ten minutes later, the doped, lumbering body of a man with the voice of a crying child reached the pickup. One useless arm hung limp at his side. The other arm was curled and cradled against his chest. It took several minutes for the crippled poachers to help each other into the cab, compose themselves and slowly, erratically, drive off.

The dog took a last look at the receding tail lights of the truck, then began to briskly trot home. Halfway there, sleeping next to a pine log, lay a young, calico feral cat. The dog stooped to a crouch, silently crept to the feline and gently

24

pawed at its tail. The cat raised its head, yawned, opened its eyes, and darted away as if it were on fire.

The dog trotted back to the huge lake home, crawled under the expansive deck and lay onto its bed of fresh cedar shavings. The Airedale pushed its muzzle into the wood curls and fell asleep within seconds, knowing its master would be there soon.

Clayton Russell arrived home that morning just after 11:00 a.m.

He was reclining on the blue leather sofa, feet propped up on the 4- by 6-foot, gray and white block of marble that served as a coffee table. His beloved friend, Winston, slept at his feet. Deep in the center of the custom cut stone table was his personal safe, which would open when he dialed a telephone number. Nobody would guess the 4.8 ton marble slab, with rough sides and mirror-polished top, was also a safe. It was waterproof, fireproof and would require a crane to move, should anyone determine it was more than a rock.

Russell was enjoying a Macanudo Portofino cigar, a premium stick that burns for over an hour, while reading a small, salty excerpt from the complete works of Benjamin Franklin. The founding father and inventor of bifocals, the lightning rod and rocking chair had written a letter to a young male friend, advising him to take an older mistress rather than a younger one. Of the reasons Franklin cited in favor of

25

mature women, one struck Russell as being particularly
astute:

*Because in every Animal that walks upright, the Deficiency of the
Fluids that fill the Muscles appears first in the highest Part. The
Face first grows lank and Wrinkled; then the Neck; then the Breast
and Arms; the lower parts continuing to the last as plump as ever;
so that covering all above with a Basket, and regarding only what
is below the Girdle, it is impossible of two Women to know an old
one from a young one. And as in the Dark all Cats are grey, the
Pleasure of Corporal Enjoyment with an old Woman is at least
equal and frequently superior; every Knack being by Practice
capable by improvement.*

Russell made a mental note to pass this knowledge on
to a younger male friend. He tossed aside the book, took
another puff of the Macanudo and was watching the floating
smoke when his telephone rang. He kept a land line, because
the mountainous terrain interfered with cell towers.

"Hello?"

It was Pamela Waters, former lover and one of the
best private detectives, female or male, with whom he had
worked. Her single fault was the insidious way she insisted
on always complying with the law, a habit acquired during
the first year she spent studying at Emory School of Law in
Atlanta. She walked out, never to return, after a professor
belittled her in Civil Procedure class. "Good evening,
Pamela. What do I owe the pleasure?"

"Clay, you owe me plenty, and you owe it to yourself
to get off your ass. Come work with me again. I have a
matter in London that may prove fascinating."

26

"I'm retired, remember?" Pam could get so excited. She always meant well but could be quite pushy when she got a bee in her bonnet.

"At least hear me out."

"OK, I'm listening." When she finished, Russell promised to consider it and call her back later.

"Don't forget." She hung up, convinced he would not call. She was worried. He had been a recluse for two years now.

Russell looked across the room at his best friend, Winston Churchill Downs, the largest Airedale from a Washington State litter four years prior. Was that blood on his muzzle? Russell examined the dog's head but could locate no wound. "Come on boy, let's go wash your face, you've been into trouble."

A few minutes later, with Winston by his side, Russell jumped off the deck and pausing to stretch, began to jog. Russell wore blue track shoes, white socks, purple cotton gym shorts and a bright yellow t-shirt. The two ran a motley workout trail several times per week. Their course lay along a rough path that wended 1.9 miles through dense, sparsely populated woods that surrounded the blue-green waters of Lake Rayton. The trail angled around mountainous terrain punctuated with a variety of exercise stations. The first: a six-foot long horizontal bar suspended between two trees 9.5 feet above the ground. Russell jogged to the bar, jumped, grabbed it with both hands, and performed a kick-thrust that elevated his body waist level to the bar. He flipped over forward and hung for a few seconds, stretching. As his mind wondered, he could hear Winston running through underbrush forty or fifty yards away. Russell was intrigued by Pamela's latest quest. She always seemed to be on some mission.

One hundred yards away, a lone jackrabbit began to lope toward the lake's edge. There were no trees on the baseball diamond-sized green slope. Visibility was clear for the larger animal as it crouched and watched the rabbit perform a final hindquarters hop that brought it to the lake for a drink. Fifty yards distant, a quartet of ducks sat on the calm lake, quacking at something. The hare watched, but its tongue didn't pause. The still, cool water tasted sweet and refreshing, and for a few moments, the only sound was the tiny plip-plip-plip of lapping. Then, very slowly, the mirror surface of the water to the right of the hare changed color: a shadow smoothly drifted over that small part of the water, a dark reflection about the size and hue of a football. The rabbit eyes cut down to the lake's surface and saw the new reflection in the water. The startled animal instantly twisted to his right and looked into the eyes of Winston. The rabbit instantly bolted away and sprinted uphill; it leapt, landed, leapt again, executed lightning cuts that ran 90° against its previous direction, and repeated various sprints again and again. The wild, desperate running pattern continued for six minutes and, incredibly, the 95 pound Airedale followed every step of the way. Winston weighed twelve times that of the hare, yet the smaller mammal could not outmaneuver him.

The rabbit was losing stamina. It performed one last 90° turn and staggered ten yards back to the lake, very close to where the chase had begun. Exhausted, its hind legs collapsed.

Winston slowly began to close the eight feet separating them. His large jaws opened, the long red tongue lolled to one side and enormous white teeth were outlined against the wet, blue-black gums. The smaller animal's heart thumped so hard that a small portion of fur on its chest jumped with each pulse. The hare began to emit a weak, shrill cry. Winston leaned closer, then used his nose to slightly nudge the rabbit and began licking its face. With the game over, the dog began to trot home.

Russell reached the second station which consisted of a large, rectangular trampoline and a sixty-foot climbing grid net attached to a pair of trees. After performing flips, twists and gainers, he climbed up and over the net and continued to run. Winston met up with his master and bounded along the trail to the third station. It was a fifty- foot span of overhead bars that Russell traversed monkey-style.

Russell's black hair was streaked with grey. His body glistened with perspiration as the morning rays of the sun shone in low angled shafts through the path that opened onto a rocky outcropping. He had exercised diligently since twelve, and now, approaching 45, his body was a physical testament to many thousands of hours of exercise. But the tanned hide was covered with scars from past trauma, including knife wounds and four bullet holes. He felt older than his age. And frequent nightmares caused him to awaken covered with perspiration. No, he did not miss certain aspects of his shelved profession.

Clayton began to slowly jog a slight incline, where the last hundred feet of the trail ended in a granite bluff. Fifty feet below was the calm surface of Lake Rayton. Russell stopped and scanned the lake as Winston began to dance, anticipating his master's next move. Russell ran forward and dove off the cliff, executing a slow, graceful jackknife before his body sliced into the cold water. Winston shook his head, barked once, then raced to the edge and leapt, head held high, and hit the surface in the precise spot Russell had, chest cleaving the water and spouting up two symmetrical wedges. Man and dog surfaced simultaneously and began a slow, relaxed swim to the dock. During his cool-down backstroke, he thought about Pam's continual prodding. Perhaps he should go back to work. Her case sounded fascinating.

Chapter 3

His Holiness

Pamela bypassed the intrusive TSA check-in at Hartsfield Airport, including customs, and boarded the private jet.

She was on a Bombardier Global Express XRS. With a 94-foot wingspan, it carried a crew of four, reached maximum altitude at 51,000 feet and had a range of 6100 miles. Being the only passenger, she felt a bit like royalty. Her invitation to Russell to join her was declined. The man remained in hermit mode.

An Asian male crew member in a navy uniform approached, took her beverage request and promptly returned with bottled water, no fizz. Looking aft, Pamela could see two spacious beds. A mid-Atlantic nap might counter the jet lag. She detested long flights and the multiple time zone changes. She walked through the tasteful forward galley, picked up an apple from a glass fruit dish and examined the luxurious living room. The carpets were of white wool, large easy chair seats were tan leather and the interior walls were laced with cherry wood trim.

A masculine voice came over the speakers.

"Seatbelts please, Ms. Waters. When you hear the chimes, feel free to move anywhere about the craft, including the cockpit. Thank you."

Pamela tossed her bag under the conference table and strapped in. Ten minutes later, with the stereo headset on and the selector dial set to Sleep, Autumn Crickets, she reclined, laced fingers across her lap, closed her eyes and reflected on the past few days. Within minutes she was asleep.

After the touchdown at Heathrow, the red carpet treatment continued.

A Mercedes limo pulled up ten paces from the steps of the Bombardier. The driver smiled, nodded politely, took her bags and held open a door. "Welcome to London Ms. Waters. I trust your flight was comfortable?"

"Yes, thank you."

In an hour they were at the Ritz Carlton Hotel, desk check-in was waived and two bellmen escorted her to The Arlington Suite: 860 square feet of plush drawing room décor, enhanced by British flourishes—fresh flowers in discreet sconces and a dozen newspapers and magazines fanned across two coffee tables. Pamela tipped a bellman and marveled at the opulent, mink-lined accommodations. The extravagance instilled a twinge of guilt, knowing how so many struggled just to feed their children.

She opened her luggage and unpacked. After a lengthy, hot shower, she put on a conservative navy Brooks Brothers' suit and crème colored open toed heels by Nina. Her client would meet her in another suite two hours from now. Pamela walked downstairs, sat at a small table in the regal Palm Court and ordered a glass of port. She tried to calmly sip it, still a bit awed by who she would soon meet.

Pamela had been born into a privileged class and traveled extensively, but she had never met this client. All communication had been by telephone. Some priceless antiquities had vanished, along with an aide. The antiquities are so rare that they cannot be sold to a typical 'fence' and could be anywhere on Earth, since the obnoxiously rich can move between borders with impunity. Soon she would meet Tenzin Gyatso, His Holiness, The Dalai Lama. In Tibet, she had read, he is also called *Gyalwa Rinpoche*, which means 'Precious Victor,', or *Yishin Norbu*, which means 'Wish-fulfilling Jewel.'

Pamela ordered another wine and reflected on the chain of events that brought her here. An emissary of the Dalai Lama had initially contacted her via e-mail. She subsequently met another representative at the Marriott Marquis in Atlanta. She was told the spiritual leader had considered a number of detectives before selecting Pamela Waters. She surmised that it was her extensive travels in Tibet and China, together with the ability to speak Mandarin Chinese, China's official language, that distinguished her from other Western investigators. Her Mandarin was rather poor, but it allowed her to travel alone and with confidence in China.

Pamela looked at her watch, rose from the table and felt butterflies suddenly rise in her stomach. Was this potential case beyond her abilities?

She had read all she could locate on His Holiness, with her research including time on YouTube. He was brilliant and loquacious and the 14th person to hold the title Dalai Lama. He fled Tibet in 1959 and the Chinese government continues to accuse him for ongoing unrest in the Tibetan region. His primary residence since exile has been in India. He travels the world meeting with heads of state and has a strong and powerful global following.

Pamela signed her tab, entered an elevator and used the key card for access to The Royal Suite. She walked down a hushed, carpeted hallway and knocked on the double doors. A pleasant looking young Asian man answered, smiled and nodded. "Ms. Waters, welcome. Thank you for coming."

The man gestured inside the spacious, lavish suite. She followed him into an adjacent drawing room. Three robed young men were standing around a large, ornate desk. One aide gestured to a pair of wing chairs positioned in front of the desk. Pamela sat, out of deference, but would have preferred to remain standing. "May I bring you a beverage?"

Pamela declined and turned her senses to the suite. It was pristine. The four aides did not speak. A pleasant aroma from fresh cut flowers filled the room. To her left a door opened, and The Dalai Lama entered.

Pamela Waters was excited. Russell certainly missed his chance! Her heart was racing a bit, and she made an effort to project outward calm as she studied the revered holy man. He looked his age, mid-seventies, and extremely healthy. Shaved head, glasses, burgundy robe with a yellow hued slash, right arm bare, sandaled feet. She had seen many photos of him and reflected that His Holiness must be one of the most recognized persons on Earth. He won the Nobel Peace prize in 1989. What were those four scars on his upper right arm?

The Dalai Lama glanced at Pamela as he quickly walked to the desk, sat down, adjusted his glasses and smiled. "Good day, Ms. Waters. So nice of you to come to me. I notice you staring at my arm. Vaccination scars, very long ago. But now, I have problem. We have problem. It is major problem for all Buddhist monks, all sincere practicing Buddhists and all true friends of Buddhists. If at any time, you need clarifications, please feel free to interrupt for questions. Do not hesitate. Do not be shy.

"I always consider myself a simple Buddhist monk," he continued. "That is the real me. The Dalai Lama is a temporal ruler in a man-made institution. As long as the people accept the Dalai Lama, they will accept me. But being a monk is something which belongs to me. No one can change that. Deep within, I always consider myself a monk, even in my dreams. So naturally I feel myself as more of a religious person. In my daily life, I spend 80% of my time on spiritual activities and 20% on Tibet as a whole. The spiritual or religious life is something I know and in which I have studied greatly. Regarding politics, I have no modern education except for some experience. It is a big responsibility for someone not so well equipped. This is not voluntary work but something that I feel I must pursue because of the hope and trust that the Tibetan people place on me." The Dalai Lama spoke in a brisk baritone and punctuated most of his nouns and verbs with quick, clipped hand and finger gestures.

"I remain optimistic I will be able to return to Tibet. China is changing. Global interdependence, especially in terms of economics and environment, make it impossible for nations to remain isolated. I am committed to my middle-way approach whereby Tibet remains within the People's Republic of China enjoying a high degree of self-rule or autonomy. I firmly believe this is of mutual benefit both to the Tibetans as well as to the Chinese. We Tibetans will be able to develop Tibet with China's assistance, while at the same time preserving our own unique culture, including spirituality and our delicate environment. By amicably resolving the Tibetan issue, China will be able to contribute to her own unity and stability."

Pamela quietly listened as her mind whirred.

"You may wonder how I was chosen Dalai Lama. After my birth, a pair of crows came to roost on the roof of our house. They would arrive each morning, stay for while and then leave. Similar incidents occurred at the birth of the First, Seventh, Eighth and Twelfth Dalai Lamas. After their births, a pair of crows came and remained. Now, the evening after the birth of the First Dalai Lama, bandits broke into the family's house. The parents ran away and left the child. The next day when they returned for their son they found the baby in a corner of the house. A crow stood before him, protecting him. When the First Dalai Lama grew and developed in his spiritual practice, he made direct contact during meditation with the protective deity, Mahakala. Mahakala said to him, 'Somebody like you who is upholding the Buddhist teaching needs a protector like me. On the day of your birth, I helped you.' There is definitely a connection between Mahakala, the crows, and the Dalai Lamas.

"Many people ask me: will you be the last Dalai Lama? Whether the institution of the Dalai Lama remains or not depends entirely on the wishes of the Tibetan people. It is for them to decide. In 1963, after four years in exile, we made a draft Constitution for a future Tibet which is based on the democratic system. The Constitution clearly mentions that the power of the Dalai Lama can be removed by a two-thirds majority vote of the members of the Assembly. At the present moment, the Dalai Lama's institution is useful to the

Tibetan culture and the Tibetan people. Thus, if I were to die today, I think the Tibetan people would choose to have another Dalai Lama. In the future, if the Dalai Lama's institution is no longer relevant or useful and our present situation changes, then the Dalai Lama's institution will cease to exist. Since 2001, we have had a democratically elected head of our administration, the Kalon Tripa. The Kalon Tripa runs the daily affairs and is in charge of our political establishment. Half jokingly and half seriously, I state that I am now in semi-retirement." The Dalai Lama emitted a brief, infectious chuckle.

Pamela Waters was absolutely fascinated, a rare state of mind for her. Before arriving she realized that she had no true concept of the charisma of this man. She now understood why His Holiness was so popular.

"When I was two years old, bureaucrats came to my remote village. They brought some belongings of the late 13th Dalai Lama. I immediately reached for a rosary—the one that had belonged to the previous Dalai Lama and put it around my neck. I was offered two canes and selected the one that had belonged to the prior Dalai Lama. Three quilts were laid in front of me and I touched the one the 13th had used. In the final test I was presented with two drums called *damaru*: one plain and the second, beautiful. I was told I smiled when I selected the plain one. Because I was able to distinguish possessions from my predecessors, I became the current Dalai Lama. I am the fourteenth Dalai Lama in a line of succession that began in the early 1200s. These historic antiquities have been carefully housed and locked in secret locations accessible to only a select few. Other than myself, only three men had access, and two of these men are in this room. The third man and the antiquities are missing. Missing, also, are some prized personal belongings. That, Ms. Waters, is the first problem I ask your friend and you to solve." He leaned back and silently studied her face.

She returned his gaze and then studied the faces and body languages of the aides, each in turn. She looked for signs of uneasiness, shiftiness, superfluous movements and saw nothing of note. They were all either exceptional performers or, most probably, innocent.

Pamela had many questions. "May I speak with Your Holiness in private?" The four aides looked to the Dalai Lama. Without hesitation, the Dalai Lama answered, "Certainly."

The aides rose, bowed slightly to the Dalai Lama and walked into the other wing of the suite, closing the door behind them. She turned toward the Dalai Lama, who was intently looking at her. She observed the cross-legged religious leader for half a minute and then asked, "Your Holiness, what is the name of the missing aide?"

"His name is Mitchell Lo."

"Do you believe he is responsible for the missing antiquities?"

"Yes and I believe he acted alone within my inner circle. From outside, he must have had a co-conspirator."

"Do you have photographs of Mr. Lo, his fingerprints, DNA samples…"

He nodded. "My aides will assist with all you need. But first we must discuss matters they cannot provide to you."

Pamela had many questions, a major one being why her? "Sir, I know you must have an incredible ability to find information. You can connect with high governmental officials and the most trained law enforcement agencies throughout the world. So why me?"

"I have thought about this for some months now. I have also asked my contacts to ask around quietly. I must be very careful, for anything I say may be misconstrued by my enemies and the enemies of Tibetans. And that is where you come in. I need you to investigate and go where law enforcement may not. Even the agents from U.S. CIA and Britain's Scotland Yard report to superiors. You shall report only to me."

"I understand that you want me to locate and return the antiquities, but what about the thief?"

"I do not want him returned. If he is arrested there will be a scandal. I do not want that. I believe his conduct shall be his punishment."

The Dalai Lama opened the desk drawer and removed a red file. "In here is our information on Mitchell

Lo. It also provides you with details concerning the antiquities and the identities of potential purchasers. General descriptions and names."

Pamela could not shield her obvious surprise that he would also know where the merchandise may have been fenced.

"For many years now, there have been increased concerns that international organizations have expanded their criminal trades from illicit drugs to trafficking of humans for sex. Even trade in organs for transplant. It is a particular problem for emerging and underdeveloped countries. Their people are desperately poor and ignorant. We have much more difficulty in protecting our people. I received information I believe to be valid, that a Dutch mafia type organization may be behind the theft, or at the very least, making significant purchases of the wares. Regrettably, while we know of its existence, we cannot confirm the identities of its leaders. It goes by the name De Blauwe Organisation. The information we have is that there is an auction by invitation only scheduled in Bermuda sometime within the month."

Pamela could not help but think that Russell would be very disappointed he had not been present to hear this.

"Your Holiness, I hope I will not disappoint you."

"That is very good that you wish to accept, but I haven't told you the second part of the problem. You may yet wish to decline, what you call, the case. One of the reasons

41

you were of particular interest to me is your knowledge of China and Tibet."

Pamela nodded in agreement.

"This crime is important in a religious and moral sense. I want to avoid all governmental scrutiny. Those valued objects, along with a few of my own, will be extremely important in finding the 15th Dalai Lama, if there is one. When I die, this position may also die, or be suspended for years. The man with the antiquities, if he does have them, he is Chinese. I do not want to get deep into the subject of China, but know this, Ms. Waters: the Chinese government *hates* and *fears* me. They will use whatever propaganda possible to discredit me."

"Sir, why would you have someone Chinese as a member of your staff?"

"He was born Chinese, but at age eight he was adopted by a Tibetan family."

The Dalai Lama's face suddenly became serious. After a few seconds he lowered his hands in his lap and closed his eyes. He remained motionless for a painstakingly silent minute and then sighed deeply. Was the man meditating?

Then he began to speak, slowly. "Gedhun Choekyi Nyima was born on April 25, 1989. Have you heard of him?"

"No sir."

"It is a very sad mystery and most likely unsolvable. I am not surprised you have not heard of him. But I want to tell you about it, because I know about how your friend, Russell, found that girl in Venezuela. I was informed by followers you met in Lhari County that you were able to locate parents of your Chinese American client, even though the Chinese government had forced his family to move from Beijing to Tibet."

Pamela was speechless, as His Holiness continued unabated.

"Many westerners have not heard of this child. But every Buddhist and most human rights proponents know of his terrible story. And I am the main reason he is in a terrible position, if he is still alive."

The Dalai Lama rose from behind the desk, walked to one of the two white sofas and sat at a corner, pulling his legs up in the lotus position. He wriggled, making himself comfortable, and began to speak in a much less energetic tone. "The Panchen Lama is the second highest lama, under my title, Dalai Lama. The 10th Panchen Lama was Choekyi Gyaltsen. In 1989 he delivered a speech in Tibet which included the statement, 'Since liberation, there has certainly been development, but the price paid for this development has been greater than the gains.' Five days later he died under mysterious circumstances. He was age 51.

"So, the search began for the 11th Panchen Lama. Monks from a noted Tibetan monastery started by using prophetic visions and the personal possessions of the 10th Panchen Lama, Choekyi Gyaltsen, to find the true reincarnation. Oracles were consulted, various divinations take place, but *one boy identified every one of Choekyi Gyaltsen's possessions.*

"The boy was a six-year-old named Gedhun Choekyi Nyima. He was born in Lhari County, Tibet, a place you have visited more than once, I am told. I, of course, was in India; but when I received his photograph and the monks' confirmation, I knew, instantly, that Gedhun Choekyi Nyima was the 11th Panchen Lama. In May of 1995 I announced the discovery to the world press."

The Dalai Lama paused again and vigorously rubbed his forehead. "Three days after my announcement, Gedhun Choekyi Nyima and his parents were abducted by the Chinese government, and they have never been seen since. In 1996, Chinese officials admitted holding the three in protective custody. No photographs of the family were produced, at least none anyone believed. One showed a boy playing ping- pong, and the other is the *back* of a boy's head! The U.N. Committee on Human Rights, backed by the support of more than 400 associations, celebrities and eleven Nobel Prize winners, asked to visit with him but were denied. In November 1999, The China Free News Association reported that Gedhun Choekyi Nyima had died in a Lanzhou prison in Gansu Province. That news group reported that, 'A major criminal had been transported from the prison to the crematorium, and the body was that of a small, emaciated child who observers claim resembled the 11th Panchen Lama.' The Chinese government denied this was true, saying the boy is alive but will allow no visitors. I suspect he may be dead, but I need to know the truth. One known photo of Gedhun exists, and a copy is in your file with computer created images of his appearance today."

Pamela hesitated and thought very carefully before replying. "When Russell and I were able to successfully accomplish our former cases, we not only knew more but did not need to avoid capture by a hostile government. Also, sir, think of the immense area. China is 3.7 million square miles."

The Dalai Lama gazed out a window. He was silent for a minute, then he turned to Pamela. "Will you spend some time to at least think about it?"

Pamela was transfixed, awed and flattered that this world figure wanted help from her. "Yes, sir, I will follow the leads for your antiquities and once again apply for a visa to China. The art objects are probably obtainable. But that lost child…" Pamela had no further words. She simply shook her head.

The Dalai Lama smiled knowingly and nodded, "Yes, yes, I agree. So focus on the antiquities first. But if you have any ideas at all on the second challenge, please tell me immediately. I have superb contacts. My friends can be your friends." He tented his fingers in a gesture of prayer.

Pamela's mind and emotions were surging. She, of all people, knew how painful the uncertainty is when a loved one is missing. Unlike death, there is no finality. Could she find a person that the Chinese government was sequestering from the rest of the world? Or, more likely, that had been executed? Very damn unlikely. But she might be able to ascertain if the young man were alive.

"Sir, I will do my utmost to locate and recover the antiquities. And I will do the same to at least update the current status of Gedhun Choekyi Nyima."

The Dalai Lama studied this bright American. She was sincere. She was also curious. Good! The curiosity about both will grow! And maybe the curiosity about the person will surpass that of the antiquities! "I will pray, every day, for your safety and success. Bring me evidence he is alive, and I will use my connections and influence to persuade the government to let him leave China."

The Dalai Lama rose, opened the connecting door and nodded to one of his aides. The man approached and handed her a small, black leather card case that held two VISA credit cards, ebony in color, in the names of C. RUSSELL and P. WATERS, respectively. "Really, sir, we don't need these cards."

"I disagree. You may need to travel in some circles that Mitchell Lo may now be in and need extraordinary amounts of cash." Pamela could not fault that logic.

"That card should take you just about anywhere you wish to go." The Dalai Lama nodded again to the aide, who handed the detective a Ritz Carlton envelope. Inside was a check made payable jointly to P. Waters and C. Russell for $500,000. "You shall receive an additional $500,000 if successful." The Dalai Lama laughed. "That check is negotiable in perhaps every country—except China!"

Pamela smiled. The man certainly had a good nature. But he was presumptuous to order, in advance, credit cards and draft a check *jointly* made payable to Russell and her. What did he know about their personal and professional relationships?

Pamela returned the warm, firm handshake. She again bowed to the older man. An aide escorted her out of the suite.

She was exhausted. Back in her room, she called Sotheby's in London and made an appointment for tomorrow. She would spend a couple of days learning more about Tibetan and Chinese antiquities. Then back to America by the weekend.

Chapter 4

De Blauwe Organisation

The Netherlands, still mistakenly referred to as Holland by many Westerners, is one of the more interesting and colorful European countries. Both an international crossroads and a many-centuries-old nation, it draws a class of wealthy people who prefer to conduct business in the shadows. In the capital, Amsterdam, No. 14 Raadhuis Straat is an old, ornate ten-story office building. On the ground floor, a bank caters to merchants.

Friday at 9:05 a.m., a man in his late twenties casually strode up to No. 14. He was of Western European descent, approximately six feet tall, thin with glasses. He carried a black, soft leather attaché case and entered the bank through revolving doors. His attire was expensive yet low key: gray topcoat, dark suit, light blue shirt, solid teal silk necktie, white cotton pocket square and black lace shoes. Crossing the lobby, he looked casually around and noted the few customers and staff. Satisfied no one was interested in his movements, he walked past the courtesy area and down a plain narrow hall to an unmarked, locked door. With a blue key, he opened the door that led to a smaller hallway that ended in a small unmarked elevator. He inserted a second blue key in a hidden slot six feet to its right. The doors opened, and he stepped into the car, which contrasted greatly with the plain, drab hallway. Hand-carved rosewood paneling adorned the walls and doors. The single button was pressed, and the elevator began a swift ascent. The doors opened onto a long hallway precisely matching the elevator's interior, and the man acknowledged he was monitored by video cameras. He nodded to one lens, then walked to the single door at the end of the hallway and again used the blue key to unlock the door. The man entered a small foyer. Over a tiny intercom speaker, a voice asked in American English, "Who are you?"

"Phillip."

After a short pause, the voice replied, "Welcome."

The door made a slightly audible click and was opened by a uniformed servant who took the man's topcoat. Phillip walked into the large boardroom and sat down. The interior of the spacious room matched the motif of the hall: richly carpeted floors, wood paneling and large, conservative artwork on the four walls. In the center of the room was a large, antique yew wood boardroom table occupied by seven men and three women. All were well dressed and of European descent. Every chair was occupied except for the one at the head of the table. A second door opened, and the Chairman entered.

Henri U. Bergmann gave a subtle, collective nod and took his seat. Ten sets of eyes turned toward him. What they saw was a pudgy, aging male. Bergmann was short. He had self loathing for his true height, always feeling it was a handicap. He used lifts in his shoes to raise his stature from five feet five inches to five feet seven. And he would hurt anyone for insinuating he was little. Bergman had dyed jet-black hair and wore a white silk shirt, maroon Grenadine silk tie and black suit. His round body was very well shrouded by the generous cut of the suit. His complexion was very pale, almost white, as if he spent no time outdoors. His movements were slow, fluid and relaxed, hinting at his lack of athleticism. In contrast to the slothful body, Henri Bergmann's beady eyes were electric: constantly moving and observing. Growing up in St. Louis, Missouri on The Hill, the historic Italian section of the city, Bergmann had been totally bored with school from the start. His personal repulsion for his height was hidden beneath his exceptionally cruel persona and disdain for practically everyone. Bergmann was not exceptionally intelligent, but what he lacked in IQ he overcame with tenacity and guile. He spoke three languages, preferred English and used it with expletives so vulgar that it belied his excellent education. Throughout high school, Bergmann lied about his age to gain employment, both legal and otherwise. His parents were not extraordinarily wealthy, but upon graduation, they were financially able to a send him abroad to study in Geneva, Switzerland. Bergmann spent his free time acquiring wealth to buy the things his body craved: food, drink, occasional drugs and frequent sex. Such a life style left its mark, aging him rapidly, and he spent money and time to cloak the abuse.

Bergmann had never felt a desire prior to sex to court and make friends with women, and few women would have been interested in becoming his friend or lover. He was lewd and had only desired the physical sensations, always having paid for sex, beginning with an East St. Louis prostitute when he was sixteen. At the same time, he began to make considerable money, first by pedaling pornography in various forms and then graduating to the more compact and lucrative business of illegal drugs. By the time he was forty, he had one of the most profitable freelance drug rings in the western Hemisphere. Had he invested well, he would never have to work again. But Bergmann always wanted more, and as a risk taker, his wealth ebbed and flowed. The ebb tide's main current was his penchant for traveling the world, ingesting, imbibing and fornicating his way across every continent. He paid top dollar for all.

The day he turned fifty, Bergmann began the week sunning himself on the island of Ceylon, the "teardrop of India," pondering his future. He made a list of 127 new enterprises, whittled it down to fourteen, then three and, on the seventh day of his professional interregnum, decided on the undertaking he now chaired.

Bergmann was the creator and Chairman of De Blauwe Organisation, an underground, international business that provided its select group of customers with the ultimate and most luxurious form of amusement: the syndicate sold people.

De Blauwe Organisation functioned solely on the whims of the private purchaser: if a fifty year-old man wanted a eight year-old boy, he could buy one; if a forty year-old woman wanted a fifteen year-old boy, she could buy one; a couple could purchase a healthy, white infant. Sixty percent of the sales realized by DBO were older men purchasing younger females, or males, for sex. White girls and boys drew the highest price, but the easiest "merchandise" was located in Southeast Asia, particularly Thailand.

The sale of illicit drugs, a sideline, was always profitable, but because of the unmanageable violence associated with drug cartels and gangs, Bergmann had been reducing income dependence on that commodity. A new and promising area, the harvesting of healthy organs, had been on the increase and accounted for most of the remaining sales. The impoverished were victimized by agreeing to sell their healthy kidneys or liver sections for a nominal sum of money. And occasionally, terminal humans were purchased, vivisected and peddled.

The State of Israel, remarkably, led in the purchase of black market organs. DBO "middlemen" bought healthy organs and arranged for their surgical removals and then sold them for handsome profits to underground connections in Israel. Those connections would then distribute the freshly harvested organs to developed countries, such as the United States and Japan. Sometimes donor and recipient attended the surgical room together. It was a great partnership, where others perform the distribution of living organs for transplant, thereby reducing the risks to DBO.

Henri Bergmann's machine ran exceedingly well, primarily because of his talent for recruiting individuals whose intelligence surpassed his. He was very selective in his choice of members for the Board of De Blauwe Organisation. His criteria were logical: in addition to superior intelligence, recruit people who are amoral and apathetic about matters of law and of the flesh. It was preferable they possessed criminal connections and political influence. Greed was assumed.

One prominent board member was Luciano Paluzzia, or Luke, a well-known figure in organized crime who had successfully faked his own death several years prior. He now traveled about freely due to extensive plastic surgery and a forged identity.

Bergmann's knack for detecting character flaws of the defrocked was evident by his addition of a former Director of the National Security Agency of the United States, Martin Johnson. Johnson's connection with NSA, the most secret arm of the U.S. government, was invaluable in warning about potential exposure.

And despite his long history of uncaught felonies, Bergmann had a high respect for the law. One always needs an attorney! Stanley Cogburn, a recent board member, practiced law in Washington D.C. and specialized in international trade. De Blauwe Organisation's legal expert was brilliant and, at least superficially, devoid of emotion.

Rewards were frequent and untraceable. Every DBO member received very generous dividends, paid in cash, in the currency of one's choice.

The DBO Chairman anticipated a brief meeting today. Everything was operating smoothly. Almost too smoothly, Bergmann thought, slightly concerned. He laced his short chubby fingers together, rested his hands on the table and called them to order.

"Welcome. Notice that there have been two replacements to the board: the departed members had to be 'removed' from our group after trying to independently market our services. Those two bastards were rewarded for their treachery with a live burial at sea. We now have, as our newest member, a talented chemist from Colombia whose knowledge in the manufacture of our necessary 'medicines' will aid the indoctrination of our Jewels in order to better service the clients that have purchased them. Our second new member, from Israel, should prove invaluable in expanding our human organ trade. We can congratulate ourselves on continued financial prosperity, which has been attained with virtual secrecy. Our Catchers have been adequately insulated from the identities of the individuals in this room as a precaution, should a Catcher find oneself in the custody of law enforcement. Some of you know the identities of our Catchers, primarily because you found them. But we shall continue to insulate the Board from our worker bees, as there is no other reason to do otherwise."

Now that Bergmann had reminded all of the stern hand and discipline of DBO, he thought it time to get down to brass tacks. Money.

"Countless thousands of people disappear all over the world every day. And a select few disappear every financial quarter." A few members of the board smiled.

Bergmann nodded to the petite elderly woman on his right, who would inform anyone who listened that her genealogy included Marie Antoinette. He extended his hand to her, much as a master of ceremonies would introduce a torch singer, and enthused, "This cunt is, truly, an artist. A live oceanic burial was a beautiful inspiration." The silver-haired woman faked a smile, offended by his crassness. Her fellow board members silently wondered which Catcher she had directed to remove the two fools attempting to compete with Bergmann. Probably Fionna. Her talents were well known among the group. One member aptly described Fionna as: BEAUTIFUL. DEADLY.

"As we enter the next fiscal quarter, I am pleased to report projected income is at an all-time high. At the end of De Blauwe's first year net profits were $13.7 million USD. The second year that figure had risen to $88.3 million. Today, twelve years later, annual net profits were just over

$1.5 billion. Our success is due, in part, to the popularity of our carefully distributed catalog: there is no publication anywhere in the world whose caliber of merchandise is on a par with that contained in De Blauwe Biblio. It is a rare and highly prized piece of art priced at $50,000 per copy."

Henri Bergmann nodded to a servant, who began passing out the new issue of De Blauwe Biblio (The Blue Book). Johnson, the NSA alumnus, accepted his new copy of De Blauwe Biblio and began leafing through a few pages. His face was impassive as he examined its contents. The sixteen, four-color photographs on each page reflected in his bifocals as he flipped through the catalog. The people in this edition, he mused, are more beautiful than ever. And none have a clue that they are for sale.

The chairman continued. "Our catalog is a very efficient and enticing marketing tool, but with limitations. It is time for our Jewels to be presented in a new setting, a new display case, one that offers, movement, along with images, and has reach worldwide. De Blauwe Biblio needs marketing through the Internet."

Several members of the board increased their focus on their leader. This was no small step. Few of the members were web savvy, most having been born in another generation and from professional positions where inferiors dealt with that medium, but all knew of the Internet's commercial potential. Everyone listened with rapt attention.

Bergmann calmly continued, "I have conferred with one of our members on the subject, and he has a proposal for us. I cede the floor to Phillip."

The slender man in the navy Brioni suit rose, fastened his top coat button and smoothed the end of his tie. "Sir," Phillip nodded once to Bergmann, put his hands behind his back and confidently, quietly spoke to his colleagues.

"This is a new opportunity for the Organisation. And repercussions will be minimal or non-existent when De Blauwe Biblio premieres, performs and reaps impressive dividends via the Internet with customers who can be reached anywhere on the planet. My blueprint for that expansion is to base the Computer System and Server in Belgium. This requires very little in capital, since it would consist of concealing our normal-size computer linked, undetected, to the mainframe of a legitimate business."

The idea of surreptitiously utilizing a legitimate business as a front brought smiles to many of the faces.

Philip, animated and charged, began to pace across the room. "I have employed an exceptional IT person to install a DBO computer in the large server room where his company's mainframe computer network is stored. Its small footprint is easily hidden among the extensive hardware already in place. A remote monitoring station will be established on a boat located in the Caribbean Ocean, with a telephone accessible to the Computer System through a privately owned geocentric orbit satellite and manned by two

IT employees who will also serve as captain and mate. Our subscription to this telecom satellite is through a Cayman Islands bank account paid by automatic withdrawal. I have been assured this financial connection is untraceable. The vessel will seldom dock, only for necessities and at varied locations. As you may know, the Cayman Islands replaced Switzerland as the location of choice for many discrete financial enterprises. Switzerland recently cooperated with the United States in identifying and seizing money deposited there by drug lords or individuals avoiding U.S. tax obligations."

As Bergmann listened, he became acutely uncomfortable with the realization he understood very little of what was being said. Phillip removed a cigarette pack size remote control from his inside left breast pocket, pressed a button and a 50 inch plasma screen began to decent from the ceiling on Bergmann's right.

"The Caymans are south of Cuba and west of Jamaica and not included on many maps. Of its three islands, Grand Cayman is the largest at 197 square kilometers. The capital, George Town, has a population slightly over 30,000 and is an ideal setting for this expansion." Phillip pressed a second button, which dimmed the lights, and a third, which instantly visualized the subject. "I have created this flow chart to assist us in understanding the schematics of my machine."

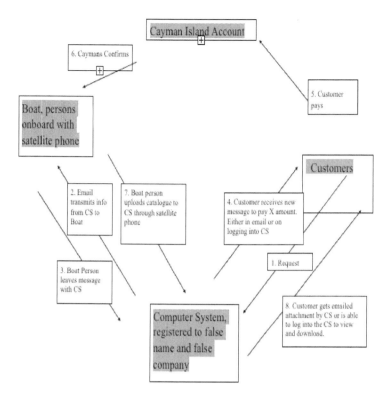

Phillip stole a quick glance at Bergman, who wore a poker face, masking ire.

Philip turned back to the screen, clicked on a green laser pointer attached to his key chain and deftly began to run through the numbers, slowly circling the various boxed sections as he described each.

"First, The Customer logs onto the website to request our catalogue. Second, the Computer System in Belgium registers the e-mail request from the Customer and sends DBO to the Remote Monitoring System. Step three, our employee at the Remote Monitoring Station replies on the Computer System. Monies required are confirmed. Our Customer receives an e-mail from the Computer System with the monies required. Step five, the Customer pays. Six, our agent in the Caymans confirms receipt of the money into the account by alerting the DBO employee operating the Remote Monitoring System on the sea vessel. The Remote Monitoring Station uploads the catalog through the satellite telephone, which is untraceable…the catalog is transferred to the Computer System in Belgium which allows the Customer to use the message on the Computer System to download our current catalog."

The group was silent, captivated by the realization of the potential for a worldwide market. Phillip sat down, and a small, satisfied smile appeared on his pale face. He looked like a milquetoast accountant who was rarely in the spotlight. After a few moments, Bergmann moved to adopt Phillip's plan, which unanimously passed. Phillip made a quiet effort to erase his smile, but could not as he envisioned his logical ascension up the DBO ladder and the eventual replacement of Bergmann. Though admired, Henri Bergmann was old and out of touch with the economies of today. Phillip also knew that, historically, the key revenue generator in a corporate environment is a logical heir to the throne. Once his plan is enacted he would, and should, sit at the head of the yew table.

Aware of Phillip's self-satisfied countenance, Bergmann congratulated his colleague. "Thank you Phillip. That is a very sound plan." But Bergmann also thought it prudent to now remind Phillip of his place. He did not trust this overly confident disciple. He really did not trust any of them. They did not reach this room by behaving like saints. Quite the contrary. And this clever bean counter needed a quick kiss followed by a slap. "That schematic looks flawless. And flawless is an apropos word for the sale of our Jewels. You are a most valuable *member* of this Board. And one very brilliant, little cock."

Everyone acknowledged the synonymic jab, and Phillip's smile slowly faded into a scowl.

For the next two hours, the committees of De Blauwe Organisation summarized their respective reports. Of unique interest was an apparent one time opportunity to purchase stolen, treasured artifacts belonging to His Holiness the Dali Lama. The board members were always looking for investments, having so much cash on hand. A sub-committee of three was appointed to report privately to Bergmann on this possible enterprise.) Upcoming Jewel assignments were outlined, and a sub-committee consisting of the American attorney and a South American surgeon were instructed to study the problem of distributing freshly harvested organs.

The board then adjourned. Members departed in the reverse order in which they had arrived: first Bergmann, via his private entrance, followed by the rest, one at a time through the hallway and private elevator. Waiting at the elevator doors were two uniformed servants who silently passed out envelopes thick with various currencies.

Every board member had at least one assistant downstairs in the lobby. Few of the board trusted each other.

Fionna arrived early to establish herself at a secluded, circular booth in the rear.

She was at The Palm Court in the Drake Hotel, Chicago. Half the tables were occupied, the patrons enjoying live harp music that began promptly at 2:00 p.m. Fionna did not care for the harp, as it reminded her of things Heavenly, and she did not believe in Heaven. Hell, maybe!

She ordered afternoon tea and pastries while waiting. Phillip was certainly not exciting, but she had learned long ago that it was easier to fuck most men for information than beat it out of them. As she looked at the collection of snobs in the elegant restaurant, she saw Phillip confidently approaching her booth. Either he's been here before or he's comfortable with money or both. She would find out that, and more, before the afternoon ended. He leaned over to kiss her on the cheek and admired her firm breasts revealed beneath the shear silk blouse. No bra, which was not visible from across the room but was delightfully obvious up close. It was an effort to take his eyes off her bosom. He instantly became aroused and quickly sat down, grateful for the private corner banquette.

The waiter arrived promptly, and Fionna suggested champagne, Taittinger. The man nodded his approval. "Superb choice." He turned and left.

She slid around the booth and pressed as close as possible, hip to hip and shoulder to shoulder. Phillip was momentarily speechless, and he picked up his water glass to think, quickly, and to soothe a suddenly dry throat. She shifted her arm under the thick tablecloth, placed it on his thigh and slowly inched her hand up. Surely not...

Then both of Fionna's hands were in his lap. She smoothly pulled down his zipper, as if they had done this before. With long, red-nailed fingers, she expertly freed his rapidly growing member. As her left hand withdrew and picked up the water glass, she calmly sipped while her right hand began one of many practiced routines. He was swelling with each second. Phillip used his table napkin to shield the bare flesh, even though the tablecloth covered both their laps.

The napkin began to undulate in a small circle, pause, and then move in the other direction. The manual stimulation settled into a lazy rhythm—four slow circles clockwise, then eight counterclockwise. Stop for 20 seconds and then repeat.

Nobody seemed to notice the silent lap dance in their midst. Now, teasing movements shifted into another direction, lightly pumping, softly, at first. Fionna delicately kissed his cheek, her lips cool from the ice water. Then she squeezed harder and focused on the tip. Phillip's eyes closed, his groan barely audible. In a few seconds he came, his hoarse climatic whispers in German. Fionna removed her right hand and rested it on his thigh. She kissed his cheek, and he laid his head on her shoulder. Across the room, their waiter was approaching with the champagne.

"Phillip, dear, I'm suddenly thirsty. Aren't you?"

The maître de was thin, silver-haired, over sixty. He stood by the arched entrance, in the at-service stance, hands clasped behind. His gaze left their table. He was not smiling but said and did nothing. While disapproving, he had seen much more than this.

For dessert, Fionna finished the second tier of the pastry compote as Phillip devoured Oysters Rockefeller. The Catcher did not need to pretend interest as she inquired of his day and slyly asked details about the latest board meeting. Phillip hesitated, and Fionna decided it required more persuasion. She suggested they move to the room he had excitedly rented at her suggestion. The couple left their table and took the elevator to the concierge level on the fifth floor. Before Phillip opened the suite door, she had his belt unbuckled.

Ten minutes after an utterly exhausted yet happy Phillip fell asleep, Fionna dressed and slipped outside, quietly closing the door. She wanted to avoid having to deal with his protestations that she should not leave so soon. She had no interest in spending any further time with him now that she had the information she needed. How interesting that Bergmann and Phillip had plans to shop for priceless Tibetan relics, and in Bermuda, no less! The question was how she could turn this information into a profit?

The Catcher had made a number of important connections over the years, first as an inexperienced but ambitious prostitute, later as the mistress to the wealthy Hispanic from Belize and then as cohort to Rafael Garcia. She kept the contacts in her laptop, always available when needed. What she needed, ideally, was a contact to get her an audience with none other than the Dalai Lama himself. Mr. High Holy might pay very well indeed to know that a group such as DBO is a buyer and that the auction is scheduled to take place in Bermuda within the month.

Chapter 5

Into Thin Air

Sally Collins, Lisa's mother, was a petite woman. She was only 30; a child bride, now widowed and a single parent. She was employed as an executive assistant at Georgia-Pacific, a paper and building products company headquartered in Atlanta. Her employer bestowed an impressive title upon her, but without commensurate salary. She often fretted that her daughter should be in an elite private school rather than a latchkey child walking home alone from a public school enmeshed by accusations that teachers and administrators changed test scores to enhance school standing.

At 6:15 p.m., three hours after Lisa disappeared, Sally said good-bye to her boss, took the two elevators down into the bowels of the parking lot, cranked up the 8-year-old VW Jetta and whined out into the traffic on Peachtree Street. She spent an economical ten minutes in Kroger's grocery to pick up a hen for dinner and arrived home at 7:00 p.m.

Unlocking the back door, Sally called out, "Lisa, I'm home with dinner."

Sally looked in Lisa's bedroom. Her daughter was not home, and there was no note on the kitchen counter. She rechecked her mobile phone to ensure she had not missed a text message or call. Nothing! An uneasy feeling crept over her.

She poured a glass of Kendall Jackson Chardonnay and sipped the wine as she walked onto the porch. The sun was setting. She began to methodically call the neighbors, parents of Lisa's friends, teachers and the local hospital. She even called family members, knowing they were too distant to have been visited by Lisa, who had only her feet and a bike for transportation. With each call, Sally became more anxious. The temperature had dropped, and she wondered if her child was hungry and cold. As Sally took another sip, she noticed a small figure shoot on a bicycle race up the street. Timmy Taylor. What does he know? She dialed his parents' number. No answer. The comfort of a local priest would be nice, but she had not taken Lisa to mass in months. Sally brushed aside fresh tears.

It was warm for March but not yet porch weather. A slight wind gave Sally a momentary chill, which underlined her mood of uncertainty. At 9:30 p.m., she called the police. And by then she could not keep the hysteria from her voice. She was switched from person to person, from uniformed police to, finally, someone who seemed concerned, a Detective Trent. He promised to be at her house at 10:30.

At 10:20 p.m, Sally made coffee, and fifteen minutes later, the front bell rang. Sally saw a large black male holding his badge up to the peephole. Unlocking the door, she extended a hand. "I'm Sally Collins."

"Detective Robert Trent."

"Please, come in."

Sally led Det. Trent into the den and began blurting out everything she had done in the past few hours. The officer appeared to be in his early sixties, pleasant-faced, plain-looking, with a bit too much weight around the middle. He listened patiently until Sally had vented her thoughts, then he questioned her thoroughly for a half-hour. Lisa's personality, school life, home life, hobbies, habits, friends, problems. "Absolutely no problems," Sally had insisted.

"May I look in her room?" he finally asked.

"Of course."

In Lisa's room, the detective did a quick examination of the drawers, closet, clothes and possessions, and then tapped the Compaq laptop.

"Does she spend much time on the computer, chatting? Is she on Facebook?"

"Yes. But no more than most kids these days."

Det. Trent finished his notes, closed the folder, looked Sally Collins in the face and with almost too much calm told her, "While there is no apparent evidence, I must always suspect foul play. The first twenty four hours are essential. Have you heard of Meagan's Law or AMBER Alert? We are going to notify all local law enforcement and news agencies. I need a recent photograph of Lisa; some of her clothing, worn and unwashed, and a shoe, her toothbrush or hairbrush. I would also like to take her computer. That's how so many predators find their prey. Those damn chat rooms and postings." Trent shook his head.

Tears welled up in Sally's eyes, and she covered her mouth with a hand.

"If a missing person isn't located within 24 hours after disappearing, the likelihood is that something is seriously wrong. The good news is that we're eight hours into that window. Dispatch will begin notifying by radio and email a description of Lisa to all the area law enforcement agencies and news media. In the morning, I'll interview the staff and teachers at Lisa's school. We need you to be accessible by telephone. May I have your cell number? Do you have someone who can come and stay with you?"

"My sister in Chattanooga will help. She'll come down."

"Good. Here's my card, with the cell number to reach me directly."

Det. Trent collected Lisa's personal effects and walked to the front door. As she let him out, Sally took one of his hands in both of hers, "Thank you so much."

The detective gave her a reassuring smile: "Talk with you soon."

As his car pulled away, Sally's sister called and said she would be in Atlanta in 90 minutes. "Sal, are you alright?"

"I don't know," she sobbed. "I just don't know."

Sally's only sibling arrived shortly before 1:00 a.m., roaring up the driveway, tapping the horn twice. The sisters talked and speculated until dawn, trying to be optimistic, offering theory after theory that would support a happy ending.

At 6:30 a.m., Sally heard two local TV stations carry news briefs about the missing girl, complete with photo. She called in to work, explained her absence and spent the day answering her phone as it rang continuously. Concerned neighbors, parents of Lisa's friends, and the inevitable crank calls streamed incessantly. Shortly after noon came the only good news, from Det. Trent.

"We've found an eyewitness who saw Lisa after school. It's a student named Timothy Taylor and I'd like you to be there when he's questioned."

Timmy Taylor! Her mind raced, as she locked her car in the school parking lot and ran up the steps to the front doors. She liked Timmy and his parents, but they never controlled the boy. He was the neighborhood wild child!

Sally found Det. Trent with two uniformed policemen, the school's principal, Timmy's mother Zan, and Timmy, in a small conference room adjacent to the library.

"Hello, Zan," Sally said as she sat down across from the young boy. "Hi Timmy."

The boy shyly waved. Zan said hello, with concern in her voice and expression.

Trent began, "This morning I asked the school administration to inquire of the student body and staff if anyone saw Lisa after she left the school grounds. Timmy appears to be the last person who saw her. " Trent's voice was flat, yet warm. "Now, Timmy, once more, please, for Ms. Collins. Alright?"

Timmy crossed his arms on his chest and looked at Lisa's mom. Mrs. Collins had always been nice to him, even when he mistakenly crashed his bike in her flower bed. She had yelled and ran toward him but only to ensure he was not hurt.

A tape recorder was on the conference table. Trent punched it on.

"Timmy: now let's begin again when you saw Lisa after school at Rohm Park."

Timmy Taylor put his tongue-tip in the corner of his mouth and looked up at the ceiling, thinking hard, concentrating before he spoke. Everyone was quiet in anticipation. He took a deep breath and began to repeat the story he had now told several times. "Lisa was walking from the sidewalk onto the grass, into the park." He was carefully pronouncing each word. "She went to one of the benches in the park, following a lady cop. They sat down on the bench."

"What happened then?"

"I dunno. I biked outta the picture."

"Timmy, how do you know it was a lady cop?"

"I know cops. She had on the dark cop uniform, the belt with all the stuff. And the car was there. A white Crown Vic."

"How do you *know* the model Ford? Could you read the name on the car?"

"No, but I know it was a Crown Vic." Timmy was getting a little nervous.

Zan Taylor interjected, "Detective Trent, I think I can help here. Timmy is an, uh, energetic boy, and he knows a Crown Victoria when he sees one, because, he's, well, been in them. Twice."

A strawberry blush crept up Timmy's neck noticeable even through his dark skin. Timmy began to pick at a dirty fingernail.

Det. Trent said, "I assume these were police cars?"

"Yes," Zan Taylor answered, "police cars. Timmy once was involved in an egg-throwing incident, and a second time there was a misunderstanding about firecrackers. In both episodes, nice officers drove Timmy home."

"I see," Trent replied, trying not to smile. This young man was simply mischievous. "OK Timmy, so the car was a white Crown Vic. Was it marked 'Police' or 'Sheriff' or anything like that?"

"I don't think it was marked."

"Now, about the lady cop, are you certain it was a female, a police*woman*?"

"Yes. She looked like Ice, but had dark hair."

"What do you mean she looked like ice? Was she pale?"

"No. She looked like *Ice*! On *Fantastic Warriors*, the TV show. This lady was tall and strong, maybe as big as Ice."

Zan Taylor briefly described who Ice and what *Fantastic Warriors* was, as Trent nodded and made notes. Then he continued, "The other thing you mentioned earlier, Timmy: you said you pedaled by again, a little while later, and what did you see then?"

"When I pedaled back by, there was the car, but I didn't see anybody. When I came around again the Ford was gone. I had gone to the Golden Pantry, bought some fireballs and I pedaled back. Nobody was there and no car."

"Thank you, Timmy. You've been very helpful. Ms. Taylor, why don't you take Timmy outside? In a few minutes, if it's OK, I'd like to take you two over to Rohm Park. We've got some lab people coming, and I want the boy there to see the place while things are fresh in his mind. Your son was very observant and has been very helpful."

Zan Taylor looked at the detective and Sally. "Whatever we can do to help."

As soon as mother and son were outside, Trent rose and shut the door. He looked at the remaining group. "Ms. Collins, if I may ask you some personal questions?"

"Of course."

"Are you wealthy?"

"No, not even close. We live from one paycheck to the next"

"Lisa's father? Is he or his family wealthy?"

"No. Nobody on his side. My husband died last year. He was in an automobile accident on I-285. There was a little life insurance, but it did not even cover all of the medical and funeral expenses. The person responsible was driving on a suspended license and had no liability insurance."

"I'm sorry. What I'm getting at is this looks like a kidnapping for ransom."

"How! Who would do something ... "

Trent held up a hand. "The last person to see Lisa is the Taylor boy, who says a uniformed female cop was talking with her." Trent nodded to another officer, "We did a quick check, and there were no Atlanta police, Georgia State Patrol or Fulton County Sheriff officers, female or male, anywhere near Rohm Park yesterday. It looks like someone impersonated an officer and took her. If it's a kidnapping for ransom, we should have heard from someone by now. And if a kidnapping, why Lisa, if there's no family money?"

Det. Trent picked up the recorder, ejected the tape, labeled it and packed up. To the principal, he said, "I'd suggest you make an announcement that Lisa Collins is missing and for all students and faculty to be very vigilant. Notify the parents, and advise them to have their kids travel in groups of three or more when going to and from school."

74

Sally Collins drove home rather poorly. She was confused and felt anxiety pains in her chest. She parked in back and entered her home with her head down and shoulders sloped. Her sister was there with two neighbors who had brought food.

"Sal, the phone's been ringing off the hook, mainly reporters. What's happened?" Sally's sister smiled, trying to be upbeat.

Sally told the group about Trent's report and the interview. She sat on a bar stool, kicked off her shoes and made a glass of ice water. The kitchen wall clock read 2:51 p.m. "Why this? Why her?" Sally closed her eyes. She held the glass to her forehead, hoping it would ease the pain.

Detective Robert Trent was sixty-two years old. He looked forward to retirement and a government pension. He had been a good career cop, having resisted the temptations of accepting bribes, which occurred quite frequently. He believed in the law, although it too often seemed the criminal element was in control. Trent sat on the curb across the street to Rohm Park. His new friend, Timmy, sat beside him enjoying a fireball. Det. Trent wanted to spit his out, because it was too damn hot. Man and boy watched the assorted crime lab technicians photograph and gather samples from the small, beautiful park.

Timmy said, "I'm ready to bite. Are you ready to bite?"

Trent smiled, remembering that it was a social no-no to hold out finishing your candy while the other guy eats his last piece. "I'm ready," he said.

"One, two, three—bite!"

Both males crunched down on the now-sweet fireball cores, then repeatedly crunched, making sounds like two ponies eating corn.

"Why so many people?" Timmy asked.

"Each is a forensic expert," Trent said. "Do you ever watch the television shows CSI or Without a Trace?"

The child nodded in the affirmative, visibly concerned. "Who would take Lisa?"

"I don't know, son."

The crime lab technicians were shuffling back toward their vehicles, packing up their equipment. Trent rose, "Thanks again, son, what you remembered was very helpful. And thanks for the fireballs." Trent opened his wallet and took out a card. "Keep this with you all the time. If you think of anything else, call me. Night or day. Deal?"

"Deal, Detective, Mr. Trent." Timmy swung onto the seat of his mountain bike, scratched off in the grass and was gone in half a minute. Timmy pondered this, his first pleasant encounter with a cop. Maybe he just might be one himself when he grows up.

Trent turned back to the park. An investigator was still there, squatting and petting his partner, a bloodhound.

"Whatcha' got Jimmy?"

The second investigator kept his gaze on the stand of bushes, and said, "Follow me." He gently tugged on the leash of a wrinkle-faced, mud-colored bloodhound that responded to his trainer's every word. "We got here what I call The Brick Wall. Some folks call it The Flying Saucer, but shit, I don't believe in flying saucers, so I call it The Brick Wall."

The Bloodhound led them across a flat grassy area, past a set of swings, toward the park bench. He patted the animal, "OK Romeo, whatta' you smell?"

The dog led them to the park bench. "Here's where they sat, " Skelton said. The dog sniffed around the bench as Skelton pulled a yellow sneaker out of a large, plastic bag and leaned over to give the bloodhound a sniff. The hound smelled the grass and then pulled his master into the bushes. Trent parted a few branches and saw the bloodhound trotting in circles. The dog whined, looked overhead at the canopy of shrubbery, sat down on his haunches, stuck out a long tongue and began panting.

Skelton translated. "The girl was on that bench, then she went to this spot right here, and vanished into thin air. Most likely the girl was boxed up. Right here, in these bushes. She was somehow rendered unconscious either at the bench or over here, wrapped up, and toted off. If she was lifted off the ground, Romeo couldn't whiff it, since trails don't cling to air for long. So this trail ends here. The Brick Wall."

Trent walked out of the bushes, and Skelton took the bloodhound across the street to urinate. He called back to Trent. "Do you need us any more here?"

"No. Thanks."

———————————

Two months passed. The only clues in Lisa Collins' disappearance were Timmy Taylor's testimony and the short trail sniffed out by the bloodhound. Trent kept in contact with Sally Collins regularly, but as time passed she became more depressed.

Though not very cyber savvy, Trent knew that kids lived by electronics, much of the technology alien to him. The Internet was a rich source for predators. Lisa's computer had been inspected by two IT forensic specialists, but they found no leads. He discovered the child's personal stash of video CDs in a locked vanity, but although he had watched them repeatedly, he saw nothing out of the ordinary.

Trent knew, however, the possibility remained open of some predator noticing her photograph posted on My Space or Facebook and following her activities and unsecured postings.

———————————

On Friday, Sally made an appointment to meet Det. Trent at the station. It had been nine weeks and four days since Lisa disappeared and with nothing new she felt more desperate than ever. "What about a private detective, Officer Trent? Can you recommend someone?"

"I know a few. Probably the best female around here is Pamela Waters. She's in her mid thirties and made news headlines solving some very cold cases. I know Pam. She can have a sharp edge to her, but it's probably a shield to make her seem as tough as the guys. She's good though. And she doesn't beat around the bush."

Trent turned and looked out a window. The veteran cop believed the girl was dead. Some as-yet-unknown Ted Bundy, Henry Lucas, Albert Fish, Albert DeSalvo, Jeffrey Dahmer—someone had carted off the good-looking little girl, done God-knows-what to her first, killed her, then effectively hidden the remains. Too late. Too sad. Too bad. The best he could do now was at least be honest with this mother. "Sally, in every major city there are detectives; some good and some not so good. But have your checkbook ready." Trent gave her half a dozen names. Sally meticulously recorded each detective the cop provided.

Trent was extremely weary. This was a nice lady who was alone; she lost her husband and now her only child. She had limited resources but was going to spend what little remained on the very remote chance her child was alive. A false hope, Trent was certain. He did not want to tell her that. But if she heard it from a PI rather than a city detective, maybe she would get realistic and move on with her life.

"Look, there is also a guy, retired now. Probably in his late thirties, but he became a detective in college, for God's sake. I forget the story. They say he could find anything. If I remember right, he was beat up pretty badly on a couple of jobs and finally decided to quit while he could still walk."

"Who is he?" Sally was excited. "What's his name?"

"His name is Clayton Russell."

"How can I find him?"

"I don't know," Trent said. "But I think Pamela Waters and Russell had a thing going some time back and she might know where he is now. How much are you willing to pay? Or maybe I should say, how much do you have?"

Sally hesitated. She would sell everything she owned and borrow all that she could. "Enough, I hope."

Chapter 6

Wanted: New Detective

The day after their meeting, Sally phoned Trent at his office.

He knew she was interested in Clayton Russell. Trent's sigh was audible. "I made sóme phone calls last night," he said. "I also sent an email to Pamela Waters, but have not yet heard back. Even if you can convince Russell to help, I think you could benefit from Pamela Waters. You heard the old proverb: the whole is more than the sum of its parts? Well, I was told Russell has a lot of ghosts that still haunt him. Sort of like Post Traumatic Stress Disorder, only its job related and not from a war.

"Pam is good; damn good in my opinion. She provides an excellent service for the money, but like all of us, she is not perfect. She has a well-known temper and can be curt, seeming to lack compassion when she may need it most. Maybe it's her method of keeping her objectivity. But cops trust her, and that's important. They will give her information, off the record information. She also has connections with the press. And, being female, she can go places where men cannot.

"She's in the Yellow Pages and on the Internet."

Sally Collins booted up her computer and quickly located Waters' website:

PAMELA A. WATERS INVESTIGATIONS, INC.
ADULTERY, CHILD CUSTODY, SKIP TRACING.
CONFIDENDTIAL, REFERENCES. *Email or call 24/7.*

Sally tapped the number and got an immediate answer.

"Pamela Waters, how may I help you?"

Sally straightened, and said, "Ms. Waters, I'd like to meet with you as soon as possible to discuss a job."

"Well, can you give me a little information about your needs?"

"Yes. I am Lisa Collins' mother. Have you seen her on the news?"

Pamela took a deep breath and steadied her voice. She had read Det. Trent's email and anticipated this call. She also agreed with Trent's last comment on his e-mail, that the child was probably dead. "Yes, I'm a bit familiar with your situation. I understand the police have reached an impasse. Let me try to reschedule some appointments, and maybe we can meet later this afternoon. Hold on for a minute."

Sally was overjoyed! Maybe her luck had changed and someone could finally help her. She would spend the time at her bank and see what money she could borrow against her house. With the economy in a mess, she was lucky she had good credit and she would sell all she had to find her little girl. She felt fortunate her employer paid her

82

for the twelve weeks' family leave. But leave time would be ending soon. And she certainly needed every paycheck.

"Sally, can you meet with me today, around 5:00 p.m.? Suite 1520, The Hurt Building, downtown. I'll tell the security guard in the lobby that you're expected."

"Thank you for seeing me so soon."

"You're welcome." Pamela gingerly hung up the receiver.

Sally's footsteps clacked across the marble lobby of The Hurt Building, echoing inside the large space. In the elevator, she peered at her reflection in the brass doors. She did not smile much. Her dentist said she had been grinding her teeth. She sighed as the doors opened. Suite 1520 was straight ahead. As Sally opened the door to the suite, a female voice said, "In here". Sally then entered a small but pleasantly furnished office.

"Pamela Waters," said the energetic, attractive woman as she rose and walked toward Sally. "I'm having water. Are you thirsty? I have soft drinks and coffee if you prefer." The female detective's handshake was strong and quick.

"Uh, yes. Water is fine. Thank you."

Pamela Waters opened a small refrigerator and poured the filtered water over ice in a large, square glass, handed it to Sally and gestured to the couch opposite a wing back chair. Sally would not have described the woman across from her as beautiful, but certainly attractive. As Sally stared, she noticed a scar above her left eye, the only blemish in a flawless complexion. It could have been cosmetically removed but appears to have been intentionally left to signify I may be female, but I, too, have battle scars. Strawberry blonde hair was cut shoulder length in a bell shape that framed her face, and the eyebrows were a half shade darker than the hair. Thin, red, tortoise shell glasses framed bright green eyes; full, bee stung lips were painted a pale red; and the perfect teeth had flashed bright-white when she smiled. She was probably five feet six inches, and her body was very shapely. The detective was dressed casually in blue jeans, high heels and a white, tailored Ralph Lauren cotton shirt. The French cuffs were held with silver, mother-of- pearl studs.

Her accent was Southern, calm and reassuring, the diction precise. She simultaneously exuded an energetic, upbeat charisma that had immediately lifted Sally's spirits. She had a compelling, magnetic aura, the rare type of charisma found in select politicians. When the detective smiled, Sally felt she had known this woman for years.

Pamela sat in the lone chair across from the sofa. She knew sitting behind the desk presented an aloof approach to people in need. Clients often needed the closeness for psychological comfort. It was amazing how much therapy was a part of the job. She shifted her posture rigidly upright, adjusted her glasses and studied the woman sitting nearby:

She was the lady I saw in the newspapers and on TV a few weeks prior, now looking a bit more tired and thinner than previous images…her nails bitten to the quick on both hands…hygiene seems fine, but little facial makeup…vintage lady's Elgin wristwatch, probably inherited from mother or grandmother…engagement diamond, but not wedding band, understandable for a widow…left foot jiggling from nervousness, perhaps she is anticipating rejection or is pessimistic…jaw muscles clenching every few seconds, teeth grinding…eyes slightly red, erratic sleep patterns presumably from nightmares…from worry…and from the only child who is probably dead.

Pamela took her ink pen, "May I make notes? It assists me in recall."

Sally told Pamela the entire story, responding to occasional interruptions by questions from the detective. She ended with Trent's recommendation of Russell. "I hope you're not offended, but I would like him to work on the case. Do you know where he is?" Sally said, haltingly, "I'm sure you're very good, alone, but..."

Pamela abruptly cut in, "Hey, I know how good I am. So, Clayton Russell's your dream detective. No offense is taken, Sally. I am very impressed by the guy myself, in multiple ways." Pamela's brief affair with Russell ended over two years ago. She had thought she was in love but decided it was more lust than love. Or maybe Clay just had too many demons, and she was simply unable to compete.

Pamela stood, walked over to the window and gazed out. "Finding the reclusive, detective is not the problem; bringing him out of retirement is problematic. It's not the money. And speaking of compensation, few people could pay him what he's really worth. Tell you what: my fee is a thousand dollars a day, plus expenses. If I don't convince him to join as a team within seven days, you just pay expenses. Then you decide what next. If he joins, Clay sets his own price."

"Great! Will you accept a check to get started?"

"I typically ask for a retainer of ten thousand, but let's start with five and see how it goes."

As Sally wrote the check, Pamela could not help but feel guilty accepting her money, because her child was probably already dead. She took the check and handed Sally a card that had her email, land line and mobile phone numbers. "I'll do my best to cajole, threaten and embarrass that lazy, genius detective you want to at least meet with us, but I can make no guarantee of his services."

Pamela smiled warmly and extended a hand, which Sally vigorously shook. Pamela watched her new client leave with a bit of a skip now in her step and her head held high. Pamela silently wished her well. *You probably have false hopes, nice lady. Even if I convince Clay this is a move for him, what will we find? A body, I fear.*

Pamela Waters had always known she was too impetuous and her first impulse as she watched Sally leave was to call Clay. But she had called several times in the past couple of years with no success. Maybe it was the fact that there were lingering hurt feelings—she certainly did not handle the separation well. In fact, she had been a damn coward about it. No person with any decency would simply leave a note to her lover and then fly out of the country for an extended period of time; especially to a place like China. Pam intentionally became incognito for months. She did not expect forgiveness, although that was what she wanted. Maybe she should drive out to see him, a surprise visit. Boy, what if he had a female friend there! Oh well, it was a chance she would take. She had gotten nowhere by telephone, and all electronic messages were ignored.

As Pamela walked to her car, the sun was setting. The security guard for her building watched as she unlocked the driver's door to her silver grey Mercedes convertible, let the top down and pulled away. It was a pleasant May evening. The oppressive heat and humidity of the summer had not yet arrived. She preferred leaving late, since the congestion on the Atlanta highways usually had eased. She would make better time to her destination without traffic stress. It also gave her time to think.

Pamela reflected upon her profession. Unlike television and films, most detective work is tedious research and surveillance. Fistfights and gunplay are as rare as human albinos: about 1 in 17,000 cases. She smiled, remembering when she first met Clay. She had excitedly rushed home, booted up the computer and found a half-page feature article in *The New York Times* from fifteen years prior. The headline read:

A College Student Tracks Down
Kidnapped Wife of Former Governor

The lead paragraph described Clayton Russell, a 20-year-old junior majoring in journalism at the University of Georgia, had "…beat the FBI and local law enforcement agencies at their own jobs: he located the kidnapped elderly wife of a former Georgia governor within 30 hours after the woman's abduction, just eight hours after the former Governor had received the first, and only, extortion call from the kidnappers."

Clayton Russell, teen college student, had located the kidnapped governor's wife by calling hotels and pizza delivery restaurants. The kidnappers were fast food addicts. He vectored in on the bull's-eye, a motel and then made a final phone call, to the FBI.

A week later, Russell received the $45,000 personal reward from the governor, which was quite a substantial sum then. The wire services ran the story, and two months shy of 21, he spent the next few weeks avoiding the publicity that hounded him. He granted two interviews: one to the *Athens Banner Herald & Daily News* and one to *The New York*

Times, refusing to be photographed. All other interviews were declined, even an offer to be profiled on *60 Minutes*.

In the last column of the article, Pamela learned that Clayton Russell's father was deceased and that his mother, Mary Jean Russell, an Athens native, was " ... very proud of Clayton, but I'm not really surprised. Clayton is very clever, and he has always been able to find whatever he has wanted."

She kept in touch with Jean after Clay and she split. They would occasionally have lunch together. What a lovely lady! And what a talented, yet strange, son.

Chapter 7

The Crime of Sloth?

The following morning Pamela drove to Sally's modest brick home on Amsterdam Avenue.

Before she could park, Sally trotted down the steps, carrying a large red canvas bag. Her client's expression was best described as stoic, the face of someone entering a strange bank to apply for a much needed loan: one hopes to be welcomed, well-received and accepted for what will be asked. Pamela was determined to raise her spirits.

Pamela's brief visit with Clay the prior evening could best be described as awkward. He did not invite her in, which was not too surprising, since she had appeared unannounced. But he looked great. She was amazed that she remained so sexually attracted to him. Could there be truth to the idea that pheromones at some subliminal level ignited attractions between humans? After all, humans were mammals. If so, he gave no indication he felt the same attraction. But at least Clay agreed to meet with them today, so her trip had not been in vain.

"Good morning, Sally," she said merrily.

"Good morning Pamela, " Sally replied climbing in and buckling her seatbeat.

"We are going to the north Georgia mountains! There's some pretty good hazelnut coffee in that thermos. Would you pour me some?"

Sally opened the steel thermos and poured two mugs of the steamy, aromatic coffee. She sighed. "I didn't get much sleep last night. I kept thinking about today and what's going to happen, what I should say and how he'll respond. I'm a little nervous."

"Relax. Be yourself. Clay will find you as charming as I did. Please remember that it is as much about the seriousness of your loss as it is the intrigue of the case."

Pamela whipped the peppy sports car around the entrance ramp to I-85 and stomped out into the light traffic. "We should make good time this early on a Saturday morning. He's expecting us just before noon."

Sally turned to Pamela, "If he does decide to help, do you think he can find her?"

Pamela cut a glance at her client. "In my bag, on the rear floor, there's a bright yellow folder. Read what I found via Google."

Sally retrieved the folder and read in silence. She closed the folder and stared straight ahead. She decided the only way she could afford him would be if she could sell her house, which she would readily do, but in this market it may not sell in time.

Within an hour they had reached the foothills of the heavily wooded Appalachian foothills. Just past Begin,

Georgia, Pamela checked the map and took the exit to 115, turned left and drove through Clarkesville, a quaint little mountain town with century old storefronts, antique stores and Victorian homes. Another two miles, and they would be at Lake Rayton, four miles from Clay Russell's home. Pamela had been there often, but its seclusion always confused her. They passed the sign that read TALLULAH FALLS 1.3 MILES and veered right at the fork in the road, then traveled another 2.7 miles and stopped. On the right, was a narrow, unpaved road, almost overgrown with vegetation. Tree branches hung to within four feet of the ground, and thin, pale green grass was threatening to grow over the hard red clay. Pamela slowly nosed the car into the woods, through the drooping branches as the limbs scratched at the canvas top of her convertible. The road wove in gentle curves, and the dirt road soon turned to gravel. After a quarter mile, the woods opened up, and the light was brighter. Suddenly, they were in front of his house. It was a very unusual looking structure. Pamela could see by the expression on Sally's face that her first impression was similar to that first visit she had had with Clay.

The house was made of wood, with dark gray, one-way windows. The dark greens, browns and purple paint blended with the woods, making it virtually invisible from 40 yards and beyond. On the other side of the cedar and stone home, small patches of blue lake shimmered through the trees.

"This is the place," Pamela said as she opened her door and got out, "let's go meet Mr. Russell."

Suddenly the passenger car door slammed inward, making a terrific bang, and Sally screamed. Pamela had forgotten to warn her about Winston. Her client had been half out of the car, and as the door snapped shut, she was squeezed away and fell backward on her rear in the gravel. Sally's eyes opened wide and blinked as she saw, two paces away, a very large dog, an Airedale, she thought, standing stock still, staring at her. She slowly skidded her butt back along the gravel in a natural impulse to put space between herself and the dog. Winston bounded once and put his nose in her face.

Pamela jumped from the car. "Hey Winston!" she yelled, "Sit!"

Winston sat down on his muscular haunches and raised his right forepaw. *Shake*, the gesture said, as the dog tilted his head 45° to the side. Sally grasped Winston's big, rough-padded paw with her slightly trembling right hand. "Hello, pooch," she whispered. Sally carefully got to her feet, tucked her shirt-tail back in and made a face at Pam, who was looking toward the house. Behind the dog, Sally saw a man walking toward them.

Clayton Russell crooked an index finger down, and the Airedale instantly lay prone in front of Sally. "Hello Pamela, Ms. Collins."

"Pleased to meet you," Sally said, as she extended her hand.

"Are you OK?"

"I'm fine. Everybody should have the pee scared out of them at least once a day. It's better than coffee." Sally laughed.

He led the women around the left end of the house to the lake side, where it was constructed almost entirely of glass. As the ladies walked up the steps and across the wide expanse of teak deck, Russell opened one of the sliding glass doors and ushered them into a massive room with a tall, angled ceiling that peaked at about thirty feet. This room dominated much of the house. The floors were wide planked, sand-colored hardwood covered with custom rugs thrown about. Two matching leather and wood Charles Eames chairs and ottomans sat in opposite corners. Centered in the room was a deep-blue, leather Chesterfield sofa with an immense coffee table in front made from a solid block of gray and white marble. Sally guessed the marble table must weigh several tons and was probably supported with reinforced floor joints. Around the perimeter of the room was a modern, black, sectional, custom leather sofa flush to the wall. A portion of the kitchen and bar was at the left rear of the room. Bright sunlight shone in through the smoked glass doors and panels, plus and three large skylights. Across the entire length of one wall was floor to ceiling bookshelves with a sliding wood ladder. Sally calculated there were at

94

least a thousand hardback books. It was apparent the recluse loved to read.

"Have a seat, please." Russell gestured into the center of the room. "Pam, if you and Ms. Collins would like to freshen up a bit, I'll brew some fresh coffee. Would you like something to drink? Coffee? Water?" He remembered that by noon Pamela would typically refrain from caffeine of any sort and drink water. When she smiled at him this morning, she was more enchanting than last night in the twilight. He had been aloof and not invited her inside because the hurt still lingered after almost two years.

"Sally, would you like to follow me to the restroom?" As they walked from the room, Sally said, "Coffee, please."

Immediately off the main living quarters was a full bath. Unable to conceal her curiosity, Sally peeked into the other two rooms: a large, very masculine bedroom with an office built into one section and a smaller but comfortable guest room.

Russell went into the kitchen and started the coffee. While it brewed, he stared, blankly, at the lake. He knew what they would ask, and he had no idea how he would answer.

The two women returned from the restroom, walked back to the large sofa and sat down. Russell sat a few feet away, crossed a leg and picked up a pen and pad from the marble slab table. Sally could feel the tension and recalled what Trent had said about their past relationship.

Pamela looked around the room. Jesus, he was still so good-looking, but why so fatigued in appearance? He had no job shackles. She had not noticed last night the increased gray in his hair. He wore black cotton slacks, black moccasins and a light gray cotton work shirt with the sleeves rolled up on muscled forearms. On the left wrist was the vintage, steel Rolex watch. At one time, Clayton Russell had been one of the foremost human hunters in America, perhaps even the world. Clay had been a wonderful mentor and lover. Some of his successes bordered on the incredible, but, once explained, the ways he had achieved such wins made perfect sense. He had applied logic, energy, nerve and, probably more important than all, imagination. Imagination is a first cousin to curiosity, and she hoped that his curiosity (plus compassion) for the loss of this child would bring him in.

Russell began by addressing Pam.

"After I spoke with you last night, I called Det. Trent, who sent me his file by e-mail attachment this morning. I had forgotten that he and I crossed paths, professionally, quite a number of years ago. He's a good detective. Not enough like him."

Sally could contain herself no longer. "Mr. Russell, I know every parent believes their child is perfect, but my daughter would not have run away, no way, absolutely not. She's only eleven years old. The Atlanta police have come

96

up with nothing. I have been interviewed by the FBI but not heard back from them either."

Sally's eyes were watery. She was on the edge. She took a deep breath, calmed herself and looked directly at Russell. "Will you please work with Pamela and look for my daughter? I'll try to pay you whatever you want. The bank has agreed to give me a second mortgage on my home. It will take a few weeks to finalize, but I have a letter of credit made payable to you for $75,000. That's all I have right now, but I will give you most of my paycheck every week and I will place my house for sale immediately. My sister and her husband don't have much, but they promised to help me, too."

Russell stopped sipping his coffee. Sally laid an envelope on the table and continued. "I want you to take this and apply it to whatever time it will buy for you to search for my daughter. I, I know you've received more money for your work, but I can get added funds, eventually." Sally began to choke up. "And that holds true if you find Lisa safe, or if you find her.... I just can't bear thinking that she is out there somewhere scared and in pain and..." Sally stopped, closed her eyes and rubbed her forehead.

Russell stood, walked over to the large fieldstone fireplace and leaned against the thick oak mantle. He looked over the heads of the two women, out through the trees and to the lake beyond. "I decided I was going to quit this profession, because I'm not certain I have anything more to give. I've done just about everything. Twice."

He walked to the sofa, sat next to Sally and looked into her eyes. "Lisa's disappearance is unusual in that some female impostor in a police uniform apparently kidnapped her. This was a premeditated plan by a professional. If it were a male imposter, I would be inclined to believe she were kidnapped, sexually assaulted and killed. But someone went to a lot of trouble to take your daughter, so while I do not want you to have false hope, I believe she is alive. I do not know for how long or in what physical or mental condition, but I do believe she is alive."

Sally, excited, started to speak, but Russell held up his hand and said, apologetically, "But I am not the person to look for her. Let Pamela take over from Trent. She's superb. Much better than Trent or anyone else in APD. Or in the Yellow Pages, for that matter. This is not for me. I'm sorry."

Sally's face slackened, but Pamela bit her lip to control a rising fury.

"Clay, if you think Lisa is alive and can be found, I'll do the legwork, make the contacts. You stay up here, cogitate in one of those leather chairs and we'll periodically huddle. We were a team once, and I screwed it up, at least personally. Don't punish Sally for my mistakes. Lisa, bless her, may just be the tip of an iceberg. For God's sake, this smells like trafficking in children!"

Both women looked at Russell. He gazed out at the lake again, then turned to the two. "I'm very sorry, but I just can't."

Pamela began to speak, but Sally waved her back, quickly stood up and with an air of cheer that was obviously false, said, "That's understandable Mr. Russell. I wish you felt otherwise, but thank you all the same."

Sally extended her hand to Russell, who gently shook it. It was apparent Sally was on the verge of losing control. Pamela slowly rose, adjusted her glasses and gave Russell a firm handshake as though all those hours in bed sharing confidences never existed. "Thank you for seeing us Clay. It's a damn shame you let such talent lapse into sloth up here in your nifty house."

Sally started to speak, but Pamela waved her back.

"No Sally, I've got the floor now." Pamela spun back to her former lover and coolly continued, "I've only been a hospital patient once, when I was born. But hey, we're all going to die sometime. Do you want to die up here, alone, reading dusty tomes by dead authors?" She gestured to the bookshelves, "Or had you rather die doing something good? You know, Nietzsche said, 'That which does not destroy us makes us stronger,' and I believe that. OK, so you got hurt. Badly. Look at all of the war veterans that come back amputees. You didn't die. Or maybe you just died inside."

There was an electric, uncomfortable silence in the room. Outside, Winston stood up to observe. Something was wrong.

Very quietly, Russell said, "Thank you, your opinion is noted." Though polite, there was finality in his tone.

"Come on," Pamela said, coldly, "let's go."

Russell slid open the door and followed the two women back to the car. Nobody talked. Pamela fired up the engine, revved it a couple of times to let their host know she was pissed and scratched off in the black gravel drive. Some small rocks kicked up as she aimed the vehicle back for the dark passage in the woods. Russell raised his hand to wave, but the women were not looking back.

In the car, Pamela kept her head straight but cut her bright green eyes to the rearview mirror. She watched the receding figure sipping coffee. "Bastard!"

A few minutes later, where the driveway met the paved road, Pamela put the car into park, and the two sat there in silence for a moment. Pamela bit her lower lip, thinking. "That SOB. You know, Sally, this is good and bad news."

"How's that?"

"The good news is: super-detective thinks Lisa's alive, which, I hate to admit, was sound logic on his part. What he said might very well be true. The bad news is that the son-of-a-bitch won't help me search for her."

"May I ask what really happened between the two of you? Det. Trent said that you two apparently were more than just business partners."

"We got too close. I got scared." Pamela put the car in gear and stomped it.

Five miles down the mountain highway, Sally held her hand up to her mouth, closed her eyes, leaned forward and said, "Pamela, please stop the car. I don't feel well."

She quickly steered the car onto the shoulder. Sally jerked the door open, ran a few yards to a tall pine tree, put one arm around it, bent to the waist and, supporting herself with the other hand on a knee, began coughing up stomach contents in rasping bursts. Pamela watched for a few seconds, then rolled her eyes in concern and disgust. She hiss-whispered "Damn him, damn him ..." Her cell phone rang.

She saw it was Russell. After two years, she had kept his number in her address book. "Yes."

"It's me. I just talked with a friend that is an FBI agent in Miami. She said she'd be interested in speaking with you about the Collins matter. It seems that there has been an increase in kidnapping of young boys and girls, typically ages 9 to 12, over the past few years in the United States and Western Europe. They suspect organized crime but have had no solid leads."

"Great," Pamela said flatly.

"May I speak to Sally?"

"Not at the moment. Something's come up." Pamela looked out the open passenger door. Sally was slowly straightening, hands on hips, looking skyward.

"Listen, tell her this: I'll do a little investigation by phone, and if I discover anything, I'll pass it on."

"Sure. I'll tell her. As soon as she's well."

"'Well'? What's wrong with her?"

"She's holding onto a pine tree, vomiting. She was polite not to regurgitate in my car." Pamela removed her glasses and began wiping them with a tissue. "May I call you when I arrive home?"

There was silence, then a notable sigh. "Certainly."

Sally slowly returned to the car. Pamela put a small box of tissues on the dash, and as Sally got in. "There are some mints in the glove box. That was Clay. I do not wish to get your hopes up, but he has nibbled and is making some calls."

"Thanks. Sorry about that. I'm so tired." Sally wiped her eyes with a tissue, opened the glove box and took two Altoids.

Within a few minutes, Sally was asleep. Pamela kicked off her shoes and set the cruise control on 71 miles per hour. She lowered the music low, and as she twirled a blonde curl around a finger whispered, "Clayton Russell. Clay. A synonym for dirt."

———————————

Sitting in a white Adirondack chair on his boat dock, Russell reviewed the file received from Trent. All female officers had been questioned and none had been near tiny Rohm Park that day. Just as puzzling, no one remotely fit the description of the muscled, mystery cop. The artist's face sketch of the impersonator was not very helpful, but a woman described as pretty, muscular, and almost six feet tall was unique.

Russell put the sheet back into the folder, dropped it onto the dock and stared out across the lake. A female pedophile is highly unusual. If the Amazon wasn't a pedophile, maybe she was a psychopath? But would psychopaths take the time and trouble to impersonate a cop? No. More likely, she had abducted Lisa for a third party. For such effort, money had to be a motive. Where there is money, there are traffickers.

Chapter 8

Heads or Tails?

Russell called his friend with the Bureau in Miami.

She had already heard from Pamela! Not that surprising, knowing Pam. According to the FBI Special Agent, the list of suspected traffickers in young children was longer than Russell anticipated. Asia, particularly Thailand, had been the bed for sexual deviants for years. Children were bought and sold with impunity. "Human traffickers of adults and children now permeated much deeper into our society," he was told. Russell also found it fascinating that illegal trafficking of living organs was on the upswing, as the need greatly outpaced voluntary donations. Seems there was a convenient overlap in both illicit trades.

Inside the house, drinking Earl Grey ice tea, Russell lay splayed on the big sofa. Next to him, Winston dozed contentedly as his master ran a hand through the wiry fur on the dog's back. He looked up the number he had not called in years and tapped it, hoping he wasn't calling too early: Erin Wallis, sole owner and operator of The Unicorn Club, one very smart, discreet brothel in New York City.

Located on the 39th floor of a 40-story condominium complex one block off Park Avenue, Erin Wallis ran The

Unicorn Club the way a fine restaurant is run: with style, taste, discretion and an ever-changing and excellent sexual menu served in a very comfortable and attractive setting. The Unicorn Club took up most of the 39th floor and could be entered from one door that sported a subtle brass unicorn just below the peephole. Anywhere from eight to twelve "Associates," as Erin referred to her employees, were usually on duty. Operating hours were from 2:00 p.m. to 3:00 a.m., Tuesday through Saturday. All major credit cards were accepted, with a 25% discount for cash.

Take the actress Geena Davis, age her by ten years, with a slimmer body, and the result would be a fair approximation of Erin Wallis. Several years ago, Erin had taken a two-week vacation to her native Australia, leaving a long-time Associate in charge of the business. The Associate had forged her employer's name in Erin's absence and then disappeared with several hundred thousand dollars from Erin's bank accounts. Erin did not want to go to the police, even though they regularly accepted numerous donations from her. Likewise, Erin did not have insurance to cover the theft. In her business, the less attention made, the fewer the problems, particularly with the Internal Revenue Service.

Clayton Russell was referred to the madam by a law enforcement officer and friend. Russell located the thief and recovered most of the money without difficulty. Russell had flown the red eye nonstop to New York. Over an early breakfast, he returned the remaining money to Erin, who had

105

been very amused at Russell's no-frills collection style. She graciously paid him on the spot, complete with an impressive bonus, and once a year, on the anniversary of that day, which happened to be tomorrow, she had phoned him for her annual thank-you-my-dear-boy ritual.

On the sixth ring, Erin Wallis answered in her slight Aussie accent. "This is The Unicorn Club. Our doors are not yet open, but our hearts and minds are. How may we help you?"

"You can tell me everything you know about any kind of person or persons who would steal a young girl for illicit purposes."

One beat, then two, then loud laughter, politely held away from the phone. "You wild young rebel! So, you called *me* for a change, and you don't even say hello before you're interrogating an innocent woman!"

"You may be not-guilty, Erin, but I don't believe you're innocent. You're just too good at what you do."

"'Goodness had nothing to do with it,' said Mae West, "and I wholly agree with her. How are you, Clayton? What have you been doing professionally or socially since we chatted last year? Are you still single?"

"Yes, just two bachelors here."

"Are you still near Atlanta?"

"Yes, roughing it in the woods. How are you?"

"The same, 400 feet above the streets of Manhattan, where a lot of poor women make their living, some on their feet, some on their backs and some doing both. To address your question: I only socialize and conduct business with adults, you know."

"Oh yes, that's a given. But I think that a young girl's disappearance may be sexually related, possibly trafficking for sex and money. I thought you may be able to enlighten me without my having to read books. Do you mind if I ask you some questions?"

"Fire away, Sherlock. I'll tell you anything."

Russell looked at his tea glass and replied, "What kind of woman would abduct a 10-year-old girl for sexual reasons? And this woman, we think, was posing as a police officer."

"Seriously, I do not know. A gay woman wants to be with another woman, not a little girl. The lady kidnapper could have taken the child for a sick threesome with a male friend. A lot of hamster-hung men lean toward little girls. Or, more likely, the kidnapping was for someone else, for money. Or maybe the woman was really a man, disguised as a woman."

"That's an interesting idea. What groups do you think might be interested in trafficking children?"

Erin said, "If the girl had been a boy and the cop a man, I would consider the abductor as possibly being somebody from NAMBLA."

"What is Nambluh?"

"NAMBLA. N-A-M-B-L-A. It is the North American Man/Boy Love Association. It was founded in 1978 by a couple of dozen men and boys. Incredible as it seems, this group is composed of gay men who believe it's proper and correct for grown men to initiate pre-pubescent boys into the joys of homosexuality. NAMBLA members are totally unabashed in their preferences; they meet regularly and try to keep a low profile. Since pre-pubescent boys turn into post-pubescent ones, there's always a market to find new children. Sometimes little boys are adopted, I hear. Sometimes they're abducted. Supposedly even bought."

"Erin, you seem to know a lot about NAMBLA."

"You wouldn't believe some of my clientele. I've got clients who are bisexual, and some who are omni-sexual. They are pretty disgusting. They will couple with anything that has an orifice and a heartbeat. Pardon my bluntness, but it's true. One of my clients is an omni-sexual businessman based in San Francisco. He told me all about NAMBLA one night over brandy in the library. Apparently, that group is very active on the West Coast."

"Is that group ever active in The Unicorn Club?"

"Mr. Clayton Russell," Erin Wallis replied, "we have various combinations of same gender activities, but all participants are of legal age."

"Is your omni-sexual client well-connected in San Francisco?"

"He knows everybody who is anybody in the Bay Area."

"Do you think he would know somebody in NAMBLA?"

"I'm certain he either knows somebody in it, or he's in it."

"Would you mind getting a NAMBLA name or phone number from him?"

"No, not at all if I can do it in a subtle manner. But why do you want to talk to someone in NAMBLA? It was a girl who was taken."

"NAMBLA may be purchasing male children through the same trafficking organization or maybe there's a North American Woman/Girl Love Association: NAWGLA."

"That's pretty imaginative, Clay. Would it help if one of my Associates cruised the Internet to see if some of the pay adult sites have any helpful information?"

"Erin, I appreciate the offer, but Pamela has taken that route and come up empty. If they post on the web, I suspect it is password protected."

Erin's voice dropped half an octave, "Do you still look the same?"

"Yes. You'd recognize me. Everything's basically the same, but I have a few more scars. How about you? Do you still turn heads on the street and cause whiplash?"

Erin laughed a brief, throaty chuckle and said, "No, I don't look the same. I look better. And you were part of my inspiration. I've spent time, money, sweat, dedication and pride to improve my physical state, and it's also good for business. I'll show you a thing or two if and when we see each other again. Are you coming this way?"

"I don't know. I'd love to visit. I've been listening to the squirrels and birds for so long I've almost forgotten how nice it is to talk to people whom I like."

"You have an open invitation to a free, luxurious, do-whatever-you-want-to-do place to stay, here, as my guest."

"I may take you up on that someday."

"I'll call my client in California when that side of the country wakes up and get a name or two from him. I suppose you wish to remain anonymous?"

"Yes. Use the name, Redmond, Sam Redmond. Thank you Erin."

"You're welcome, honey. Chat you up later."

He stood, stretched, poured another iced tea, slid open the main front sliding glass door, which perked Winston into attention, and went outside. From a shadowy place under the deck, he retrieved some of the old practice throwing knives kept in a leather sling. He walked fifty paces into the woods, where the trees and bushes were particularly thick. Inside a small clearing, he lifted the seven-foot tall, solid wood wheel, propped it against the old oak and brushed off enough leaves so he could see the shadowy silhouette of a crouching male figure.

Sitting on the ground, Russell tapped a knife on his shoe and thought of what Erin had said.

Devil worshipping. Skulls for sale. NAMBLA. Omni-sexual people.

Russell imagined the silhouette figure on the wheel was a satanic worshipper. He jumped up and whipped away three 14-ounce Vipers in a blur, striking the target once in the neck and twice in the chest area. For half an hour, Russell practiced with the throwing knives: overhand, underhand, side throws, spin-and-draw throws. Yet again he had been reminded of all the evil in the world. Here, sequestered in nature, the customary irritant was merely the chatter of squirrels.

At 2:00 p.m., Pamela called Clay. She wanted to discuss her findings on human trafficking of children. No answer. She left a brief message and said she would call back later. She resisted the impulse to ask if he was in a hammock reading.

Winston's loyalty to his master was unquestionable.

He rarely left his side and when doing so, did not stray far. At 9:26 a.m. Winston was two hundred yards from the lake, when the dog saw something on the water that made his muscular body stiffen. A quarter mile out on the smooth cove, a lone boat was slowly cruising toward the general area of their dock. The dog could see four human shapes in the boat, saw one shape lift a hand to its head, lower the hand, and two seconds later, the dog heard the human cough. Very slowly, the Airedale began walking backwards, keeping its eyes on the boat. As soon as Winston blended into the shadows of the woods, he turned and ran. Racing through the trees, the dog quickly reached a narrow, worn path and sped along it for 300 yards, kicking up dirt and leaves until he reached home.

The Airedale ran to the east side of the house, pushed his snout into a mass of ivy that covered the wall and pulled out a weathered, green tennis ball attached to a wire. He backed up a few feet, jerked his head once to the right, sharply yanking the wire, then excitedly pranced around to the lake side of the house and sat down at the foot of the deck stairs, patiently watching the lake. A sliding glass door slid open, and Russell stepped out onto the deck and slid the door shut behind him. He leaned against the rail, took a sip of coffee and raised a small pair of Nikon binoculars up to his eyes.

There were four dark silhouettes in a 14-foot Jon boat. The occupants were too far away to see any more detail. Russell lowered the binoculars and waited for the vessel to get closer. Under dark eyebrows, the pale blue-gray eyes narrowed slightly, watching the slow progress of the boat, now some 50 yards from his boathouse and dock. His clean-shaven face was unlined, except for a slight dimple in the chin and a two-inch scar that barely appeared along the left jaw line. His wide shoulders drooped slightly, but the waist and hips were narrow and the hands and wrists showed sinewy strength under tanned skin. Watching the men approach, his face exhibited the pain and character lines at the corners of his mouth and eyes from years of rugged physical encounters. An astute observer would see the small, pea-sized scar at the right lower side of the neck, just above the collarbone. The bullet had entered from above and perforated his right lung. The other bullet scar was a nickel-sized one on the front of his left thigh, the exit scar quarter size. Fortunately, it had just nicked the femur.

Russell wore tan, ankle-cut desert boots, soft khaki slacks, a medium-width pale-brown belt and a black cotton corduroy shirt with black bone buttons, sleeves rolled halfway up the forearms. On his left wrist was a stainless steel Rolex Oyster Perpetual Datejust with the Tapestry dial. He looked like a seasoned, professional football player the day after a big game: clean, groomed, rested, wearing casual-yet-expensive clothes; but his carriage, face, expression and demeanor hinted he earned his income more with his mind than his body.

As the boat continued to approach, Russell raised the binoculars again and saw what he had suspected. The four figures were all men, and the four utensils were a rifle, two baseball bats and something he could not quite distinguish. An electric trolling motor powered the boat.

113

Russell went back into the house, picked up a phone and started to call the sheriff. Instead, he opened a hollowed out yellow pages phone book and removed a .38 Smith & Wesson revolver. He hesitated here also, then put the pistol back into its hiding place.

He dumped the coffee from the mug, then filled it with Tabasco sauce and liquid drain cleaner, 50-50, added two tablespoons of cayenne pepper, put the mug into the microwave and hit high for one minute.

Ding.

Russell retrieved the coffee mug, reached into a drawer, put a few items into his pockets and took a deep breath. Then he walked onto the deck, steaming coffee mug in one hand, the other in his pocket.

The Jon boat was fifty feet from his dock. He heard muted curses as they tied the boat and began to walk up through the trees. They trudged in single file, their loud, tramping feet shuffling leaves and dust on the sloping path.

The first man, sixtyish, wore work boots, overalls, a dirty denim shirt and a mud-colored cardigan sweater with holes in it and an old straw hat with a green plastic visor in the brim that cast an eerie emerald glow on his deeply-seamed, white-whiskered face. He held a baseball bat in his right hand and an almost empty fifth of Early Times Bourbon in his left. The second man appeared to be in his late thirties and wore cowboy boots, jeans, a gray, sleeveless sweatshirt and a red Peterbilt cap. He carried a baseball bat. The third

114

man looked to be about forty and wore an oil-stained mechanic's jumpsuit, black work boots and a week's worth of salt-and-pepper beard stubble. The man lacked the little and ring fingers on his right hand. In his left, he held a rusted, black machete. The last man seemed to be in his thirties and wore mustard-colored athletic shoes, dirty olive workpants, a black sweatshirt and a soiled Atlanta Braves baseball cap turned backwards. He carried a deer rifle slung in his arms upside down, the way Davy Crockett carried muskets in the movies.

The four men stopped twenty feet from the deck. Beside Russell, two paces away, stood Winston, frozen in a point.

The older of the four men, keeping his eyes on Russell, turned his green-cast face slightly to the left and hoarsely whispered, "Izzat him?"

Machete-man grumbled, "That's him, daddy. That's Clayton Russell."

Without moving his lips, Russell whispered softly, "Winston, en garde." The Airedale remained still, but his muscled haunches rippled slightly.

The old man looked insolently at Russell, took a long pull from the bourbon, licked his lips and said, "D'yoono who we are, Mr. fuckin' Russell?"

Expressionless, Russell said nothing. High above in a tree, a blue jay began to warble. At the lake's edge, a large fish broke and slapped the surface.

115

"You shore fucked up this fambly!" the old man growled. "These two boys here," the old man jerked his head sideways, "spent a whole, helluva lot o' time in a Fedruhl shithole, and you are the reason they did! Whatchoo gotta say 'bout that!"

Clayton Russell remained silent but quickly reflected on the four shabby men in front of him. This was the male contingent of the clan Meechum, from Albany, Georgia, and the two younger brothers were a particularly obnoxious, deadly pair whom Russell had encountered almost a decade before.

Dwight and Billy Meechum burglarized the home of a prosperous, retired Atlanta couple, torturing the two with pistol whippings and cigarette burns until Mr. Rosenthal revealed the location of his safe. The homeowner was forced, at gun point, to open an old Mosler vault in the floor. Before leaving, the two burglars blinded the couple with one of Billy's hooked carpet knives, a tool from his job. "Dwight did the holding, and Billy did the cutting," as the criminals testified at their trial, ".... so those Jew bastards wouldn't be able to finger us."

Mrs. Rosenthal suffered fatal injuries, but her husband survived. He hired a succession of detectives to locate the brothers the Atlanta police said, sheepishly; "had just vanished." A friend of the widower referred the victim to Clayton Russell.

"Find those animals, whatever it takes," Marc Rosenthal had instructed Russell, offering him a substantial retainer and a staggering sum at the time should he succeed. The detective convinced his client to submit to hypnotic suggestion, and Mr. Rosenthal responded with a subliminal recall pearl. The brothers had mentioned "... humpin' the whores at Whitelaw's after the liquor at Firewater's." He recalled the names Dwight and Billy, described a 'flag eye' and his assailants' south Georgia accents. Russell located the two establishments, Whitelaw's and Firewater's, just outside Albany. It took Russell a week hanging out at Firewater's before he finally heard a redneck native call out, "Yo Billy... Dwight! Get your asses over here!"

Russell surreptitiously taped several minutes of the trio's conversation with a recorder hidden in his denim jacket. He stepped outside and phoned Mr. Rosenthal in Atlanta, who verified the voices as belonging to his assailants. He then returned to Firewater's with a plan to taunt Dwight, the brother who had a chilling, unmistakable feature: an artificial eye whose art was not a replica of an iris and pupil but of a Confederate flag. When Dwight stepped up to the bar for another beer, right next to Russell, the detective said, "Hey Popeye, do you mind if I go outside and fuck Olive?" Russell had walked quickly out the door and to the pickup truck with camper he had rented, where he pretended to fumble with the keys as he readied for them. The brothers Meechum were going to do it fast, with fists,

117

but Russell won, with a leather glove and brass knuckles on the right hand, partnered with blackjack and wrist-strap on the left.

Within five minutes the Meechums were sleeping soundly, trussed in the back of the camper. By morning Russell had deposited the two, handcuffed to each other, around a tall light pole near the Atlanta City Hall.

And now, apparently paroled, they had located him in seclusion and were looking for revenge.

"Talk to me motherfucker!" the old man bellowed.

Russell had decided the old man was well-positioned to strike first and also an intoxicated weak link.

"Cat got your tongue, cocksuckah?" Dwight Meechum piped up, lifting his bat a few inches.

Russell pretended to take a sip. The fumes from the mug's contents stung his eyes.

"Goddam, look a' that... this shakin' sack o' shit's so scared he startin' to cry! I'm gonna take first crack, and you boys can clean up."

The old man shook his bat a couple of times, took a last pull from the Early Times bottle, tossed it aside and began to slowly move toward the deck.

The Airedale began to quiver, and Russell calmly whispered, "Winston, heel."

In a flash of brown fur and bared fangs, the huge dog leapt from the top stair step and bowled papa Meechum over snapping his jaws onto the man's left heel, sinking the large

118

teeth through sock and flesh into the man's heel bone and began horribly shaking the leg and dragging the man backwards in the dirt. The dog simply obeyed the literal command: *Destroy the heel of the nearest antagonist.* The old man screamed and vainly tried kicking the dog in the muzzle with his free leg, but the dog was shaking so furiously that papa Meechum's leg just punched air.

The other three men jumped back, and Russell acted instantly: in a blur, he dropped to one knee and hurled the coffee mug at the man with the rifle; the mug hit the man squarely in the chest, shooting a generous splash of the liquid up into his nose and face, causing him to drop the rifle and join his father's screaming; Russell whipped a silvery object out of a front pocket and swung the object hard, like a pitcher winging a fastball. The razor-sharp, 10-ounce Viper II knife whirred through the air and cut into the gunman's sweatshirt, slicing into the solar plexus, sinking to the hilt in the man's diaphragm, causing him to immediately blackout, sink to his knees and fall on top of the rifle. The knife wound was not mortal. It was an old commando tactic for taking out a sentry before the person can scream.

Russell knew the fight was almost over. Now, flat on his back and stirring up an increasing cloud of dust, the elder Meechum was screaming so shrilly that he just hissed. Every third or fourth kick connected with the dog's shoulder or muzzle, but the blows had little effect. The dog seized a better jaw clamp on papa Meechum, and now the animal's teeth began to further crack and splinter the heel bone. The man's screams changed key, reflecting the heightened level of pain. The two conscious sons, temporarily paralyzed, now rushed to the father, looking for an angle from which to attack the thrashing dog. Winston shook and moved so quickly, it was difficult to find a good position from which to strike. As Dwight attempted with his bat, Billy Meechum shook the blade, then hurled the three-foot machete at Russell's head and jumped for the rifle. Russell ducked down to the left, and the machete rang off the wooden frame of a sliding glass panel as he pulled out another Viper and vaulted over the deck rail. Billy turned over his brother, Russell whipped the second knife at Billy's leg and the stainless steel blade sank into the back of the man's right knee. Billy grunted with the pain and dropped down on the injured knee, howling in agony, but managed to grasp the rifle, twist and aim the weapon at Russell, who had now picked up the father's dropped baseball bat. Russell cocked and swung, whacked the rifle out of the man's hands, then reversed motion to crack Billy's jaw, knocking him unconscious. As the second brother fell on top of the first, Russell turned to see the largest Meechum lift his bat high overhead, preparing to smash it over Winston. Russell sprinted and swung the metal bat, blocking the third son's weapon so forcefully the six-foot-four man spun around almost 360°. Remarkably, the large man did not drop it until Russell side kicked him in the stomach and used the heel of his right hand to strike him under the chin with a short, chopping uppercut. The three Meechum brothers were down, and the father continued to be shaken like a giant rat, which, in Russell's mind, was a benevolent metaphor.

"Winston, that's enough," Russell said, and the dog immediately released the mangled leg, backed up three paces and waited for the next command.

"Uhhh... ahhh... ARRHHHHH!" roared William Lamar Meechm Sr., as the newspapers and TV news programs would later reference him. He began to pound the dirt with his fists in fury and pain, causing twin dust clouds to rise up on either side of the horizontal body. The old man bared his teeth in rage. The green-visored straw hat was gone, and the top half of the man's head was bone white, contrasting with the tan, enraged face. Flecks of pale brown liquor foam and small, white spittle bubbles outlined the gash of his mouth. As he sat up on one leg, turning to Russell, the old man belched out the threat, "I'm going to take that fuckin' club and stick it up your mutherfuckin.... " Russell ended the crude threat with a solid bunt to the man's right cheekbone.

As Russell tossed the bat aside, he congratulated his companion. "Good dog, Winston." The Airedale walked over, sat and lifted a paw to shake.

Russell dragged the four men to a two-foot thick pine tree, removed the blades from the bodies, arranged them in a circle around the tree and then handcuffed them to each other: ankle to wrist to ankle to wrist.

He went inside, phoned the sheriff's office, then took a leisurely shower, knowing the deputies were at least a half hour away. He dressed in a burgundy knit shirt, khaki slacks and brown boat shoes. Twenty minutes later, four county cars roared up, blue lights on, sirens off. The officers exchanged Russell's cuffs with their own, placed the men in the back of two cars and the junior deputy completed an incident report with Russell.

He watched the strange caravan leave his property and disappear into the woods. "Unbelievable," he said.

Russell went inside and threw an extra change of clothing and his toilet kit into a soft leather carryall. He activated the security system, petted Winston, unlocked the camouflaged pet door, filled up the dog's food and water bowls, locked up and walked downstairs to the three-car garage. His current vehicles were a dark green Range Rover, a navy blue 740i BMW that had been custom-made into a convertible and a BMW K 1200 S motorcycle with sidecar that could hurl Russell from 0-60 in 4 seconds. Russell put his bag in the trunk of the 740i, started the engine and touched the center garage opener. By 5:45 p.m. he had reached the outskirts of Atlanta. It was rush hour but not too bad going against the thick stream of traffic leaving the city. He exited onto Ashford Dunwoody Road, passed the mall, turned right onto Mount Vernon and then left onto Jet Ferry.

Why was he going to Pamela's house unannounced? He flipped the switch that put the top down. The unseasonably cool air felt refreshing on his face and through his hair, clarifying his thoughts.

Within a few minutes he arrived at the three story split level mansion and parked. Her mother and father had died only months before Russell met Pamela, and they left her enough inheritance to live comfortably. As he walked to the door, he suspected she was not home. He still had a key to her residence but knew not to use it. He would wait for her to arrive home.

Suddenly he was very tired.

When Pamela saw the weathered wooden sign with the sunken letters, carved and painted cattle-brand style, that read ROHM PARK EST. 1953, she reduced speed. There was the single wooden park bench and behind it the stand of trees that Trent had included in his report. A few people were walking up and down the street. A mom with a dog. A dad coming home from the bus stop, carrying a tired leather briefcase that matched his worn face. A young girl, walking alone, as Lisa Collins probably had that day.

She drove the car slowly up and down the street a couple of times to familiarize herself with the neighborhood. When people disappear, searches often extend far away. Yet, in any of these innocent looking, half-century old brick homes, Lisa could be chained in an attic, buried in a basement or planted in a garden. Jaycee Dugard had been kidnapped and kept hidden in a backyard for 18 years.

Pamela Waters looked at many of the houses with sharp eyes and an ever-suspicious mind. None of the houses look neglected. This was not a neighborhood of boarded, broken windows. No home appeared sinister enough to possess the tangy, acid-sweet aroma of a decomposing body. People were friendly and returned her waves. Dogs wagged tails when she made smooching sounds.

Pamela drove back to the park, shut off the engine and got out. She tried to envision a 10-year-old child talking to a strange female officer and then, what? She stood up and walked back to the stand of bushes behind the bench, where she found a narrow opening and squeezed into the greenery. It was an interesting and cozy little space. The kind of space where two small kids would play doctor or two slightly older kids may smoke pot. Where two teens in love would couple or where an adult abducted a child. She would talk to Timmy but wanted to see Sally at home first.

Pamela drove to the Collins' house, raised the windows of the car and locked it. She had skipped her usual blue jeans and wore a skirt and blouse with flat shoes. Walking up the steps to the long front porch, she estimated the house to be about 80 years old. Manicured ivy covered most of the small front yard, and colorful flowers lined the window boxes that ran the length of the wide porch. Three sets of French doors opened onto the porch. Looking inside, she saw a living and dining room that seemed recently refurbished. She pressed the bell and saw Sally Collins walk down the long hallway to the door. Still in her work clothes, she brushed back her hair with one hand and opened the door.

"Hello, Pamela," she said quietly. "Come on in, please. May I get you something to drink? There's fresh coffee, juice or water."

"No, thanks. I'm fine. Sally, I know we went through a lot of this before at my office and on the drive to Russell's place. I also know you have been through it repeatedly with the FBI and local police, but I would like to take a look myself."

"Sure. You know, I used to caution Lisa constantly about strangers, but I never warned her about the police. She was to call on them if she needed help." Sally breathed deeply, pain showing in her face. "So, if that policewoman had anything to do with this, I'm sure Lisa would not have suspected anything."

"Has Lisa consumed alcohol or drugs, to your knowledge?"

"No. Are kids really starting so young? I was asked so many questions like that. It's that computer. I've been reading a lot about the way a predator can locate someone by Internet. Do you think that is how they found Lisa? They saw her on the Internet?"

Pamela suspected that was precisely how Lisa was selected, but why tell Sally that now? "I don't know, yet. Det. Trent released your daughter's computer to me after he received your call authorizing him to do so. I doubt I will find something they missed, but I hope to inspect it this weekend when I have some additional time. I also want to review Lisa's personal CDs."

Pam followed Sally down the hallway and into a small room with sky-blue walls, white trim, a small coal-burning fireplace and a few pieces of white furniture that roughly matched the wall trim.

"Have you changed anything in Lisa's room?"

"No. I want it to be the same as she left it when she returns home."

For the next half hour, Pamela dissected Lisa Collins' room the way a skilled watchmaker examines an expensive timepiece. She remembered how Clay and she would pore over every square inch of every piece of evidence. She looked at the child's clothing, games, doll collection, even removed the vents to explore for hidden drugs or maybe a diary of which her mother was unaware. If you want to know an adult, ask the secretary, not the spouse. But for children, their lives are revealed among their personal effects and computers. And for anyone, regardless of age, who uses the internet socially there are no secrets. All can be revealed in a hard drive and on the web.

"I understand Lisa did not keep a diary, to your knowledge, but she posted on Facebook. Anywhere else, like MySpace?"

"Yes, she did. And she had three photos of herself posted with just her first name, not her last."

Pamela made a mental note to discuss this with Clay and Det. Trent. (She was more certain now that Clay was going to be of help, but how much she could not guess.) Photos of a beautiful, young female like Lisa would be an enormous enticement to Internet predators. As Pamela extended her hand and thanked Sally, the mother stared blankly at the detective and robotically shook her hand.

Three minutes later, Pamela pulled in front of the Taylor's house, where she sat in the car for a few moments, thinking. Then she drove away to a Chevron convenience store she had passed at the corner of Virginia and North Highland Roads. She recalled her conversation with Trent and Timmy's affinity for fireballs. She phoned the Taylors, identified herself and asked if she could drop by briefly. Pamela returned to the Taylor's house, trotted up the steps of a residence much like Lisa's, and before she could knock, the slender, dark-haired woman opened the door and smiled broadly. "Hi, I'm Zan Taylor. Come in. Timmy's back in the sunroom. Would you like some iced tea?"

"No thank you."

Pamela followed her through a slightly more modern version of Sally's home. In the very back of the house was a

127

bright 15 by 20-foot sunroom. It was filled with lush green plants, four bright pieces of wicker furniture and Timmy Taylor, lounging on a loveseat. The boy wore tennis shoes, jeans and a rumpled, canary yellow sweatshirt with a Batman logo. He was reading Mad magazine.

Before Mrs. Taylor could make the introduction, Pamela nodded to Timmy's magazine. "Do they still carry Spy vs. Spy?"

"Uh, yeah," Timmy replied, a bit surprised that someone this old would know what's inside Mad magazine. "But it's not funny this time."

"Your mom told you why I was coming here?"

The boy sighed. "Yep."

"Timmy, I know you have told lots of people what you saw at Rohm Park the day Lisa disappeared, but maybe we could go over there and walk through it together."

"Mom won't let me ride on that street any more," Timmy said with a touch of defiance, cutting a glance at his mother.

"It'll be OK with the three of us," Zan Taylor quickly countered.

"Good." Pamela reached into her jeans pocket, pulled out an Atomic Fireball, removed the wrapper, looked at the two and innocently asked, with arched eyebrows, "Either of you want a fireball?"

Zan shook her head negatively, but as anticipated, Timmy vigorously nodded yes. Pam tossed one to the boy.

She then quizzed him about the day. Few adults would have better detailed recall of two months prior than this child. Pamela was impressed. He looked out the window, tongued the fireball from cheek to cheek as he answered her.

"So when that school day was over, you left, on your bike, and started pedaling home?"

"Yes ma'am."

"Let's go take a look at the park."

When they arrived at Rohm Park, Pamela said, "Timmy, show me where the white car was parked, so I can park in the same location."

"Pull up some more. A little more. More. Whoa!"

Pamela turned off the engine. "Let's get out. I want you to walk down the street like you're riding your bicycle— act like you're holding the handlebars, if you wish—and tell me everything you saw, heard, smelled or wondered about."

They exited and Timmy held up his arms to grip imaginary bicycle handlebars.

"I was pedaling down this hill," as he began to walk down the street with Pam beside him. "And I saw the car. A cop car. Then I saw Lisa and the pretty cop. She was really tall." Timmy was speaking slower and more distinctly than usual in a mature effort to use correct language. "They sat on that bench, and Lisa wasn't happy."

"How do you know she wasn't happy?"

"She was frowning."

"Was the policewoman touching her?"

"No."

"Then what happened?"

"Then I coasted down the hill. To that corner." Timmy pointed to the intersection 40 yards away. "Then I came back," he continued, re-gripping the invisible bicycle as he turned around, "and pedaled back up the hill." The boy began to walk up the hill.

"Why?"

"I wanted to see what they were doing."

"And what did you see when you pedaled back up this hill?"

"I saw the car. I saw the bench, but nobody was on the bench. My legs were hurting a little from the steep hill." Timmy began walking slower, making more exaggerated steps, lifting his feet higher, hanging out his tongue in mock fatigue. Zan Taylor, leaning against Pam's car, was fascinated. Her son seemed almost hypnotized. "I looked in the car. There was nothing in it."

"What do you mean nothing?"

"No cop stuff. No window between the front and back. And the front looked different. I didn't see a police radio or anything on the dash like, you know, no cop stuff."

"Anything else?"

"The window was open, and I could smell suntan lotion, like at the beach. And pancakes, blueberry pancakes, like mom makes."

"Then what did you do?"

"I turned around right here." Timmy angled 20 feet in front of the car. "And I coasted back down the hill, then went home, 'cause my legs were tired."

"When you biked by the car, the last time, did you look back at the bench?"

"Yes. It was empty and I still did not see anybody."

"Did you look at those bushes?" Pam pointed to the stand of bushes where the bloodhound had lost the scent.

"I don't know. Maybe, but I don't remember seeing anything."

"I could use another fireball, Timmy. What about you?"

As she drove mother and son away from the park, Timmy asked Pamela questions about all the gadgets on the car. She answered curtly, her mind in other places. At the Taylor's house, Pamela thanked Zan, then said to Timmy, "Thank you very much. You're a super smart guy."

She extended her hand, Timmy shook it, felt the palmed fireball and smiled at her wink. He put on his poker face and quickly pocketed the candy.

Pamela left and drove to Rohm Park for a third visit to the crime scene. The sun was getting low, and her mind began to stray. Twilight was a favorite time for love making with Clay.

She parked where the abductor's car had been, got out, walked over to the park bench and looked around. Why would the car have smelled of suntan lotion and blueberry pancakes? The two are not complementary. There's no such thing as pancakes that taste or smell like suntan lotion, is there? Don't think so. Is there a suntan lotion that smells like blueberries?

She returned to the car and pulled Trent's report out of her briefcase. As she flipped through it, she saw no reference to the smells. Standard incident reports always note the weather. It had been clear. She fastened her seatbelt, started the car and drove away, slowly, replaying everything Timmy had said. As she headed home, she could not remove the suntan lotion/blueberry pancake thoughts from her mind.

Half an hour later, approaching her home, she saw Clay's car. He was behind the wheel, asleep. Her heart raced, and she felt those old familiar butterflies in her stomach. Why did she react like a lovesick teenager around him?

Chapter 9

Healing Old Wounds

Russell fell asleep listening to classical music on the radio. He was startled by the light tapping on his car window. He opened one eye and saw a long, slim finger with a pale, pink nail briskly tap the driver's side glass. The fit body he knew so well was visible from the neck down. He lowered the window.

"Clay," she looked at his face, "Jesus, you're exhausted. Come on in." She opened his door.

Russell signed and slowly got out. He forced a smile. "Thanks. It's been a long day."

As he straightened up she saw brown blood drops on his shoes. "What happened to you?"

"There was a scuffle at the house. Trespassers. Remember the Meechums?. Sheriff Tomberlin has custody of the bunch."

"Is Winston hurt?"

"He's fine. Home alone and most likely sleeping."

Ten minutes later, his shoes off and feet up, Russell told her about the Meechum encounter. Pamela made her trademark tossed Caesar salad, baked potato and steak. Russell ate like a condemned man on death row and began to yawn.

She removed his bag from the car as Russell showered for the third time that day. He put on a large, white terry robe hanging from a hook on the door. It was clean and fresh. He was touched that she had kept it, a gift from her to him on Valentine's Day, three years prior.

For a quarter hour they discussed the Collins case. For five minutes they discussed their shelved romantic relationship. And for two minutes they kissed, slowly, without speaking.

Pamela opened her eyes, brushed the black hair off his forehead. "Separate bedrooms tonight, OK?"

"Platonic is fine with me."

"I'll be in the pink palace. You can sleep wherever you wish. First one up in the morning makes coffee, O.K?"

"Sure."

Pamela paused, for a moment. She rarely was at a loss for voicing an opinion, and especially so with Russell. "Clay, you're too old to be getting into altercations; especially with hillbillies. Why didn't Winston and you just drive away and call the sheriff? What the hell were you thinking?"

"I was bored and pissed. They were trash and trespassing. I must admit that I also wanted to see how well I could thump them. Correction: how well we could thump them."

Pamela looked into the blue eyes, studied the tan face and had a quick image of what he might look like dead, horizontal in a black suit and casket. She instantly erased the thought from her mind and gave him a quick kiss on the forehead. "Typical male, thinking with the wrong end."

A few minutes later Russell was asleep, snoring lightly. Pamela stayed awake another hour, curled on the sofa. She sipped wine and thought about the Collins case and her plans for tomorrow. She also thought how nice it felt to have her good friend in her home for the night.

Russell rose at 7:30 a.m. He looked into Pamela's room. Her cat was curled up on the end of the bed, but Pam had already left. A hot carafe of coffee in the kitchen with a note next to it said to make himself at home, please inquire among his female friends about any suntan lotion that smells like blueberries and if he needed to reach her, just call the mobile number.

He felt at home. Pamela was good at giving orders, and today he did not feel offended. He went into her office, booted up the computer and read newspapers and magazines online for two hours. At 9:45, he made a second pot of coffee, poured a fresh mug and called the most expensive store at Lenox Square shopping center in Buckhead.

"Good morning, Neiman Marcus, how may I direct your call?"

"Ladies' fragrances, please. Felicia Marsh."

Felicia had the best aromas and the most beautiful legs in Atlanta, which was no surprise: she sold expensive perfumes and ran marathons. Russell hoped she was working that day. If anyone could help, she could.

"Ladies' fragrances, how may I help you?"

"Felicia, it's Clayton Russell. How are you?"

"Clay! I'm fine. Well, is this a social or business call?"

"It's business. Have you ever heard of a suntan lotion or cream with the aroma of blueberries? Or blueberry pancakes?"

"It sounds like Nudus Bleu suntan oil. It feels wonderful and is one of the world's finest tan enhancers. It's favored by nudists. Nudists who have money, I might add. Wheat and blueberry are added to moisturize the skin, plus dye it a darker hue. It works quite well."

"Where would I purchase it?"

"We used to carry it here at Neiman's. But we didn't sell enough, so it was discontinued. Several places in Europe continue to carry it. The Cloister hotel on Sea Island also carried it in the past. Do you know it costs about $80 for six ounces? I can special order it if you are interested. We can have it for you within three days."

"Yes. Please order it in the smallest size available." He gave her his credit card information, FedEx number, slowly hung up the phone and said, "Son of a bitch."

The following afternoon, Russell found the package from Sea Island in his post office box. He rushed home, sat on the deck and studied the small box.

YOUR SPECIAL ORDER FROM The Cloister, it read on the outside.

Russell opened it and looked at the six-ounce tube of Nudus Bleu. A stylized painting of a nude man and woman was on the dark blue label. He unscrewed the gold cap and squeezed some of the indigo cream onto a palm and sniffed it. Coppertone and blueberry pancakes. Pam was correct; the kid had accurately described the smell. An attractive, extraordinarily tall, athletic woman dressed as a police officer and who used Nudus Bleu had abducted Lisa Collins.

Did the woman come from Europe? Had she stayed as a guest at The Cloister? Russell thought he had a thread. But if so, to where?

Two lengthy hospital stays? That's the rearview mirror—look through the windshield. He fished out a quarter from his front pocket.

"If it's heads, we take the case, Winston. Tails, we go to Jamaica for two weeks' vacation." He tossed the quarter. Eagle. He flipped the coin again. Eagle. He repeated the action a third time, finally uncovering George Washington.

"Heads it is, Winston," he said without emotion. The dog's tail wagged a few token thumps on the dock in reply.

At sunset Pamela and Russell sat on his dock with Winston next to them, splayed out flat, almost asleep. They discussed faux police, Nudus Bleu, NAMBLA, serial killers, the red-eyed mother, an empty stand of bushes, Lisa Collins and a street pantomime by the little boy who had last seen her.

Russell wore khaki shorts and a peach colored Polo golf shirt with old black tennis shoes. His nut-brown skin was sullied in half a dozen places visible to the eye where foreign objects—lead, steel, wood and human teeth—had perforated, leaving small jagged places that no longer tanned. Inside was scar tissue on one lung and, Pamela was certain, his heart. But on the outside, the slightly flawed exterior, with two small sections of early gray hair at the temples, were the only evidence of higher than normal mileage.

Pamela was dressed in a loose white cotton skirt that fell mid way down her calves. Her figure was enhanced by the teal colored tight fitting spandex top with spaghetti straps. Flip flops had been kicked aside, and her perfume, the toss of her hair and soft giggle suggested she was at his home to flirt and not merely discuss business.

"Clay, it's getting cool. Let's go up to the house."

When they were inside, Russell locked all the doors, turned on some low ceiling track lights and then stretched out on the long sofa.

"Clay, do you mind if I put on some music?"

"Go ahead."

Pamela walked to the audio section of the massive bookshelf wall. She tilted her head and looked at the classical discs. The usual works from noted composers were in a long row, then the discs segued into movie scores. She selected the soundtrack from the Kubrick film Barry Lyndon. As the music began, Russell remarked, "Isn't that a bit dramatic?"

"Yes, my friend, and so is life." She went into the kitchen, poured a glass of Kendall Jackson Merlot and adjusted the controls for the intercoms on the eaves of the deck for music to play softly outside. She then walked outside and sat side-saddle on the deck rail to survey the boats and lake. For several minutes she replayed her time with Russell, from the moment they met until now. The affair had the shape of a classic bell curve: meet, touch, kiss, bed, more bed, less bed, friction-and-harsh words, then adios. What a damn, stupid shame. And what caused the break? It was not a single incident, just two headstrong personalities that had meshed and then separated. One thing that they could never agree upon was who would move in with whom. Both loved their respective homes and space. How trivial when compared to the bigger things. Pamela bit her lip. And now they were together, again, because of a mystery and perhaps a tragedy. She brushed away a single tear; then shrugged off the sadness. Since a little girl, she had been able to gradually shift into a positive frame of mind and mood. She walked back inside, grabbed Russell's hand and pulled him up off the sofa.

"Let's dance. I'll lead." And lead she did, with her left hand clasping his right, her right hand splayed wide at the base of his spine and her feet, now free of shoes, lightly tip-toeing across the shiny oak floor.

"I can't remember the last time we did this." Russell laughed and held her closer.

"I can." Pamela's expression was serious. Russell was clueless.

"Pam, I'm not sure…"

"Hush, Clay." She put a finger on his lips. She held both of his hands and began to walk backwards, toward the master bedroom. He went with her, hesitantly. She gave him a sharp tug, and he picked up the pace.

"Pam, do you think we should…"

"Quiet. Sometimes you think too much. Besides, you said I could lead.'

Chapter 10

Unraveling Threads

On July 26, Russell rose before dawn, left Pam sleeping in his bed and ran the workout trail with Winston beside him in total blackness that slowly went through varying shades of gray.

The smell of rain was in the air. He showered and dressed in a white sweatshirt, faded jeans and tennis shoes, then penned a list of things he wished to accomplish that day. He peeked into the room and she smiled, sitting up in bed and drinking coffee. While out on his run, Pamela had called Sally. She could hear excitement in Sally's voice when told that Russell and she would be working as a team. Compensation was deferred for Clay, and it was agreed that $1000 per day plus joint expenses would cover them both. Sally had almost lost hope. Stunned, she stammered, "Why, that is incredible. I just ... "

"We'll discuss it later," Pamela interjected. "Let me go now—but do us a favor, soon: drop by my office with additional photographs of Lisa, the more recent the better. Also, if Lisa has any birthmarks, scars, tattoos, moles or other distinguishing marks on her body, would you describe them in detail and note where they were located? If I'm not there, leave it with the receptionist downstairs. Take care, see you soon."

Sally, dazed, had slowly tried to hang up the phone without looking, missed the cradle, and then got it on the third try. She closed her eyes, put both hands up to her mouth, leaned against the refrigerator and began to quietly weep. Oh God, she prayed, please help them find my baby alive....

Now Russell walked to the bed and kissed Pam on the forehead. "I'm going to see whether we can get some leads through the Adam Walsh Foundation and make some calls on that list of missing children you obtained from the FBI agent in Miami."

An hour later, after scrambled eggs for both and sausage for Russell, Pamela gave him a very long hug good-bye. "I've got some leads I want to follow. I also need to call London. It seems some very valuable relics are missing."

Clayton Russell watched as Pamela picked her things off the table and briskly walked out, waving over her shoulder without looking. She was always in a hurry, he mused.

Russell went to work. The Federal Bureau of Investigation kept a computerized file on all reported missing people, and he wanted more details. He called the Atlanta field office, (404) 679-9000, said he was the new partner of Det. Trent, APD, and asked to speak with the investigating officer for all kidnapped children occurring within the past two years. Special Agent Warren Cooper came on the line, and Russell asked him whether any of the missing children cases involved abduction by someone wearing a uniform? He was told only one reported, in San Francisco, and the agent gave Russell a direct line number to the detective division of the San Francisco Police Department.

"We had a similar missing person case about 18 months ago", the officer explained. "A 12-year-old boy vanished. Straight kid, from what I remember, nice looking. Parents were divorced, and he lived with his mother. One Saturday, mom and son are shopping, son gets tired, and the mom suggests the boy go to a park to wait for her. According to the mother, her son set out toward the park, and that's the last she saw him. The kid never turned up. anywhere."

"So, other than the park angle, what's the similarity?"

"There was one eyewitness who saw the boy after the mother. A teenager swore he saw the child talking to a woman in the park, a nun. The nun was never identified, though. We suspect she was an imposter."

Russell's scalp began to tingle. He sat straight up in his chair, "Do you remember anything else?"

"No, but I didn't handle it, another detective did."

"Is he still with the department?"

"Yes. In fact, he'll be here in a couple of hours, if you want to talk to him."

"Yes I do. It's very important. Can you take a message?" Russell gave his name and number to the detective, who assured him that his call would be returned. "That case upset the department quite a bit, especially the lead investigator. You'll hear back."

Russell thanked him, hung up the phone and stared out the window. "Son of a bitch!" Another uniform! Effective means to lure children of all ages.

Russell had spoken with John Walsh several times in the past, and the two men had immense respect for one another. Russell greatly admired the fact that a man whose young son had been abducted and brutally murdered could establish the Adam Walsh Foundation and then a few years later create and host the television show *America's Most Wanted*. To date, the show had helped in the successful location and arrest of over 1100 felons. Russell had a great appreciation of the media's power to find a person or thing. And he was not so naive or egotistical to think that any one person, or team of persons, could locate a child who had so utterly vanished. But someone among the millions of viewers of that program might be able to help do so.

Russell first called the office in Florida and ordered a package on child safety. He then dialed John Walsh's mobile number and immediately connected.

"Hello."

"John, this is Clay Russell. Hope I didn't catch you at an inconvenient time."

"Hey, Clay, it's good to hear from you. I'm on the road but can certainly chat. How are you?"

"I'm great. Congratulations on your 1100-plus collars."

"Thank you. We're proud of our record, and it's nice to be in a line of work that actually does some measurable good. How about you? I haven't heard from you in a couple of years."

"I've been out of the loop for a while, sort of retired, I guess, but I'm working on a case now that's hit a wall. I think it might be a good one for your program."

"What are the facts?"

"Four months ago an eleven-year-old girl, A-student, vanishes in Atlanta after school. Mother is a widow with limited financial means, so ransom has not been the motive. We think she may have been kidnapped by some child trafficking ring. An interesting twist is the M.O. may be associated with the disappearance of another child, but male, around the same age, in San Francisco recently."

"Who is 'we'?"

"A Det. Trent, Atlanta PD, handled the initial investigation. No leads. Timmy, the last person to see the child was a boy about her age. Lisa was sitting on a park bench, talking to a policewoman. We believe a woman impersonated a police officer and forcibly abducted the child. My initial information on the kidnapping in San Francisco is a woman impersonating a nun abducted that child as well."

"Hold on, Clay, I'm pulling over, so I can write this down."

Russell heard muted traffic sounds and then, "O.K: What is the mother's name and contact number?"

"Sally Collins. 404-876-5305."

"Atlanta, you said? I'm going to have one of our producers call and see if she'd agree for us to conduct an interview and tape a segment. Three months ago?"

"Yes."

"Mm ... I wish I had known earlier. Where are you going with the case?"

"I intend to continue to pursue the thread in San Francisco. The disappearances are so similar."

"You know, the criminal mind is truly amazing and perverse. I'm near the airport. I've got to run, but AMW will check this out. Good luck with the hunt at your end."

"Thanks."

Russell pulled an O'Doul's from the refrigerator, added a lime wedge and slid the beer into a mug holder as his telephone rang. It was the Inspector from San Francisco P.D., calling about the missing boy. The two men discussed details, exchanged information and noted the similarities of both disappearances.

The west coast inspector sighed deeply. "The only clue into the missing boy's case was the eyewitness account of him talking with a nun in Golden Gate Park."

"Any details?"

"There wasn't much, just like on your end. The witness said the boy was sitting on a park bench with a nun who appeared to be between twenty five and forty five years of age. Poor description, but we believed the witness to be reliable."

"Why?"

"He was a sixteen-year-old Mormon teen who was articulate and observant. You know the Mormons pride themselves on integrity. And his is a very good family. Tragically, the witness died a week after we interviewed him. Hit and run. We found the car, stolen. No clues, other than the young man's blood on the front fender."

"You sound upset."

"I am. Some person or persons went to a lot of trouble to take the child. And I think the same folks killed our witness to keep him quiet."

"What makes you think that?"

"He was a smart kid and physically fit. No caffeine, alcohol, tobacco—typical, Mormon kid. He ran cross-country. On his body, the upper arms and the back of his neck, we found multiple bruising. From the evidence, we concluded he was probably grabbed while jogging and thrown in front of a car. We've got a missing boy, a dead witness and no more leads. We recovered some DNA but could not get a match when running the sample through the FBI database. I suspect it may be because the criminal or criminals were foreign."

"Why foreign?"

"I don't really know, Mr. Russell, just a gut feeling I have."

The two men promised to exchange files and keep one another abreast of any new developments. He would send his file to Det. Trent in Atlanta, along with the taped interview of the witness. Before they hung up Russell told him to expect a call from John Walsh. Maybe connecting the two cases via mass media would generate a solid lead.

Winston was down at the dock, wagging his tail, looking at something in the shallow lake water. Russell cut loose with a wolf whistle, and the Airedale instantly turned, spotted Russell and bounded off the dock and up the path. Winston leapt onto the deck, shook his haunches and tail, sat and raised a paw. Russell shook it, and then pointed to the spot by the big chaise lounge. "Lay down, boy." Winston trotted to the spot and flopped with a noisy whump. Russell sat on the lounge chair and began petting Winston, who quickly fell asleep. Anyone observing this scene would have thought it a tranquil, peaceful vignette. And such it was, for the dog.

Clayton Russell's clean, handsome, lightly tanned face showed no emotion, but his clear blue eyes darted with fierce, energetic movements that displayed the intensity of the mind behind them. The commonalties of the two disappearances were chilling, but in San Francisco the eyewitness was deliberately pushed in front of a car.

Russell called Pamela at her office to let her know Timmy may be in danger. It had not occurred to him before now that the only eyewitness in the Collins matter, a child, may also be vulnerable. She picked up on the tenth ring, they talked for a minute, and she told Russell she would leave her office immediately. This type of news should be delivered in person.

Pamela hung up and looked at her watch. Zan should be home with Timmy by now. She closed her office, told the lobby security that she would not be back and rushed to the Taylor home.

She rang the bell and again rehearsed how to approach the idea that Timmy could be the target of a professional assassination. Al Taylor came to the door, his wife having called him at work to tell him to leave early. Al led Pamela to their sunroom, where Zan was waiting.

Pamela explained the possible connection between the two kidnappings and then told them, "The San Francisco inspector thought the teen witness had been murdered. Forensic evidence suggested at least two people held the young man and shoved him in front of a moving car."

Al Taylor's complexion suddenly paled. Zan asked, "How do you suggest we protect Timmy?"

"I recommend you really keep a very close eye on your son. Remind him not to talk to any strangers. No cops, nuns, teachers, coaches or anyone he does not know. I also suggest he keep what he saw the day of Lisa's disappearance

149

a secret between us. Whether you explain to him why you are initiating certain restrictions, well, that's your decision as parents.

"Also, John Walsh, the host of *America's Most Wanted,* may do a segment on the Collins' disappearance. Do not let them interview or identify Timmy. They should certainly understand your concerns, and if not, well, just tell them 'No'."

Pamela rose to leave. "I'll keep you posted. Tell Timmy he owes me a couple of fireballs."

"What?" Zan mumbled. "Oh, sure. Thanks."

Pamela left and drove by to see if Sally Collins had arrived home. She saw her on the street, getting her mail. Pamela waved, rolled down her window and after repeating the latest information, encouraged her to cooperate with the Walsh group. "But don't let them have Timmy's name, whatever you do. And be sure to tell Det. Trent. We want to avoid placing the boy in any danger."

"You know, I've never seen that show. I don't watch much TV."

"It's a good program. Think of it as an adjunct to the internet as another way to distribute information to millions so that they may be your eyes and ears."

Pamela drove directly home. She needed research leads on the Dalai Lama treasures.

Russell leaned back and stretched, pleased with their accomplishments.

The sun had set behind the mountains, and Lake Rayton slowly changed from blue to pewter to black. He was tense but excited that he may be on the verge of something. And he had not realized how much he missed that feeling. At this moment, some person or persons as yet unknown may be planning to abduct another child.

Russell went inside, stripped, tucked a large towel around his waist and walked down to the dock. He tossed the towel on a chair and dove into the lake. He swam downward at a steep angle for twenty feet, enjoying the chilly caress of the water much colder than at the surface. He used a slow breaststroke to climb up, then rolled onto his back and began using the elementary backstroke at a medium pace. He heard a noise from the woods and saw Winston race down the path, pound across the dock and make a mighty leap into the water.

For fifteen minutes, Russell and the dog swam out to the main body of the lake and slowly returned. As the sky darkened and the evening softly rolled over the land, he found himself feeling a bit like a child the night before Christmas. He was excited about being back into "the game" and, he had to admit, being with Pamela again.

Chapter 11
Delta to NAMBLA

Russell drove the Rover to Clarkesville's post office where he rented a box. He noted it was scheduled to be closed next year because of cost overruns by the U.S Postal Service. In his box were a dozen pieces of assorted envelopes, bills, a birthday card from his mom and two Express Mail packages. He hurried back to the house, poured a tall glass of iced tea with a lime wedge, dropped the mail on the large marble coffee table and opened the package from the Adam Walsh Foundation. As he sped-read the various brochures, Russell noted some alarming statistics from the U.S. Department of Justice:

- ***More than 58,000 U.S. children are abducted annually. Although the vast majority of children return from abductions, forty percent of kidnappings by strangers are murdered***

Sadly, the stats had risen. Russell booted up his computer and found an e-mail from Det. Trent with an attachment from Inspector Webb's case. The interview with the Mormon boy was remarkably similar to what Timmy described. Also attached were color photographs of the crime scene, one shot of the boy and several disturbing

photographs of the eyewitness, David Robinson: the body
shots revealed post mortem bruises consistent with fingertips,
but no fingerprints had been lifted, and no DNA was
recovered except that belonging to the victim. The assassins
had probably worn gloves.

Russell opened the large package from McMillan
Gun Specialties. Inside, surrounded by unsalted popcorn,
was the ugly, black, plastic box. Taped to the outside was a
note from Steve McMillan.

Clayton,
I've calibrated the sight, and it's dead-on. This
system is a honey. Don't
tell anyone where you got the loads. Hey, what
loads? (Catch my drift?)   Steve

The box contained one of the world's better designed
handguns. It was a Glock 19, slightly smaller than the other
Glocks, easier to carry and conceal. Invented in 1963 by
Gaston Glock, an Austrian who wanted to design a better
pistol, the Glock is fondly embraced by many law
enforcement agencies. It has no external operation controls
and is light, fast and safe. The all-black Glock Russell held
in his right hand was just under 7 inches long, weighed less
than 21 ounces unloaded, held 15 rounds and required only
10 pounds of pressure to pull the trigger. Custom added to
this pistol was a Viridian Green Laser Sight.

Included in the firearm package were four plastic
packs marked FOR MILITARY USE ONLY and holding
twelve Glaser bullets. Russell thumbed the dozen Teflon-

tipped shot-filled bullets into one of the two clips and slapped the clip into the butt of the gun. Like a child with a new toy, he walked out onto the deck and drew a bead on a small oak sapling forty feet away. The Viridian GLK sight was attached below the barrel. He gently squeezed the trigger, and when the bright green laser splash appeared on the slim tree, he pulled the trigger harder. The gun roared like a small cannon, and the Glaser slug instantly tore with surgical precision along the green beam of light and punched the small tree with the force of a mule kick. Bark flew away from the tree in a starburst, while splinters of wood exploded out the backs and sides of the trunk as the pellets inside the slug erupted. For a moment, the tree was motionless, and then the upper half slowly toppled over and softly crashed on the ground. He looked at the pistol and slowly shook his head, genuinely awed by the power and accuracy of the weapon.

The detective went inside, looked around for a place to hide the Glock and settled on the inside center foliage of a large potted fichus tree. He snapped off a branch at waist level near the trunk, hung the gun by the trigger guard and practiced reaching for it three times with his eyes closed.

Russell telephoned Erin Wallis in Manhattan. After her recording, he requested a callback. An hour later, after a run with Winston, he caught his land line on the third ring.

"Yes."

"Dear boy, you should say 'Yes, Erin, my sweet, when I call again, it will be a local call, and we'll have dinner at one of the city's nicer restaurants.' "

"Yes, Erin, my sweet, and whatever makes you happy, do you have a timeline as to when you may be able to help me with some information?"

"I'm on the verge. I should know something later tonight. Will you be up late?"

"It doesn't matter. Wake me."

"Yes sir. Later."

"Thank you Erin, my sweet. And remember, I'm Sam Redmond."

Russell clicked off the phone. Erin was loyal, but naive, and he had to feed her as little information as absolutely necessary because he was concerned she might unintentionally blow his cover. He yawned and looked at his watch. 4:30 p.m. His jog didn't clear his mind very well. But he knew something that would. He put on a Leo Kottke CD, climbed up into the spacious loft overhead and for the next 90 minutes, he listened to Kottke's masterful 6 and 12-string guitar work while he lifted light weights.

Was he trying to remain fit or simply blunting emotional vexation? It was apparent Pam and he needed to talk matters over and not simply make assumptions about the scope of their relationship. But what did he want? And what did she really expect?

At a few minutes past nine, Russell was sprawled on the sofa reading *Practical Trivia* by Julian Minnow. Under the heading, *How To Tell The Temperature In Warm Months When You're Not Near A Thermometer*, he discovered:

> A cricket's metabolic rate is directly related to the temperature.
>
> One can tell the temperature by listening to a cricket's chirps. Count the number of times a cricket chirps in 15 seconds, add 37 to that number, and it will total the temperature in Fahrenheit degrees.

Interesting, certainly; useless, probably!

The phone rang, and Russell reached for it, keeping his eyes on the book.

"Hello."

"Clayton, this is Sally. Sorry to bother you. I tried to reach Pamela first." And without waiting for a response, "The *Most Wanted* people just called and asked me so many questions I worried I may have given the wrong answers. They're interviewing me for the show tomorrow! I wondered if you could provide some advice. Det. Trent's going to be interviewed, too."

"When's the segment going to air?"

"This Friday, I think."

"Sally. Just be honest. But it is important not to mention any names other than your daughter. Call me after they've finished shooting and tell me how it went?"

156

Russell's Call Waiting did the double click.

"Thank you. I will call back tomorrow."

He clicked the phone off and on. "Hello."

"Do you have a pen, Clay?" Erin asked, breathless and animated. She gushed, "I have a name. I spoke to him briefly. He is a college professor at Stanford University. Early forties. He's apparently very active in NAMBLA, eager to sign up new men—always recruiting new boys—and he's waiting for you to call. His personal number is 415-220-0179, and he has your first name only- well your name, Sam."

"What did this Archie Reese say?"

"He was curious about you. I said you were a good client of The Unicorn Club, but I preferred you answer his questions. His full name is Archibald Reese, no middle name, and his office number is 415-239-7648."

"Thank you again, Erin. Please call and tell him to expect my call, that I'm planning a trip to San Francisco. Remember to always use the name Sam, please. OK?"

"Sure thing, Sam, dearest. and I'll call the guy as soon as we've hung up. Have a nice trip to California. And remember one very important thing."

"What?"

"Wrap that rascal, Clayton."

Russell laughed and said, "I have no intentions whatsoever of getting one millimeter beyond the handshake stage, Erin."

"Good. A flaming heterosexual. Stay that way."

"I will." Russell's line clicked again.

"Watch yourself. So long."

Before Russell could set the phone in its cradle, he heard the click-click.

"Russell, this is Bob Trent. How are you?"

"Couldn't be better. How about you?"

"I'm OK. Well, you sure whacked the damned hornet's nest with that TV show. The Chief is unsure about the publicity APD is going to receive. Some believe it might reflect poorly on the department." Det. Trent sighed. "You know, a few years ago, Atlanta, Dallas and Miami kept swapping off the honor of being the murder capital of the country. Child prostitution is also a dirty problem that's continually swept under the rug. Now we have a cop kidnapper."

"Why are you telling me this?"

"I guess I really called to see why you don't want your name mentioned."

"Trent, I'm pursuing a lead. A gossamer-thin lead, I might add, in another city, and I don't want publicity."

"OK, but I thought you might also want to know that the *Most Wanted* people were pretty firm. They said they'd air the Collins segment with or without the APD's permission. Does that surprise you?"

"No. Not really. John Walsh and company play hardball. So do kidnappers and murderers of children. I'm glad the good guys can play hardball, too. Aren't you?"

Trent was silent for a moment, and Russell wondered what the older detective was thinking. "Yeah, well, maybe I'm just getting tired. I think I'm ready to retire."

Trent hung up without another word. Russell looked at his watch. 9:41 p.m. Three hours earlier on the west coast. Perhaps Archibald Reese was home from work.

Russell called Reese's number.

"Hello." A nice, formal, accent-free voice.

"Mr. Reese?"

"Speaking."

"My name is Sam Redmond. Erin Wallis, from New York, may have told you to expect my call."

"Oh, yes," Reese said politely.

"Good. I was wondering if we could meet while I am in San Francisco. I fly in tomorrow."

"Will you be here very long?"

"Two days, maybe three."

"We can meet tomorrow if your flight is early? When do you get in?"

Russell had no idea, but he said, "Around lunchtime."

"Let's meet at 5:00 p.m. in Golden State Park. There's a fountain at the north end."

"That would be splendid." Russell described himself and said he would be carrying a *U.S.A. Today.*

"Good, Sam. I look forward to meeting you. And please call me Archie or Arch. Uh, how did you hear about the organization?"

"I have known about it for years. Ms. Wallis filled me in on it. I thought I'd check it out and, maybe, take the plunge, so to speak."

"Are you from Georgia?"

Russell's mind raced. Should he tell him? Why not? It would keep the lies and possible mistakes to a minimum. "Yes, outside Atlanta."

"Did you know we have chapters in various cities? Small but growing. We're big in New York and San Francisco."

"I had heard rumors."

"Would you like to visit one of our pleasure spots?"

"Yes. I imagine the 'Frisco groups are bigger, more active and more liberal. I travel to the west coast a lot."

"Ha! We're liberal everywhere, Sam. You'll see." Reese had a chilling laugh.

"To tell you the truth, Archie, I'm a bit nervous."

"Oh, don't worry. You won't be nervous for long. I promise. Our organization is, well, it's a slice of heaven."

"You're getting me excited."

"Good. That's the whole idea."

"Gosh, this is thrilling. I'll see you tomorrow, at 5:00 p.m., in Golden State Park at the north fountain. Correct?"

"It's a date." Reese laughed again as Russell said Good-bye and hung up.

Russell said, "Oh boy," as he set down the phone which drew a mild sigh from Winston, sleeping in a corner. He called the airlines and booked the earliest non-stop from Atlanta to San Francisco leaving at dawn. First class, first row, window. To locate a hotel, Russell pulled up MetaCrawler on the computer. As he did so, he glared at the fichus tree that held the new Glock pistol. Should he bring it to California? No. It's probably unnecessary. But there would be no harm in packing a couple of Viper knives.

Chapter 12

The Flesh Wish Book

As the jet descended through the ash-colored clouds that partly shrouded the skies of San Francisco International Airport, Russell again wondered how he should play it with Archie Reese: homosexual, heterosexual or bisexual?

Pamela was considerably more liberal. She condoned alternative lifestyles and effectively argued NAMBLA gave homosexuals an undeserved reputation. She had almost convinced Clay homosexuals, male and female, preferred consenting adults. "A pedophile's behavior was deviant and it had nothing whatsoever to do with gender preferences. They just prey on innocent children," she would repeatedly remind him.

Russell decided to pose as a wealthy, quiet, bisexual man who was narcissistic, lonesome and bored.   His costume was expensive, casual, and conservative: charcoal gray cotton slacks, a navy blue striped, cotton button-down shirt and an oversize maroon, cotton cardigan sweater that effectively played down his physique. The aircraft squelched to a fairly smooth landing and quickly taxied to the gate. Russell was first out, and he unhurriedly walked through the airport. He purchased a half dozen newspapers and magazines, stepped outside into the cool air and caught a cab.

"The Stanford Court, please. There's no rush." He settled into the back of an extremely clean, early model Cadillac Seville. The cab moved out into traffic, and Russell began scanning the papers with particular attention to the personal ads. He did not find the word NAMBLA, but neither was he surprised. He did not really expect the organization to be that flagrant.

As the cab reached Nob Hill, he set the newspapers aside and began to think this was probably a snipe hunt. True, he was pursuing a logical thread: a semi-underground sub-culture that might lead to an omni-sexual one. It was a sensible guess but an extremely long shot. The power of television, on the other hand, would probably do far more toward finding Lisa, if she were still alive. In just two nights' time, the kidnapping of Lisa Collins would be told across America and in much of Europe and South America.

At the Stanford Court Russell paid the driver and entered a beautiful, marble-accented lobby. He checked in as Sam Redmond, applied $2,000 cash toward his room, and five minutes later he was in 419, with a panoramic view of the Bay Area.

He spent a few minutes freshening up and then slipped a couple of the Viper knives into his pockets. For air travel, the knives were sheathed in lead-lined leather in specially made slots in the corners of his soft leather bag. Only once, in dozens of trips in the past, had he been asked

163

to explain the knife x-rays. He displayed them to airport security in Miami, along with a badge that identified him as a deputy with Rabun County Sheriff's Department. Even now, post 9-11, his baggage passed through security unchallenged.

He took the elevator to the lobby and stepped outside to hail another cab. "Golden Gate Park, north end, at the fountain."

Russell looked at his watch. 4:35p.m. He saw the large fountain up ahead.

"You can stop here."

The cab driver eased over to the curb. Russell gave him a twenty and got out.

This end of the park was sprinkled with the usual collection of characters one would expect to see. Mothers with strollers, food and beverage vendors, street artists and musicians, lovers here and there, an elderly man sitting on the edge of the fountain feeding pigeons.

He sat down on the fountain wall a respectable distance from the pigeon feeder and began reading *USA Today*, the prearranged signal. Minutes later, a man said, "Excuse me—are you Sam Redmond?"

Russell looked up to see a very well-dressed, slim, dark-haired man standing a few feet away. The man wore a gray plaid suit, expensive dress shoes, white shirt and deep purple bow tie. He resembled a successful, stylish Frisco attorney instead of a pedophile. But, then again, what does a pedophile look like?

"Yes, I am."

"Archie Reese," the fortyish man said, extending his hand.

Russell stood up and shook it.

"It's five on the nose," Reese said, looking at his watch, "Bobby will be joining us in ten minutes. Let's go over there." Reese nodded to a nearby bench, out of earshot from the pigeon feeder.

"Bobby?" Russell asked as he rose.

"Yes, Bobby. A special friend."

They walked to the bench, Reese sat down and motioned for Russell to do the same.

"Thank you for seeing a stranger," Russell began.

"I'm glad to do it. It was Alexander Jordan who called me. And if Alex says it's OK, then you're fine with me."

"Who is Alexander Jordan?"

"A very discreet, older man. Long-time prominent resident. He and I met socially. It was he who introduced me to NAMBLA."

"Well, it sounds like a fascinating group."

Archie Reese smiled. "NAMBLA is frequently misunderstood, and we are all asked to avoid conflict whenever possible. What do you know about NAMBLA?"

"Practically nothing."

Archie Reese turned away from Russell and looked at the various people in the park. Reese's face began to beam.

165

Before he spoke, he reached into his right coat pocket. Russell heard a distinctive click. Probably a recorder.

"There is too much hate in the world and not enough love. Society should not judge us by what particular flavor of love we choose to enjoy. At NAMBLA, we believe that it is good for a man to love a man, and acceptable for a man to love a boy. Many boys or young teens are confused as to their sexuality, and NAMBLA gently assists boys in recognizing and accepting their homosexuality. When those boys mature, they, in turn, will guide other boys into our world. And the cycle beautifully perpetuates. Does this make sense?"

"It makes perfect sense," Russell answered softly, but the reference to boys left him sick at his stomach. He wondered how young? "What you're saying is, truly, wonderful," he lied.

Archie Reese turned to look at Russell, reached out and gently squeezed Russell's hand. Russell squeezed back and smiled slightly.

"Sam, each of us prefers to have one 'special' young friend." Reese looked over Russell's shoulder and smiled.

Russell followed Reese's gaze and saw a dark-haired, slender boy walking toward them. The boy was smiling shyly. He looked to be about twelve. Why wasn't he in school? Who are his parents? The detective wondered what occurred when the boys matured. He found it overwhelmingly difficult to resist the urge to notify the

166

police immediately. He made a mental note that once he knew it would not jeopardize the investigation, he would report Reese to various authorities.

"Hello, Bobby," Reese said.

"Hello AR," the boy replied.

Man and boy kissed, and Bobby sat down on the far side of Reese. "Sam Redmond, meet Bobby."

Russell extended his hand, "Pleased to meet you."

"And you, sir." The boy's soft hand had a firm grip.

Reese looked intently at Russell's face, and after a few seconds, quietly asked, "What exactly do you want from NAMBLA, Sam?"

"What I want is something that … "

Reese held up his hand. "Bobby," he said pleasantly, "would you get us some mineral waters? Three, please."

"Sure, AR," Bobby happily replied. Reese gave the child a crisp fifty.

When Bobby was several yards away, Russell continued, "What I want is a companion like you have." Russell pointed to the retreating boy. "I want someone to love, to lead, and spoil. I'm lonely, but I'm very financially secure. I could take very good care of someone—someone who is special."

"Would you like to attend our next NAMBLA meeting? We'll have another one in three weeks."

"I appreciate the invitation," Russell said. "And I absolutely adore young males. But I also adore young females. What I desire most is a boy *and* a girl."

Reese started to speak, but this time Russell raised a hand. "Money is no object. I would happily compensate you or a third party for any introduction you could make."

Reese smiled quietly, "I may have just the thing for you, Sam, something with which you could net two lovebirds with one stone."

"What do you mean?"

"I have a friend who has access to something that may enable you to realize your wish, but I need to speak with Alex first. Where are you staying and for how long?"

"The Stanford Court. At least two nights."

"I'll call later today and let you know what I've found."

"I appreciate it, Archie. I cannot tell you how much I value your help."

"You're welcome, love." Reese smiled and patted Russell on the left thigh. Bobby walked up with three small Evians.

"Sam, I'm sorry, but we need to run. We're due at dinner soon. I will phone you later tonight or in the morning." Reese stood up. Russell also rose.

"I look forward to hearing from you, Archie." The other man nodded.

Russell watched man and boy walk away, holding hands. Bobby turned to look at Russell, who waved. The boy raised his water bottle in return.

Russell had to get to a safe phone, fast. He used his cell phone for convenience, but he preferred certain land lines that were more secure. It took increasing talent and effort to find them, but he did. He found one a block away, in a hotel lobby. He dialed the long distance number, tapped in his credit card number and glanced at his watch: 8:45 EST.

"Hello, this is The Unicorn Club, how may I help you?"

"I need to speak with Erin Wallis. This is Clayton Russell."

"She is talking to a new member right now, Mr. Russell."

"Please have her call me the instant she is free at 415-233-5179."

"I will see that she gets the message, sir."

"Thank you very much."

Russell hung up the phone and waited. Five minutes later he picked up the receiver on the first ring. He explained where he was and why, then asked, "Erin, I predict you may receive a call asking about me; what does your client know?"

"Almost nothing. I told him you were a sometime customer from Atlanta. Quiet and a good friend of The

Unicorn Club with no real preference on age or sexual orientation."

"If you hear from him or anyone associated with NAMBLA, please provide them a more detailed sketch of me?"

"Of course. What kind of profile do you want?"

"Extremely wealthy, very liberal, but trustworthy and discreet. State that I am very generous to liberal causes. I inherited my money, and I play. And Erin, remember that my name is Sam Redmond. Not Clayton." He always used false names as a subterfuge. Pamela preferred the straightforward honest approach. It was amazing how effective she could be with simply identifying herself and asking for assistance to resolve most questions. But she had only been a hospital patient once, when she was born.

Erin agreed, "Yes sir, Mr. Redmond. Sam."

Russell began walking up the one-way street to look for a cab. He saw one, whistled it to a stop, got in and named his hotel. He slouched and held his head. The entire matter gave him a headache. He now had little doubt Lisa had been prey to organized traffickers of children.

"Please stop by Tiffany's," he said to the driver. He wanted Reese to know that Sam Redmond had deep pockets and was generous.

———————————

Archie Reese reflected on his interesting encounter with Mr. Redmond, who seemed like a nice guy and kindred soul. He called Jordan, whose pedophile appetite raged so fierce that he maintained another home in Thailand.

"Ahoy," Jordan answered, as always.

"Alex, it's Archie. I hope I'm not disturbing you."

"No. What prompts this call?"

"I met the nice man today who was referred to us through a high end brothel in New York. He's interested in making a new young friend. Actually, two young friends, a boy and a girl. He seemed most sincere, and I was wondering if you still had the catalog? And if so, perhaps you would let me show it to him?"

"Archie, I really do not think it is safe to show that to a stranger."

"I know, and usually I would agree, but he was initially referred to me through you, remember. I called the sporting house in New York, which my new friend frequents, and the madam verified this fellow's background."

Alexander Jordan looked at his jewel-encrusted, Vacheron Constantin tank watch and sighed heavily. "I suppose I can do what you ask, if you can meet me at my apartment in the next half hour. And do not let this fellow out of your sight with the catalog. Do you understand?"

"Of course."

"What you are about to see," Archie Reese proudly enthused, "is unique and thrilling. There is nothing like it in the world."

171

Clayton Russell and Reese were having lunch, al fresco, on The Terrace at The Ritz Carlton, Stockton Street. Reese was impeccably dressed in a tan suit with a tasteful sliver of white cotton pocket square showing, aqua silk shirt and a lilac Nelson Wade custom necktie. Russell wore a charcoal gray cotton turtleneck, sky-blue worsted wool single button blazer, black slacks and a pair of Edward Green mink suede loafers. The shoes, from a satisfied client, were hand-made, from London. Russell thought it ridiculous to pay $1,400 for a pair of shoes, but it would underline his image as a man with coin to burn. Reese nursed a Bloody Mary and Russell a club soda. The café was three-quarters full at 11:40 in the morning.

Reese had specified a corner table for privacy. The two men sat side by side, as lovers might do.

"See this?" Reese said, in almost a whisper, tapping the cover of his menu. "This is one of the finest food menus in San Francisco." Reese's eyes were bright with excitement. "And this," he breathed…Russell could barely hear the man…"is the finest flesh menu in the world! " Reese squeezed Russell's knee, left his hand there and slid it to mid-thigh. He opened up The Terrace menu to reveal inside a cornflower blue nine-inch by twelve-inch brochure with gold reverse type on the cover that read:

De Blauwe Biblio XII

DBO 2378

Reese handed the catalog to Russell and said, "Take a look, Sam. Everything on this menu is very, very special." It did not take Russell long to grasp the concept. A horrible concept.

Men, women, teens, boys, girls, even infants …were represented therein. All professionally and yet candidly photographed with only a number for identification. They were of all races, all ages and all very attractive. One elderly woman looked especially beautiful, as did many of the younger girls and boys. Page after page, 48 in all, filled with head and body shots of people. About 60% of the photographs were young boys and girls, preteens. And on the back, the name:

De Blauwe Organisation

P.O. Box 32216

Zurich, Switzerland

www.DBO.merchandise.com

"Who are these people in the photographs?" Russell asked.

"These people are for sale!" Reese gushed, "For sale, forever, for the select few who can pay!" he whispered.

Russell closed the catalog. "Archie, how can that be? How can you buy a person?"

"I don't know except this group does it. They deliver. Believe me, if you can pay, you can play for keeps."

"Don't tell me Bobby came from this?"

"No, no. Bobby came from a perfectly legal source that I was very fortunate to discover. He was adopted. But the owner of the catalog has purchased people from this source. It's amazing but true."

"How does one do it?"

"Alex just said that if a customer is interested, go through the email, click on the link to the DBO blog and post a notice. The e-mail is designated on the last page. Tell the Organisation the ID number of the individual desired and how you wish to be contacted."

"Unbelievable, " Russell said. "Do you mind if I look through it some more and write down a few numbers?"

"Not at all," Reese said, taking a sip from his drink.

Russell uncapped his pen, and as both men intently studied the photographs, a nearby voice suddenly said, "Well! Have we made a choice?"

Russell was slightly startled, but Reese exclaimed, "Jesus! What the ... "

The hovering waiter wore a puzzled look, and as Reese began to pull himself together, Russell raised his menu higher, to keep the catalog out of sight, then coolly asked, "What are the specials today?"

The waiter said, "Squab Au Vin, which is superb, and a new dish, Kobe Steak Tartare. Both come with our luncheon salad and house dressing, garlic parmesan."

"I'll take the Squab," the detective replied, "and a Heineken, on the rocks with a twist of lime."

174

"Two Squabs," Reese said, "and a double Bloody Mary for me."

Reese began to light a cigarette. The waiter collected Reese's menu and reached to take Russell's, until the latter said, "I'd like to study this more. Everything looks so delicious."

"Very good, sir." The waiter gave Russell a sincere smile, Reese a faux one, and then turned away.

"My God," Reese said, "there's adrenaline in my system! Shit, this catalog makes me so nervous. Forget the fact that it's illegal, the damn thing is incredibly expensive."

"How much?"

"Alex said he had to pay $50,000 just to get the catalog. Money up front but it would be applied against any future purchase." Reese looked at his watch. "I've got to return this within an hour."

"Unreal, Archie. Unreal. Well, let me make some quick choices."

Russell continued studying the photographs, finally jotting down the numbers associated with the eight boys and nine girls, the name and address of De Blauwe Organisation and its email address. He closed the menu, let the catalog slip into his lap and passed it to Reese, who quickly returned it to his briefcase.

Both men silently nursed their drinks for a few moments and pensively ate their lunch. Reese patted

Russell's knee and said, "So, what do you do for a living, Sam?"

"I manage my investments. I have large blocks of stock in a few very select group of companies. Then I enjoy life. I spend six months of the year in the States, for income tax reasons, and the rest abroad. I vacation in Europe and Japan. I have good friends in Australia."

"And your home is in Atlanta?"

"One home is there. I also have an apartment in New York."

"Where do you live in each city?"

"In New York I live on 38th Street. In Atlanta, atop a high-rise condo on Peachtree Street. Both under assumed identities."

"Oh, really? Why?"

Russell smiled at Archie and said, "Because of my extracurricular activities. You understand, don't you?" Russell patted the hand that was now glued to his thigh. He picked up the tab and inserted cash. "Thanks for the most entertaining lunch I've had in a long time, Archie. That catalog and the 'merchandise' are truly fantastic."

"You're most welcome, Sam." Reese tossed his napkin on the table. "Shall we?"

"But first I have something to show you."

Russell pulled a small gift box from inside his coat and handed it to Reese. "Please, for Bobby and you."

Reese took the small bag, removed the rectangular Tiffany's box and opened it. Inside were small and large silver and gold cable, matching friendship rings. "I guessed at the sizes," Russell said.

"My! They are beautiful!" Reese said. The rings disappeared into the bag, and the bag was quickly stuffed into a coat pocket.

"Thank you so much, Archie." Russell stood and shook the man's hand. "I'll make inquiries about the catalog and the exquisite inventory I noted. And, if you like, I'll give you my catalog once I've ordered from it."

Archie's eyes sparkled. "I'd love that. Here's my card with the home address. Thank you Sam."

"Take care. And please thank your friend for me." Russell looked at his watch to accelerate the parting.

"I will. Good-bye, Sam." Archie Reese walked off in the opposite direction.

Fifty yards away, wearing a black warm-up suit, Alexander Jordan snapped off the last shots on the 35mm Nikon with telephoto lens: a four-shot series of Clayton Russell walking and getting into the cab. Jordan lowered the camera, watched the cab pull away and he looked at Reese, walking toward him, waving with a lowered hand, twittering his fingers. Jordan, with senatorial countenance and thick silver mane of brushed back hair, looked arrogantly at Reese and said, in a vulgar hiss, "Well, AR, you'd like to fuck him, wouldn't you?"

"Of course. But he wasn't interested."

The two men walked off together, across the park and toward Jordan's home. They had decided to spend the afternoon together, just the two of them, and both men were looking forward to each others' company. There was no emotional warmth, but they were both highly skilled at pleasing each other. The children they molested were considered fresh and firm young flesh, tight and pleasing receptacles for their seed. Or as Pamela observed, "It's just a sick, illegal, unnecessary dimension for practicing adult homosexuals. Ditto for heterosexual perverts!"

In his hotel room, Russell's first action was to wash his hands. He just felt dirty. He then shed shoes and jacket, emptied his pockets and lay down on the king size bed, hands laced behind his head. He looked at the ceiling and thought about Archie Reese, Bobby and that catalog! De Blauwe Biblio. Christ, what a publication! Just like the old Sears catalog was a wish book, but a flesh wish book.

Russell closed his eyes and again marveled at how a succession of unrelated events had brought him in contact with the unusual. What was that short story by de Maupassant? *The Piece of String.* A man picks up a length of string, and, through a chain of escalating events, it ultimately kills him.

Russell's jaw muscles clenched. He'd love to get his hands on De Blauwe Organisation. It seems that the group was an organized crime syndicate that operated worldwide with impunity. And in first-world countries to boot.

So where was Lisa Collins in the scheme? Russell decided this De Blauwe Organisation was certainly worth investigating. If *Most Wanted* does run the Lisa Collins segment Friday and, by remote chance, De Blauwe Organisation is connected to the girl's disappearance, they may go into hiding, and keep it up indefinitely. He needed to move before the show aired.

Russell picked up the phone to call Erin. After a "One moment, please, sir," and a minute of sensual music, Erin came on the line.

"Well Clayton, this is becoming habit-forming. What's up phone buddy? Are you still on the West Coast?"

"Yes, but I'd like to come to New York tomorrow, and meet around dinner time. Are you open?"

"I sure am. What about 7:00 or 8:00 p.m.? Will you be alone or will your female companion accompany you?"

"Alone, and it's business. I want to make a proposal."

"My stars, I can't wait. Welcome to the Taj Mahal of sex, my friend. It must be a heck of a proposal if you're coming all this way." Erin was intrigued by Clayton, even though she had learned long ago that while some men were better than others, most should not be trusted.

Russell hung up, called Delta Air Lines and booked a flight that would leave San Francisco in time to arrive at LaGuardia by tomorrow afternoon. He looked at his watch. He'd call Pamela and let her know about his detour to New York.

Pamela was stepping out of the tub when she heard her mobile phone. She smiled, hoping it was Clay, and ran to answer.

The two discussed their day and agreed they would meet Sunday. He could tell from her tone Pam was displeased he was seeing Erin, but she said nothing.

Chapter 13

A Most Wanted Young Girl

The jet began a long, low swoop over the Flushing Bay, and Russell thought about three words: De Blauwe Organisation. The jet's tires screamed twice as they softly bounced on the runway. He was first leaving the plane. Moments later he approached a young blonde woman wearing a sweatshirt that read *The International University – Vienna.*

"Excuse me."

"Yes?" No accent.

"Do you speak German?"

The woman smiled, "Ja, of course."

Russell showed her his boarding pass, on which he'd written De Blauwe Organisation. "Do you know what these words mean?"

"Yes. It means 'The Blue Company' or 'The Blue Organisation'."

As he turned the pass over, "And what does this phrase mean?"

She replied, "De Blauwe Biblio. It means 'The Blue Book'."

"Thank you."

Russell turned to leave, and the woman said, "Sir?"

"Yes?"

"Those words, by the way, aren't German, they're Dutch."

On the cab ride into Manhattan, Russell pondered this latest information. A Dutch-named company with a Swiss mailing address. So, if De Blauwe Organisation is European-based, maybe *America's Most Wanted* is not carried there. But Russell knew an organization with such an international reach would have extensive contacts. The story would probably be on YouTube within hours or twitter as it was being viewed.

In front of the Fitzpatrick Hotel, Russell paid the driver, retrieved his luggage and gave it to the desk to hold. He wasn't due to meet Erin for another hour. He went into the long wooden bar, now one-quarter full, and found a relatively un-crowded seat at a corner. He ordered an O'Doul's. The bartender was a middle-aged, white-haired Irishman. He spent a few minutes mentally composing the letter, then went into the lobby and asked the concierge for stationery. Sometimes email was not the appropriate medium, especially for a brothel in New York.

At 7:30 p.m. Clayton Russell walked into the elegant lobby of the high-rise complex where The Unicorn Club conducted business. A slim, silver-haired doorman held open the door and raised an inquiring eyebrow.

"I'm here to see Erin Wallis."

"She is expecting you, Mr. Russell. Please go up." The man gestured to a bank of four elevators.

Russell took the quiet ride alone to the 39th floor, stepped out, rounded a corner and immediately saw the small, brass unicorn logo that glistened under key lighting on door number P-7. He pressed the doorbell, and a moment later, the door was opened by the madam herself. He extended his hand to the older, beautiful, raven-haired woman. "Hi Erin. Long time."

Erin Wallis delicately slapped Russell's hand to the side and said, "Give me a kiss, handsome fool." She gave him a very warm hug, and he kissed her on the cheek, near the ear. She smelled of sandalwood and flowers. "Come in, and let me have a look at you."

"You're more beautiful than ever, Erin."

"I was about to say the same. Gosh, I had forgotten how fit and strong you are. And that face. Clayton, you could earn a very good income just escorting wealthy older women to the theater. Honest."

Russell smiled. "I'd get fat."

She lovingly squeezed his left bicep. "Jesus! I doubt it! If you ever think of switching careers, I can connect you with some exceptional ladies." Erin's expression became serious as she looked over his face. "You look the same, except for ... have you been in pain within the past couple of years?"

"I spent some time in the hospital three years ago. Two stays, in fact. Why do you ask?"

"There are some more character lines around the corners of your eyes. And I do believe you have more gray at the temples and streaked throughout that full head of hair. You've aged a bit, on the surface. Something I struggle to continually conceal, cosmetically." Erin laughed, and added, seriously, "What put you in the hospital?"

"I was on a large boat that exploded just as I jumped overboard. The explosion added some impressive distance to my leap. I had to swim quite a way to shore and ended up spending three weeks in the hospital and months in rehabilitation. But I'm fine now. Just some scars from the burns."

"You said you were in the hospital twice?"

"The other time, about a year before the boat explosion, I had a run-in with a Mexican drug cartel. Not too far from here. I was briefly tortured before escaping and shot twice. Fortunately, my connections enabled me to receive timely medical care."

"Goodness, Clayton. What a dirty dangerous business you are in." Erin shook her head. "I have a friend who lives ten blocks away, recently widowed, loaded, and just the other day, she asked me if I knew of a discreet, younger man who could accompany her to a function or two a week. Dorothy is about 60, she makes me look like a boy, and, believe me, any boats you stepped on with her would be better described as yachts. The only explosions would be corks popping."

Russell laughed and thought that it sounded too good, but he'd quickly bore. "I'll keep it in mind, but what I'm interested in now concerns another widow. And her daughter."

"Let us convene in the library, Mr. Russell."

Russell followed Erin down the carpeted hall, and as he looked at the tasteful furnishings, he reflected that The Unicorn Club was as he had remembered. Subtle colors, tall ceilings, airy, flowers everywhere and pastel leather sofas. Light classical music could be heard throughout.

The library was a corner room with floor-to-ceiling bookshelves built around two tall windows that provided a great deal of light. On one coffee table was a medium-sized covered silver server. As they sat on a sofa, Erin said "Voila," and lifted the cover. "The best from Carnegie's Deli. I took the liberty of ordering hot pastramis, tuna-melts and a lot of trimmings. I hope that's acceptable?"

"I love Carnegie's. How about half of each?"

Erin served the food on two blue and white China plates, poured coffees and for a quarter of an hour, she and Russell talked about her business. The Unicorn Club did not feel the economic downturn adversely impacting most of the working class. Ninety percent of her clients were regular

185

customers that included CEO's from Wall Street, politicians, the old names that live off their trust funds and entertainers from all levels of celebrity. New referrals were carefully screened, and she had several recent and wealthy customers from Europe and Asia. Police cooperation and protection were at an all-time high, thanks to the combination of Erin's discretion and generous quarterly contributions to the department's slain and disabled officers' fund. "I like to think that profits from 'the act of life' can help those families who have been hurt by injury and death," she said.

"Very poetically put," Russell commented. "And an interesting cycle. May the blue knights be on your side forever."

"Since The Mayflower Madame in the 1980s, journalists have attempted to destroy careers by revealing men's indiscretions. I don't think a reporter has ever been inside here, knock on wood, but in the meantime, I'm salting away the profits. I hope to add to my retirement investment for another three years, sell this business and go back to Australia. I have one living relative in Australia, a younger sister married to a successful rancher. I want to move back to Melbourne, visit them frequently, be a patron of the arts and maybe find a nice gentleman for my golden years."

"Where do I sign up?"

Erin laughed and said, "Let's talk again in three years when I am sixty five. I'm sure you will be on my short list."

"I'm very flattered." He was amazed at her poise and beauty. He also admired the confidence she had in admitting her age. So many women would shun the thought. He took another sip of his coffee, and for a half-hour Russell brought Erin up to date on the case, relating all the material facts. He ended by telling her to watch *America's Most Wanted* tomorrow night for the Atlanta segment.

"You're certainly stirring things up, Clayton. I've seen that show a couple of times, and law enforcement must be thankful for the help. I think it's fascinating." Erin looked directly into Russell's eyes, smiled warmly and said, "What would you like me to do? You did not come here in person to tell me to watch some television show."

Russell glanced out the windows to the clear blue sky and then at Erin. "The most remarkable things I've encountered in this case are the female kidnapper, De Blauwe Organisation and the catalog. The United States and Europe have joined other emerging and under developed countries in human trafficking. That catalog, Christ, it'll make you shiver. Whether or not Lisa's disappearance is connected to the organization, I'd like to learn more about them. I don't know how you feel, but it's anathema to me that such a thing can happen, anywhere. What I'd initially like to do is order De Blauwe Biblio, the catalog, through you, try to learn more about them and, possibly, purchase a person. I may get nowhere, but, for some reason, I don't feel that way."

187

Fine curiosity lines gently appeared between Erin's eyebrows. "Mother Mary, Clayton. How would I purchase that catalog?"

"I think by just sending them an appropriate query, then paying for it. Apparently it is the money that talks. Pay $50,000, Reese said, and you get a catalog and down payment on the purchase. I need to try to get these people to act in person, off the web."

"That must bloody well be the world's most expensive catalog. Well, I guess I have to be careful on that one. Well, what should I say in it?"

Russell pulled the piece of Fitzpatrick stationery from inside his jacket and handed it to Erin. She put on bifocals to read:

A very special client of mine has some singular requests, and rather than try to fulfill his desires locally, we would like to consider using your company. Could a representative meet me here and deliver your catalog? Money is no problem, including travel expenses. Please feel free to contact me at (SIGNATURE, PERSONAL ADDRESS, EMAIL INFO)

"Erin, I suggest you offer to pay $25,000 up front and the rest upon delivery. And I understand they may have a website to download a copy through some secret password, but I need a hard copy version hand delivered. Tell them you are too old fashioned. One reason I need your assistance on this is because I want to interrogate the delivery boy. It is virtually impossible to verify the source of an Internet site."

Erin was amused. "Of course, I'll do it for you, let me get my secretary.… "

"No! Don't get anyone else involved. You and you alone. Send them an e-mail and then follow instructions. Don't mention my name to anyone, and don't call me except from a land line that you know is a secure phone. Call collect, anytime."

"My, are we a bit paranoid? It's just a catalog, for God's sake."

"Erin, I don't think the people in that catalog are willing models. Nobody was looking at the lens of the camera. The shots were high quality, and I think they were candid. I believe these people aren't being sold of their own free will."

"You mean th …"

"I think the people featured in that publication get kidnapped, drugged, somehow indoctrinated and then sold. I think De Blauwe Biblio is the Sears wish book catalog of slavery."

Slowly shaking her head, Erin replied "That's almost impossible to believe."

"I know. But I'm willing to ante up some serious money to see if I am correct."

"And I thought *I* was in a controversial business."

"Erin, I really appreciate your doing this. Please be very careful, though. After today, secure land lines only and not a word of this to anybody." Russell suppressed a yawn that he could not quite conceal.

"A bit sleepy?"

"Yes."

"Would you like to take a nap, with or without company?"

Russell could not suppress his smile. "You know, I'm very tempted to do just that, but Pamela and I are trying to patch things up. I'd like to go to LaGuardia immediately and get the first flight home."

Erin picked up a telephone, pressed one button and said, "Please bring the car around to the front. Mr. Russell will be going to the airport now."

"I can take a cab, Erin."

"No you cannot, because I won't let you. And anyway," Erin looked at her watch, "in about 90 minutes, a plane lands from The Bahamas with four guests we need to pick up anyway. My driver will have a little extra time to wait for their arrival, that's all."

Russell stood up and turned to Erin, who extended a hand. He gently clasped it and pulled her up. "Clayton, I wish you could stay longer."

"Me too." Russell kissed her lightly but full on the lips, backed up a half step, lifted her hand, kissed it and said, smiling, "Please show me out, Ms. Wallis."

Erin sighed, theatrically, mocking their flirting disengagement. "Of course, Mr. Russell, right away, before I get an overwhelming case of feminine humidity."

She held his hand and slowly walked him to the door. Along the short walk, they passed two associates, both of whom were drop-dead beautiful. The detective recognized one. He had seen her in cosmetic TV commercials for years. At the door, Russell turned and looked over Erin's shoulder to make sure no one was there, then he put both hands on her remarkably slim waist. "Thanks again." He kissed her lightly on the neck.

"Good-bye Clayton. Safe travel. Now, I'm off to write the strangest letter of my life. I'll give you an update as soon as I hear anything." As he turned and walked away, she looked at his rear end and cooed, "Ooo, zee nice derriere, too." He patted his right buttock and heard her low, musical laugh as she closed the door.

Yes, it was no surprise that The Unicorn Club was so popular.

On the street, a black Chrysler Lincoln Town Car limousine was waiting with its engine running. A young, pretty petite lady was leaning against the car. Russell guessed her age to be about 24 and was wearing sunglasses, a navy, double-breasted suit and bright yellow necktie that was a shade brighter than her shoulder-length brown hair. She raised a hand.

"Mr. Russell?" She stepped forward and shook his hand. He noted she had an impressive grip for such a small person. "LaGuardia, right?"

"Yes, please."

Ninety minutes later he was in the air, and six hours after that, he was pulling into his garage, with Winston prancing excitedly beside the car. As the ivy-covered garage door hissed down, Russell exited and knelt down to hug his dog.

"Good boy, yeah. I missed you too."

The following day was uneventful. Russell exercised, showered and ate a light meal. At dusk he noticed a UPS package leaning against the sliding glass door. Inside it were a disc and a thick 9x12 envelope. The detective sat on the large leather sofa, kicked off his shoes and slid open the panel to his bookcase revealing a 65-inch Panasonic plasma TV. He picked up the remote and switched to Fox. On the envelope, the return address read: *America's Most Wanted, P.O. Box Crime TV, Washington, DC 20016.*

"Oh boy, Winston, we have something to read during the commercials." Clipped on top of the stack of reports was a handwritten note.

Dear Clay,
I thought you may be interested in the enclosed information. If you didn't know, we're using that story as our lead segment tonight, at 9 on Fox. Thanks for the tip, I'll keep you posted.
John Walsh

Russell removed the note and looked at the brochures:

- *Investigator's Guide to Missing Child Cases*;
- *Children Traumatized in Sex Rings*;
- *Child Molesters: A Behavorial Analysis*; and
- *Child Sex Rings: A Behavorial Analysis*.

The four were published by the National Center for Missing & Exploited Children. Setting aside the materials for later, Russell patted the sofa.

"Winston, come watch this." He wished Pam was here too, but she said she had work to complete, so he agreed to tape the show to view later.

The opening musical chords of *America's Most Wanted* began, and a minute of quick-cut montage crime images played across the screen as the announcer dramatically previewed the show. Other segments were touted, then came the one that began, "And up front on *America's Most Wanted*: in Atlanta, a young girl disappears after school, and the last person she's seen talking with a policewoman. But according to this detective…" A freeze-frame shot of Det. Trent came to life, and he said, "We can find no police officer, man *or* woman, who spoke with Lisa Collins on the day of her disappearance. We believe someone impersonating a law enforcement officer abducted the child."

With the first commercial break, Russell muted the sound and went to the kitchen to make a drink. He returned to the sofa, petted Winston and pressed the sound back on.

"Good evening. I'm John Walsh. Tonight we'll profile three people in these unrelated cases, all of whom have vanished, leaving precious few clues. Two are fugitives from justice. The third person, however, is an innocent 10-year-old Atlanta girl who is believed to have been abducted."

Walsh narrated a masterly distillation of the case, which included interviews with Sally Collins and Det. Trent. Particularly chilling was the dramatic re-creation of the abduction in Rohm Park. The little girl portraying Lisa bore a good resemblance, and the actress portraying the policewoman was unnerving: coal-black hair, beautiful jaw line, dark Ray-Ban sunglasses. After talking with the girl on the bench for about a minute, with Walsh providing voice-over narration, the policewoman simply clamped a hand over the girl's mouth and manhandled her into the stand of bushes.

The policewoman emerged from the bushes, now dressed in jeans and a leather jacket, carrying a large burlap bag over her shoulder. The woman put the sack in the backseat of a white Ford and slowly drove away. The segment ended with a photograph of Lisa, height and weight superimposed, and Walsh said, "If you have any knowledge concerning the whereabouts of Lisa Collins, or if you see anyone resembling her, please call, immediately, 1-800-

CRIME-TV. There is a substantial reward, and the line is answered 24 hours a day, seven days a week."

"Up next: a Texas ..." Russell muted the sound and sipped his drink. He wondered what kind of response the show would generate and when Erin would be contacted by De Blauwe Organisation?

Russell could not sleep. He kept recalling the image of the policewoman; exceptionally tall, tanned and athletic. She was wearing Nudus Bleu purchased at Sea Island. He decided to ignore the lateness of the hour and rose to call Pam.

"Hello Clay. *You* may be a night owl, but I enjoy my sleep. What's up?"

"It's that policewoman and blueberry suntan oil. I did some checking and called an aroma professional. There is a very high end suntan lotion called Nudus Bleu. In this country it's sold only at The Cloister on Sea Island. Maybe the impersonator spent a day or two there, sunbathing and waiting for a green light to get Lisa. Anyway, would you please check with The Cloister, sniff around and see if you can sweet talk some guard into letting you look at the security tapes? If this lady is as striking as Timmy described, someone should remember her, regardless of the name she used."

"It sounds like a long shot, Clay. From suntan lotion to kidnapper? This could wait for tomorrow don't you think?

Why don't we discuss it at brunch? We can plan out the week together. Would you mind coming here and bring Winston? My cat won't mind. And if she does, she'll get over it. Working 24-7, and I'm exhausted."

"Sure, see you mid-morning."

"Bye, now."

Pamela looked at the clock—2:14 a.m. "Kitty, kitty," she called. Duchess, the longhaired calico, came running, leapt on the bed and purred deeply as she rubbed her face upon the pillow. Pamela lifted her with one hand and placed her on the end of the bed. Pamela then walked across the ostentatiously decorated master bedroom suite to the kitchen for a glass of water. The king size canopy bed was centered across a room with dimensions grand enough to include a full suite of furniture, fireplace and entertainment center. It was pink on pink with white accents in satin and lace. No one, except Russell and a couple of her dearest friends, had seen this room. It was a side of Pamela few people would know.

She returned, the water on the bedside table, closed her eyes and was instantly asleep.

————————

At 8:45 a.m. Pamela's phone rang. She tapped on the brass touch lamp, opened her tired eyes and saw it was Clay.

"Hey Hon. I guess the sun has been up awhile."

"You have not called me Hon in quite some time. That is Hon with an O and not a U, correct?"

"What? Oh, yeah, I get it. I'm still asleep and have not had my first cup of coffee. Kindly get me off your speakerphone, Attila. Are we still on for brunch? I have almost no food in the kitchen. Could you pick something up to cook or would you prefer to go out? Sunday is a great day for brunches if you're interested in crowds. I also heard the weather was expected to be a sizzling 99 degrees with 85 percent humidity."

"I'll swing by Natural Foods and be there by 11."

Pamela turned off her i-Phone, rolled over and decided it was time to face the day. Duchess watched her put on a robe and shuffle around the furniture, through the spacious sunken living room and to the kitchen. She sleepily made coffee, opened a can of Friskies tuna and set it down for Duchess. Pamela had no interest in food until after her morning caffeine fix. She did not care for colas and other carbonated drinks, but chocolate and coffee were daily dietary supplements.

When Russell arrived, the two enjoyed preparing a meal of eggs and pancakes. He devoured the country ham, but Pamela passed. Once again she was determined to faithfully follow a vegetarian diet, fortified with fish, milk and eggs. She preferred serving meals at the kitchen bar and often complained that the furniture was too expansive for just one person.

Her mother died of breast cancer when she was fourteen. Her dad traveled in his job, was rarely at home, and she was reared in the Waters' mansion by a Jamaican immigrant. Carol Brakespear, a large jovial woman with coal-black skin, had no children of her own. As a result, she and Pamela soon became very close, with the latter still calling the former Mother. Thanks to Pam's financial means and generosity, her surrogate mother resided comfortably in an upscale assisted living home ten minutes away.

Pamela's father died several years ago, leaving his only child with a substantial estate. She remained in the family home and kept numerous antiques but redecorated the master suite and most of the first floor. She left the second floor and guest cottage virtually untouched and moved her father's things into one of the four upstairs bedrooms, along with mementos belonging to her biological mother. Then she closed the door, along with many memories.

Russell had encouraged Pam to sell the place, but she would not discuss it. She complained that the residence was too big, yet she just could not part with the only home she had known. Not yet. The shrine upstairs was slightly unsettling to Clay, but perhaps her loss of family explained in part why Pamela adored his mother. Then again, Jean Russell was an exceptional lady.

The two detectives carried coffee to the overstuffed linen couch in the living room to discuss their past week and plan ahead. The afternoon quickly passed, with a lengthy conversation that included the time spent apart over the past two years. They cooked dinner, and when Russell rose and made a comment about driving home, he was thankful she asked him to stay. He never presumed too much with Pam. She was an unpredictable pistol, and some very surprising things could set her off, in a variety of moods.

As she turned out the lights, Pamela decided to pack an overnight bag in the morning and drive to The Cloister very early, in order to avoid Atlanta's traffic.

Then she took Russell's hand and led him into her pink room.

On Tuesday, Pamela called from St. Simons and woke Russell at 3:30 a.m.

"Go turn on your computer, and open your email." He looked at his clock and silently swore, but she was excited and must be on to something important.

Russell yawned, "Good morning to you, too." He padded over to his desk, hit the start button of the computer and resisted the desire to make coffee. "Why call in the middle of the night?"

"I just finished uploading the photographs and wanted you to see. This is great stuff."

"I'm looking at your email attachment and the photo labeled number 1: a swimming pool. Will this get better?"

"Patience, smarty. That's an establishing shot; The Cloister's small but exclusive seaside pool. Open up number 2."

"Got it. Nice looking woman in a turquoise tank suit."

"Study the lady, Clay. That woman stayed at The Cloister three days. She bought their whole supply of Nudus Bleu from the spa. She even had them special order a case of it."

"What's her name?"

"They don't know, really. She was staying there under the name of Kleven, F. Kleven. But the room, and all her charges, were billed to a yacht, about a mile away. A boat called The Samaritan. Next shot, please."

"Alright, photo 3."

"Welcome to the Palmaire Marina, five minutes from The Cloister. That white 80-footer is The Samaritan. The Palmaire has a better video security system than the hotel. There are more valuable things to steal. Look at 4."

"Same shot at night."

"Now hit 5. And look at the white car in the parking lot, middle left."

"A white Crown Victoria."

"Open 6."

"Woman taking something out of the Crown Vic."

"Hit 7."

"She's carrying a sleeping child. But with dark hair."

"Ever heard of hair dye? Now 8."

"Woman's taking the girl to The Samaritan."

"9."

"How did you get these so damn fast, Pam?"

"Later. 9."

"Woman's walking away from the boat. No kid."

"10."

"Woman's at another car. A Jaguar."

"Open 11 through 15."

"She's putting something in the Jag's trunk; a security man is talking to her; he gets in the car with her; car goes into shadow; red brake lights, apparently from the Jag."

"Clayton, that security man was found the next day. Or at least part of him was found, by fishermen who saw an alligator moving the partial corpse around. His head and the upper fourth of his torso. Apparently the reptiles eat some, move it, eat some more later. They had to shoot the 'gator to get the remains."

"Alright, you've got Nudus Bleu, a dark haired child, and a Crown Victoria, which is a popular resale car. That still doesn't confirm much."

"Look at the last one, 16."

Russell leaned closer to the screen. The extreme blowup was of the woman carrying the girl, shot from the rear. The child's shoes were eggshell and blue saddle oxfords. The back upper portion of the right shoe had a ragged, V-plug hole.

"A dog had chewed Lisa Collins' shoe two days before she vanished. That's her shoe. That's Lisa Collins,

201

Clay. If we locate The Samaritan, we're way up the pipeline."

Chapter 14

Jewels and Catchers

Since the *America's Most Wanted* airing of the
abduction of Lisa Collins, calls came in from locations
throughout the country reporting sightings of the child. The
AMW staff dutifully passed the tips on to law enforcement
authorities but with no success.

On Thursday morning, six days after the program's
airing, Pamela was in her office reading a book she had
received from Clay. He had highlighted factoids from the
book *Child Rings: A Behavioral Analysis:*

> The U.S. Department of Justice's 2000
> *National Incidence Studies on Missing,*
> *Abducted, Runaway and Throwaway Children*
> *in America (NISMART)*, estimates the number
> of stereotypical child abductions at between
> 200 and 300 a year and the number of stranger
> abduction homicides of children at between 43
> and 147 a year (see References).

Approximately half of the abducted children are
teenagers.

Pamela appreciated Clayton's efforts in expanding
her education on a subject. He was a voracious reader. She
sipped her coffee and skimmed to the next highlighted
passage:

> Although child molesters frequently
> claim that sex is only a small part of
> their "love" for children, the fact is
> that their primary reason for
> interacting with the children is to have
> sex.

The two detectives were convinced Lisa had been abducted for sexual purposes and that she was alive, especially after obtaining the security camera photos. Pamela was determined to locate a yacht named The Samaritan.

She set down the book and studied the recent photographs of Lisa that Sally had emailed to her. The child was very pretty, Pamela thought.

Pamela was childless, but she could imagine Sally's pain and loneliness. God's fist, it seemed, had really hammered the Collins' home. The father dies in a car accident, and the daughter vanishes after school. That is a 66% casualty rate, the kind of losses that would force most armies to surrender. Pamela wondered if Sally had contemplated suicide. *Maybe she should encourage her to seek counseling. No, Sally was Catholic and also held hope that her daughter was alive.*

Russell came in from his morning exercise run and swim with Winston when the telephone rang.

"Hello."

"Good morning, Clayton, it's Erin. Are you having a good day?"

"Yes. Not happy, but productive."

"Well, hold on to your hat, honey—guess who just called?"

"Who?"

"A very smooth, eerie-sounding man with an equally spooky name: Mr. Krieg. He said he works for De Blauwe Whatever-It's-Called. He's asked to personally deliver some literature to me."

Russell sat up straight. "You're serious?"

"As a heart attack."

"What did you tell him?"

"I said I'd reserve a room at a hotel, in Manhattan, where we could meet, and if he would call me back in half an hour, I'd tell him which hotel. He said he could be in New York Monday and would call late that morning."

"You talked a few minutes ago?"

"Yes, dear boy. He phoned the club, and I asked him to call another number in five minutes. Then I trotted across the street to a pay phone at the Hyatt."

"Great. Look, would you call the 70 Park Avenue Hotel and reserve a suite? Book Sunday night, so the room is ready for Monday."

"OK. He also told me that he required half of the $50,000 in US currency in advance. He gave me a wire transfer number to a Cayman bank account. The balance is due at delivery. Clayton, this is wild ."

"When this Krieg calls, see if he can meet you there between 2:00 and 4:00 p.m. on Monday at the Park Avenue hotel. Tell him the room will be in your name, you'll wire the money this afternoon, and he can confirm the deposit by Monday. I'll reimburse you for the amount. Let's meet for a drink on Sunday, around 5:00 p.m. Where would you suggest?"

"What about the bar at the Four Seasons?"

"Sure. Give me your account number, bank name and its wire transfer code. I'll call my banker and have it in your account by tomorrow. Thank you so much, Erin. You need to get back and wait for this guy's call."

"Don't mention it. This is fun! Later!"

"Hold on a minute, this isn't fun. This is very serious. Make no mistake. These are extremely dangerous criminals, Erin. Please call me back when the meeting is arranged."

Russell slammed the phone down and stared vacantly out at the lake. He began to regret placing Erin in danger. It was time he spoke with his attorney. He called the long-ago-memorized number, hoping Sidney was in town.

Seconds later, Sidney Bressler came on the line. "Clay, lad, what's it to be: lunch, dinner, drinks, a game of squash; all of the former and ladies afterwards?"

"Actually, lunch or drinks would be in order, but it's work Sidney. Can we meet today? I need some legal advice, so your time would be billable. Do you still gouge your clients at $450 an hour?"

"For you, I would charge $450 per *and* you get to pay for the lunch for using the 'G' word. Let's do lunch today. Where?"

"2:00 p.m. at Chops in Buckhead. And Pam will join us, if that's OK."

"Pamela Waters? She still talks to you?"

Sidney Bressler, 58, left his black Mercedes CL 600 with the valet in the adjacent parking lot and walked across the street to Chops, just off Peachtree Road on the ground floor of a high rise office building in Buckhead.

Bressler was rare among the professional field: attorney, certified public accountant and licensed stockbroker. The three hats that justified the title elegantly embossed on his business card: *Attorney & Certified Financial Advisor.* A decade before, when Russell's financial worth began to escalate from his notoriety, he hired Bressler, who built a portfolio into a financial machine that provided enough after-tax income to ensure Russell's early, permanent retirement, despite the márket crash of 2008. Russell had an appreciation for Bressler's mind, which could quickly absorb input, rapidly actualize throughput and output multiple scenarios with intelligent percentage likelihoods for each.

Bressler was rapier-thin, balding with gray hair. In various social columns he had been referred to as the best-dressed Jewish lawyer in Atlanta, an appellation borne out today by a tan Mani suit, silk necktie from Paul Stuart and dark brown Gucci loafers. Bressler entered the restaurant, paused, looked at the various tables and told the hostess, "I'm here to meet somebody who I don't think has arrived, but ... "

A voice behind Bressler hissed, "Hands up."

The attorney raised his arms, slowly turned and said, "Jesus Clayton! My heart..."

Russell interrupted, "Attorneys don't have hearts."

Bressler smiled at Pamela. "Ms. Waters, you look great, but I can't say the same about your companion."

The hostess led them to a spacious booth, and they ordered crab cakes and unsweetened ice tea. Bressler also requested a Caesar salad, adding, "Hell, bring me a Long Island Tea, too." The waiter bowed and left for the kitchen.

Russell raised an eyebrow. "Isn't that a bit heavy for lunch?"

"Sometimes," Bressler replied, "but I see a new client across the room, a jackass, and a little buzz will relax me. Great drink, the Long Island Tea. I wonder who invented it?"

Russell replied, "Some matrons on Long Island came up with it, so sympathetic bartenders could secretly serve them a 4-shot drink during high tea."

"Well, I think it is a perfect lunch drink." Bressler glanced at a passing waiter with two martinis. "Hey," he said, "why are martinis like women's breasts? One is not enough, and three are too many."

Pamela was not amused. She had only agreed to attend because Clay assured her it was business. She did not like nor respect his attorney friend.

Bressler intuitively felt Pamela's disdain and instantly became serious. "So, what's cooking?"

Clay brought the attorney abreast of everything in the Collins matter. Bressler took copious notes on a legal pad, jotting with the right hand and eating his salad with his left. He paled considerably when Russell told him about NAMBLA. Informing most adults, especially a parent, about NAMBLA and De Blauwe Organisation was a one-two punch. Bressler, recently divorced, had two sons. The eldest graduated from Harvard and followed in his dad's footsteps but practiced in DC. The younger, age 12, resided with his mother in Florida.

Once the waiter had served the second Long Island and was out of earshot, the attorney leaned forward, propped his elbows on the table and asked, "Are you ready for some advice? Alert the FBI, the State Department and then get out. Erin Wallis and her association with the Alexander

Jordan types, and her profession, are illegal. The latter, alone, is reason enough to distance yourself from her. You've done your part getting *Most Wanted* to showcase the crime on national TV. If the child is alive, some viewer of the show will probably speak up. Curtain falls, you take a bow, we all applaud."

"Sidney, you're advice is sound. But if any federal or state authorities begin to make noise about NAMBLA or De Blauwe Organisation, members may go into hiding and the trail turn cold. Now's the time to move."

"Clay, get your exercise in a country club. Sharpen your mind with chess. Walk away from this."

"I've already decided. I'm going to buy a copy of De Blauwe Biblio, via Erin Wallis, from Mr. Krieg, for 50K."

Bressler's eyes narrowed. "You're kidding."

"Pam and I are going up there Sunday. I want you to start a file on this whole thing, in case we need a documented chronology later. I need you to watch our backs."

"Jesus! You are off your fucking rocker. That damn catalog is legal dynamite. Get caught with that thing and you could catch some real heat. And if the authorities think you are involved with buying a person, my friend, they'll put you *under* the jail."

Russell smiled. "I have a good attorney."

Pamela suddenly felt nauseous and was glad the lunch concluded.

Bressler finished his drink and put cash under the tab. "Very well," he said. "Keep me abreast of things starting after contact with Mr. Krieg. Clay, do you know German? We Jews do. 'Krieg.' That's German for 'war'. Don't become a casualty. And Pamela, don't let Clay take you down with him."

In Amsterdam, the Secretary and Records Custodian for De Blauwe Organisation took a sip from a floral china cup as he brought up Erin Wallis' name on the computer screen. He studied the information, noting her age, profession, address, estimated net worth and the one truly subjective piece of data on the screen: her Trust Quotient. The arbitrary rating given was 94%+. Under Chronology, he entered the data, "Krieg to deliver De Blauwe Biblio, XIV, 2383 hard copy to E. Wallis, 70 Park Avenue Hotel, New York City, U.S.A." Before closing the file, he typed, "Referred By: A. Jordan."

In the opulent, over-decorated apartment, Alexander Jordan viewed his candid, long lens photographs.

Jordan pursed his thin lips. He was displeased with what he saw. True, one cannot pinpoint a pedophile by appearance, but the usual reticent Jordan had an uneasy feeling about the stranger. He again cleaned the lens of the large, tortoise shell magnifying glass and scrutinized

Russell's body, sitting in the park with Archie Reese. He slowly shook his head and telephoned Reese at work.

"Archibald, my friend, I need more information about your new acquaintance, Mr. Sam Redmond. I would rather not discuss it over the phone. Please come by?"

"Well, alright. Say about at 7:00 p.m.?"

"No Archie. Leave work and come over now."

Before Reese could reply, Jordan hung up the phone.

Russell jogged back to his house just as twilight faded into darkness.

Winston had lagged behind in the woods and now bolted from the trees, passed Russell, leapt onto the deck and began lapping at his water bowl.

Inside, Russell noticed the phone message light was blinking, and he touched on the speakerphone.

"Clay, it's Erin. We're on as planned. See you at the Four Seasons Sunday at 5:00. Toodles."

Russell smiled, picked up the receiver and called Pamela. Yes, she was ready to join him in New York. No, she does not need a ride, she would take MARTA. Just call back with the flight. She was on her way to visit her nanny and take her to dinner. Saturday morning she was running in a marathon, but would touch base afterwards.

At a few minutes past 5:00, Erin Wallis walked into the Four Seasons bar.

She looked like she owned the place and was obviously there often. Bartenders waved, and servers nodded. An emerald green silk cocktail dress clung to the impeccable body, and her shoulder length hair was woven in a ponytail of three raven braids. The dress, trimmed with thin ribbons of black, beautifully matched the color and sheen of her hair.

Russell stood and walked through the crowded bar to greet her. She kissed his cheek, then he led her over to their table and whispered, "I think we're OK today, Erin, but we probably shouldn't meet in public any more."

The waiter appeared, "Welcome Ms. Wallis. What's your pleasure today?"

Erin smiled at the young man, "Hello Andrew. Stoli, please, on the rocks with lime."

Pamela felt the old jealousy rise. She knew it was foolish but continued to be in awe of this woman, who had to be at least 60. Her looks and charisma were ageless.

Erin graciously extended her hand which Pamela readily shook as she smiled.

Russell patted Erin's hand and said, "Let's talk business first, all right?"

"You have the floor, sir."

"Here's the balance due for the catalog." He handed her a thick envelope from his private banker that contained five, 50-count banded packs of $100 dollar bills. Back at your place, take the money out of this envelope, and put it in one or two envelopes of your own, then burn my envelope and flush the ashes down the toilet."

"You're serious?"

"Erin, you're not going to believe this catalog. It's very disturbing, to say the least. I don't want it traced back to us if anything goes wrong."

"Clay, all of a sudden you're frightening me."

"Good. You need to be wary." The drinks came and Russell thanked the waiter. Erin smiled as she lifted her glass. "Salud, Clayton and Pamela."

"To good health and happiness," Pamela replied. She liked Erin, despite the competition she felt. The madam was as kind as she was beautiful.

Russell interrupted the toast, "Look, tomorrow get to your hotel suite as soon as possible and call me. I'm in room 1605, registered as Sam Redmond. Pamela has an adjoining room in her own name. We'll come to your suite and set up. Then we wait."

"I'll have hors d'oeuvres and drinks brought up."

"Fine. When Krieg arrives, encourage him to talk. As a first-time customer, you're curious as to how they work. You have a client that may be interested in buying, but you don't want any subsequent problems."

"This will be an easy role for me to play, because most of it's true anyway. What else?"

"We're going to set up a live video feed, so we can monitor the transaction and make sure things go safely. The

214

catalog will surely be packaged. When you open it, touch the publication only with latex gloves. There are a couple of pairs in here." Russell handed Erin another envelope.

"For fingerprints?"

"And other forensic evidence, such as oils, hair, fibers."

"Yes sir." Erin stirred her drink and finished it. "Kiss me off to work, Clayton. I've got to pay for these threads."

Russell rose, and as he kissed and lightly hugged Erin, he gently pulled the back top of her dress just far enough to see a label that informed him the elegant frock was

Created for
Ms. Erin Wallis
By Richard Tyler

"Tomorrow!"

She walked out of the bar at a leisurely pace, swinging her hips in a seductive manner and leaving a wake of appreciative stares from the men. Pamela smiled.

At 2:00 p.m. on Monday, Erin waited in her king suite on the 14th floor of the 70 Park Avenue Hotel, at the corner of Park and 38th.

She sat in a soft leather wing chair, sipping water with fizz. She glanced at the large floral arrangement that now adorned the top of the tall bookcase. Pamela had brought the flowers that morning at 11:30, positioned them on the bookcases and suggested that Erin attempt to get Mr.

Krieg to sit in the opposite wing chair. The two detectives decided against a "bug." With current equipment, it's too easily revealed. But Pamela wanted him facing the doorway, to get a clear view. Russell was concerned about Erin and hoped she could appreciate the danger she was in. This was much more serious than in-call prostitution.

The phone rang, loudly, causing Erin to jump.

"Yes?"

"Ms. Wallis, this is the front desk. There is a Mr. Krieg here who says he has an appointment with you."

"Please send him up."

"Certainly."

Erin opened her purse and removed the old, but mint condition .22 Smith & Wesson Escort, a small, nickel-plated gun that held five, long rifle hollow point bullets. She pulled back the slide and let it go, jacking a bullet into the firing chamber. She flipped the catch from safe to fire and put the gun back into her purse between the large Unicorn Club envelopes holding $25,000.

Soon, there were two knocks at the door. Erin stood up, smoothed her dress, and slowly opened it. The man was tall, thin and older, maybe 70. He wore a dark gray chalk-stripe suit, white shirt and blood-red tie. He looked like a cold, wealthy, asexual gent who had made his money in caskets, funeral homes and cemeteries. With white, close-cropped hair, dark brown, almost black eyes, thin angular face and pokerfaced expression, Mr. Krieg looked like Death. He only lacked robe and scythe.

"I am Mr. Krieg." He extended a long, sinewy hand. His voice was a husky tenor with no accent. Erin lightly pressed the skeletal claw.

"I am Erin Wallis," she answered, forcing a smile. "Please come in."

She stepped aside, and Mr. Krieg slowly entered, leaving a mild aromatic trail of some strange cologne. What was that smell? After a few seconds, Erin realized the man smelled of cloves. What the hell? Screw that, focus, focus! She knew her opening performance must be outstanding.

"Please have a seat," she said, gesturing to the opposite wing chair.

Mr. Krieg hesitated, walked around the living room and glanced into the adjoining bedroom. Finally he sat down and held his hands in his lap. Erin sat in the other chair, looked at the man and smiled again. The man's irises were so dark, she could not tell where they ended and his pupils began. His eyes looked like a cat's at night.

"Please help yourself to some food." She gestured to the silver platter on the coffee table. "May I get you a drink?"

He politely shook his head.

"Do you mind if I smoke, Mr. Krieg?"

"No."

Erin lit a slim Capri, inhaled deeply and blew the smoke up. "Thank you for coming. How was your flight?"

Mr. Krieg smiled slightly and said, "Uneventful." It was apparent he had no interest in casual conversation.

"Mr. Krieg, you are here because I wish to purchase your catalog, and, in all likelihood, your company's, uh, products. But I would like to know enough about your organization, in general terms, of course, to help lessen any post-purchase anxiety on my part." Erin re-crossed her legs, rested her elbows casually on the arms of the chair, tented her fingers and raised an eyebrow.

Mr. Krieg's smile was thin and artificial. "I would be glad to open your eyes."

When Erin heard the phrase *open your eyes*, her sphincter muscle tightened, and her heart began beating faster. She wanted to close her eyes and have this person gone. He was cadaverous and cold. Maybe it was the clove aroma? She quickly re-focused on the man's words.

"The company, if it exists, is a private business controlled by a board."

"What do you mean, if it exists?" The conversation made Erin uneasy. Maybe the guy suspected this was a ruse? She reached into her purse, repositioned the gun, removed another Capri and nestled the purse beside her left thigh.

Mr. Krieg blinked twice, smiled and continued. "De Blauwe Organisation, if it existed, would probably charge a premium price to provide an ultimate service to select individuals. It may sell people—Jewels, if you will—for marriage or more often simply for sexual pleasure. DBO may also locate donors of healthy organs. You understand the hungers of the flesh. There are so many very ill, wealthy people who need a healthy liver or kidney and do not wish to wait on some organ donor list mandated by your government. De Blauwe Organisation may, in theory, help them locate a donor. But I am here because of your interest in the catalog and Jewels, not organs. Yes? You seem quite healthy."

Erin tried to smile. Her throat was dry, and her palms were wet. "How do you make a Jewel, uh, acquiesce?"

Again, Mr. Krieg's mouth smiled, but his eyes didn't.

"With the proper medicine, and indoctrination, I would imagine anyone might be converted into a Jewel. And DBO may provide the indoctrination of the Jewel and unlimited supply of special elixirs with each purchase to ensure client satisfaction. However, a year's supply may typically be all that is necessary."

Erin was visibly shaken. She reasoned that after a year, the prolonged use of such "elixirs" would render the victim dependent addicts, incapable of self-will. Or dead.

Mr. Krieg made throwaway gestures with his gaunt hands and continued, quite candidly and relaxed. "Once a client contract has been secured and a Jewel has been selected, the abduction, perhaps 'mining' is a better term, do you think? Mining and delivery might be carried out by a three-stage process. First, a 'Catcher' might locate, subdue

219

and mine a Jewel. The Jewel then may be 'put in the box' where the merchandise is kept quiet. The box may then be passed to a Conductor, whose job may be to polish the Jewel: clean it, make it smoother and prettier, perhaps even some cosmetic surgery and begin the indoctrination process. Once the Jewel is polished, the Conductor might then pass the package on to a Presenter, who may be someone, such as me, who then would present the Jewel to the new owner."

Erin's face was calm—she was an expert actress—but her knuckles were unconsciously gripping the chair. She noticed the tension and relaxed her grip, hoping Mr. Krieg had not observed. Until now she thought Clayton was overly cautious. Now she agreed.

"Thank you for enlightening me." She reached into her purse and removed the thick envelopes. "This *might* be a down payment for such a catalog. *If* it existed, of course."

Mr. Krieg emitted a rather unpleasant chuckle. "If such a catalog existed, I imagine it would be too heavy for one person to carry. However, I would be glad to take your package, which, now I remember, contains money you owe me from a friendly wager, right? And then, perhaps, who knows?" Mr. Krieg held out both arms. "An act of God may cause such a catalog to come your way. Maybe within the hour, but one must have *faith*. Do you have faith, Ms. Wallis?"

"Don't you have the catalog with you?"

"No. But your down payment, and the balance, could, perhaps, make one appear shortly after I depart."

Erin wasn't sure what to do. Should she let this ghoul leave with Clayton's money, on the hope that later, the catalog would be delivered to her? Was this guy a con man? Clayton was sure the catalog was real, so Erin agreed. Any further hesitation on her part may make the ghoul suspicious.

Erin politely replied, "Yes, one must certainly have faith if one is to make any progress." She stood up to end the meeting. "Thank you for coming here today. I hope you have a pleasant journey back to... " Erin wanted to say Transylvania, "to your destination."

Mr. Krieg nodded and gave a Mona Lisa smile. "And thank you Ms. Wallis. I wish all our clients, if we did have clients, were as beautiful and charming as you." Mr. Krieg walked to the door and silently let himself out. Erin walked to the door, hesitated for a few seconds, then opened it and looked out into the hall.

It was empty.

How did he vanish so quickly?

She closed the door and leaned against it.

It was as if the man had not even existed. As if he had been a ghost, a character from a bad dream. Except she could still smell cloves.

Erin picked up the phone and called Russell's room. No answer. Strange. She clicked off and called room service.

"Yes Ms. Wallis? May we help you?"

"Please send up a bottle of Tanqueray, ice and three limes."

"My pleasure, Ms. Wallis."

Erin went over to the window and began to chain-smoke Capris. She gazed down to the street far below, looking for a man-thing with gray hair and a $25,000 bulge in his funeral suit.

The knock at the door made her jump. She pulled the pistol from her purse, went to the door and asked, "Who is it?"

"Room service."

She looked through the peephole to confirm and let the server in. An hour later, sipping her third gin on the rocks, her mobile phone rang. The address stated 'public caller.'

"Hello?"

"Ms. Wallis, this is Mr. Krieg. I am calling from a jet that has just left New York. It is such a beautiful day, not a cloud in the sky. Thank you for your consideration, Ms. Wallis. I appreciate the high denominations and the clean, crisp notes." A slight pause, some static, then, "There is a gift outside your hotel door. From God. Perhaps." Click.

Erin hung up and quickly went to the door. She cautiously opened it, and the DSL package -plopped on the floor. MS. E. WALLIS was printed on the front.

Erin picked it up, saw no one in the hall, closed the door and bolted it.

"Damn!" She had forgotten about the gloves.

She carefully set down the envelope, put on a pair of the latex gloves and picked up the envelope again. Using a sharp penknife she gingerly opened it.

The cover was a glossy, deep blue, and in red type was the title:

De Blauwe Biblio
XIV   2383

Erin, mesmerized, slowly and carefully turned the pages, touching them only on the edges. The photos were just as Mr. Krieg had described. Fully half of the people appeared to be between nine and sixteen years old, all attractive, and below each photograph was a five-digit number—ordering codes, she guessed. She wondered how many of these people, these Jewels, were still going about their lives, unaware that they were being merchandised this way in a slave catalog? Redheads, blondes, brunettes, bald, Asian, African, Nordic, men, women, teens and children. The next-to-last page was particularly disturbing. This section contained small blocks of copy with very sweet descriptions of many types of infants but no photos. In the lower right hand corner of the page, the copy read, "Describe your small Jewel here," followed by ample blank space, then, "We guarantee you will soon possess the tiny gem of your dreams."

Erin set it on the coffee table, roughly stripped off the latex gloves and filled her glass halfway with gin. She went to the window and stared into the distance. Sipping the drink, she slowly shook her head in disbelief and began to quietly weep.

At 11:00 that evening, Russell and Waters were stretched out in the half-empty first class cabin, a bright full moon visible out the window, as they thought about the day's events.

Four hours earlier, they left Erin Wallis, noticeably high and upset.

"That catalog is the most immoral thing I have ever seen in my life," she had softly said. "I will never, ever, be able to get the dirt off my hands after having touched that hellacious thing. Mr. Krieg and his colleagues should be drawn and quartered. What he and those people do is sub-human. They're reptilian. Clayton, if there is anything I can do to help stop those people, just let me know, and I will do it. If you can hurt them in any way, I would be goddamned proud to help you."

"Right now I want to get the catalog out of town and have it analyzed. Can you call me in Atlanta sometime tomorrow evening?"

"Yes. Of course." She wiped an eye with a tissue and turned away.

He picked up the envelope and carefully put it into his attaché case.

"Erin, are you alright?"

"Yes, but go, soon, please. I need a good cry, and I'd rather do it alone."

"You've been a great help. Thanks." Russell then hugged her, Pamela kissed a moist, salty cheek and they left.

In the cab ride to LaGuardia Airport, Russell called Bressler and gave him an update.

In the air, flying over Washington D.C., when most of the passengers were quiet or asleep, Pamela switched on an overhead light. Wearing latex gloves, Russell opened his attaché case, removed the catalog from the envelope and began to carefully turn the pages.

What they saw was beautiful and horrible. The quality of the design, layout and photographs were exquisite, on a par with Architectural Digest; it was the disgusting contents that shocked. A buffet of beautiful people for sale.

As he turned the pages, Russell remained quiet. Pamela cursed in whispers periodically. On page 17, Pamela suddenly gasped, and her finger quickly pointed to a face in the center of the page.

It was Lisa Collins, a head and shoulders framing, bright sunlight, the child smiling broadly. The photo appeared to have been taken no more than a year ago.

Pamela began to cry.

Russell closed his attaché case and turned off the light.

Chapter 15

Ordering a Jewel

"I can't believe you would even consider ordering someone from a publication like this! And Pam, you've got a good head on your shoulders, why are you going along with this insane idea?"

Sidney Bressler was so agitated, he paced back and forth across the highly-polished oak floor in Russell's great room, his loafers clicking soundly on the wood then making no noise as he tread across the plush area rug. Pamela was content to let the two friends argue it out. Outside, the temperature was rising quickly and predicted to reach the high nineties. The humidity was oppressive and the hot August winds consistently huffed at the trees and shrubs. Winston lay stretched on his side next to the sliding glass doors, happily asleep on the cool floor. He would occasionally open one eye to observe the status of the heated debate.

Pamela was drinking ice water and seriously considered a Bloody Mary. Russell sipped on a tall iced tea with lime, and Bressler was loudly slurping down his third Scotch-rocks-twist. He had arrived two hours earlier, at 9:00 a.m., and the entire morning consisted of discussing the pros and cons of ordering a Jewel, the detective making logical points in favor of the former and the attorney arguing for the latter.

"Sidney, I'm telling you, if I make this thing official, turn over the catalog to the FBI or State Department, all key players will vanish. Wherever they are, these people operate through the Internet. For years our government and, I dare say, all governments, have known about human trafficking but turn a blind eye unless it bites them politically and shames them into addressing the issue. Then they arrest a few convenient locals and pat themselves on the back for a job well done. On the rare occasion foreign governments cooperate, and here they may, considering the sensationalism of this stuff, it will, undoubtedly, take weeks of red tape. By then, you can bet the farm De Blauwe Organisation will have disappeared. Documents will have long since been shredded and anything else incriminating. I doubt they have qualms about murder irrespective of age of the victim."

"But you and this Manhattan madam are ordering a little girl, just like you're ordering a friggin' pizza?"

"That's right. First, we try to order Lisa Collins, though I think she's already been purchased by someone out of the country."

"Why another country?"

"Because it's been over two weeks now, and no solid lead has resulted from *America's Most Wanted*. I think if she was in this country, and alive, somebody would have reported her by now. First we'll try to order her, and if she's not for sale anymore, we order someone else, somebody similar, so it looks like we're shopping for a particular type. When the Presenter delivers our Jewel, we eventually pass the girl onto the Red Cross, Amnesty International, the State Department, whomever. Then we snatch the Presenter, crack open that person, go up the DBO pipeline and, hopefully, find Lisa."

"Who's going to pay for the Jewel?"

"Me."

"How much?"

"We don't know yet. Several hundred thousand, certainly."

"And you, personally, are going to pay that?"

Russell nodded, got up and poured another tea.

"Clay, to use their parlance, when a 'Jewel' is bought, does the 'Jewel' come from an existing 'inventory,' or is the Jewel mined?"

"Please elaborate."

"If you buy a Jewel, are you paying for another girl—now free, happy and innocent—to be drugged, kidnapped, kept drugged, abused and, possibly, killed? Or does the new Jewel come from an inventory of kids they've got warehoused somewhere?" Russell began to reply, but Bressler held up his hand and continued, "How in the world can you justify that?"

"I never considered that before."

Pamela had not either, and she did not like the idea. Maybe she could not go along with Clay after all. She decided to make that Bloody Mary.

"Sidney, look at the big picture. For every kid pulled out of the blue hole, at least that person is in a better place. Every Jewel purchased increases the odds of causing a fracture in that organization, a leak in their boat. Maybe the boat will even sink. If you can tell me another way that will not tip off the criminal minds, counselor, speak up."

Bressler had no counter, but he was worried. Very worried.

"I might even get the money back somewhere along the way. Plus save a few more captured children. Stop the flow of illegal organs. Who knows where it may lead?"

Emotionally exhausted and physically inebriated, Bressler picked up the De Blauwe Biblio. "What have you learned about this rag? You've had it for a week now."

"A forensic lab we hired found no fingerprints. The paper is from England, the ink is from Italy, and the photos could have been uploaded on disk from anywhere. The company and catalog names are Dutch, and the mailing address is a Swiss post box with a Cayman bank account. It's like the United Nations published the catalog. Did you notice the stitching on the catalog?"

Bressler looked at the spine. "Yellow stitching. So what."

"That stitching is 22-karat gold thread, Sidney."

Bressler's face screwed into a puzzled expression.

"The creators of this publication consider the catalog an art form, and take real pride in their work. I'd like to meet the character behind this machine."

Bressler put the catalog down on the marble coffee table and sat on the large leather sofa. "OK, you order a Jewel, you get it, her, you get your little breathing gem, and you 'appropriate' the person who makes the delivery. How exactly do you propose convincing them to help you? To tell you anything?"

"I've got some ideas."

Bressler shook his head in exasperation. "Do you want to retain me for the trial?"

"What trial?"

"Yours. For slavery—the Mann Act—kidnapping, drug violations. The penalties include life in prison, Sherlock. Pam, I do hope you are listening to me."

Pamela shook her head. "Guys, I find both arguments compelling. I just haven't decided yet. But we do need to tell Sally Collins something. She has a right to know."

Clayton hesitated. He did not want to argue with Pam, too. "I don't know. Seeing her daughter in that catalog may alarm her to the point where she could take unilateral action that would make too much noise." Russell heard a little voice in his head ask *Aren't we being a bit God-like with ...* He pushed the voice into a closet and slammed the door.

231

Bressler crossed a leg in exasperation. "Well, I've got kids. If I were in her place, I would want to be kept abreast and to know the truth. What has your madam friend done?"

"On Monday, she sent a letter to De Blauwe Organisation, requesting to purchase Jewel #79947, Lisa Collins. We're waiting for a reply. I expect to hear she's been sold, but I'm hopeful their arrogance will lead to mistakes."

"What the devil makes you think they're that arrogant?"

Russell calmly answered, "Their products. Their delivery. The quality of their distribution. Also, how many people know what I know about Lisa *and* have a copy of this catalog? Nobody. So I'm going to strike while the iron's hot. I'm going to go up the pipeline and see what I can find. See if I can locate her."

Pamela looked at her lover and his lawyer and sighed. Men!

———————————

Three days later, at mid-morning, Russell answered the phone.

"Clay, this is Erin," she said excitedly, "great news!"

"What?"

"I received an email this morning, with a blind sender address. Let me read it to you."

"Where are you?"

"I am on a payphone in a closed booth at a midtown hotel. It's safe. Listen:

> 'Dear Ms. Wallis: We regret the Jewel you requested is not available. May we suggest Jewel 80032. Wire $200,000 USD to our Cayman account. The fifty thousand advanced for the catalog has been applied to the balance with another $150,000 due at delivery. You may accept the offer by simply wiring payment, or, if you need further information, post on our blog. Kindly provide several alternative dates, times, and locations for delivery. We shall notify you 24 hours in advance. Thank you for your interest in De Blauwe Organisation.'

Was Bressler correct, Russell thought? By ordering Jewel 80032, was he initiating a kidnapping? The goal had to justify such an action. Otherwise, someone else would eventually purchase the child and he could not get closer to locating Lisa.

The worm had been put on the hook, the line was tossed into the water, and before the ripples had subsided, the cork had started bobbing. Russell, nervous with anticipation, nevertheless kept his voice very calm as he spoke and confirmed the financial details.

The madam laughed. "This is great, Clay! I can't believe it's happening!"

"Erin, please appreciate the danger you are in and don't think of it as exciting or fun. This group should be treated with the same respect given poisonous snakes. Please don't forget that."

"And don't you forget I'm a big girl. I've been pretty successful in a hardball business myself, too, you know. Send me your mad money, and I'll pass it on to those evil people."

"Thanks Erin."

"You're so welcome, dear boy."

Russell hung up and called his banker at Colony Square in midtown Atlanta and scheduled an appointment for 2:00 p.m. He would liquidate some investment bonds and sign a short term note for the balance. He glanced over at De Blauwe Biblio.

Pamela and Bressler were right. Sally was entitled to be informed. She should not bear needless suffering when there was hope.

That evening, after wiring $150,000 to Erin Wallis' bank account in New York, Russell picked up the book John Walsh had sent him; The Sexual Trafficking In Children— An Investigation of the Child Sex Trade, by Daniel S. Campagna and Donald L. Poffenberger. He highlighted passages he thought pertinent.

> Minors will continue to be the most sexually exploited group in the United States. Those believed to be involved in sexually exploitive activities here may number as many as 1.2 million.

> When the commercial element is present, the victim is compelled to exchange sex often in order to survive... The relationship is

234

maintained at the victim's expense; it may include pornography sessions, multiple adult lovers, and drug dependency. In all cases, those exploited are eventually discarded.

The sexual traffic in minors, like drug trafficking, is an international phenomenon with the opportunities enhanced by the internet.

Under the chapter Pedophilia, Russell highlighted:

Although it is usually assumed that most pedophiles or child molesters are males, we have observed an increase involving females.

Under Pedophile Organizations and Publications,

Russell noted several amazing groups, the first of which he

was now personally familiar:

They strive to justify and rationalize the illegal behavior of their members and readers. For example, the North American Man-boy Love Association (NAMBLA) advocates intergenerational sexual relationships between adult and underage males. NAMBLA claims chapters in Boston, New York, Los Angeles, San Francisco and Toronto. Membership is unconfirmed.

NAMBLA contends children and adults can have satisfying emotional and sexual relationships based on consent, not bound by age limits. An adult male attracted to an underage male is, they say, entitled to establish a nurturing relationship based on mutual trust and respect. What is ignored in this argument is whether a minor's immaturity renders him incapable of giving consent to an extraordinarily complex and potentially damaging relationship with a seductive adult.

What a euphemism, "intergenerational relationships." He wondered what Bressler would say if told, "Your 13-year-old son is having an intergenerational relationship with his 40-year-old coach."

Russell tossed aside the book. He walked outside and looked up at the bright stars visible in patches through the limbs of the swaying pine trees. He wondered when Erin would again hear from De Blauwe Organisation. And why could Pamela not find The Samaritan? What was the connection with the Dalai Lama's artifacts? He would not even think about that missing kid in China. That gave him a real headache and restless nights.

Emotionally spent, Russell went to bed.

———————

Five days later, when Russell and Winston returned from a swim, the sole message on the answering machine was, "Guess who? They called, and the Jewel is being delivered Monday night. Call me!"

Chapter 16

To Catch A Presenter

The child was to arrive with her escort around 11:00 p.m. at Erin's apartment. Russell thought that in the pipeline to the DBO heart, a Jewel was a minor vein with limited information, whereas a Presenter was an artery.

The Unicorn Club's personnel physician, Jose Gonzales, was on call to join them and examine the child prior to her trip back to Atlanta. Though medically trained, the doctor was not licensed to practice medicine in the United States. Obtaining his degree in Mexico, he was never licensed here but maintained a successful, albeit, exclusive private practice treating Erin and her girls.

Russell continued to worry about Erin's involvement. With the disappearance of the Presenter and Jewel, would De Blauwe Organisation assume disloyalty and personal flight with the money? Russell would be gone, but could Erin safely cloister herself within the protection of The Unicorn Club cocoon? Would an extended vacation in a faraway secluded resort be safer? Maybe now would be a good time to take that early retirement she frequently mentioned.

Russell glanced again at his watch. 11:03 p.m. He cautiously pulled back the drapes and looked at the dimly lit street far below. The torrential rain storm that swept through in wild, angular sheets a half-hour earlier had now subsided to a drizzle. A New York City uniformed beat cop walked by, pausing to turn and look over his shoulder at a homeless man who was huddled in a nearby doorway. Russell wondered if the man were a spotter of some kind.

A yellow cab eased up to the curb outside the building. Russell raised and focused the small Nikon binoculars. The left rear door opened, and a young blonde girl wearing a long black rain coat and sunglasses slowly steeped out. Another figure emerged. It was a woman. She was difficult to discern, but appeared to be thirty-something, rather plain looking, wearing a tan trench coat and carrying a black physician's bag. On her head was a white nurse's cap. The Presenter placed a protective arm around the girl, and the two trotted through the light rain to the outer door, where Russell lost sight of them.

Turning to his friend, Russell asked, "Erin, are you OK?"

"Yes, I think so. I just wish this were over. I don't feel well. This does not seem right."

"What do you mean?"

"I just have a bad feeling about what we're doing. I've got chills."

"Pamela should arrive soon. Your role is almost complete. Once I can return this Presenter to a secure place in Atlanta for interrogation, you're through."

"I sincerely hope so."

The phone rang, causing Erin to spill a dollop of the drink in her lap. "Bloody hell!" she hissed.

Russell quietly rose, as Erin picked up the receiver. "Hello?"

"Ms. Wallis? Your Jewel is here." A pronounced German accent. "May I deliver her now?"

"Uh, you're in the lobby?"

"Yes."

Erin bit her lip and replied, "Then I will buzz you in. I'm on th…"

"39th floor," the woman interrupted.

Erin hit the code and hung up.

Russell touched her shoulder, smiled encouragement, padded over to the closet, closed the door and put his eye to the peephole.

Erin made a fresh drink, took a deep breath and smoothed back her long black hair. She forced a smile, which lit up her face enough to mask the nervousness.

Two long minutes later, the doorbell rang.

Erin calmly walked to the door. Russell heard it open and her say, "Welcome to The Unicorn Club. I'm Erin Wallis." Russell tightened the blackjack strap around his right wrist.

"I am Ms. Scala," said a female voice. German? Swiss?

"Please, come in," Erin continued.

The door shut, and Russell saw the trio walk into view. The Presenter introduced the child as Lorena. She handed Erin a large black leather clutch bag, explaining, "Lorena has been successfully indoctrinated, but if necessary, you can totally control your Jewel with these medications. Instructions are written on dosage and effects; energetic, sensual, sleepy, and asleep…for 12 hours. We do not advise frequent use of the elixirs, as they may tarnish the luster of a Jewel."

Within the dark black leather case, Erin could see vials of liquids, syringes and bottles of pills with labels.

Russell's heart was beating so fast, he thought she would hear it. The woman was moving his way. He slowly turned the knob of the closet door. When Ms. Scala was ten feet from the closet, Russell burst out, causing both women to jump.

The Presenter sprang against the wall and reached into her purse, but she was immediately checked; Russell let fly with a backhand, and the blackjack smacked her right wrist, fractured it and sent the purse sailing across the room. The woman clutched her right forearm, and before she could react, Russell came across with the blackjack just hard enough behind the right ear to render her unconscious. As she began to fall, he caught her and laid the limp woman on the floor, face down. From behind a sofa cushion, he retrieved the roll of Gorilla Tape and began trussing up the Presenter, cutting off strips with a Viper. He secured tape around both wrists, behind her back, bound her ankles together and wound the tape around the legs up to the knees. He used a triple loop of tape to connect the arms and legs, putting her in a tight hog-tie. From his hip pocket, he removed a white cotton handkerchief, stuffed it in the woman's mouth and wrapped two loops of tape around her jaw and head, careful to leave her nose free to breathe. With his thumb and forefinger he opened her eyelids. Static, pale green eyes stared into mid-space, but the pupils were reactive and shrank slightly with the increased light.

Russell sat down beside the trussed Presenter, rested his arms on crossed legs and took a deep breath. He had broken a slight sweat, more from nervousness than from the small physical exertion, but he felt good. This is going smoothly. At any rate, they were safe inside The Unicorn Club. All doors to the hallway were secured.

Russell glanced at the young teenager cowering in a corner. She seemed alarmed, yet fairly calm. She must be drugged.

Erin whispered, "Well, you certainly wrapped that package in a jiffy. I've never seen anyone move so fast. What do we do now, cowboy?" The madam's attempt to be relaxed was betrayed by her face. She had become quite pale, and the smile was forced. She also felt nauseous and cradled her midsection.

Russell nodded toward the girl. "Why don't you see if you can calm her a bit?"

Erin attempted another smile as she walked toward the girl.

Russell leaned over the unconscious woman and searched her pockets. From the thin tan raincoat over an arctic white nurse's uniform, he removed a wallet that contained a passport identifying her as Sofia Scala from Florence, Italy, plus a considerable amount of dollars and lire. In her shoulder purse he found an assortment of cosmetics, along with a small aerosol tube that looked like pepper spray, the brand name and instructions printed in Italian. He began to frisk her body, starting at the tightly buttoned collar. Centered between her breasts, he felt a small, hard, rectangular object. He quickly undid buttons and discovered the matchbook-size plastic box with two wires disappearing into her bra.

"Jesus Christ, Erin, she's wearing a wire. Call Pamela so.... "

BOOM! BOOM! KRAAACKK!

Erin's door smashed open, the lock side splintering as it flew against the interior wall. The force of the final blow was powerful enough to imbed the doorknob into the wall. Erin's door was soundproof, and for something to hit the double-enforced, oak slab that hard was incredible.

Russell stared at the thing that had blasted the door. The silhouette blocked out nearly all the light from the hallway.

He was six-and-a-half feet tall and had the build of a weightlifter. A second after sizing up the room, he reached into his coat and withdrew a long pistol. Before he could aim, Russell let fly with a Viper, and the sharp, steel sank deep into the back of the man's gun hand between the second and third metacarpals. The gun slipped from the right hand, but the man quickly caught it with his left. Just as he grasped the gun, Russell's first jump kick caught the man square on the chin, snapping his head back a foot, but he somehow managed to grab Russell's ankle with the left hand. Russell was pulled up in the air, horizontal, but with his other leg, he kicked the chin again, causing the large, shadowy head to snap back a second time. The man dropped the gun and let go of Russell, who fell, rolled, stumbled back against the corner bar, regained his balance and grabbed a tall, wooden barstool. The man yanked the knife from the back of his right hand, dropped it on the floor, then reached down to pick up the gun. Russell quickly spun around 360°, swinging the stool in a blurred arc. The centrifugal force was tremendous as it smashed into the man's left forearm, breaking it. The gun flew out of his hand and across the room. The man roared, showing he was mortal. He leapt up and, considering his size and the dual injuries, executed a very swift and accurate flying sidekick. The large black boot caught Russell in the solar plexus and sent him backwards a dozen feet, where he tripped and fell but rolled and bounded up on his feet. He had managed to tighten his midsection in time, but held his middle with one arm, trying to pull in the rolling pain. Russell looked at the giant's left arm, which now hung straight down, useless. A compound fracture of the radius showed all the way through the dark shirt sleeve, splintered bone protruding in an ugly red and white shard. He charged and lashed out with a very quick, straight right leg kick to the groin, but Russell sidestepped it and used one arm to grab the man's ankle and kept the kick going up, up. The giant was lifted off the floor and fell flat on his back with a crash that shook the room. He quickly rolled to the right, scrambled up and charged Russell again. As the man reached him, Russell grabbed the giant's lapels, twist-turned him and used the larger man's thrust and heavy momentum to pile-drive him headfirst into the large brick wall of Erin's fireplace. The noise was sickening, and as the giant groggily tried to stand, Russell whipped out the blackjack and began hitting the man on the head: left, right, left, right. The clopping blows took effect. The man slowly sank to the floor, his knees struck the flush marble hearth, then the unconscious body toppled to the left and became still, as the large, oil painting of a lake above the fireplace fell free, bounced once on the mantle, then landed upside down on the floor, the action punctuating the fight. As Russell straightened up, the fallen man grunted, and Russell grabbed the large brass poker from the fireplace set. He swung it back like Ruth about to send one over the fence. But the intruder finally became still.

244

Russell leaned against the wall. He coughed up a teaspoon of blood, verified it came from a cut inside his mouth, and then wiped it off with the back of a sleeve. He went to Erin. She had picked up the man's gun, and was pointing it at him. She started to cry and slowly sat down on the sofa, trembling.

"Are you OK?" Russell whispered, hoarsely.

Erin nodded twice, silently.

Russell went to the closet and from a small duffle bag removed two sets of handcuffs. He knelt down beside the man and noticed that blood had stopped seeping from the arm and head wounds. He felt the side of the giant's neck. No pulse. Russell put the cuffs in his pocket.

"You two stay here and try to get Pamela on the phone!"

Russell ran down the hallway and banged open the exit door. He raced up the stairs, shouldered through the door, onto the roof and then froze. The helicopter was about fifty feet in the air and rising. Inside beside the pilot, Mr. Krieg clicked off several photographs of Russell with an infrared camera, which depicted him in the lens-finder, pale green in color, his hand over squinting eyes, hair flapping wildly from the blades' downdraft. Then the copter quickly banked west and disappeared into the night behind a skyscraper.

Russell admired the intelligence of the assignation; it was simple yet brilliant! The DBO Presenter and Jewel entered from the street, with their backup muscle and exit transportation poised on the roof. They affirmed what he thought: do not underestimate this group.

Russell limped across the tar roof, then down the stairwell. His midsection throbbed with pain. He hoped there wasn't internal bleeding. He held his bleeding side and slowly walked back to Erin's suite.

As he neared the broken doorway, he heard a strange, scuffling sound.

He broke into a trot just in time to see Erin, ten paces away, back out of her doorway, saying, "No! No!... " PHUTT-PHUTT-PHUTT. Muffled snaps from the silenced gun sent three bullets into Erin's body: the first one hit in the shoulder, spinning her around 180°; the second slug struck the small of the back, propelling her against the opposite wall; and the third one kicked up her dress at the left hip, then she slid to the floor. Russell raced to the doorway. The young girl still pointed the gun at Erin, pulling the trigger, bullets punching into a wall. Russell bounded to the dazed girl, her face vacant and emotionless. He pulled the gun from her hand and pushed her face backward hard enough to send the girl flying across the room and crashing into an end table.

"Goddammit!" Russell dashed back to Erin and gently rolled her over. She was conscious and trying to speak, but the words were gibberish. Russell picked her up and laid her on the large sofa as Pamela ran into the room.

"Clay, someone T-boned the taxi two blocks from here…" She saw the carnage and wrecked room. "Oh my God."

Russell grabbed the nearest phone, called the lobby and before the doorman could speak, said, as calmly as he could, "Find Dr. Gonzales. He should be in the building. Get him here, fast."

Russell hung up, ran to the bathroom, snatched several white towels from a large stack and returned to Erin. In the few moments it took the Unicorn's physician to arrive, Russell made crude but tight bandages on the three wounds, using a Viper to first slice off clothes, then cut strips from the thick terrycloth towels and bind them around her body. Two of the wounds seemed to be bleeding much less, but the hip wound was continuously seeping crimson.

Dr. Gonzales entered the room, expecting to examine a runaway child but took one look at Erin and said, "She must be taken to the nearest hospital immediately."

Russell told Pamela to stay with the girl."

He punched 0 and a female voice answered, "Yes?"

"Erin's hurt," he replied, forcing calm into his voice. "Have an Associate bring a car and Dr. Gonzales and I will meet her at the lobby entrance. Hurry! We need to get to a hospital, fast." He hung up and turned to Pamela. "Can you stay here and prepare for a long car trip home?"

"Of course." Pamela began to cry. "But what…"

"Trust me."

Russell glanced at the girl. Was she playing possum? He spent a precious minute trussing up the girl with Gorilla tape. He carried Erin into the hall directing Dr. Gonzales to prop up the smashed door and frame in place behind him as Russell ran to the elevator. The doors opened immediately, he popped the lobby button, held Erin close to his body and tried to think clearly. He trotted across the lobby, as the horrified doorman stared, Russell yelled, "Let us out!" The shocked man held open the door. An associate was at the curb with a back limo door open. Within seconds they were speeding north.

Erin was still unconscious. Russell held her in the rear seat as Dr. Gonzales applied pressure to the bandage over the hip wound.

"When we get to the emergency room, tell the ER staff an intruder broke into her home. Say nothing more. Call me at Erin's suite as soon as you can."

The young woman at the wheel was sobbing, but she drove like a pro. Within moments they screeched to a stop at the emergency entrance of Park Forest General Hospital.

"Hit the horn! Again!" Russell demanded, elbowing open the car door and lifting Erin out with Dr. Gonzales at his side.

Two male orderlies smoking next to an ambulance tossed their cigarettes aside and ran to them.

"Gunshot wounds," Russell said, as he handed Erin to the two large men. The orderlies joined hands to make an arm stretcher, and Russell placed Erin on their locked wrists and forearms. "Shoulder, hip and small of the back. I'm an undercover police officer, and I need to return to the scene." Then he ran to the corner and whistled down a cab.

Russell got in, gave the address, "Hurry, emergency! Here's $200, run the lights!"

He sat back in the cab, pulled out another handkerchief and wiped blood off his hands. Erin's blood. Innocent blood. And it was his fault!

Back at The Unicorn Club, he took the elevator to Erin's floor. Pamela was pacing. "Clay, what do we do?"

"We leave town, pronto. "

Russell frisked the dead man and found two speed loaders. He put one in his pocket, picked up the ugly .38 revolver, popped the empty cartridges onto the floor and snapped the loader into the .38, releasing six bullets in the chambers. He opened a drawer next to Erin's bed, got out a condom and tore it open. He put the condom on his right hand, lightly held the gun and with his left gingerly wiped the weapon clean. Holding the gun by the condom hand, he went to the dead giant, laid a folded towel over the face and fired two rounds into the corpse's forehead, for the forensic folks. It might help muddy the waters.

Russell tossed the spent speed loader, gun and bloody washcloth into the trash bag. He sat on the sofa to rest and think. Five minutes went by, in silence. Then the sleeping girl on the floor sighed, causing him to start. The phone rang. When Russell answered the Unicorn physician reported that her prognosis was poor.

"She's lost a lot of blood. It could go either way. They're operating. Jesus. How could this happen to her?"

Without answering, Russell asked Dr. Gonzales if he could speak with the young driver, who handed the phone to the young driver.

"I need you to return to Erin's suite as soon as you can."

"I'll leave now. Dr. Gonzales says he will wait. By the way, when she gained consciousness for a few minutes the first thing she asked was if you were alright. She told me to do whatever you say. She could square everything with the police."

Russell blinked back tears and then pulled himself together. "Hurry back."

Pamela sat quietly, waiting for instructions. Russell found a tumbler, added ice and four fingers of Grey Goose vodka. He took a large sip, touched the cold glass to his forehead, closed his eyes and then rested the glass over his sore midsection. He slowly stood up and walked to a phone on one of the undisturbed tables in the wrecked room.

He called his friend Bressler, spoke for a minute and then turned to Pamela.

"I'm exhausted. Can you drive?"

Chapter 17

Armed Forces

The road trip from New York to Georgia was long, tedious, more so because Clayton Russell could not alleviate his feelings of guilt.

The Unicorn Club's navy Cadillac limousine had blacked out windows, and Russell sat in the front, his visor mirror adjusted so he could continually check on the occupants in the rear.

Pamela kept the car on cruise-control at the speed limit. They did not need to be stopped by police. Every two hours they stopped in rest areas, where Russell and Pamela went into the back of the car and gave the Presenter and Jewel water. They received no food and were not allowed out. Their hands and ankles were restrained with cable ties Russell had purchased at an all-night supermarket. The discomfort the captives felt soiling themselves were minor factors compared with the risk of periodically escorting them into restrooms. Russell's focus was to arrive home as quickly as possible without complications.

Two hours into the 850-mile drive, Russell told Pamela what he intended to do. She kept her eyes on the road, listened intently and periodically nodded. When finished, he asked her opinion.

"I hope it works. If it does, it's brilliant. If not, well, we may have a bigger problem. But I don't have a better idea."

Russell slouched down in the seat, put on his sunglasses and slept.

The following evening at Russell's home, Sidney Bressler sat in an Eames chair, sipping Scotch and soda. He was very uneasy and had serious misgivings about what he termed "rogue rashness" in Russell's plans. He advised Russell to let the proper authorities take it from here, but his counsel was declined.

Russell wore tennis shoes, jeans and a white knit tennis shirt. He was quietly pacing, staring at the floor, deep in thought.

Dr. Jackson, a respectable-looking elderly man, sat on a small chair. He wore pale green scrubs and latex gloves.

Pamela stood beside the doctor. She was at parade rest, feet slightly apart, arms behind her back, one hand holding a wrist. She wore jeans and a scrub top.

But the most curious-looking person in the high-ceiling great room was Ms. Sofia Scala, the Presenter. She was in front of the massive bookcase, strapped to Russell's Soloflex bench, now positioned at a 45° angle. A sheet covered her body up to the neck, and silver auto-towing tape, tightly cinched around the sheet, bound her to the bench. The unconscious woman's face was pale yet clean, the light brown hair tied in a ponytail. There was a funeral silence in the room except for Russell's soft, steady pacing and the occasional clink of ice cubes as Bressler nursed his drink.

Dr. Jackson filled a syringe, swabbed a small section of skin at the base of Ms. Scala's neck and injected the contents into the Presenter's body. The woman's complexion segued from pale into pink. Her eyes opened, blinked for a few seconds and began to dart around the room, assessing the unknown venue and strangers. She quietly asked, "Where am I?"

Russell walked toward the bound woman. "Ms. Scala, we are interested in one of the Jewels your company recently abducted, a young girl, and we want her returned. We expect you to tell us how to locate the child. Lisa Collins."

Stepping closer, the detective held up a photograph of Lisa. Sofia Scala ignored the photo, studied Russell for a few seconds, turned her head toward Dr. Jackson, glanced at Pamela and said nothing.

The room was silent. Even Bressler was frozen, his glass held in mid-air, inches from his face. The attorney had no idea what his friends planned to do if this stranger did not voluntarily cooperate, but the attorney was no simpleton. His mind was in a flurry, as he had doubts about this "physician." And what was Russell doing, being the shepherd of such? The woman should be in the hands of the FBI. He took a hearty pull of his Knockando rocks.

Russell continued, "Ms. Scala, you have received an epidural to block pain. Every time you refuse to answer my question, the doctor will remove a finger. Do you understand?"

The woman said nothing. She merely looked outside at the trees.

Russell nodded, and Dr. Jackson reached under the sheet and extracted the woman's limp, paralyzed right arm. He firmly grasped her right hand, placed it on a tray held by Pamela and spread her fingers. In a quick motion, the doctor neatly sliced off the end of the woman's fourth digit at its lowest joint. Bright red blood began to steadily seep out of the wound. Dr. Jackson elevated the hand a few inches, and Pamela covered the stump with a small white bandage, taped it and looked at Sofia Scala.

The Presenter's expression had rapidly changed from composure to tight-lipped stoicism. Amazingly, she turned her head away and stared at a wall, as if nothing had happened.

Bressler gasped, "JesusMaryMotherOfJesus!" He finished his drink with one gulp, bolted up and stumbled to the bathroom.

Dr. Jackson turned toward Russell, who stood over his victim and studied Ms. Scala. He could imagine what she was thinking. She was trapped, like a mink in a steel cage. Should she reveal what she knows and risk retribution from

DBO for squealing? Or would this man kill her anyway after she answered the questions?

Russell looked at Dr. Jackson and nodded again.

Slowly and methodically the physician amputated each digit of the right hand. As Ms. Scala's chest slowly rose and fell with deep breaths. Russell recognized the look of fear. He knew it firsthand. But she said nothing. Pamela quickly put a large gauze bandage around the five stumps and applied pressure.

Bressler, quite pale, returned with another drink of courage. He scanned the faces of the people in the room. "Holy fucking shit! Goddammit, FUCK!" the attorney yelled, as he flung open a sliding glass door, did not bother to close it, walked stiffly out onto the deck and vomited over the rail.

Small rivulets of sweat were slowly running down the sides of Sofia Scala's ashen face. Her eyes were half-closed and her expression totally slack. She dry-swallowed and in a barely audible, hoarse voice said, "Water. Please."

Pamela went to the kitchen, filled a tall glass with tap water, found a bent straw in the cabinet and held it to the exhausted woman's lips. She eagerly sucked and emptied the glass in four pulls. She leaned her head back, slowly looked up at the tall, vaulted ceiling and quietly said, "Here is what I know."

Russell hopped over to turn on the stereo tape recorder in the large bookshelf. The shotgun microphones spaced in the shelves could pick up a voice anywhere in the room. In an emotionless voice, Sofia Scala began to speak.

"Fionna. She caught the Collins Jewel."

"Who's Fionna?" Russell asked.

The Presenter took two deep breaths and then continued. "I just know her as Fionna, a Catcher."

"What can you tell me about how this catcher Fionna locates and kidnaps her victims?" Russell asked, wondering about the Nudus Bleu suntan lotion.

"She entices children in chat rooms or selects them from postings on Facebook and My Space. To appropriate Jewels, Fionna likes to impersonate with the use of uniforms."

"Where did she deliver the child?"

Sofia Scala closed her eyes for a moment and inhaled deeply. "Fionna delivered the Collins child to me at The Cloister, where I was a guest on *The Samaritan*."

"What is the name of her buyer, and what else do you know about him?"

"His name is Anthony Montero. He lives near Maracaibo in Venezuela."

"How are payments made?"

"I do not know how all the financial transactions take place. After presenting the Jewel, I received my cash commission by direct deposit into my personnel bank account in Switzerland." Sofia Scala looked at Russell. "You know, the Organisation's usual procedure with someone who has been exposed is extermination. If you free me, I won't survive. No matter where I go."

The Presenter again closed her eyes for a few seconds, then opened them and stared into mid-space. Her right arm was resting on her stomach. No blood showed through the new bandage Pamela had applied. The arm slowly slid off her body and hung by her side, limp. Dr. Jackson positioned the slack arm on her body, at a slight elevation, and taped it to the woman's covered torso. Russell turned, left the room and walked to the kitchen where he poured a Brandy on the rocks. No. it would be iced tea tonight.

Softly, Dr. Jackson advised his patient that he was going to administer a mild sedative and general anesthetic, to induce sleep. He removed a syringe of clear liquid from the tray and injected the contents into the woman's left arm. The effect was immediate. Her mouth parted, and her head rolled to one side. He checked her pulse at the wrist, opened each eye to look at the pupils, then lowered the sheet and with his stethoscope confirmed that her rapid heart rate was decreasing. After a few seconds he removed the stethoscope and put it into his bag.

"Clayton," he said, "do you have any bourbon?"

Russell poured an Old Grand Dads on the rocks and handed it to the physician, who took a swig as he glanced at the sleeping Presenter.

Bressler had been listening from the deck, but with his back to the scene, staring at the lake. He turned around and glared at Russell. Frowning, he slowly returned to the large room and started to say something, but closed his mouth and planted his feet. He stared hard at the doctor. Russell, stone-faced, sat down, took a sip of his drink and observed Bressler.

"For the love of God," the attorney boomed, "What in the hell do you think you were doing!? And, you, a medical doctor! You've just ruined the hand of a young woman! Sure, she's a harpy, but did you have to do that? Why didn't you just slap her around a bit? Chrissakes! You two are both ghouls! And you," Bressler turned to Pamela, "I am so stunned, I do not know what to say. I would never have imagined you could be so callous. And what about the illegality of all of this! Has anyone considered that?"

Bressler poured more Knockando in his glass and added cubes. The man was on a roll and could not stop. "Clay, my *friend*...I knew you had eccentricities, but this takes the shit-eating cake! What's next? Put out one of her eyes! I'm getting out of here. Shit, I need a cab. Do you think I can get one to come out here and find this fucking place? This torture chamber in the woods?" Bressler killed his drink, closed his attaché case and headed for the door, a bit unsteady.

"Sidney, come here. I want to show you something."

Bressler stopped. Still scowling, he tossed his briefcase onto the sofa, loosened his tie, removed his suit coat, took another swallow of the Scotch and flopped onto an Eames chair.

Pamela assisted in removing straps from the Presenter's right shoulder, which was covered with silver duct tape. The surgeon gripped the shoulder with both hands, braced a foot against the slanted bench, gave a hearty tug, and the woman's right arm snapped off her body, with a very loud SQUATCH!

"Fucking A!" Bressler yelled. "God-DAMM!"

"Relax Mr. Bressler, please observe." Dr. Jackson held up the limb. "This is one very real feminine arm from a medical school that no longer needed the cadaver." He removed a ring from the corpse's third finger. "This is Ms. Scala's ring, placed on the cadaver's hand, to heighten the illusion. Attached to the base of the cadaver arm is this elastic bladder which releases blood when pressure is exerted. And this is human blood," Jackson tapped the plastic bag, "recently purchased from a pliant employee of the local Red Cross. Snip the cadavers' fingers, and the blood runs out, creating a most realistic tableau for the restrained woman."

He removed a similar rigged arm on her left side, which would have enabled him to continue, should it have been necessary. "I'm glad we did not to remove anymore fingers. I don't know if I could have continued acting in the role of a butcher." Dr. Jackson carefully placed both of the detached arms on the tray, picked up his drink and sat on the couch with a sigh.

"Christ Clay!"

"Sorry Sid. I thought you'd perform better if you thought the ruse real. Forgive me. Do you think I would actually do that to anyone?"

Bressler answered, "You've done some things I would never, could never do. And you're supposed to be square with your attorney. Fuck, man! I've aged four years."

"A Georgia Tech grad student rigged the arms. It's not the most brilliant thing in the world, but at least the Presenter will still be able to play the violin. Or take it up."

"Shit, Mr. Detective. Or should I say Dick?" He looked down at both sides of his pale lemon, tailored dress shirt. Sweat stains the size of pizza slices were under each arm. "Jeez Louise. Are you happy now? Did you get what you want?"

"I think so," Russell answered.

"What a day," Dr. Jackson commented. He picked up the arms with blood bladders and left for the kitchen. Pamela carefully sliced through the tape holding the woman's real arms, secure against her body. Ten minutes later, the Presenter was in a deep sleep, sedated and strapped in a guest room bed.

The doctor returned to the great room. "This has been a most interesting house call, but I do hope I shall never be called upon to repeat this or anything like it."

Russell handed him an envelope.

"Before you leave, Doc, how about looking at some of the drugs we found in the Presenter's kit?"

The man spent a minute examined the vials and syringes in the kit, then replied, "Without a toxicology analysis, I can only assume these are a number of hallucinogens and stimulants. I'm reasonably certain the medications in this bag include phenobarbital and Halcion, as well as illicit street drugs, such as methamphetamine, cocaine and ecstasy. Those people have, in essence, a 'turn-me-on,' 'turn-me-off' portable pharmacy that can manipulate moods, but used for a prolonged period, or in excess, would probably prove fatal. Most of it can be administered orally, anally or by injection. To turn a victim into a willing participant with drugs can be accomplished, but it would take, uh, repeated sessions." The physician handed the kit back to Pam. On his way out the door, he hailed, "Goodbye, Mr. Bressler." The attorney smiled slightly and gave a token wave as the man walked outside to his car.

Pamela looked at her lover and noticed the deep circles beneath his eyes. "Clay, I need to spend time tomorrow on the computer. Some leads I received from Sotheby's in London. Those antiquities must be exchanged someplace, and if rumors are correct about the Organisation, which I believe is a damn logical link, that is where I/we need to be. Think about it. In the meantime, mind if I take a swim? I need to exercise and unwind."

A minute later Pamela trotted down to the path to the lake. She dropped towels onto the polished teak dock planks, removed her nurse uniform, bra and panties and placed them in a neat stack. She began stretching before her swim.

Russell looked up and down the lake to ensure some stunned fisherman hadn't dropped his rod and reel. He kept his eyes on Pam as Bressler emerged out of the woods, zipped up and stood beside his unique friend.

"Would you look at that," Bressler said, nodding toward the dock. "An hour ago, I wasn't so sure, but maybe there is a God. I never realized Pamela was such a free spirit. Damn, brains and a body." Bressler paused at the foot of the deck's steps and admired Pamela. He knew she was very fit, but he had no idea her body was this exceptional. She dove into the lake, surfaced and began a relaxed, backstroke across the cove.

Bressler considered getting Russell's binoculars but instead asked, "What do you intend to do with Ms. Scala?"

With no emotion, Russell answered, "Get rid of her somehow. I'll think of something."

"And the child?"

"Pam will try to find her parents. The girl is very confused, apparently from drugs and indoctrination by her kidnappers. Pam's going to create a web page with photos entitled 'Where Does Lorena Belong?' I won't be surprised if she uncovers the girl's identity and family fairly soon."

When Pamela finished her swim she joined the two men for a casual meal of green salad with fresh grilled tuna. After dinner, the three friends discussed ways to locate Anthony Montero.

Bressler also had some ideas about where an exchange may take place between members of the Organisation and the antiquities. The female detective had almost forgotten about her other client.

"There aren't many people in the world with the resources to fence merchandise that hot. The richest, like Carlos Slim, Gates, Buffett, the Walton heirs, aren't crooked. So my bet is on the richest person in the world who is also crooked: Roger Vogel, the billionaire. Have you heard of him?"

"Who hasn't," Pamela replied. She knew world finance and economies much better than Russell who looked a bit puzzled. "Clay, Roger Vogel is an entrepreneur who 'turned' a number of struggling companies, then sold them for impressive profits. In 2000, Vogel began a successful takeover bid for Investments Overseas, with holdings of $200 billion. When the firm ran into financial difficulty, no white knight was willing to get involved. Vogel saw his chance and began a protracted battle to assume control of the company. Vogel was accused of looting the company of hundreds of millions of dollars. Many prominent figures with international business and finance were tied to the mess, receiving money from one party or the other for support. Among the accusations against Vogel were that he parked funds belonging to IO investors in a series of dummy corporations, one of which had an Amsterdam address that was later linked to some mid eastern prince. It's rumored he broke into a Swiss bank vault to obtain shares. The allegations were unproven, as Vogel fled the country and spent the next several years relocating between nations that lacked extradition treaties with the United States. Many people, indeed, would like to find him. Almost as much as they would like to find his money. Rumor has it he lives on a big mystery yacht."

Bressler added, "Sources say that the Feds, Interpol and who knows what other international law enforcement agencies are after his ass but can't get enough to nail him. His usual place of residence is that yacht or a personal island he owns near St. Thomas. When he does venture out, the agents that follow him say he enjoys visiting Bermuda. If Pamela can find that ship of his, you may find Michael Lo and the Dalai Lama's stolen property." Bressler rose from the table. "I appreciate the meal. Maybe I'm sober enough to drive home."

At the front door, he paused. "I suggest you keep all your thoughts and actions in a Word file, and before you venture out 'into the field,' send me the file." Bressler stared at the strangest friend he had ever had. He wanted to remember him clearly, as Clay Russell was this day. His friend just might get himself killed this time. "Ciao, you two. Break a leg."

"Bye, Sid," Russell said. "Lose the long face."

The attorney walked out the door. A minute later they heard the big Mercedes start and drive away.

Pamela and Russell held hands in silence and walked into the bedroom. As they undressed, there was a comfort with being together that transcended sex. Pamela knew her lover was preoccupied, and she was just tired. Tomorrow the two would begin a search for Anthony Montero. Maybe they would hear some positive news about Erin.

Pamela's last thoughts before sleep were about the two missing children, Lisa and the long-vanished Asian child. The Panchen Lama will keep for another quest.

Focus on Lisa Collins.

Chapter 18

Locus Montero

Russell rose before dawn, quietly left the warm, sleeping Pamela and tip-toed out of the bedroom. He made coffee, took a hot mug onto the deck and with Winston at his side, watched the sun rise. It was early September and autumn was in the air. Before he finished his first mug, Pamela gave him a hug and leaned her head on his shoulder.

"Well, P, how to connect the dots? We're pretty sure we know who has Lisa and that she's in or near Maracaibo. And if Bressler's right about Vogel, and we locate the wealthy Russian recluse, we not only may recover His Holiness' treasures but have an opportunity to identify, if not capture, key members of the Organisation. Do we split, or head in one direction and hope we don't lose the other? Bermuda and Venezuela are both in the Western Hemisphere, but that's about all they have in common."

"Lisa first," she replied. "The girl is more important than relics."

The following day at noon, an emergency meeting of De Blauwe Organisation began in Amsterdam. After the board members were seated, Henri Bergmann entered and took his place at the head of the table. Despite the subject, he spoke without emotion.

"For the first time in the existence of our organisation we have encountered a major challenge. Some might call it a problem. I prefer the word 'challenge'. Anything that temporarily intrudes on our enterprises can be overcome, as this certainly shall."

The board members were electrified. Everyone became perfectly still. Bergmann's words, per se, were astounding. And his delivery—flat, smooth, almost as if he were bored—magnified the electricity.

"We have a 'leak.' A Jewel delivered to a New York brothel, and the Presenter, possibly with the money have vanished. The Presenter has an excellent record. I do not believe she vanished of her own volition. I believe she was abducted, seriously injured or killed. I do not have all of the details yet, but I am confident I shall soon be fully informed. Her bodyguard, who also has a flawless record, has vanished. A popular television crime show, *America's Most Wanted*, recently aired a program that showcased one of our Jewels. This particular Jewel was mined in America, in the State of Georgia, in a suburb of the city Atlanta. The abductor was profiled, portrayed in a generic police officer uniform and bore a striking resemblance to our premiere Catcher, which was an accurate portrayal. All potential leaks shall be cauterized promptly. Payment for your presence today will commence in two minutes, then you will leave. I would like

Numbers 4 and 8 to remain and discuss cauterization. And for those of you interested in the Vogel display next week, you may wish to exercise particular caution. We have never had law enforcement sniff this close. Are there any questions?"

Number 7, Hans Mueller, a nondescript, middle-aged banker from Hamburg asked, "This television show, *America's Most Wanted*, was our Organisation in any way mentioned or alluded to?"

"No, but we cannot assume the producers of the program are unaware of us."

Mueller followed up. "The people connected with the program: they are professionals and have no personnel information, but what about the Jewel's mother and her neighbors? Should they be terminated?"

Two of the DBO members glanced at Mueller, appreciating the question as they stared at Bergmann. The CEO had anticipated this question. He tapped a fingernail on his Royal Delft coffee cup, waited for the nearest servant to fill it, and then answered, "De Blauwe Organisation is a machine with no superfluous parts and no unproductive members. Periodic staff changes are needed, but since there are so few moving parts in our machine, there are fewer parts to repair. Our machine is intact and vital. However, DBO should maintain the lowest possible profile. The Jewel's mother and neighbors may be monitored. They shall remain untouched by us."

Bergmann's eyes swept across the faces of the board. He looked at their foreheads, not their eyes, a practice that helped him regard people as objects, rather than humans. "DBO works from the shadows, and though we should be more wary, especially any persons here who plan to attend the Vogel auction, we will remain calm. If we make ourselves more visible, people who were not aware of us, may become so. It is regrettable that our finest Catcher has been compromised."

A few of the board members decided Bergmann may actually have an attraction beyond mere business and professional admiration for their star Catcher.

Bergmann placed both palms flat on the table, the visual cue to his staff that the meeting was adjourned. After the DBO members departed, Bergmann quietly addressed Numbers 4 and 8. "Here is what I wish you to do."

For a half hour, Bergmann gave the two males specific orders and an exacting timetable for them to complete their tasks.

In San Francisco, Alexander Jordan regretted loaning De Blauwe Biblio to Archie Reese. After studying the long lens photos he had taken of Reese and Redmond in the park, the stranger's face and mannerisms looked odd. Jordan decided to report his suspicions and sent an email to the DBO address listed in his catalog.

To Whom It May Concern,

270

*Attached are several photographs. I permitted
a trusted friend of mine, to show the De
Blauwe Biblio to an acquaintance of his.
My friend, Archie Reese, is on the left. The
acquaintance, right, claims he is Sam
Redmond, from Atlanta and New York. At
the time, I thought it harmless to let my
friend borrow the catalog. In retrospect, I am
concerned Redmond is not what he purports
to be. I thought you would want to know. I
prefer to remain, Anonymous.*

Jordan placed the letter and photographs in a large envelope, added a piece of stiffener and addressed it to the DBO Swiss post office box. Initially he thought it unwise to include his home address, but greed overcame reason. De Blauwe Organisation must have incredible coffers; perhaps he would be rewarded for this information. Jordan added his private address and sealed the envelope. Tomorrow he would mail it, first class. Surely, DBO was not dangerous. Their interest was to sell sex.

It surprised Pamela Waters at how easily she located the residence of Anthony Montero. But her luck ended with her efforts to confirm whether Vogel was anchored off Bermuda, even after calls to a friend at Interpol. The Dalai Lama was convinced the antiquities were to be auctioned there within the month. There would be no choice but to fly to Bermuda and hit the pavement the old fashioned way, two gumshoes, snooping.

271

A long day on the telephone and the Internet
narrowed the search for the Venezuelan. Russell's agent
friend at the FBI Miami office convinced her she had the
correct person. Special Agent Beth Willis and her partner,
Maria Sanchez, had tried to connect this Anthony Montero to
dozens of drug-related murders in the south Florida area
during the past decade but were unable to compile sufficient
evidence. "I know what he has done, and how dirty he is, but
can't prove it," Sanchez told Pamela. She agreed to send
Pam photographs of his estate, which were soon delivered via
e-mail.

> Dear Ms. Waters,
> Rancho Recito is 50 miles north of
> Puerto Miranda. It's a coastal city
> between two bodies of water, Lake
> Maracaibo and the Gulf of Venezuela.
> Señor Montero has an estate, some
> 900 acres, with a half-mile of beach
> on the Gulf. If you plan to visit, do
> not go alone. Best Wishes, M.S.

Now, in her downtown Atlanta office, she studied the
color photos from PDF files downloaded and printed.
Pamela increased the halogen desk light to its brightest level
and carefully moved the 10-power jeweler's loupe over the
photos. Satellite pix, maybe? Great resolution! Not
surprising, since the FBI's work involved surveillance. It
was an understatement to say the drug king's Rancho Recito
was an impressive estate. Seven buildings connected to the

272

main mansion via a web of brick pathways. Every structure was arctic white, with walls clad in what appeared to be painted fieldstone, the roofs of pale orange Spanish tiles. Two kidney-shaped swimming pools were connected via narrow canals to a very large, freeform pool laced with fountains. The main pool also had a huge, rock waterfall interspersed with palm trees and a variety of flowering plants. Brown-skinned sunbathers of both sexes lounged in and around the pool. Most of them wore small, brightly colored bikinis, thongs and trunks. Some were nude. In one series of photos, the attire, decorations, buffet tables, white-smocked serving staff, numerous drink stations and varying displays of affection suggested a party.

The compound was heavily guarded. Men with tropical suits appeared on guard, with white-wire earphones and dour expressions. Pamela paid particular attention to the figure that Agent Sanchez had circled and identified with a grease pencil: *Anthony Montero.* He was probably in his fifties, with black hair, bone-white teeth and a large and beefy body. Pleased with her find, she kicked off high heels, opened the small fridge in the adjoining break room and poured a large glass of V-8. She returned to the privacy of her office and called Clay. She would give him the good news first.

Chapter 19

The Floating City

Pamela promised she would only investigate the leads in Bermuda and return to Atlanta within two days. She assured Russell she would avoid doing anything to draw suspicion and jeopardize their upcoming plans to visit Montero's compound. "Please curb your enthusiasm," he had asked.

Despite being only 640 miles from North Carolina's coastline, Pamela had never visited Bermuda. So she spent a day crash-reading about the territory, and on the flight to the island, she sped-read Fodor's Guide to Bermuda.

Tourism is Bermuda's second largest industry. Glancing around, Pam could easily see that fact from the flow of people. The island was discovered in 1503 by the Spanish explorer Juan de Bermudez and first settled by shipwrecked English colonists in 1609, waylaid en route to Virginia. The prime businesses are finance and insurance.

The only source of fresh water is rainfall. Water is collected on roofs and catchments and stored in tanks. Its latitude is akin to Savannah, Georgia, but the winters are warmer and the summers cooler. Beautiful pink beaches necklace the island, and numerous sea wrecks, coral reefs and shallow water with superb visibility make it a haven for skin and scuba divers.

Much to the detective's delight, one cannot rent a car in Bermuda. Until the U.S. visited in World War II, cars were entirely banned. And now, only residents may own autos. Buses and taxis abound, as do rental mopeds, motorized bikes and bicycles. She had flown in one-way on a vintage, Lear Jet 23. That kind of bird would blend in better at the small airport at Bermuda International in St. George's Parish. From there, a short taxi ride deposited her at The Royal Palms Hotel, a 32-room boutique establishment. Like so many buildings in Bermuda, it was pink and trimmed with white; the collars matching the cuffs of the pink and white beaches. She had chosen a "Superior Mini Suite," which was basically a king bedroom with kitchenette. It was perfect; feminine, clean and cheerful.

Now, a few minutes before noon, Pamela sat at Hannah's Harbor House, an outdoor café, enjoying raw oysters and iced tea. She had walked the five minutes from her hotel to Hamilton, the island's capital.

Among the assortment of boats moored in the calm Atlantic were a handful of luxurious private yachts. From her bag, Pamela pulled the L.L Bean binoculars and trained them on the most impressive yacht in the harbor: The Marco Polo, from Miami, displayed in neon blue letters on the white stern. A dozen people were sunbathing and laughing on the three large decks. The boat was at least 120 feet. Tethered to the rear swim platform was a small, tri-hull runabout.

Pamela was drawn to a woman sunbathing among the group. She would periodically rise, presumably from a deck lounger, and walk about the upper and lower decks. Topless and wearing only a gold thong, she was totally unabashed about her superb body. The woman was very tall, clearly an athlete and striking, with red hair drawn up in a bun under a straw hat.

Pamela sharpened the focus on the binoculars. She found herself intrigued by the woman and could not understand why. Did she know her? Should she know her? The redhead's skin was a flawless, tanned, honey gold. On her right hand was a ring with what looked like a very large emerald. On her left wrist, a Breitling watch.

Pamela stood up. None of the café patrons took notice—tourists often gawk at yachts. She watched the redhead walk down steps to the lower, stern deck. Now Pamela could see the woman's entire body, as she sat in a deck chair and slowly thumbed through a large magazine. Pamela walked a dozen paces, to the café's rail, and refocused. It wasn't a magazine, but a catalogue! In the redhead's hands was the centerfold—a beautiful, four-color photograph of one of the missing works of art, Guru Padma and His Eight Emanations! So, the near-nude amazon will be attending Roger Vogel's Ultimate Auction, Priceless Lost Art of Tibet!

Pam lowered the binoculars, went back to her table and sat, looking out to sea, thinking. Several minutes later, she glanced at the other diners. Seated only three tables away was the errant monk, Mr. Lo!

She could not believe her luck! The deer had waltzed into the hunter's sights. Then again, she should not be surprised. It was a very small island, just 21 square miles, and this restaurant was a gem among the seaside dining establishments. She adjusted her gray sunglasses, pretended to study the Fodor's guide and observed the thief.

Lo wore a white Polo cotton dress shirt with the sleeves rolled half up. Tan khaki slacks and blue boat moccasins. His only visible jewelry was a large, black, diver's wristwatch. No sunglasses, but a navy baseball cap with gold scrambled eggs on the bill, shielding the Asian's face from the pleasant, bright sun. The waiter served him coffee, followed by a fruit platter. Lo checked his watch, made a phone call on the cell, consumed his breakfast at a leisurely pace, then settled back in the chair and looked out at the harbor. His back was turned to her, and the man was motionless. A half hour later he ordered smoked salmon on toast. After one bite, Lo suddenly stood up and approached her table.

Her heart began to pound, but she consciously studied her book and did not give Lo any overt notice. In her peripheral vision, she saw the man stop five feet from the table, wait a few seconds, then he cleared his voice and spoke.

"Excuse me?"

"Yes?" Pam looked up and still held onto the book. She acted as if she were mildly disturbed at her solitude being broken, though her mind was now racing.

"Fodor's is a superb organization. They are one of my longtime clients."

Ah so, Mr. Lo, lying like a rug! I do believe the crook is trying to pick me up. She set the book down on the table. "I've found Fodor's pocket guides are most helpful when traveling to new places. Are you in the travel business?"

"No," he answered. "But I travel extensively, for business and pleasure." Lo pointed to the condiments on Pam's table. "May I?"

"Certainly."

Lo picked up a bottle of green hot pepper sauce.

Pamela took off her sunglasses and smiled. "What line of work are you in?"

Lo looked at this attractive lady dining alone and was curious about her. "I am an art broker," he answered. "I buy and sell."

"Really." She added enthusiasm to her voice. "That is one of my pastimes. I collect art. Do you have a specialty?"

Lo uninhibitedly studied Pamela as she crossed her bare legs. "I am currently negotiating select works of the late Mr. Andrew Wyeth."

"Do tell! Christina's World! The Helga pictures! I would love to own a Wyeth. I possess a few works from Winslow Homer and Howard Pyle. Are you familiar with those fellows?" Pamela was dumbing down her vocabulary. She wanted the man to think she had money but was unsophisticated.

"Of course," Lo answered, with slight disdain. "Their works are a bit pedestrian for my tastes. Homer, I can understand. But why would you care for Pyle?"

She decided to poke the thief with a sharp stick. "I like Pyle's subject matter. You know, Robin Hood, pirates, rogues and thieves. They fascinate me. I wish I had the cojones to be a master thief."

"Yes," Lo said without hesitation. "I would imagine master thieves possess much nerve."

Pamela decided to push her luck. "Might I see the Wyeth pieces you're offering?"

"I am sorry, but that is not possible. Since Mr. Wyeth died, his works greatly increased in value. I find myself in the fortunate position of being the broker for works of Mr. Wyeth currently up for acquisition here in Bermuda."

"Is it at a local art gallery?"

"No. It is a private affair. We are conducting an auction for a select group of bidders." Lo smiled and began to turn away. He decided this lady was too inquisitive. Plus it was time for an appointment.

"Would that auction be open to another individual, in return for compensation?"

Mitchell Lo's smile returned, polite, but equally apparent it was quite insincere. "The event is just nine days hence. All the invitees have accepted."

"I will pay you five thousand in cash for one chair at the auction."

Lo's left eye began to twitch.

"And if you provide me with two chairs, I will give you ten thousand, USD."

"I am afraid all of the chairs are filled. But if someone should send their regrets, I will notify you. Where are you staying?"

"I have to fly back to the States for a few days, but can return once my business is final. What if you give me a number where I may reach you?"

"I would prefer you provide me with a number. Then, I shall inform you of any change."

Pam stared back at the Asian. Damn! She wrote a number on a napkin and the monk tucked it into his pocket with a wink. "I hope to hear from you," she said. The number was to a land line Pamela kept for situations such as this. It was an unlisted land line number that went to a recorder.

Lo's cell phone went off, playing the first eleven notes of My Favorite Things. He looked at the number, excused himself and began walking swiftly toward the beach.

Pamela picked up the binoculars and trained them on the monk's back. When Lo reached the ocean edge, he took off his shoes and began to roll up his trousers. Pamela trained her binoculars out to sea and saw the cigarette boat a quarter mile away making for the shore. She packed her bag, put cash under a water glass, left the café and once outside broke into a swift jog. Within three minutes she was on the beach, a hundred yards south of Lo. The monk was standing knee deep in the surf. A bright yellow, motorized raft was pulling away from the cigarette boat.

The King George Marina and Boat Club was a good 300 yards to her right. She ran toward it, quickly, and within a minute, looked at the trio of short docks, decided to pick the near one and trotted out onto the white concrete pier. Most of the slips were occupied. Halfway down the pier, she saw a moderate size fishing cruiser, a Hinckley named Jaws. A young black man was sitting in the stern, working on a scuba tank regulator.

"Ahoy Jaws!" Pamela shouted and put on a big smile.

The young man looked up, slightly startled, but returned a smile and answered, "Ahoy to you, my lady. How may I help?"

"Is your boat for rent?"

"Every day the sun shines."

"What about right now?"

"Uh, sure. How many are in your party?"

"I'm the party."

"And where would you like to go?"

"I'd like to just cruise around and look at some of the yachts."

The man smiled and gestured to a stern seat.

She climbed aboard the 55-foot cruiser, and he said, "My name's Marlin, just like the fish."

Pamela replied, "And I'm Pam Waters, a tourist in a hurry."

Marlin asked, "How about ninety minutes on Jaws for $200?"

"Fine." She gave him two hundreds.

When they were past the docks, Pamela said she wanted to get a closer look at the super yacht. She had never seen anything like it. As Marlin straightened their course toward the huge ship, Pamela asked, "What do you know about that strange vessel?"

Marlin smiled and sighed, "If I win the lottery. Check out her lines, and I'll tell you about this one."

Pamela made a quick visual sweep of the ship from stem to stern. "It looks like a scaled down oil tanker."

"It's a former freight vessel. Chinese. Now it's the latest product from Shadow Marine. A fellow named Tom

Gonzales founded the company. Shadow Marine does conversions of freight vessels into ultimate luxury yachts. Gonzales saw that the problem many yacht owners had was super-sizing in order to make room for their various runabouts, helicopters and lengthy guest lists for parties. Shadow Marine utilizes the ample load capacities of freight ships. The ships are gutted, and the storage spaces are cleaned, tiled and paneled…the results being new areas for lounges, billiard rooms, spa pools, entertainment theatres, dance floors, bowling alleys, you name it. At first, you might think they are just converted barges, but no: Shadows are tip-top yachts; floating mansions; and this one, I've been told, is a palace, with marble floors, chandeliers, curving staircases and a gymnasium with workout room. There is a bowling alley in there and a mini-casino, with roulette and card tables. Wet bar stations are on all four levels, or, floors, if you will. My uncle has been aboard a couple of times. He owns Hamilton Plumbing Crafters. He re-tiled the foredeck swimming pool. There are three swimming pools on this baby; two above deck and a rock-grotto pool inside, complete with waterfalls and marine animals. The interior pool is saltwater. Ocean water is piped in, filtered and channeled into the grotto pool. The owner, Mr. Vogel, has a dozen parrots that live in the pool grotto room. Small tropical fish swim about in its lagoon. That indoor sea pool is the size of an Olympic swimming pool. The ceiling in the grotto is painted like the sky. A fake sun, with bright, tanning floodlights, slowly moves across the ceiling, in time with the real sun. Ocean sounds play on the stereo. Waves, pelican and gull calls. At twilight, the faux sun disappears on the 'west end' of the grotto, and soon the full moon begins to rise. The moon is pale yellow, lit by LED bulbs. It moves across the ceiling sky in the same cadence as the real moon. The stereo ocean wave sounds continue, interspersed with occasional fog horn calls and buoy bells. That ship is a floating city."

Pamela Water's heart began to pound. "What's its length?"

"The Allure class was the biggest Shadow Marine conversion, several years ago. It was 220 feet. This is the new baby from Shadow. She notches in at about 330 feet. It is a football field length, plus both end zones."

"What's her name?"

"What time is it? Her name varies with the days of the week. The last time I saw the stern, she was The Gold Mind. Last month, she was Eye Dare You, with a spooky artistic icon above the name: the all-seeing eye, an ancient symbol for divinity. It's that eyeball above the pyramid on the back of your U.S. dollar bill. She's been here about five weeks."

Pamela gave the Russian a silent salute. The billionaire on the run had created his own mobile, luxurious sanctuary; a refuge that could sail the seven seas and refuel vast stores at whatever friendly port that did not enforce extradition laws. It was a personal, private, saltwater Switzerland. No, Switzerland is too large. This was a mini-Monaco. A mobile principality fueled by dirty money.

"Marlin, let's circumnavigate the ship, from 80 yards out, and rubberneck."

"Many boats do."

Pamela returned to the stern deck and gazed over the starboard side of the cruiser while the pilot began a slow, clockwise circle of the ship. They came about the massive bow. She noted that although the hull had numerous portholes, the glass was smoky and mirrored. One could see out but not in. When the port side came into view, she saw a rectangular outline on the hull, approximately 15 by 40, that was probably a retractable swim platform. She looked topsides and saw nobody, but any number of people could be sunning or playing unseen, from this angle. They came about the stern, and Marlin eased the cruiser further out. The name du jour came into view. Today she was Eye Dare You. She focused the binoculars on the all-seeing eye. The cyclops orb from atop the U.S. currency pyramid engraving stared back blankly, daring them to get closer.

"Marlin, please head toward shore, and when we're 300 yards away, drop anchor, if you've got enough chain."

The pilot throttled full ahead, and the Hinckley quickly planed level. In five minutes, they were anchored, with the engine cut. The only sounds were small waves lapping their hull and the occasional gulls that would fly around the cruiser, see there was no food and then squawk away.

Pamela pondered the good ship Eye Dare You, imposing in size, even at this distance. Inside, she surmised, were Lo, the crooked billionaire on the lam, and antiquities taken from His Highness the Dalai Lama. One e-mail or phone call from her and The Dalai Lama could alert the Brits or the U.S. Coast Guard. With his position and connections, His Holiness could have USCG cutters and copters surround the ship, come aboard and reclaim the stolen artifacts, if Vogel did not first have them destroyed. She decided the antiquities were too valuable for anyone to destroy, even a criminal with pockets like Vogel's. Instead, Vogel would hide them, but they may not surface again for many years. Pamela thought it best to call her client to let him decide.

She went below and closed the sliding door to make her private call. She was relieved the signal was adequate. She located DL in her address book and dialed the office of the Dalai Lama.

A man answered. "The Office of His Holiness the Dalai Lama."

"I do not have a secure line, so apologize that I may not identify myself, but it is urgent that I speak with His Holiness. I am working on an important matter for him."

"One moment, please."

Even after having met the Dalai Lama, Pamela realized she was intimidated by His Holiness; well, not the man but his position. Pamela's father had continued to take her to church as a child after her mother died, but she found herself not particularly religious. Still, she could imagine how a Catholic might feel about phoning The Pope.

When His Holiness answered the phone, Pamela did not express the usual niceties but launched into the problem.

"Sir, it's your friend from America. No names, please. I have reason to believe that I have located your misplaced items aboard a ship, along with your missing colleague."

"Excellent. Excellent! Oh my, you have found them! And no one has been harmed?"

"No." Pamela wanted to add, not yet, but refrained. "Sir, you have two viable options: one is to request military aid and board the ship. The downside is that before boarding, the items may be destroyed or, more likely, hidden and not resurface for many years. Do you understand?"

"Yes, yes my friend! That is a most logical assumption. So, what is my other option?"

"Sir, the second option would be for me, with the help of a friend, and one or two assistants, to get aboard and attempt to retrieve the items. I believe those possessions are slated to be sold at auction in nine days."

"Can you do this safely?"

"I do not know, sir. There are no guarantees."

"I wish to have the treasures returned, but proceed with utmost caution. Remember this: I have many friends, in many places so they, too, are your friends. Call any time. I will be praying for you."

"Thank you your Holiness, sir. Goodbye."

"Bless you."

Pamela clicked off. She looked across the calm sea. A pirate ship, certainly, if there ever was one. Could they pull it off? There was a kidnapped child in South America, and the head of the Organisation responsible for human trafficking would probably be attending an auction of the Dalai Lama's treasures. Too farfetched a coincidence? Not really. Big criminals and big crimes often intersect.

Pamela climbed the stairs and walked out onto the aft deck. Marlin observed his fare studying the big ship. The Bermudian wondered what this attractive, blonde woman really wanted. He believed she told him only as much of the truth as she needed. Yes, she was probably an American, based on the clothes and language.

Pamela turned to Marlin. "Your uncle, can he get me aboard that ship? Perhaps he could think of some plumbing excuse. I will pay handsomely if you will arrange such a visit. And I'll be returning in a week."

———————————

Fionna enjoyed her afternoon aboard the Marco Polo.

She added another layer to her tan. And as she had privacy from the public, she did so with a thong or nude.

After Phillip had so willingly revealed Bergmann's travel plans, she simply could not resist the opportunity of investigating the matter and perhaps filching a couple of relics for herself. She was disappointed to have not been granted an audience with His Holiness the Dalai Lama, but the nice reward his office gave her for the information about the stolen antiquities eased the disappointment. It had to be the easiest $50,000 she had ever made, certainly just for information via two long distance conversations. Then a phone call to a totally unrelated source in Miami and she not only wormed her way into an invitation to visit the Marco Polo, but she also convinced her host they should meet for a few days' relaxation in Bermuda. The owner of the Marco Polo, with whom she had slept with two years ago in South Beach after a party, had jumped at the opportunity to have her aboard. He wanted to repeat their brief affair, but Fionna immediately made it apparent that was impossible. Recent surgery, she lied. How unfortunate for us both. It was not morality that kept her out of the captain's bed. This was a business trip. Huge potential money. She was in the shadow of a crooked billionaire and immense treasures, and all her faculties, senses and intelligence were focused on the contents of that ship.

As the sun dropped lower in the sky, the Catcher made an excuse to go ashore. She wanted to shop. A steward offered to accompany her, but she declined. The steward suppressed a smile. The wild, redheaded guest had again fucked his boss into deep sleep. So what is more natural afterwards than a shopping expedition? Typical woman.

Two crew members piloted the small dinghy ashore. They dropped her at the Hamilton Ferry Terminal. She would call and tell them when to pick her up.

It was 5:00 p.m. Fionna decided to rent a moped and ride through the tiny island, maybe bar hop and grab a bite to eat while she snooped. She was wearing yellow shorts, white tennis shoes, an athletic bra and light grey sweatshirt for the cool evening. She had a small backpack across her shoulders and looked like a typical, moneyed tourist on the island. She paid cash for 24 hours' rental of a black moped, fired up the small engine, and turned right onto Front Street.

There was a lot of activity on the road, which more resembled what one thinks of a boulevard, as evidence of wealth abounded. The island was a rock, with all greenery manicured, including the trees. The few vehicles permitted on the island were top-end: Lexus, Mercedes, BMW and one 60's era Rolls Royce. She left the main road and began climbing a steep hill toward a residential section. The view overlooked the harbor and spanned much of the island's east side. At one home, Fionna saw a custom, kids' tree house, three stories high, crafted around a magnificent banyan. "Some parents are ridiculous," she remarked aloud to herself. At the fifth home, a medium-size adult party was in full swing. The ground floor of the mansion was brightly lit, and a good-sized crowd milled about outside. She recognized the music. Herb Alpert and The Tijuana Brass, a group that hinted at the age of the party inside, which was verified as she passed the first window of the downstairs living room. They all appeared sixty and over, probably fifteen couples or more. Two very happy ladies were laughing as they tripped through the dynamic throng, armed with bottles of champagne, fueling the soiree. The home was wired for music throughout, including the grounds. As Fionna passed, nobody seemed to notice her, and when she turned to motor toward the beach, party sounds segued into the soft crashes of the Atlantic.

She parked the moped and began to walk slowly down a steep narrow path that extended about a tenth of a mile before it ended at the beach. A few lights could be seen out to sea. Her attention was on the private yacht that looked more like a tanker. She slung the bag over her shoulder and forged ahead. In the bag was a new bat watching guide. If anyone intercepted her and asked questions, she would say tonight was devoted to studying bats. In particular, Townsend's big-eared bat, *Corynorhinus townsendii*, a species of vesper bat. She had wondered, as she packed, whether Bermuda had bats on the island but decided it was too late to be overly concerned with such detail.

Fionna opened the bag and removed the night vision binoculars. They were ATN PS-23 Night Vision goggles, which could be head mounted or hand held. Their design allows the user to read and function in zero light areas. An automatic brightness control protects against excessive light, shutting off the infra red illuminator in seconds. When the lenses detect loss of excessive light, the unit reactivates automatically. With the IR on, the binoculars would provide power for 10 hours. A small camcorder could be attached, but Fionna did not want the added gear. She would remember what she saw.

She focused on an object in the sand, about 75 yards away. It was a big, dead jellyfish. She could vividly see every dried, gelatinous tentacle. When she lowered the binoculars, the invertebrate turned into a small, black shadow.

She took off her shoes, threw them into the bag and stepped onto the cool soft sand. She waded into the water and slowly headed north toward several large rocks about 150 yards from the shoreline. The rocks would provide a secluded buffer from pedestrians walking along the beach. The water reached waist high before she climbed onto the ledge of the rocky station.

She lay prone on the rocks, raised the binoculars, looked skyward, then panned down to the water, sweeping left to right. She could see everything in vivid detail but just in black, white and varying, light shades of green. It was an eerie, Halloween-like tableau.

Fionna aimed the binoculars toward the yacht rumored to hold the sacred treasures in its belly. She thumbed the focus. Only a few upper deck lights were on.

Fionna had just wedged into a comfortable flat spot, when she glanced over her shoulder and saw an odd moving shadow 60 yards south southeast on the soft sand of the beach. She adjusted the focus on the binoculars: two men, one carrying a tote bag and the other dressed in a black wet suit, with gray horizontal stripes on the shoulders and along the ribs. At the water's edge, they stopped and stood still, facing the Atlantic. For five minutes, there they stayed, and then the man with the tote bag removed something, held it in front of him, aimed out to sea, and the beam from a powerful light flashed three times, quickly, then flashed four times, each flash longer. The sequence was repeated twice more. From the vessel, Fionna saw the light signal repeated.

She positioned herself on one knee to get a better look. The craft was over 250 meters away. In the foreground, through the binoculars, she saw it a few seconds after she heard the distinctive thunder of the engine: a cigarette boat was coming in fast, close to the shore. One of the figures turned its head sharply to the left. Fionna zoomed in on the face and saw it was an Asian. Those sneaky slants, she thought. Eyes in slits so narrow that you can blindfold them with dental floss, she had once heard in a rude comic bark. Swift and stealthy, hard to detect on radar and difficult to intercept by the Coast Guard, cig boats are a favorite with smugglers. It was a smart way to ferry a man out to rendezvous.

Phillip claimed to know only that the fence was a billionaire named Vogel and the artifacts were lifted by someone trusted by His Holiness who would be delivering them in Bermuda. This guy in the surf? Smart money said yes.

Fionna panned back to the beach and saw that the man in the scuba suit was already in the surf, swimming out to catch his ride.

Forty yards out in the ocean, Fionna watched two dark figures help the man into the boat. It instantly revved up, turned and roared away to the huge, strange vessel. His companion who remained ashore flashed a beam three times and got the same answer from the mother ship. Then the man turned and headed back toward the pathway that lead up to the road above.

She watched the receding lights of the cigarette boat and waited. Would the man return soon? On impulse she formulated a plan to intercept the man in the wet suit when he returned. She only hoped he was dropped off alone and met no more than one other on shore. She was confident she could out maneuver two men and persuade the wet suit to reveal what information he may have. This place was reasonably isolated, and people rarely are mugged and murdered here. A body may never be discovered if properly weighted and dumped at sea. Fionna heard what she thought was the cigarette boat, but no lights were visible. She focused the binoculars on the sound. Sure enough, there it was, about three hundred yards out, making a beeline for the beach, all lights off. Why was the boat hiding now? Fionna panned left and right on the ocean. Nothing. She did the same up and down the beach. She trained the binoculars back on the cig boat. Fifty feet from the shore, it did an expert 180, churned the surf once, touched reverse and stopped dead in the water. The man in the wet suit jumped into the sea, chest deep. He quickly waded to the sand and began to jog quickly up the beach toward the pathway to reach the public roadway. The cigarette boat had not moved.

Suddenly, the boat veered toward her. Adrenaline coursed throughout Fionna's body, prompting the two primitive Fs: fight or flee?

She set aside her binoculars and crouched. When the first man leapt out of the boat and churned in the water toward her, she waited until he was fifty feet away. Since a teen, she had learned to use knives to protect herself. As a stowaway, one of the sailors taught her some tricks in exchange for sex. She would practice incessantly and was now at her peak, with agility, coordination, hand-motor skills and strength. She could put the tip of a blade into a quarter-size mark at this distance. She hefted the blade by the tip and hurled it. The knife sank into the man's chest. As he frantically clawed at the blade, she was on him in the surf within seconds. She pulled the knife from his body, slit his throat and turned to face the driver of the boat.

She heard the sound of the pistol chambering a round and quickly dived beneath the surface. The water was black and should prevent penetration of a bullet. She swam along the sandy bottom for almost a minute then surfaced. The boat was thirty feet away, idling, the driver was standing, scanning the waves. She stood up chest high in water and side-threw the blade. He grunted, collapsed on the boat's side, dropped his weapon in the ocean, then he fell into the water. She quickly reached the man as he floundered in the water, grabbed him from behind and expertly broke his neck. She pulled the blade from his body and looked around. She saw nobody. The cigarette boat was drifting out to sea. She swam back to the beach, retrieved her backpack and jogged to her moped above.

She fired up the little engine and soon reached the Hamilton Ferry Terminal. How could she board the ship and engineer a burglary onboard? She phoned the Marco Polo and soon two crew members arrived to ferry her back to the yacht. She had been out for quite a while and had no purchases from her faux shopping trip. She noted the crew members' curiosity, but they'd get over it. As one man took her backpack, he saw she was disheveled and soaked.

He wondered what she had been doing but did not dare ask.

Chapter 20

Cauterizing

The meeting was held in Suite 318 at the Hotel Plaza Athenee in Paris.

Two men in disguise, seated in lavender easy chairs at opposite ends of a coffee table, identified themselves only as numbers 4 and 8 of DBO. Fionna Marceau sat opposite the table, on a matching sofa. Dressed in upscale, casual, street smart European clothes, she was drinking espresso and smoking a Cohiba Robusto cigar. The two men wore dark, conservative suits, yet both had on black ski masks. Only under exceptional circumstances would a DBO board member meet directly with a Catcher, but this kidnapper had proven to be of immense value. Number 4 conducted the meeting.

"Thank you for meeting with us so promptly," Number 4 began. "The DBO pipeline has leaks in New York and San Francisco. The individuals responsible must be removed." He showed the Catcher a photograph. "This is Sofia Scala, formerly a superb Presenter. On a Jewel delivery to New York City she disappeared with the funds she was to have collected for the delivery along with her partner. We believe the purchaser, a brothel owner who services the wealthy and powerful, to be dead. When Ms.

Scala is located, she is to be discretely and permanently removed. This second photo is of a man who appeared on the roof of the New York apartment building as the delivery was unraveling. He was also photographed in San Francisco with two NAMBLA members that have access to our catalogue. When he is identified, he must also be eliminated."

Fionna quietly listened as the masked board member described her assignment with the two targets. She knew the identity of Number 4. Only two Americans were on the board, and this man must be the lawyer. She had identified all members of the DBO board, including that crass Chairman bastard, Bergmann. But she pretended otherwise. Men so underestimated women. And DBO "believed" the whore house owner to be dead. Shouldn't they confirm her death?

Number 4 continued. "The NAMBLA members, Alexander Jordan, and Archie Reese, along with Mr. Reese's young boyfriend, Bobby, must be killed as well."

The second board member, No. 8, finally spoke. "You shall receive half payment now and the balance when the job is complete. $250,000 for each cauterization."

Fionna calmly inhaled deeply from her cigar, blew smoke toward the ceiling, and smiled. "What an interesting challenge. May I begin in New York?"

Though it was the last thing Russell wanted to do, he thought it prudent: return the wounded Presenter to New York.

With the aid of amphetamines prescribed by Dr. Jackson, he drove the sedated Presenter back to New York City. 880 miles, right on the speed limit, quick fuel and rest stops, 16 hours. At 3:40 a.m. he left the anesthetized Ms. Sofia Scala behind a large cardboard box in an alley near Lenox Hill Hospital at 77th and Park. He phoned the hospital, described the woman and her location and Lenox Hill medics were immediately sent to investigate. Within the hour, she was in a private hospital room, under a Jane Doe.

Sofia Scala awakened late the following afternoon. A detective from the NYPD questioned her, but she refused to identify herself. She decided to play a drugged, dumb junkie and simply leave in the early hours after midnight. Just mug a staff member, get jewelry and cash, change out of the hospital clothes, go out on the street and then leave town. It would be a smooth exodus, something she had done before. The Presenter was tired and still groggy from the sedative. She turned on her side to nap and rest.

Fionna made numerous calls that day. She began with hospitals in Manhattan: "My sister from Berlin is visiting New York. She disappeared two days ago and is suicidal with delusions of identity." She would then describe Sofia Scala in detail. Several hours and many calls later, the Catcher found her prey at Lenox Hill Hospital.

That evening, shortly after midnight, a nurse wearing a pale green lab coat walked into the hospital. The nurse carried a clipboard, stethoscope and a look of concern as she approached the man at the information desk. "Where is the German Jane Doe?"

The bored attendant was in the middle of a crossword puzzle. He gestured with a pen and replied, "401, end of the hall."

The nurse quietly entered the room and paused to make sure the patient was sleeping. She went to a closet, removed a spare pillow and slowly rolled Sofia Scala over, face down. As the Presenter began to stir, the nurse put the pillow over the back of the woman's head and fired five shots from the silenced .22 caliber long rifle pistol. The nurse carefully removed the pillow and turned it over 180°, so as not to spill any blood. She put the pillow back into the closet, turned the corpse onto its back and adjusted the hair to hide a few blood drops. As a final touch, she tucked sheets around the body, to enhance the ruse of sleep.

The Catcher left via the stairwell. She flagged down a cab and pondered her next tasks. Phillip was so naïve and readily influenced. He would tell her anything she asked. He could not, however, protect her from Bergmann.

––––––––––––––––––

Archie Reese and Bobby were relaxing on a bench in Golden Gate Park, enjoying the afternoon sun. Reese was dozing, his arms folded, legs stretched out with ankles crossed and classical music playing on his well-used iPod. Bobby sat quietly next to him, reading a comic book.

Twenty feet away, a young mother pushing a baby carriage slowed in front of them, stopped, and then reached into the carriage to do something with her infant. She fired a small, silenced, machine pistol, from inside the carriage. Four bullets entered the boy's torso, the pinstripe fabric of his Polo shirt flicking minutely. Bobby grunted twice, twitched slightly and slumped on the bench as the comic book fell to the ground. Reese awoke and turned to see why his ward was agitated. The mother fired into the man's torso in a circular pattern. Reese slumped, his head dropped and the eyes slowly closed. The young mother laid the boy's head in the man's lap, removed a checked stadium blanket from the carriage and calmly covered the body. Any blood seeping through would not immediately be apparent. A father and son were napping. Mom returned to the carriage, adjusted her baby's blanket to hide the pistol, then resumed her walk.

Sixty yards away, Alexander Jordan lowered his binoculars, horrified. At first, he could not understand why Bobby and Reese had suddenly slumped. But when the strolling mother covered them with the blanket and resumed her walk, he dropped the binoculars and quickly backpedaled a few feet, instinctively putting distance between himself and what he had witnessed.

Jordan lived ten minutes away and decided to seek sanctuary inside the luxurious safety of his home, to think. He walked, shakily, at first. But with each succeeding block, the cold sweat dried and his self-confidence increased. He had a good idea who had killed Archie and the boy. He thought—no, he knew—DBO would not dare touch him. The Organisation was just acting on his helpful letter. Archie was crass, common and careless. Fucking Bobby was one thing; parading him out in public like a prize-winning poodle was vain and stupid.

When Jordon reached the security of his high-rise condominium in Pacific Heights, he paused outside the wrought iron gate. Twenty yards away, a handsome, young male jogger in a burgundy Fila tracksuit had finished a run and was resting, hands on his hips, stereo earphones around his neck. The jogger was thirtyish, sported a SFPD baseball cap, sunglasses and had a full, trim black beard. The man turned toward Jordan, looked him over, smiled and nodded toward the magnolia trees to the left of the gate. Then he tapped his crotch, once, with a forefinger. Jordan's vanity and penis began to swell. He nodded back at the jogger and tapped his forehead, twice, to signal, *You proceed first, and I'll follow in two minutes.*

The jogger disappeared into the thicket of magnolia trees.

A quick rendezvous with this stranger would be just the trick to relax him, Jordan thought. He had enjoyed

302

numerous trysts there. It was a known and popular spot for gays. The liaisons were convenient, clean and anonymous. He did not dare bring a zipless fuck into his home. After two minutes, Alexander Jordan adjusted the erection to the left side of his slacks and walked into the trees. Within seconds, he was dead.

Fionna Marceau slowly withdrew the ice pick from Jordan's chest. The initial stab, in his right eye, had probably killed him, but she made sure with a heart puncture. She removed his Vacheron Constantin, watch, two rings and the cash from his wallet. For the watch, she could get several thousand on the street, and more at a pawn shop. She put the cadaver in a giant green plastic leaf bag and hoisted the body by the ankles 25 feet up in a tree. The hoisting was easy, thanks to a pulley and cable she installed the previous night. With cooler weather, decomposition would not reveal the body for days. Fionna knew the authorities would probably write it off as another 'Frisco fag murder.'

She resumed her jog but as a female.

Pamela suggested dinner, al fresco.

Russell was too exhausted to sleep, so the detectives decided to discuss their plans over dinner. They sat at a remote table at Taco Mac in the Virginia-Highlands, next to a large oak. Russell ordered a Heineken, rocks and lime and for Pamela, the house merlot. After the drinks were delivered and the waiter took their order, Pamela pulled a large quilted envelope out of an over-sized gym bag, placed it on the table and pushed it toward Russell.

He turned in his chair and surveyed the other patrons. The patio was about half full. Nobody seemed interested in them. He opened the envelope and removed a number of 11 by 14 color photos. The quality was outstanding. Brilliant color, sharp focus, amazing detail. Small features of buildings could be easily discerned, along with faces of guests and servants.

Russell was delighted. "How was this done?"

"Agent Willis wouldn't be specific. I was only told these were taken via satellite and aircraft. We're lucky that they want him and are not too proud to accept our help."

"It's much more than I expected. These shots that you've marked with Post-It notes, especially the ones labeled 'Montero;' are they positive IDs?"

"Beth says the Bureau swears by it. Montero is a recluse who rarely leaves the compound."

"So there's no evidence that revealed Lisa?"

"Nope. The FBI believes Montero's mafia is aware of the aerial surveillance. If we want photographs of someone they don't want seen, we'll need a shooter on the ground, from a safe distance. Maybe from the mountainous jungle outside."

Russell finished his beer and signaled the waiter for another round. "I know an excellent outdoors photographer. Manny earns a living taking candid shots of wild animals. If available, he could do it. Whether he agrees or we find someone else, I think that's the next logical step. And if she's there, I slip in and slip her out. We have no diplomatic relations with Venezuela. The two governments hate each other. So you can't expect help from the Chavez government. Worse, if tipped off, they could inform Montero, and he would just kill the child."

Russell's tone was low key and subdued. She watched him look up at a languid, circling hawk. Slip in and slip out? Alone? Pamela thought he was daft. She grabbed his chin and made him look at her.

"You mean *we* slip in and out Clayton. But let's assume we get photographic confirmation Lisa is there, look at all the 'barriers to entry,' as they say in marketing. Multiple barriers to entry, with the same, *or more,* barriers to exit."

Russell noted that Pamela's reaction was like Bressler's. "Pam, if Lisa is proven to be there, I intend to go. I have several ideas, all of which need at least one, preferably, two other persons. But I don't want it to be you. I'm firm on that."

Pamela removed her glasses and stared back. "Yeah, well, I'm not firm on that."

After sleeping late the following morning, Russell met with Manny Ruez and brought along the FBI photographs of Montero's estate.

Ruez was a friend and former National Geographic photographer. The detective asked if the photographer could, safely, get close enough to the compound to capture high quality telephoto shots of people on the grounds. Of very special interest was a young blonde girl who recently would have celebrated her eleventh birthday. Russell was honest with his friend. He told Manny the truth about the owner's profession and reputation. Without hesitation, the talented photographer agreed to go.

"I've traveled throughout South America shooting wildlife for National Geographic. I'll have that ID, plus enough nature paraphernalia that if questioned, I should be OK."

Russell, very pleased, fronted him a retainer plus expenses and said he would appreciate the results as soon as practical.

"Clay, once I've snapped any and all people within the compound, I'll get to the nearest 'net connection and email them to you. But I can't simply fly in and set up my tripod. I need to camp out in the mountains for a few days. Maybe a week or more."

Concerned they may miss the auction, the two detectives decided to visit Bermuda and see if they could close that part of the case. And with luck, maybe meet someone in the Organisation.

Chapter 21

Pre-Auction Party

Marlin kept his promise and arranged for Pamela and Russell to meet his uncle, the plumber. Now that they were executing a plan, Pamela was ambivalent about changing priorities from Lisa to the artifacts, but the time constraints made perfect sense.

Uncle Cliff stared at the two Americans. "All you two need to do is follow with the tools and hand me what I ask for." He was worried. Tourism on the island was down. Hell, the whole world's economy was shot, and he needed the money.

Russell put both hands back in the front pockets of the worn, red canvas jumpsuit and sat down on a corner of the stern sofa, next to Uncle Cliff. Pamela preferred to stand. She was uncomfortable in the overalls, which fit too tight across her chest. Good thing she was a 36C and not any fuller.

A small runabout had ferried Uncle Cliff to Jaws ten minutes prior. The Bermudian plumber was pushing 70 years old and had muscled, veined forearms and hands. A black version of Popeye. His rather plain and dour ebony face was seamed by sea and sun. As Russell shook his hand, he slipped the plumber $500 in cash. "You'll get another

307

$1,000 upon our safe return from this house call. Sound fair?"

The older man checked the amount, nodded and put the money in a large, worn leather wallet attached to his belt by a bronze chain.

"What do I call you, Uncle Cliff?"

"Just Cliff will do," he answered. "What your $1,500 buys you, stranger, is about an hour on that thing. It's like no yacht I can imagine in Heaven or Hell. Marlin here gave your lady friend good marks, and he can size up a person real good. So I told him I agreed to help and called the head mate on that thing, saying there might be a problem and we need to check the pipes."

"Suddenly I'm thirsty," Russell said. He went below and returned with a large bottle of water and a six pack of Red Stripe beer. The detective downed the water and one beer, then opened another and quickly drank half of it. Pamela looked at Russell, puzzled. He winked at her, as he finished the second Red Stripe.

Uncle Cliff opened one of the scarred tool boxes, removed two caps and handed them to Pamela and Russell. They matched Uncle Cliff's cap: black cotton with script on the front which read *Hamilton Plumbing Crafters*. Pamela twisted her hair in a ponytail, pulled it through the hole and secured the cap tightly on her head. Cliff gave a sharp whistle and pointed to the ship. Marlin nodded and put the Hinckley in forward.

As the stately cabin cruiser slowly motored to the ship, they could smell and taste the odd flavor of salt sea air and diesel exhaust. At forty yards away, the enormity of the yacht felt threatening. The port side of Eye Dare You began to blot out the light blue, twilight sky. Two Caucasian uniformed deck hands descended an angled steel ladder amid-ship. They motioned to Marlin, waving him in. The pilot used one hand to manipulate the Hinckley's JetStick, a single knob that allowed the cruiser to move in all directions with small twists and nudges. The boat turned precisely on it axis, then with a touch of the stick sideways, moved laterally towards the immense ship. In seconds, Jaws slid up neat to the 20-foot platform at the base of the ladder.

Marlin tossed bow and stern lines to the men. Pamela and Russell stood up behind Uncle Cliff. She saw Russell finish his third Red Stripe beer, which was curious. It was not like Russell to drink on a job. Russell grabbed the heavier of the two tool boxes. They would obey Uncle Cliff with grunts and "OKs," the fewer words the better. What Russell missed in the ship, he was confident she would observe. Passageways, doors, portholes, exits, hiding places, staff and—if the opportunity presented—take some mobile phone photos. Uncle Cliff stepped off Jaws onto the base of the ship's ladder, said something to the first deck hand and then beckoned for Russell and Pam to follow.

"Thanks for your help, Marlin," Russell yelled back as he began to climb aboard.

"Good luck." Marlin discretely made the sign of the cross on his chest. Catholic, Pamela, noted. The church had provided Sally immense comfort these trying months. Maybe she should give it a try again. Feeling somewhat ashamed that fear had fueled her religious thoughts, she was reminded of the saying, "There are no atheists in foxholes."

For Russell, Marlin's signing was also an unpleasant omen. He slowly rotated his neck and heard some cervical joints crackle. He took a deep breath and followed the two deck hands and Uncle Cliff up the ladder. Then the plumber and his two assistants walked into the bowels of Eye Dare You.

Inside, as his eyes began to adjust from the sun to artificial light, Russell paused, stunned. He could hear Pam catch her breath. This was no yacht. And the word "ship" did not really apply. This was another world.

The huge room was obviously a crew lounge. Half a dozen men in khaki uniforms sat in leather chairs and on a sofa eating early dinner from lap trays. One man sat on a wheeled mechanic's stool, working on a large pile of ropes at his feet. In front of the black sofa, a loud, wide-screen TV blared UFC fighting. On the sofa, two men turned to look at the three visitors. They could not remove their eyes from Pamela.

The lead deck hand pointed to a double door. "This way, Cliff." As they passed through the doorway, Russell leaned close to Cliff and whispered, "Show me as many rooms as you can." The plumber nodded.

Pamela tried to keep the butterflies out of her stomach, but she could feel the nausea rise as they moved through the large vessel. It was through shear tenacity that she overcame her fear. The initial plan was to separate, have Russell hide and somehow get the relics ashore. A rather flimsy design, she thought. Perhaps they would come up with something better.

They entered a spacious banquet room, at least one hundred feet by one hundred-fifty. Along the sides were stations with glass encased cabinetry, all locked, and with what appeared to be a laser security system surrounding the valuables. Some of the auction items were on display, but it did not look like the Dali Lama's treasures were among them.

Directly ahead and in front was a podium and gavel. The center of the room had seating for about two hundred. Pamela whispered to Russell, "The auction room." Russell whispered to Cliff, "The room behind the podium—get us in there."

Uncle Cliff tried the large double doors. "Could you open this?"

The crew member unlocked the doors, pulled one open and flipped a switch. The big room blazed with powerful ceiling arc lights. It was filled with a very mixed collection of the auction inventory. On the left side of the room were bigger items: statues, furniture and life-size portraits; the remaining two thirds of the storeroom were filled with tables on which laid tagged objects. As they followed Uncle Cliff to a far corner with a network of exposed stainless steel pipes, Russell and Pamela glanced at the objects they passed. Each gold foil tag had a number. The items were amazing: guns, knives, jewelry, a tiara, swords, ornate boxes of silver and wood, photographs, three brass helmets, plus many things that neither could identify. Uncle Cliff set his tool box down beside the largest pipe, which ran floor to ceiling. In a low voice, he told Russell, "We need to start a leak."

"Cliff, you occupy the guard. Ask him questions for a couple of minutes. I'll create a leak."

"Sir," Uncle Cliff said to the guard, "have you noticed any changes in water pressure throughout the ship? How's the hot water?" The series of questions continued. The guard gave cursory replies.

Pamela walked over to a long table covered in red velvet. As she approached, her pulse raced: the antiquities from the Dalai Lama, at least two dozen pieces! She pulled the cell phone from her front pocket and began snapping photographs, careful to keep her body between the phone and the guard. After two minutes, Russell called out, "Hey, there's seepage in this corner." The plumber and guard walked over to see a sizeable puddle, apparently coming from the base of the starboard wall behind the pipes. "I just hope it ain't ocean water," Uncle Cliff said. He got down on one knee and began to rummage in his tool box. Pamela turned away from the guard, to hide her smile. She suddenly knew why Russell had consumed so much fluid.

The plumber adjusted some screws and after two minutes stood up and turned toward the guard. "I need to come back with some O-rings and, maybe, new brass fittings and lock nuts. I can do a temporary fix in a couple of hours. For a permanent repair, I can come back tomorrow."

The guard's expression was extremely serious. "Do whatever is necessary to fix the plumbing. We have a very important social function here tomorrow evening. It must not be disturbed. And this room," the guard glanced around, "is the last place we need water damage."

Cliff replied, "I'll take care of it..." He looked at the guard's pewter name tag, "...Mr. Jansen. We'll be back around sunset."

Five minutes later, aboard Jaws and pulling away from the tanker, Russell asked Uncle Cliff, "Can you keep up this plumbing charade to get us back aboard before and after tomorrow's auction?"

"Probably," the older man said. "But I don't think you can do that piss in the corner trick again."

Back on the island, Pamela suggested they all go to her room at The Royal Palms Hotel.

Half an hour later, Pamela clicked through the cell phone snapshots. "They're all here," she said, excitedly, "every stolen item! Do we go for them ourselves or call the Dalai Lama and suggest he call Washington or London?"

"Cliff," Russell asked, ignoring Pamela's inquiry, "can you bring on board crates with plumbing fixtures? Containers large enough to hold the antiquities?"

"Sure, I can," Cliff replied, "but if we make the switch and get those crates off and back to our homes, what will convince Vogel we were forced to do the theft? A lot of damn ifs, and stealing from thieves is something else. I can do it, but it will cost you more, and I don't want Marlin in danger."

Marlin glared at his uncle but knew not to argue.

Pamela rose and walked outside onto the balcony. She raised her binoculars and focused on the Eye Dare You. "I want a chair at that auction. I need Lo to invite me."

For an hour Pamela led the discussion with Russell, Cliff and Marlin on how to get back aboard the Vogel yacht to appropriate the antiquities. Key to everything was having Pam on the ship, before, during and after the auction. She was fairly certain a direct communication to Mitchell Lo may do the trick. On hotel stationery, she wrote:

Dear Mr. Lo,
We chatted briefly at Hannah's Harbor House café. After careful consideration, I have

314

decided to invite myself to your fascinating auction. All I wish to do is bid on some artwork. My dear friend, Sir Richard Hugh Turton Gozney, Governor of Bermuda, may be curious about the intriguing ship Eye Dare You, in particular its cargo. But I would prefer an invitation from you. I look forward to your reply.

Ms. Waters

Room 215

Pamela called room service and asked for a courier. She showed the note to Russell, who asked, "Why use your real name?"

"Why not? That's how I'm registered here." She sealed the note in an envelope. "So, what do you think?"

Russell was suddenly weary. He did not know if she was amazing or just plain rash. "I think it will probably get you on the ship. Getting off, however, may not be as easy."

When the courier arrived, Pamela instructed him to deliver her note to Eye Dare You and wait for a written reply. She handed the man $100. As the messenger left, Uncle Cliff and Marlin followed, with a promise to get the crated fittings on the ship.

Within an hour, the courier returned. An embossed card admitted her to the cocktail party preview in four hours and the twilight auction tomorrow.

As Jaws slowly cruised toward Eye Dare You, Pamela studied the other launches arriving at the party.

Although her knowledge about boats was limited, she knew that vessels with lengths under 40 feet were classified as cabin cruisers and over that length were termed yachts. Both were moored here. In a country where the per capita income is $90,000, it was obvious that guests whose earnings far exceeded that were turning out for the event. Moneyed moths attracted to a very bright, illicit flame. The smaller craft were directed to the rear port side swim platform of the giant yacht. Buoys festooned with lanterns formed a wide V along the 90-foot wide teak deck. Marlin piloted the Hinckley behind the line of six similar sized vessels depositing passengers in small groups.

Pamela rose and took the hands of two dark jacketed men who welcomed her aboard and gestured inside. Her date stepped off Jaws, she clutched his offered arm and they entered the massive ship.

Pamela gave a gentle squeeze to the strong arm. She did not think anyone would recognize Russell or her. He was now in a tux, with his hair combed back and wore a pair of light gray Ray Bans. Pamela had quickly rinsed her hair an auburn to match the knee length cocktail dress. It plunged low in the back revealing her tailbone but with only a suggestion of cleavage in the front. She had thrown a T-shirt and pair of gym shorts in her purse and opted for slippers over heels. As a back up, she thought. Running in the dress was problematic.

They ascended an immense curved marble stairway, then down a long paneled hallway, through a living room/foyer and into the banquet room auction site. Russell saw half a dozen men in tuxedos standing against one wall. He whispered to Pamela, "I'll go hang out for a while with the guys." Without moving her lips, she breathed, "Pray for us, Clay." As he walked off, she steeled herself and began to mingle.

In any other place, the scene could be mistaken for a very high end, exclusive charity event. A sea of black— tuxedos, cocktail dresses, ball gowns—with splashes of color from purses, shoes and pocket squares. But this affair was illegal, and the crowd was unusually quiet. Which wasn't that strange, Pamela decided. An extraordinary collection of crooks, with many dark secrets among them. A female servant took her drink order, returned with the flute of champagne and Pamela sipped it slowly as she began to inspect the crowd.

Mostly men, fortyish and older. Many of the women half the ages of their dates. And other than Russell, just one man she recognized. Mitchell Lo.

Pamela walked directly to him, smiled to the young blonde woman at his side and said, "Thank you, sir, for the invitation."

"You are welcome," the monk thief replied. "I thought you might bring your friend, the Governor."

"No," Pamela answered and forced another smile, "just my date."

"Well, enjoy yourself. Please excuse me." Lo guided the woman to one of the bar stations.

Pamela looked at the retreating back of the Asian. Her dislike of the man was growing into abhorrence. Regardless of what Lo had crafted into his current persona, she looked forward to yanking the carpet from under his patent leather pumps.

She spent another ten minutes casually milling in the throng. Servants plied the guests with lavish canapés and cocktails. Suddenly Pamela saw her: the striking, redheaded sunbather. Pamela moved to within three feet of the woman's right elbow, turned away to pretend interest elsewhere and began to eavesdrop on the conversation. Two men were vying for her attention, with personal questions. She answered with phrases so low that Pamela could not decipher the words. What was that smell? An aroma from the female. Blueberries and pancakes. Nudus Bleu. The policewoman! Lisa's kidnapper!

Pamela's heart began to pound, and she moved away a few feet away to better study the woman. Dark red hair. Bare arms with well-defined muscles. About six feet in height. It had to be Fionna, the top Catcher for De Blauwe Organisation!

Pamela did not want Fionna to see her staring. Her mind raced—she needed to locate Clayton. Christ, it's all on this ship! The kidnapper of Lisa Collins, the Asian thief and the Dalai Lama's antiquities!

Suddenly a voice came over loudspeakers. "Excuse me. Excuse me."

Pamela looked toward the podium. A very tall, middle aged man in a midnight blue tuxedo smiled and lifted a champagne flute. He adjusted the microphone and said, "Welcome, ladies and gentlemen. And welcome, also, those of you who are not ladies and gentlemen. Thank you for coming."

Few of the guests laughed, and the speaker ignored his lame bon mot.

The man continued. "My name is Mr. Miller. I will conduct the auction, tomorrow evening at seven sharp. This affair will be, assuredly, unprecedented in history. Never before have such rare and priceless treasures been available at an auction. Please, study these incredible offerings, enjoy the evening and do not hesitate to ask or request anything from the wait staff or myself. And now: behold the treasures within the good ship Eye Dare You."

The lights slowly dimmed, as the music rose: The Moldau by Smetana. On one side of the room, lighting within a glass case began to glow and then brighten. The next glass case did the same, followed, one by one, by all the glass display cases on both sides of the room. The effect was incredibly moving and elegant. It was as if a giant flower was awakening, proud of what was inside. The crowd began to murmur and move, gravitating toward the dramatically lit pieces. Pamela moved to the end of the starboard side row of display cases. She wanted to observe the guests as they passed in front. Not one person looked at her face; they all gazed down into the chest-high glass tops, intent on the items artistically laid out on what appeared to be turquoise silk. The Moldau segued into Philip Glass' Closing, a light flute and piano instrumental that helped underline the haunting, exciting mood in the gallery. Finally the music settled into a continuous loop of Glass' theme from the motion picture *The Illusionist*. The entire affair—ship, food, drink, music, illegality—was stirring the crowd into a new level of excitement, as promised by the auctioneer. It also gave an extra shiver to Pamela's spine to know that she, like a lamb in a wolves' den, was in the middle of what was likely one of the most concentrated gatherings of moneyed criminals ever assembled in one room. How many of these people have killed or commanded others to kill? Will anyone here die tonight? She closed her eyes for a second to summon a dose of courage and calm, when someone grasped her elbow.

"What the f…" she quickly stopped.

It was Clayton, smiling. "Hey, stay cool. Are you alright?"

"Yes," she said, "it's just this place. The theatrics, the crowd. Jesus, Clay." She pulled him aside two paces, away from the display case. "I feel like we're a couple of ants trying to swipe cheese from a giant rat."

"Yeah, well, if we're ants, we'll just out-think the vermin on this barge." Russell looked out at the assemblage. "What a paradise for a pickpocket. Though I doubt if any sane pickpocket would lift a wallet in this group."

"Clayton, Fionna is here."

Russell's eyes narrowed. "Birds of a feather, flocking together." He kissed her on the cheek and moved closer to whisper, "I think our man from DBO is also a guest. Look behind me at the short pudgy fellow speaking with the host, Vogel."

Pamela gazed at the line queuing along the display cases. She wondered how he had recognized the host and, even more so, how the DBO chairman had revealed his identity?

"His name is Bergmann. Henri Bergmann."

"Clay, how did you…"

"Later. For now, let's watch each others' backs."

For an hour the two detectives feigned interest in the showcases while they continued to scrutinize guests and eavesdrop.

As the gathering thinned and individuals began to leave, Pamela and Russell made their way to the rear swim deck, where Cliff and Marlin were tied up. They silently cast off and motored away.

Twenty minutes later they regrouped in Pamela's hotel room.

"Cliff, Marlin, please excuse us for a moment," Russell said. He guided Pamela into the bathroom and shut the door.

"Pam, I think we ought to tell our guides about the Dalai Lama's stolen antiquities and pay them more to help us."

Pamela bit her lip. "OK. Sounds logical. Let's brief them and see what they say. But let's use those two as little as possible." She tapped a knuckle on his chest. "Only as needed. That ship is a dangerous cesspool."

They returned to the suite. Russell went to the window and looked out across the harbor at the dark yacht as Pamela addressed the Bermudians.

"Gentlemen, we have a proposal. We need transportation tomorrow to and from the good ship Eye Dare You. You will be well compensated, but I must warn you it could be dangerous."

Marlin looked at his uncle, who was studying Pamela. Cliff's reply was somber. "Ma'am, compensation is most welcome. And cash is good. Cash is king. But on that boat, I didn't see much good. That boat is full of crooks. A big basket full of bad apples. Before we further rent out our skiff, how 'bout filling us in on your business with that pirate ship?"

Pamela adjusted her glasses. "Certainly, Cliff. My client has retained me to recover certain possessions of his that were illegally appropriated. My client's possessions are on that pirate ship, which is an apt term. I intend to reclaim those possessions, and your role as competent ferrymen will be greatly appreciated."

Cliff nodded. "OK. And who is your client?"

"My client is His Holiness, The Dalai Lama."

Cliff was poker faced. Marlin became animated and piped up, "The Dalai Lama? *The* Dalai Lama? From Tibet?"

"Yes."

Marlin said, "That's kind of hard to believe."

"Damn hard to believe," Cliff seconded.

"Can either of you gentlemen work a computer?"

Cliff jerked a thumb at Marlin.

Pamela turned on her laptop and opened the Google home page. "Marlin, please." She gestured to the computer. Marlin sat at the desk and put his fingers on the keyboard.

"Hit 'DalaiLama.com'."

The Bermudian went to the Dalai Lama's website.

"Scroll down, and on the lower right, hit 'Contact'."

The young man obeyed. Pamela handed him her cell phone. "Now, call that number."

Marlin pressed the number, Pamela took the phone and switched it to Speaker. After four rings, an Asian male said, "The Office of His Holiness, The Dalai Lama."

323

Pamela moved closer to the phone and said, "This is Pamela Waters, in Bermuda. May I please speak to His Holiness, for just a few moments? It's important."

"Yes, Miss Waters. Hold, hold."

Pamela drummed her nails on the desk, slightly impatient yet confident. Thirty seconds later, the deep voice of the Dalai Lama cheerfully boomed.

"Pamela! Hello, hello!"

"Good evening, Your Holiness. Sir, I want to let you know that we are making excellent progress, and within a day should have some significant news."

"Superb! And you are well? You and your friend?"

"We are fine, sir. Thank you for asking. I just wanted to touch base."

"Bless you! Be safe, my friend!"

"Goodbye sir." Pamela ended the call. "So gentlemen, are you with us?"

Without hesitation, Marlin said, "Count me in." Uncle Cliff nodded, adding, "Me too. And cash is king."

Pamela opened the top drawer of the teak dresser, reached in and tossed a brick of currency to Uncle Cliff. "That's ten thousand, U.S. More upon completion. May we proceed?"

The older man put the money in his pocket. "Let's go."

Pamela smiled. "Good. Now, Clayton. Our plan of attack, in macro terms: should we use stealth or strength?"

Russell knew exactly what she was thinking. "I vote for stealth."

"Why?"

"The ship is too big. It's well guarded. If we try strong arm tactics to remove the antiquities, and get caught, someone will probably die. It could be mass confusion. I think cool and quiet is the smart option."

Pamela began to slowly pace, her arms crossed. "I see that point. And if anyone could quietly retrieve the goods, it's you." She smiled, "Helped by me. But I greatly disagree with stealth. I think we need the assistance of some big guns, as you put it. And His Holiness is key there."

Something was bothering Pamela. Something on the ship, in the display cases. What was it in that one case? That long baton that looked so gaudy? What the hell was the thing? Suddenly it hit her.

"Oh my God, they've got that damn sceptre!"

The three men watched Pamela frantically work the keyboard of her laptop. In two minutes she sat back and shook her head. "Those sons of bitches! Those thieving fuckers! Clay, look at this."

Russell leaned over her shoulder, studied the photograph and immediately understood. He, too, had seen the dazzling item in the front, starboard display case. The Sceptre with the Cross.

On the website royal.gov.uk, at The Crown Jewels link, there it was. The Sceptre with Cross, sometimes called

St. Edward's Sceptre…created for King Charles II in 1661…redesigned after discovery of the Cullinan Diamond, a jewel of 530 carats…last used officially by Queen Elizabeth II at her coronation in 1953…and famously stolen twenty years prior during a mysterious fire at the Jewel House in the Tower of London, repository for the Crown Jewels.

Pamela was stunned. How in the world? Stealing the treasure, she could understand. But by who? And where had it been? It had to have been with a major criminal, someone who would only trot it out to parade in front of a few in his or her inner circle. The British Government, with financial backing from The Crown, had offered a £1,000,000 reward for its return, with no questions asked. But the antiquity had not appeared, in any form, until now. Tomorrow, a key component from British coronations for three and a half centuries would be sold to the highest bidder. Suddenly, the Dalai Lama's antiquities shared equal billing with the greatest missing treasure from the United Kingdom.

Pamela Waters now had a newfound respect, and, she admitted, fear of the people on the huge, dark ship. With that kind of booty in its hold, she had no doubt what would happen to anyone trying to steal from the thieves.

Stealth or strength? Which way to go?

Russell asked, "Pam, do you have a photo of the Sceptre? I saw you snapping a lot."

"I don't know." Pamela quickly tapped through her phone's images. "Yes! Here's a good one."

Russell said, "Then let's go with strength. E-mail that photo to the Dalai Lama, and then ask him to call Queen Elizabeth."

It took twenty-one minutes for respective officials and aides to connect the two world leaders.

After being put through four telephone transfers, a British male finally told the Dalai Lama, "Yes, please hold for Her Majesty. It should be just a moment."

Click. "Is this the Dalai Lama?"

"Yes, yes, Your Majesty! Hello!"

"To what do I owe this pleasure?"

"It is no pleasure, Your Majesty. It is problem."

"Please elaborate."

"Tibetan sacred objects have been stolen. A fellow monk stole. The sacred objects have been found. On British territory."

"Oh, my! Your Holiness, may I also put my secretary on the line?"

"Yes, yes."

A pause, then, "My secretary is with us. Please go on."

"Tibetan sacred objects are on a ship…"

Queen Elizabeth II interrupted, "Your Holiness, a ship, within which British territory?"

"Bermuda. Very large ship, at anchor, Bermuda."

"How might we help?"

"Also on that ship is…" The Queen could hear paper unfolding. "…also on ship is, quote, 'The Sceptre with Cross, St. Edward's Sceptre…from 1661'."

"Oh, heavens! You are sure?"

"Yes! Yes! A woman in our employ, American, on the ship, sent us a photo, from her phone. We can send to you."

"I would welcome such a photo. The Sceptre was stolen, years ago. Yes, please send the photo. Then our diplomatic staff…"

The Dalai Lama interrupted the Queen. "Ma'am, no time for diplomacy! No time!"

"Why not? Is the ship moving?"

"No, but all stolen items on ship will be sold tomorrow! At auction! Dirty, dirty auction!"

"Oh, my. Heavens. This ship: what is her name?"

"Ship name is Eye Dare You. E-Y-E…Eye Dare You. Large yacht. Owner is Roger Vogel, big criminal."

Another pause, then, "I have heard of Mr. Vogel. Please wait."

The Dalai Lama patiently held the line for five minutes. Then, "Your Holiness?"

"Yes, yes!"

"I have another gentleman on the line: Major General F.H.R. Howes."

"Yes! And who is Howes?"

"Major General Howes is in charge of what we call the RM. Major General Howes operates the Royal Marines. Now, Your Holiness, please tell Mr. Howes all you know about this ship."

"All I know, I just said. Mr. Howes needs to talk to Mr. Russell. Mr. Clayton Russell."

For an hour, Clayton Russell conveyed to Major General Howes all he had observed aboard the Eye Dare You.

Howes and his second in command referred to a blueprint of the Eye Dare You, obtained from the builder, Shadow Marine in Ft. Lauderdale, Florida. Of particular interest to the British were the ship's crew and weapons. Russell told the RM high command that the crew was international, looked tough and that they were heavily armed. The British also asked details about the location of the Sceptre and specifications of the display case. Russell answered as best he could.

The Major General ended by verifying Russell's cell phone number, assuring him the Royal Marines would provide a countdown for Zero Hour, 10:00 p.m.

Russell asked a final question. "Sir, what exactly will happen at 'Zero Hour'?"

"At that time, Mr. Russell, thirty-six Royal Marines will board and take command of the rogue ship Eye Dare You."

Chapter 22

Going, Going, Gone

At 7:00 p.m., the auctioneer looked at the audience and smiled.

An hour before, over cocktails, the attendees were given bidding paddles with numbers and black velvet domino masks, to shield their identities. Most had donned the masks. The auctioneer rapped his rosewood gavel on the podium, calling the affair to order.

"Welcome, ladies and gentlemen, welcome. This will be an evening unlike any other you have experienced. Should you need anything during the proceedings, kindly alert one of the servants, and you shall be provided. Every item shall be presented here, front and center. You will see features and details of each piece on the television screen behind me. American dollars are the medium of exchange. Salient points about the provenance of each item shall be related. You may rest assured that every exquisite piece is authentic. There are no forgeries or fakes in the magnificent inventory. So please open up your minds, and your pocketbooks. Now, let us begin."

Pamela Waters sat at the end of row two, on the port side. Like the majority of the audience, she wore a black mask. She also wore a black, low-cut cocktail dress and was confident people might be able to recall her hair color and shape but not her face. Running shoes and leather gloves lay in her black bag, on top, which she planned to don five minutes prior to Zero Hour.

As she lightly fanned her face with the bidding paddle, number 28, she studied the people around her. Seated at her right elbow was an elderly French couple, their English superb but accents obvious. The woman had chatted on to her companion about trifles, most happily, and the man (her husband?) had answered with monosyllables and grunts. A quarter hour before, when the man pulled back a chair for the woman, Pamela had seen the pistol and shoulder holster under his left arm. She was not surprised but thought the man slightly careless. He should have kept the tuxedo buttoned.

Black clad servants, six men and six women, stood at parade rest alongside the port and starboard walls. They too wore masks. At a high end Halloween party, the masks would have added a touch of lively spice; but here it underlined the criminal element of the crowd and possible danger.

"And now, ladies and gentlemen," the auctioneer enthused, "may I present Item Number One: the weapon that killed the 16th President of The United States, Abraham Lincoln!"

The room became absolutely quiet. A tall male servant carrying a red pillow walked up the center aisle. The auctioneer made a show of putting on white gloves. At the podium, the servant bowed slightly as the auctioneer delicately lifted the small pistol. He held it up, pinky extended, and the image came to life on the flat screen TV behind and above him.

"Behold, the single-shot derringer that ended the life of Abraham Lincoln on April 14, 1865. On that evening, just six days after the surrender of Robert E. Lee, John Wilkes Booth entered the presidential box at Ford's Theatre in Washington. It was 10:15 p.m. Booth shot Lincoln in the back of the head, at point blank range. The president, the first of four American chief executives assassinated, died nine hours later. This beautiful pistol was created by Henry Derringer of Philadelphia. It is six inches long, with a 2.5-inch barrel. The projectile was a .44 caliber lead ball. Notice the finely crafted trigger and mountings, composed of German silver. This singular instrument of death was found on the floor of the box at Ford's Theatre shortly after its discharge. For well over a century it has been displayed in the museum in the basement of that historic building, until six months ago when it was removed during wee hours for the express purpose of exchange in this auction."

"I hereby open the bidding with one million dollars. Yes, number 14, one million. Do I hear one million and a quarter? Yes, to you 34, one and a quarter. Do I hear two, two million? Yes number 7, two million. Do I hear three? Three million it is, to number 53."

The auctioneer turned the pistol around and tapped the hammer, trigger guard and wooden butt of the weapon with a conductor's white baton. "Look, ladies and gentlemen. This derringer weighs only eight ounces, yet it brought down a man who was six feet four inches. Think of the thrill you would have with this historical treasure in your pocket or purse. From Booth, to Lincoln, to you! Do I hear four million? Yes, number 19, four million dollars. Do I hear five, five million? Thank you number 11, five million. That is most generous. But now, ladies and gentlemen, for a little demonstration."

The auctioneer swiftly marched to the nearest portside window, which a female servant opened. He held out his right arm and cocked the pistol, the close-up action displayed on the TV screen. The audience gasped.

"Ladies and gentlemen," he shouted, "imagine I am Booth on that evening!" The auctioneer fired: the loud explosion rang in the room, accompanied by flame and smoke from the derringer. Several women screamed. Someone dropped a glass. The auctioneer yelled, ""Sic semper tyrannis!" Then in a calm voice, he said, "Who will bid seven million? Yes, number 40, seven million. Oh, my, I almost forgot! Yes, come here, quickly!" The auctioneer gestured to a male servant, who trotted up to the auctioneer. He handed the auctioneer a knife. "And this, ladies and gentlemen, is the dagger Booth also carried that night. It is the hunting knife used by Booth to stab Major Henry

Rathbone, also in the presidential box. I will add this to the pistol…and ask for ten million. Who will bid ten million? Yes, madam, number 33. Thank you. Now, touch and feel these treasures for a few moments."

A servant placed the pistol and knife on a gold tray and handed it to a man in the front row of the audience. The bidder hefted the derringer, then passed the tray to his neighbor. The macabre offering slowly made its way among the audience, many of whom declined to touch or examine the weapons. When it came to Pamela, she lifted the pistol, slowly brought the barrel to her nose and delicately sniffed it. She smiled and passed the tray to the French woman. Then she raised her paddle and said, "Fifteen million dollars."

Two minutes later, the Booth relics were sold for $22.5 million, to a man somewhere behind Pamela.

Pleased with her small performance, she ordered club soda in a Champagne flute. Having established herself as a player with ample coin, she had paved the way for bidding on the Dalai Lama's artifacts, should she decide to go that way.

Noticing several audience members moving to exits with their cell phones, Pamela did the same. She found privacy in a "Lady Powder Room" one deck below. She locked the door, raised the black mask to her forehead, looked in a small ornate mirror and freshened her lipstick. Then she phoned Russell.

"Hello number 28," he said. "How are you doing?"

"I'm fine and focused. Christ, I can hardly believe this thing. Where are you?"

"I'm topsides," Russell answered, "with a dozen smokers. There's a big monitor up here, too, piping in the auction. Booth's pistol! Jumpin' Jesus on a pogo stick!"

Pamela looked at her watch. 7:21. Two hours and thirty-nine minutes until Zero Hour, 10:00 p.m. "Clay, I better get back. Wish me luck."

"Break a leg."

"Watch your ass."

"And you, yours."

Pamela readjusted her mask, opened the door and walked right into a woman half a head taller. Fionna!

The Catcher was dressed totally in black: a tight, cotton jumpsuit with black pearl buttons and matching vest; thin, leather jacket that looked like Versace; and unusual black flats which resembled ballet slippers. Pamela caught a whiff of perfume. No, cologne. Cool Water, a man's scent.

Fionna pulled the domino mask down around her neck and said, "Hello. I, also, need to make a call."

Christ! Had the woman heard? Pamela pulled herself together. "I must keep my partner aware of the sales. Do you need to call a partner too?"

Fionna Marceau's smile was slight and patronizing. "Oh no, honey. My partner is here. Excuse me." She moved past Pamela and into the small head. As she began to close the door, Pamela asked, "Have we met before?"

Fionna looked the detective up and down. "Perhaps. Were you in Rome last month?"

"No."

"Are you in The Lifestyle?"

"No. I don't swing."

"Pity. You don't know what you are missing, honey." Fionna closed the door and locked it.

Pamela walked ten paces down the hall, opened her purse and turned on the small electronic receiver. As she thumbed up the volume, she heard Fionna say, "Nosey cunt," then the sound of running water. The grape-size bug she had slipped into the leather jacket was good for 24 hours.

When she returned to her seat, the auctioneer was touting The Birds of America, a magnificent illustrated book from original drawings by the author, John James Audubon.

"Yes, ten million, from number 14. Thank you. Come now, this volume was 'donated' from the Houghton Library, at Harvard university. Did you know, ladies and gentlemen, that the good Mr. Audubon, in order to capture these beautiful images, first shot and stuffed all the glorious birds?" Several men in the audience laughed. "So be generous. Do I hear twelve million? Thank you number 23. And now fifteen? Good, fifteen million from number 30." After showing the book to a man in the front row, the hammer price came down at $14 million.

Pamela looked over the audience. She did not see Russell, but in the back Fionna had buttonholed a slim man at one of the corner bars. Pamela quickly put in the tiny earphone and adjusted the volume of the remote.

"…dear, I do not want an introduction, just point him out. Is Vogel in this room, Phillip? Come on. Tell me, sweet."

Pamela heard the man whisper, in a European accent, "The last row, second chair. He's seated to the right of Henri."

Two very large men stood within arm's length of Bergmann and Vogel. Bodyguards, obviously, for the DBO head or billionaire fugitive. Perhaps both.

Pamela's head began to swim. There were too many significant characters in too small a space, drawn together by the largest collection of purloined artworks and antiquities ever assembled at auction. It was difficult to remain calm. She turned her attention back to the auctioneer.

The lights slowly dimmed by three quarters, and a single spotlight shone on the auctioneer. "My friends," as he spoke, "we come to a highlight of tonight's offerings. It is one of the world's most treasured missing pieces of art. This painting has been 'on permanent loan,' as it were, since March 18, 1990, from the Isabella Stewart Gardner Museum of Boston, Massachusetts. Voila: The Storm on the Sea of Galilee, by Rembrandt van Rijn!"

Another spotlight illuminated the portside door behind the podium. A servant opened the door, and two female attendants carried out a dark painting in a gilded frame, roughly four feet by five. As they placed it on an easel by the auctioneer, he continued.

"Created by Rembrandt in 1633, 'The Storm' depicts Jesus miraculously calming the waves on the Sea of Galilee. The fourteen people in the boat are Jesus, his twelve disciples and the artist himself. He is the crewmember looking at you, ladies and gentlemen. This is considered part of the largest art theft in the history of The United States, and it is an honor to have such a masterpiece up for bid here tonight. I open the bidding at ten million."

The initial bid was instantly accepted, soon went through the teens and was hammered down at $22.5 million. The auctioneer led the audience in brief applause, then he slid back a sleeve and looked at his watch.

"Soon we will pause for a brief interlude. But first, this…" The auctioneer dramatically removed his wristwatch and held it at shoulder height with both hands. "Behold, a Lord Elgin wristwatch, appropriated ten months prior from the Park Avenue New York home of Ms. Caroline Bouvier Kennedy. This watch was given to her father, the 35th President of The United States, John Kennedy, on his birthday in 1952. Perhaps the party with Mr. Booth's pistol would also like to possess Mr. Kennedy's watch? I open the bidding at one million."

Within three minutes, the JFK Lord Elgin watch sold for $5.5 million.

The auctioneer smiled broadly. "What a wonderful beginning. We will now pause for a twenty minute interlude. Offerings will continue then. Thank you."

As the lights came up and the audience began to talk and mingle, Pamela handed her Champagne flute to a server and asked for another club soda.

She felt a slight chill and attributed it to the eeriness of the evening. Millions of dollars were exchanging hands illegally, the crowd was laced with crooks, and memorabilia from dead presidents added to the creepiness. Dead presidents on two levels, she reflected.

The server returned with her drink, and she took a sip. Something was in the bottom of her glass. She held it up to the light of a chandelier. It was the bug she had placed in Fionna's jacket.

Pamela's heart began to race, and she felt her face flush. She walked unhurriedly toward a door, let herself out onto the deck and, ensuring nobody was watching, she dropped the glass over the rail into the ocean. The hunted had turned on the hunter. How much did the Catcher know?

Pamela turned and looked at the large picture window of the ballroom. The crowd was in small groups, conversing, some animated but most serious. She gazed up and saw a man on the top deck looking at her. He raised a hand. It was Clay. She signaled to meet her and walked to the bow of the ship where he appeared at the rail, ten feet away.

"Clay, I'm blown." She told him about the bug.

"Amazing," he said. "When the fireworks start, watch where she jumps. I'll be close."

Pamela looked at her watch. "It's about time to head back in. Let's meet right here at ten minutes before Zero Hour."

"Deal."

The lights in the ballroom dimmed and brightened three times.

As the attendees began to be seated, the auctioneer adjusted the podium microphone and resumed. "Welcome back, ladies and gentlemen. Now, for my favorite listing of the evening. A collection."

A photo of The Dalai Lama appeared on the screen.

"This man has provided priceless antiquities, by way of a colleague. May I present the treasured antiquities from His Holiness, The Dalai Lama."

Up the center aisle walked two servants carrying a table with a white cloth draped over the contents. They placed it next to the podium, removed the drape and revealed the dozen stolen relics.

"Ladies and gentlemen, what you see are the sacred objects that are used to select the men who sequentially hold the title of Dalai Lama. These extraordinary pieces are centuries old. Each item, alone, is quite valuable, per se. Together, this collection is priceless. The new owner of these antiquities will have the power to determine the next

Dalai Lama. Since we are all realists, we all know that the Dalai Lama is a religious charlatan, a mere puppet who guides millions of fawning disciples. Now, who will be the new puppeteer? Who will soon control millions of people, spread over every continent? Who will accept the opening bid of twenty million?"

Six paddles were raised.

"Ah, splendid. Now, twenty-five million?"

Four paddles remained raised.

"Fifty million?"

Two paddles remained. A few in the audience whispered.

"One hundred million?"

The room became absolutely silent. Bidding had been extraordinarily swift and now appeared to plateau. Pamela could see the backs of the two paddles, both on the front row. They remained aloft. She rose and walked to the port side of the ship. As she moved forward, the auctioneer increased the bidding. "These are the world's most sacred missing antiquities. Now, do I hear one hundred ten million?"

She came abreast of the front row. The paddle near her descended. The last paddle was held by a small elderly Asian man in a black suit.

"One hundred ten once…twice." The auctioneer paused dramatically. "SOLD, to number 7, for one hundred ten million dollars!" The announcer led applause, and most of the audience joined in.

Pamela studied the new owner of the antiquities. She was not surprised. The buyer was Asian, probably Chinese. Since 1959, the Chinese Government had hated and desired control of The Dalai Lama; now that dictatorial authority may have achieved a new level. The small Asian man watched attendants carry his new possessions inside the storeroom behind the podium. He remained in his seat, focused on the auctioneer, who began to tout the next item.

Pamela returned to her chair and feigned interest on the speaker. The chess game aboard the ship had taken a new turn, creating more questions while providing no answers. What was Fionna up to? And Bergmann? How tight are Bergmann and Vogel? How do Mitchell Lo and Phillip factor in? The only people Pamela could count on for certain were Russell and, presumably, the Royal Marines. She looked at her watch. 9:01. Forty-nine minutes before she would meet Clay. Then the British invasion.

At 9:50 p.m. Pamela walked to the bow of the ship. She gripped the teak rail, hard and repeatedly, to relieve tension. Russell walked up and slowly lit a cigar.

"Are you ready?"

He sounded amazingly calm. It immediately relaxed her, somewhat. "Absolutely. Got on my running shoes. Did you see who bought the collection?"

"Little man, Chinese. I peg him as an emissary from organized crime or the Chinese government. Either way, Hop Sing's going to be hopping mad when we abscond with his purchase. Mad or sad, he won't be in a position to do much. This place will be too lively."

"Everything on track?"

Russell took a puff of the long Macunudo. "Locked and loaded. I meet the paratroopers here at Zero Hour. Uncle Cliff and Martin are moored and watching. I'll call you in the auction room one minute prior to the raid there."

"Are you as calm as you seem?"

"No. That's why I'm smoking."

Chapter 23

Zero Hour

Clayton Russell was amazed at how quietly it began and how quickly it was over.

Major General Howe had said that the first Royal Marines would come from the sky. Standing on the bow of Eye Dare You at 9:55 Russell looked up. He heard nothing but soon saw that stars were winking off and then on in four black areas which were growing larger. The quartet of black shapes grew bigger and descended onto the foredeck of the massive ship, thirty feet in front of Russell. The four marines' landing was totally silent, the sounds of the boots and parachute canopies masked by the peaceful ocean waves.

One Royal Marine quickly ditched his chute and walked up to Russell. As Russell tossed his cigar aside, the soldier tapped the stripes on his left shoulder, indicating he was the troop commander.

"Fleming?" Russell asked.

The soldier wore a beret, camouflage uniform and facial greasepaint. He remained silent, nodded, held up his left hand with palm flat to indicate single file, then placed his hand briefly over his eyes, the field signal for ambush. The four Royal Marines rapidly marched off, with Russell following closely.

All of the soldiers carried short rifles. Russell's telephone briefing had informed them that the weapons were capable of firing in single rounds or bursts, but these rifles were also outfitted with Taser pistols under the front stock. Right away Russell saw the soldiers' method of ambush operation.

Two male crew members leaning against a rail, smoking, looked toward the five men: both immediately reached into their coats, the two lead marines aimed their rifles, bright green laser dots appeared on the startled men and Russell heard a double click. The pair of Taser X26 pistols fired four probes, two striking each man in the torso, dropping them like logs on the steel deck. One marine quickly handcuffed each man's wrists behind their back, used a third set of cuffs to connect the two men and finished the encounter by placing a strip of black tape across their mouths. Russell marveled at the efficiency and professionalism of the soldiers. They had been aboard the ship for barely one minute.

Fleming, the leader, raised binoculars and looked out to sea.

Russell whispered, "What's going on?"

Without moving, Fleming replied, "Waiting for the distraction. Fireworks, cruise ship."

Several seconds later a lone rocket arced up from the ocean a mile away and exploded, revealing the outline of a Norwegian Cruise Line ship. A multitude of fireworks followed, brilliantly lighting up the sky, ship and ocean, followed by the delayed sounds of explosions.

Fleming said, "Russell, take us to the crew lounge."

Russell jogged ahead and opened the door at the top of a service stairwell which led directly into the main crew lounge, at sea level. He led the marines down thirty steps and paused at the connecting door. He looked at Fleming, who nodded. Russell slowly twisted the knob, pushed the door open and stepped aside.

The four marines rushed in and caught a lone male crew member carrying a food tray. He was instantly Tasered, cuffed and taped. Fleming spoke briefly into a cell phone and then nodded to one of the marines, who opened a shore side door. One hundred yards away, Russell could see a dark vessel speeding toward the Eye Dare You. The LCVP MK5 is a landing craft that resembles the amphibious boats which deposited Allied troops on the beach at D-Day. This one— 15.5 meters long and loaded with 32 additional troops— quickly tied up to the ship and unloaded all but two marines. Now 34 Royal Marines, each armed with the Taser-rigged rifles, lined up in single file. Lingering doubts Russell had about the abilities of the British to secure the ship now vanished.

Fleming pointed to the end of the line, and the last two marines broke away and flanked Russell. They were to follow him, find Pamela, accompany both detectives to the auction storeroom, help them retrieve the Dalai Lama's possessions and get the antiquities on board Jaws, which should soon be tied up to the LCVP boat. The other marines would focus on the Queen's sceptre.

The marines at Russell's disposal were both at least a head taller. The one to his left said, "Mr. Russell, I'm 'Cain,' and this is 'Abel.' The plan is for our main force to secure the auction ballroom, contain all crew and any hostile guests and secure the sceptre; during that exercise, myself and Abel will escort you and Ms. Waters to retrieve certain antiquities, then to your departure vessel. Is that acceptable, and are there any questions?"

"No questions, Cain." He watched the marine chop the air twice, the silent signal to attack, then Fleming opened the main door and they all rushed forward.

As the three dozen men trotted up the empty stairs, Russell phoned Pamela.

"Yes?"

"Breaking through in a few seconds, get to the rear starboard corner of the room!"

"Got it!"

Russell was excited—the world's most exclusive illegal affair was about to end, its attendees surprised shitless when 34 British marines raided their party! What an inspiration to have a joyful visual and audio decoy outside the port windows of the ballroom! He and his two escorts were at the end of the trotting column. He flexed his fingers. Just a few more seconds before the lead marines would burst into the rear of the ballroom.

Then...Russell heard a clamor ahead, followed by two extremely loud explosions; stun grenades, he had been warned, which would cause five seconds of blindness to anyone looking toward the rear of the room and temporary deafness for twice as long. People began screaming. Russell elbowed his way up through the large camouflaged bodies and jagged to the right rear of the room, searching for Pamela. The marines were barking orders to the guests and crew, "Everyone on the floor, face down!" A bartender brandished a pistol and was able to get off one shot before two marines sprayed his torso with bullets; the barman next to the dying server put both hands on his head and dropped to the floor.

There she was! Russell grabbed Pamela's hand, and they ran toward the podium. He glanced over his shoulder to see Cain and Abel at their flank, keeping tight at four and eight o'clock. Abel suddenly sprinted in front, and stiff-armed a fat male guest in the chest who was about to collide with Pamela. The fat man bounced off the big marine's rigid right arm, spun, hit his head on a marble column, sank to the floor and did not move. The detectives were now halfway across the room. It was pure bedlam, in black tie. The shocked guests continued to scream as they lay on the floor. The auctioneer ran for an exit, was hit in the back by a Taser and quickly handcuffed.

As they passed the podium, Pamela looked at the cruise ship fireworks still erupting. The entrance door to the auction storeroom behind the podium was open. A large male crew member, one of the assistants who had helped move larger auction items, suddenly appeared in the doorway, on his way out. In one hand was a sword tagged for auction; seeing the marines he instantly flung the weapon aside, just as Russell struck the man in the face with the heel of his left hand. Russell felt the man's nose break, and he fell aside. Russell and Pamela entered the large storeroom, the two marines at their heels. The room was brightly lit, the merchandise glittering and, from across the room, turning in their direction, was a sole masked woman.

The Catcher had been placing merchandise in a large canvas sail bag. At her feet was an unconscious crew member, probably a casualty of hers just seconds prior. Had the crew man at the door been her accomplice? As the detectives and the accompanying guards moved forward Fionna whipped a shiny item from the sail bag. The instant that image clicked in Russell's and Pamela's minds, the Catcher's pistol discharged, half raised, as a Taser shot from Cain hit her. The marine's X26 Taser pistol released a blast of compressed nitrogen that launched the two barbed darts at roughly one-fifth the speed of the average bullet, but it was fast enough—the darts passed along the green laser light and pierced the clothing across her solar plexus; 1200 volts of electricity seized Fionna Marceau's body in an iron grip, the two attached wires delivering current which pulsated in a series of 100-microsecond jolts; her powerful skeletal muscles locked, and she drew up into a partial fetal position before twisting slightly to the right and sinking to the floor. She jerked slightly, as the marine held the trigger for five additional seconds of current. Fionna lay on her side, moaning slightly. Abel already had out a set of handcuffs and ran to the fallen woman.

Pamela picked up her canvas bag as they stepped over her body. Reaching the table filled with Tibetan antiquities, the two continued filling the bag. Cain, reloading his Taser pistol, walked toward the ballroom door, to keep anyone else from entering.

As Abel knelt down beside Fionna and pulled her left, limp arm up to put on handcuffs, the last thought the young marine had before dying was, *She shouldn't be...*

Fionna lashed out with her right hand and sank the ice pick into Abel's left eye, all the way to the wooden handle. The man immediately became unconscious and collapsed. Fionna saw that the other backs were to her; unaware of the kill. Clamor in the ballroom masked immediate sounds. Keeping her eyes on the others in the room, Fionna slowly rose and withdrew the ice pick from the corpse; with the other hand, she removed the commando dagger from his belt and quietly walked toward the six-foot-five quarry at the doorway. She tightly gripped both weapons and focused on the two areas of penetration; then, from two feet away, she thrust, simultaneously. Being ambidextrous was an enormous edge—the ice pick to the right ear and the slashing dagger across the throat caused the marine to simply drop to his knees, as if in prayer. His hands began to reach up but stopped halfway as the brain blacked out. Fionna gripped the fabric at the man's armpits and dragged the heavy Brit out the door. Keeping to the wall, she kept the body face down, being careful to avoid stepping in the blood trail now smearing across the marble floor.

The auction room was still noisy chaos but becoming more controlled as the marines went about their duties. One marine near the auctioneer's podium caught an image to his left. He turned to see a woman kneeling beside a fallen marine in the corner and hurried over to the pair.

"Excuse me, miss, please step aside!" The marine barely glanced at the woman.

She stood up and said, "Please help him!"

The marine saw considerable blood on his colleague and knelt down. As he began to turn over the body, his head sank, and the woman twisted the ice pick in the left ear canal, then spiked it back and forth. Thanks to considerable gear on the new corpse, she was easily able to position the man in a kneeling pose that gave the appearance of one concerned marine attending to another. Fionna palmed the weapon and walked off to blend in with the crowd. Outside the panoramic starboard window, she saw a military helicopter heading for the yacht.

She walked out of the ballroom and into the foyer, tossed aside her mask, ran up the spiral staircase and went topsides. The Lynx Light Battlefield helicopter had just landed, and more Royal marines were storming off. Seeing blood on her left hand, she smeared some on her forehead, ran up to the lead marine and said, "They've killed two soldiers!" The marine beckoned others to follow.

Fionna saw that the sole man in the copter was the pilot. She faked an injured stagger to the aircraft, climbed aboard and sat in the co-seat. The stunned pilot looked at her, saw the blood and before he could speak, she stabbed him deep in the thigh then positioned the ice pick below the marine's right eye. Holding it there, she tore off his helmet, unplugged his radio and yelled, "Up, fast, Miami!"

When the pilot hesitated, she quickly jabbed the ice pick totally through his right cheek and repositioned it under the eye. She yelled, "Both hands in sight, for the whole ride." The pilot nodded, slowly, as she removed his sidearm. He immediately got the craft airborne and banked west.

With the antiquities packed, Russell and Pamela hurried out of the room, failing to see the first dead marine. Their minds were on a speedy exodus. They ran through the ship, down to the crew lounge and out onto the boarding ladder. Marlin helped them aboard, and Cliff aimed Jaws toward the lights of Hamilton.

Down in the hold, Russell took off his tie. "I wonder what happened to our escorts? And what they'll do with that crazy bitch?"

Pamela lay down on a sofa and replied, softly, "I hope they hang her. That crazy bitch shot me."

Chapter 24

Negative Doubts, Positive Proof

When they were together, Pamela preferred to stay overnight at Russell's place. There were too many memories at her own that she had not yet escaped.

Her bullet wound could easily have been fatal, had the marine not spoiled Fionna's aim with the Taser strike. The .22 caliber hollow point struck her right thigh, mushroomed and lodged in the muscle. Fortunately it missed the femur, and bleeding was minimal. She was left with a slight, temporary limp and tiny new scar.

Russell was unusually depressed having been denied the opportunity to have Bergmann and the others arrested on Vogel's ship. Somehow, the head of De Blauwe Organisation, along with Phillip and Mitchell Lo, had escaped in the frenzied but quite successful raid. Vogel's ship had been impounded by the British Government, and he was in Westgate prison, awaiting extradition to England. The only auction items that escaped confiscation were the Tibetan antiquities. Russell and Pamela enjoyed that and other successes.

While in Bermuda, Det. Trent had emailed to say he located a relative of Lorena. The girl had been flown to

Boston. Russell and Pamela decided to bring Trent into their confidence when no immediate leads had surfaced. She had been in captivity for several years and was so indoctrinated that she needed professional therapy. Her parents had died in a terrible fire, and it was assumed their daughter burned with them, so the usual sources of missing persons were not available. DNA revealed that a maternal aunt was her only surviving relative.

Erin survived and was recovering, slowly, but healing nevertheless. After Russell returned the Presenter to New York City, he visited her in the intensive care unit. Pamela flew to New York with the sole purpose to help Russell convince Erin to go into hiding.

She had advised the brothel owner, "You need to take a long sabbatical to visit your family in Australia. Recoup at your sister's ranch there." Surprisingly, there was much less resistance than Pamela had expected. The two women had developed a mutual respect for one another, and both loved and admired Clay. Dr. Gonzales agreed to assist in the operations of the Unicorn Club in Erin's absence, which left Erin with a poor excuse for staying once discharged from the hospital.

Now Pamela was sitting with her back propped up in Clay's bed, her sore leg on a pillow, reading the email from his photographer friend.

Clay,

I think I got some good shots; take a look at the young blonde. Used a Nikon 500 mm with a silent motor. I will overnight a CD. No creatures beyond 20 feet heard or saw me. Only problems were the usual bugs and one very curious boa. Love the jungle.

Manny

The attachment was opened and contained dozens of color shots of the compound to aid Russell's entry and exit. There were a number of shots taken of a young blonde girl. A red-haired girl who seemed to be about the same age was also with her. The blonde appeared to be Lisa Collins, but he wanted a damn good second opinion before he jeopardized his ass in some foreign country on the property of a criminal. He replied, thanking Ruez for his work and closed down.

They agreed Russell would take a late flight to PhotoOps, a high-tech Miami company specializing in the analysis of photographs, videotapes and films. PhotoOps first made international news when the group debunked many "recently unearthed photographs" that had purported to show proof of more than one shooter in Dealey Plaza on November 22, 1963, the day President Kennedy was assassinated.

Once again Russell would call upon his contacts at the Bureau in Miami to call in a favor and encourage PhotoOps personnel to prioritize his job upon arrival. He needed to confirm that the Venezuela drug lord held Lisa captive.

After a late breakfast, Pamela kissed Clay good-bye and drove home to pack for London. Carefully wrapped in a new trunk were most of the Tibetan antiquities. Russell and she were unable to recover everything stolen, but the Dalai Lama should be pleased. Both detectives were convinced the other treasures were hidden away in the belly of that pirate ship of Vogel's, but they were satisfied with what they retrieved. She held in her hands the 16 x 24 painting of "Guru Padma and His Eight Emanations," dated 1912. This priceless artwork displayed three rows of three figures each, brilliant colors of orange, aqua, cobalt and gold. The middle and bottom characters were perched on a variety of pedestals, though one of the seats was a reclining tiger. Three Asians, one African, one Siamese, one oriental, one mulatto and one fiery character that appeared to be Satanic with tiger underneath. The top three figures sat upon clouds. In the center sat a kingly looking figure, the Lotus-Born Master, crowned, right hand holding some sort of small scepter, and left hand with a bowl of something unidentifiable. The background was a beautiful sky: gradations of gray, light blue and sapphire. Though intricate with detail, there was a remarkable symmetry about the work: it was as if an artist with a wildly colorful palette had been restrained by an architect, so each figure and its vivid colors had been put in their own respective space on the canvas.

Pamela was no collector of art, but if she had an instant longing for this masterpiece, heaven knows what an art connoisseur, one with extremely deep pockets, would pay! Mitchell Lo had certainly stolen some exquisite items. Among the recovered were a sacred text on woodblock prints, a *cho-goe* ceremonial robe, ritual implements tooled from human skulls and a mantra rosary with 112 carnelian beads. These religious possessions of the Dalai Lama were irreplaceable, and now she was returning them.

His Holiness' pilot remained on call in Atlanta to fly her to London. If the plan did not go awry, she would meet Russell later this week in Switzerland.

Two days later at dawn, tired and unshaven but highly wired, Russell was on his porch with coffee, enlarged photos, magnifying glass and the report PhotoOps had printed out at 10:33 p.m. last night. He had been at the elbow of the Miami technician who made the blowups during the entire process. The technician concluded that the photographs of the blonde girl were, with 90% plus certainty, identical to the photos provided by Sally of her child.

Russell knew his friend Manny had probably not yet returned to the States and would give him a call later. Once in the jungle, he knew Manny would want to stay awhile, but the detective was suddenly anxious. He sent a follow-up email message instructing Manny to leave promptly and not return to Venezuela. He would explain later.

Russell then booked one way flight arrangements to Zurich and an indefinite stay at the Arabella Sheraton

Atlantis Hotel in Zurich Center. Too bad he could not have coordinated the flight over the Atlantic with Pamela.

Chapter 25

Across Continents

Russell arrived in Switzerland and before checking
into the hotel, drove his rental Volvo to the Widder Hotel at
Renneg 7, located on a side street in the heart of Zurich.
From the business office, he sent an international telegram to
Anthony Montero:

> *Dear Senor Montero:*
>
> *As a valued customer, the Organisation is offering a*
> *complimentary copy*
> *of the latest edition of De Bleu Biblio. Accompanying*
> *this gift are special elixirs and toys. Please wire if*
> *and when you may receive a member of our company.*
>
> *Cordially,*
>
> *De Blauwe Organisation*

The Arabella Sheraton Atlantis Hotel was five miles
from Zurich in the woods at the foot of The Uetilberg, a
small mountain and the highest point in the region. The
property had acres of jogging trails, spacious bedrooms that
are spartan by American standards but well upholstered and
soothing. The hotel amenities included two restaurants, a
bar, health club, sauna and 24-hour room service.

Russell called Pamela to tell her he was staying on the
fifth floor in a "monochromatically soothing room"

(according to the literature) that had a balcony with views of forests and the spires of Zurich. He hoped she would arrive soon. Her company would help ease the impatience and frustration of waiting.

She called that evening, gushing with excitement from her meeting with His Holiness. "Clay, you should have seen that man's face when I walked into the hotel suite. There were six other monks with him. One quickly bolted the door behind me. I unpacked the antiquities and, one by one, delicately handed them to him. He in turn passed them to his colleagues, who immediately began packing each. When I apologized about our not returning all, he asked his companions to leave us alone. In private he said, 'Pamela, first, I am so glad that Mr. Russell and you were not hurt, at least not seriously. Second, it is a miracle that you found them. Third, another miracle you could infiltrate a pirate yacht, both of you, and get off the evil boat with sacred objects. Fourth, you accomplished all so quickly and with discretion, so the public, and Tibetans, may never know treasures left their home. No apology necessary! Oh, bless you!' Clay, I'll tell you all later, but the net is that case is closed. Then the meeting ended with him giving me an envelope. Back in my room, I opened it. The check is for the agreed fee, plus a bonus for my injury."

Pamela had concluded by asking if she could remain in London for a while longer? She was the Dalai Lama's guest. She would see him back in the States. Would you mind?

"No, of course not," he lied.

To help fight the blueness of being alone, he spent his time jogging, walking, reading, chatting with guests in the restaurants and bar and waiting. On his fourth day at the Atlantis, Russell made the third of the daily phone calls to the concierge at the Widder Hotel and was told a telegram had arrived for him. One hour later he read the short message:

Greetings:
I appreciate the gift. My staff and I shall be at Rancho Recito the remainder of September. I extend my home and hospitality to your member and a guest.
Regards,
A. Montero

Russell was thrilled that a second person was invited. But it was not uncommon for most cultures around the world to open their homes for weeks at a time for friends and family. It was polite. Only Americans, it seemed, had issues with their personal space. He hesitated about bringing Pam, but she could be invaluable in retrieving the child if there was trouble. And Montero would undoubtedly be charmed with her, even if children were his preferred sexual choice. He thought for a minute about who he should be and then replied:

Dear Senor Montero:
Please expect my companion and me on September 15th or 16th.

Due to uncertainties of connecting flights, I shall need some leeway
as to time of arrival.
                    Sincerely,
                    Mr. Rush, DBO

The following day at noon, Russell was back at his home on the telephone with Pam.

Pamela did not like the plan but was not creative enough to suggest a better one.

She phoned him to voice her concerns. The risk was too high that the drug lord would kill Lisa if his compound were openly raided with the military types.

"Let me understand, Clayton: I am to accompany you to Montero's estate under pretense, locate Lisa and then we just sneak her out!"

Russell was on his deck, enjoying the beginning of fall. Switching the phone to the other ear so he could more conveniently pet Winston, he tried to convince her they should be able to return to Atlanta within a few days.

If we return, she thought. "Are you positive this will work? Are you sure you want to do this?" Pamela realized she was biting her lip hard enough for it to bleed. "I'm pretty sure it will work, and I am absolutely certain I will try. Look, if you don't want to risk it, I understand. I can go alone."

"No. If you go, so will I, but only if you permit me to notify a special agent working in the country so he can be close by. Our Americans working undercover may not be able to intercede in a timely fashion, but it provides us with some back up."

Russell agreed. The American government was unreliable. Politicians always worried, first, about political ramifications, but our agents on the ground would do what they could to protect American lives. What did Jesse Ventura, former Governor from Minnesota call the politicians in Congress? "Chicken hawks!"

Pamela hung up without saying goodbye, closed her eyes for a minute, then picked up the phone and began making some calls. First, she needed to locate a trustworthy, bilingual Hispanic knowledgeable about Venezuela.

After four phone calls, Russell finally located Eddie Dempsey, a freelance pilot who could fly almost anything. Eddie made pretty good money, but he was continually bored, loved to fly and enjoyed being out of the country.

"Howdy," Eddie yelled, over considerable background crowd noise.

"Eddie, it's Clayton. Got a minute?"

"Yeah, hang on, it's loud in here. I'm walkin' and talkin'... OK, you're coming through. Clayton Russell?"

"Yes. Where are you?"

"Buster Hyman's. I was on the deck. They're having a Rate Her Rack contest. You won't believe some of these ..."

"I believe it, Ed. Listen, want a job? Fly from here to South America and back? Small cargo pickup."

"Legal cargo?"

"Of course. Can you fly a seaplane?"

"Yup, not the big ones, though."

"The smaller the better, just as long as you've got the range."

"How much cargo?"

"Three passengers and a large trunk down there and four people back. You may need to make a hasty departure from Venezuela."

"Angry Latino husbands, Clayton?"

"You know me better than that."

"Alright then, when?"

"Within a few days, but you'll have to be flexible. And we'll need to fly as far under radar as possible."

"Clayton, are you sure this is legal? I prefer to file a flight plan."

"We can't. This is a mercy flight to rescue an abducted child. And if our government or theirs knew, they could blow it, in a fatal sense."

"No shit? This is a serious gig, Clay."

"So don't be cheap about the cost of rental. Get us a good bird."

"Piece of cake, pal."

"$5000 for you and I pay all expenses?"

"It's a deal."

"Is this number the best way to reach you?"

"Yup. My cell. With me all the time."

Two days later, Eddie Dempsey called to say he had a Seawind 300C, which was, "the best amphibian you can rent." He agreed to meet Russell at the Shalimar Yacht Basin and Marina in Destin, Florida.

On September 11, four days before they were scheduled to arrive at Montero's estate, Pamela showed up at Russell's place just after midnight. She had the top down on her car. In the back was a large trunk.

"I've got it all; the trunk, the toys and a guy who was highly recommended through a friend at Venezuelan Consulate in Miami. It took me so long because he was the 12th guy I interviewed. His name is Simon Rey. He's the son of Ambassador Rey, in DC. I met with him. He's 28, grew up in Caracas, went to the University of Miami, dropped out after two years, fought as a professional boxer for three years, and for the past five years he's been a hunting and fishing guide, based out of Miami. He's a South American Ray Leonard. He asked for $1000 a day plus expenses."

"Splendid."

They unloaded the trunk from Pam's BMW and went inside. After placing it on his marble coffee table, Russell surprised her by complimenting the luggage. "It's absolutely beautiful."

"The gentleman asked for a trunk, and this one's a pearl!"

"Louis Vuitton?"

"Yes sir. It was made in 1905 and has the original hardware, solid brass lock and leather exterior."

"Where'd you get it?"

"It's mine, inherited from my great-grandmother. I want it back, Mr. Russell."

He gave her a dry look. "You'll probably get it back. Let's look inside."

She fished an ornate brass key out of her pocket, unlocked the large center latch, raised the lid and said, "It's the world's sexiest trunk."

Russell looked at the contents of the 6-inch deep removable tray and, practicing the face he would use with Anthony Montero, tried to appear unimpressed, but it was difficult. Carefully arranged in a near-perfect jigsaw pattern was a cornucopia of sexual paraphernalia: about two dozen toys, straps, ointments, ropes, electrical devices and at least half a dozen items Russell could not identify. Some of the toys were extremely colorful, and all appeared to be of a quality more apropos of Hammacher Schlemmer rather than Target.

Russell picked up some restraints labeled Alligator Cuffs. He felt the insides and said, "Hmm, fleece-lined."

Pamela adjusted her glasses and facetiously added, "By the way, all of these trinkets are new. None are mine."

Pamela's expression suddenly changed, "I forgot something that might give us some extra time down there." She ran back outside to her car.

The 368-mile drive from Atlanta to Destin, Florida was uneventful and boring. By twilight, they reached the Shalimar Yacht Basin, parked and walked around the docks. After finding a good place to meet Eddie, they checked in to the nearby Fairfield Inn as husband and wife. Russell called the pilot, verified a dawn pickup two days hence for Russell, Pamela and Simon Rey. The Venezuelan would drive to the panhandle from Miami. Then they all fly to Venezuela, where Rey said his cousin would be waiting at an isolated location on the coast a few miles from the port city Maracaibo.

After a short, fitful sleep Russell spent a day and a half at the hotel's business center reading about Venezuela while Pamela enjoyed the surf. September was off season and the crowds gone.

The country, he read, is a third larger than Texas and borders most of the northern coast of South America on the Caribbean Sea. Mountains divide Venezuela into four primary areas: the Maracaibo lowlands; the mountainous region in the north and northwest; the Orinoco basin; and the Guiana Highlands, south of the Orinoco, which comprises nearly half the nation.

As with much of Central and South America, the production of opium and coca attributed substantially to their GNP. Without American purchasers to the north, the farmers would have switched to food crops. But the United States' profits from illicit drug trafficking was irresistible.

The next day, Russell exercised for a half hour while she slept in. They packed, went downstairs for coffee, checked out of the hotel and then walked to the marina. Ten minutes later, they saw a speck in the sky near the horizon line.

Eddie Dempsey had said the plane was a Seawind something, and this one was a beauty. White and sleek with a single prop at the top center fore of the tail. The craft was very agile, as demonstrated by Dempsey doing a sharp drop and then swooping down within forty yards of where the detectives were standing on the end of the dock. Dempsey gave a wave, banked the plane sharply out to sea, rolled the craft once, did a loop, banked back toward the dock, dead-on, smoothly touched down on the calm sea surface, slowed the plane, turned it 90° and stopped in the ocean fifty feet from his passengers. The pilot slid open his window and yelled, "Hey sailor, need a ride?"

Russell grinned at the colorful flier. "Lemme get a bit closer. I'll throw you a line."

Pamela's feeling of dread lessened somewhat. Now she only had butterflies in her stomach. The man was certainly capable at the stick, and that aircraft could turn on a dime. She thought that only a military jet could out-maneuver it, should they be chased.

Dempsey nosed the plane up to the dock and tossed a bright orange rope to Russell. When the engine shut down, Russell and Pamela pulled the plane up to the dock. They tightened it up against the marina's new, clean boat bumpers, and Dempsey reached into a large denim coat pocket, pulled out a can of Pabst, popped it, touched the can next to Russell and Pamela's coffee cups and said, "Morning. What do you think of the bird?"

Russell smiled at his friend. "Looks like a winner. What are the specs?"

"It's a modified Seawind. This one was lengthened, like a stretch limo. It'll hold four people, with cargo space for about 12 large suitcases. Wingspan 40 feet. Sea level top speed, 200. Cruising speed, 180. Extended range, 1460 miles. Takes off from water in about 1000 feet. Landing distance, about 700 feet. It's an amphibious Porsche. Should be perfect for whatever you're importing or exporting. Especially if we're being pursued."

Russell looked at his watch. "Our Venezuelan guide should be here within the hour."

At noon, the pilot and crew were halfway to Jamaica, where Dempsey had arranged a refueling stop near Half

Moon Bay. Dempsey and Simon Rey had hit it off from the first few minutes, and the two continued to amiably chat well after takeoff. Russell and Pamela had settled in the back. Russell closed his eyes…

…and found himself bound to a chair. A large silhouette backhanded Russell's face but he did not feel pain. Only fear. He could not see a face. In an accent Russell could not identify, the man demanded, "Where is our Jewel! Where is she!" but he could not recall where the Jewel was. He heard Pamela plead, "Clayton, tell him where the girl is! He will kill us both if you don't tell!" "No, I don't know where she is." He suddenly heard a strange metallic sound, a smashed pumpkin sound, a plop—as if a grapefruit had hit the floor—and when the shadow stepped aside, an angular pool of light shown across the floor displaying Pam's severed head as it slowly rolled across the tiles, leaving a blood trail, as she continued to speak and look at his face, once per revolution. "Look what they did to me. No, no, no. Now they're going to do it to you. No, no, no. Poor Clayton, poor Clay, poor Clay, poor…

"…Let go! Let go of the *door* Clay! Dammit!"

Pamela repeatedly shook him, fiercely. Russell, slowly segueing from sleep to consciousness, was trying to open the shotgun door of the seaplane. Simon Rey had a

371

firm grip on his forearms and gradually relaxed the grasp as Russell came to and slumped back into the seat. For a few seconds, the only sound was a reassuring, steady drone of the Seawind's engine. Everyone knew it was a nightmare. Russell would not reveal what the dream had been. He was glad to be sitting behind his two male companions. He was scared, having a panic attack, he wanted to hide it from the pilot and he damn sure wanted to hide it from Simon Rey. But Pamela knew. No hiding it from her.

Russell was sweating, nauseous, light-headed and saw white sparks in his peripheral vision. Suddenly, an acid gorge rose in his throat, which he was barely able to contain. He closed his eyes for a moment, rehearsed the plan again in his mind and, overcoming his doubts, knew they could succeed. He squeezed his hands into fists for a full minute, then relaxed them and opened his eyes. "Hey Eddie, could I have one of your beers?"

"Sure Clay. It won't be long now."

One hour later they refueled at the Glistening Waters Restaurant & Marina at Falmouth, Jamaica, just east of Montego Bay. The weather was flawless, and Dempsey kept the Seawind at top speed.

Just under five hours after leaving Jamaica, he pointed to the horizon and said, "Lady and Gentlemen, welcome to Venezuela."

Chapter 26

Precious Jewels

They were flying three kilometers above and ten kilometers away from the Gulf of Venezuela. The Gulf was bordered by the Caribbean Sea to the north and the Venezuelan states of Zulia and Falcon on each side. To the south lay Lake Maracaibo, the largest lake in the continent. Dempsey relaxed. The maritime activity was moderately busy, perfect for a small seaplane to land and take off without much notice.

As they passed over the Gulf and began descending toward Lake Maracaibo, Simon Rey touched Dempsey's shoulder. "There, to the right of those two freighters, the 25 story building, that's the Del Lago InterContinental Hotel Maracaibo. To the right of it is the marina, the Nautical Yacht Club. We'll touch down in the Club's harbor, tie up and my cousin will meet us tomorrow with a four wheel drive."

Ten minutes later, the Seawind was docked and secured in a slip located near the guard station. While Dempsey checked them into the 50-year old lakeside Hotel

Maracaibo, Russell and Pamela sat with Simon Rey at the hotel's poolside Cabana Bar. After ordering Carta Blancas and a shrimp platter, Russell began to prep their guide.

"Pam told me you're familiar with this area and have been to Rancho Recito."

"Yes. Even though Montero is corrupt and violent, my government tolerates him. And so, if not out of respect then certainly out of fear, when invited as a guest, one attends."

Russell looked out across the flat waters of Lake Maracaibo and casually scanned the dozen or so people around the pool. No one appeared to be interested in the three newcomers. "Simon, for your protection I'll tell you just what you need to know and nothing more. We are Mr. and Mrs. Rush. Tomorrow morning we leave here for Rancho Recito. When we arrive, Pam and I will deliver a trunk of gifts for the drug lord. Leaving could be tricky. I need your cousin and you to wait outside the compound for our signal. We may be on the run."

The young man sat expressionless. Russell could not read him. He did hope Pamela was correct about his integrity.

Russell handed Rey an envelope. "Here's $10,000. I'll give you another $10,000 once we've boarded the seaplane and are airborne. I increased your pay so you can reward your cousin for his silence."

"I appreciate it and understand. Do not worry, he can be trusted."

"Good. When I conclude my business inside with Mr. Montero, Pam and I will return with the trunk. We then depart. No delays. Your cousin's bringing a four-wheeler, right?"

"Yes. It's a Range Rover, black, and he will deliver it promptly by 8:00 a.m."

Rey toyed with a final shrimp on the platter. "Mr. Russell, the trunk: are you delivering something *to* Montero or taking something *away?*"

"Both. What we are doing is, technically, illegal but morally justified. Montero would be very unhappy if he knew our true mission. I cannot discuss anything further, but I promise to answer any other questions on our way home. Are you able to handle it if someone recognizes you?"

"Si. I find the idea of Montero's displeasure exciting. Our families have never been friends. We merely tolerate one another out of necessity. I also get a kick out of kicking assholes."

Russell smiled. He felt the same way about assholes. "Wear casual, comfortable clothes, a hat, sunglasses and shoes for running. Wear a Timex or other nondescript watch."

Pamela added, "Have the vehicle clean, with nothing to connect us to that car. Be equipped with some weapon for protection, a knife or a gun, if you can handle it." Russell did not agree with the gun but kept silent. He would pack Vipers.

The three discussed additional supplies, then stood and shook hands. Rey placed the list in his shirt pocket and walked away. Russell signaled for the check. Mr. and Mrs. Rush returned to their room to discuss permutations and possibilities concerning the next day. Russell verbally practiced his patter as Pam critiqued. He hoped it would be in front of an audience of only one adult, and his partner agreed.

By 8:35 a.m. they were on the road.

Rey drove, Russell sat shotgun and Pamela was in the rear. Rey wore camouflage pants, white denim shirt, tennis shoes, a black Nike baseball cap and oversized sunglasses. Russell wore a crisp blue and white seersucker suit, white button down Tommy Bahama shirt, no tie and dark brown Timberland boat shoes. And Pamela was a sight to see. Russell had forgotten how seductive she could be. She wore a slinky silk green floral dress, cut low in front and tea length. The neckline revealed just enough cleavage to be enticing, and the full skirt gave a hint of the thong beneath with no other under garments. She would have preferred tennis shoes and blue jeans, but this was show time. All Latinos like pussy, though she would never say that. Flat sandals were laced securely around her ankles, and she had donned contact lenses in lieu of glasses, heavy on the eye make-up and Black Orchid perfume. Montero may prefer children, but she expected his guards would be interested in an adult woman.

The Rover was packed with rudimentary camping gear: first aid kit, road flares, a large Igloo Marine 72 cooler stocked with food, beverages and several specialty items hidden beneath the ice and tray. When they left the hotel, the countryside soon became flat and verdant. As the terrain became hillier, there were fewer residences. The first clue they were nearing Rancho Recito was two nondescript men in khaki safari suits holding machine pistols and playing cards in the bed of a new pickup truck. They wore matching, plain white baseball caps with very long bills that obscured their faces. Both men stopped their play to watch them drive by. Russell raised a hand. One man waved back. Pamela looked in the rear view mirror to see the other man pick up a cell phone, probably to report ahead.

A mile later they saw a posted warning:

PRIVATE PROPERTY. NO TRESPASSING.

They drove over a steep hill, made a slight turn and stopped at the hill's peak. In the beautiful valley below, easily recognizable from the photos, was Rancho Recito.

Russell assumed they were being observed. He asked Rey to retrieve the binoculars from the glove box. Russell slowly panned with the field glasses, keeping one hand in his pocket to project confidence and nonchalance. A brunch party was in full swing at the main pool. Servants briskly worked the gathering, with multiple guards throughout the grounds. He handed the Nikons to Pamela. She noticed one guard with a very large pair of binoculars looking directly at them. After Rey viewed the compound Russell suggested they proceed.

They began the descent and within minutes were at the steel ornate gate. A burley, armed man in khaki uniform, wearing an earphone, raised a hand, then pushed out his palm, gesturing halt. He approached the driver's window.

"My wife and I have an appointment with Montero. My name is Mr. Rush."

"Drive through, and park on the main circle. Enter the front. Mr. Montero is expecting you."

A few feet from the front door, one of the guards frisked Russell. Another guard searched Pamela with unabashed pleasure, fingertips lingering over the lines of her thong. She took off her glasses and winked, which she did to stop him and it worked, instantly.

Rey was asked to wait in the Rover, where the guard gave the vehicle a cursory search. He opened the cooler, glanced at the contents and shut the lid.

Russell and Pamela were then led through an immense wooden front door. Pamela was perspiring from the heat and humidity, but it masked her nervousness as they entered the large, cathedral ceiling foyer. From here they followed a curious servant. The young man wore a tuxedo.

In silence he gestured with crooked fingers and extended arms to indicate where to follow. The couple's minds and emotions were racing as they casually noted all they saw: furniture, doors, windows and wait-staff. Their departure may have to be swift.

After the foyer, they passed through a short hall, a small semi-formal dining room and a medium-sized library. There sat a young couple laughing and texting on their i-Phones. The servant led them through a small sitting room with fireplace and finally a large, open Mexican tiled veranda that adjoined the main pool area.

Fifty feet away, near the largest of the three fieldstone waterfalls that gently cascaded water into the huge pool, a dozen people in various levels of bathing attire sat at the feet of the big frog in his pond. Anthony Montero was the nucleus of a motley cadre of obsequious guests laughing, applauding and paying homage to the reclusive criminal. The servant bid adieu with a final gesture, to which Russell gave a polite nod. He pulled his hands from his pockets, affectionately grasped Pamela's hand and coolly observed Montero and friends.

Montero saw them and raised an index finger. The drug lord said something through a crocodile smile, clapped twice and the group dispersed.

Montero briskly walked up to his visitors. "Buenos dias, Senor and Senora."

Pamela extended her hand, and Montero bowed, kissing it lightly. "Senor, you are so fortunate to have such a lovely creature by your side." Had Pamela not known what a monster he was, she could have been charmed.

"Thank you, Senor", Russell replied.

Montero guided them to a wrought-iron four top table. The noise from the waterfalls would shroud their conversation. Pamela was itching to get the program moving and to get the hell out of there.

Montero politely asked, "Do you like margaritas? You must be thirsty from your drive."

"That would be excellent," Russell answered, then looked at his watch. "But I apologize that we only have an hour to spend in your company. We have a tight schedule, and it is the policy of DBO that we conduct external meetings as quickly as possible." Pamela smiled but declined, asking only for a bottle of water, "No fizz please."

"Certainly! It is you who are doing me the courtesy of this visit. Whatever you wish you shall have."

"Fine," Russell said. "Now, I must instruct my driver to retrieve your gifts, then we shall depart within the hour."

"That is not necessary," Montero quickly gushed, smiling slightly. "One of my people will inform him." Montero glanced over Russell's shoulder and raised a hand.

Without looking behind, Russell emphatically said, "Mr. Montero, I have to personally inform my associate.

Unlike you, I have superiors who insist I follow a certain protocol. I know you understand. My wife shall remain."

Montero's slight smile faded, but slowly returned, a bit brighter. Russell had no idea if the man were suspicious or was not used to someone countering his suggestions.

"Yes. Of course."

"Thank you," Russell replied, rose and quickly walked the route from which they entered. It was an effort to calmly do so. He could feel his armpits trickling cold sweat, the droplets falling down inside his shirt and onto his waist. The seersucker coat should hide any perspiration stains. He would wipe his face dry the moment he felt he wasn't being observed.

In the foyer, Russell's silent guide nodded and held open the door. Russell nodded back and forced a smile. Outside he counted six guards between their vehicle and the gate. From the Rover's rearview mirror, Simon Rey saw Russell approaching. Rey could not gauge anything from Russell's expression.

At the open driver window, Russell quietly said, "Let's get the trunk in quickly. I'm not sure what Montero will do, and I left Pam poolside. I presume he'll direct us to a private room. If so, I want you to stay just outside the door. I don't know how long Pam and I'll be alone with him. Ready?"

"Yes sir," Rey replied.

Russell lifted the Rover's rear window and lowered the tailgate. Rey took out the 2-foot by 4-foot Magliner platform hand truck. They loaded Pamela's trunk onto the dolly. As they wheeled it toward the mansion, Russell kept one hand in his pocket and began to softly whistle "We're In The Money." When the butler opened the foyer door, Russell began to quietly sing. He hoped all who observed would think the visitor was harmless and a bit loco. Judging from the look one suited guard now cut at Russell, he was succeeding.

The young servant led them to ornate carved wooden double doors in the central section of the sprawling mansion. The servant pointed at the top of Pamela's antique trunk and made a gesture with his hand to "open it up."

Russell produced the brass key, unlocked the center latch and lifted the lid. He smiled and politely asked, "Would you like to try the mink handcuffs?"

Surprised at such a suggestion, the man quickly shook his head, turned, opened the large doors and pointed toward the room's interior.

Russell slowly closed the trunk and locked it. He didn't ask to see under the tray! First hurdle passed!

He and Rey walked in. The room was large and richly furnished with opulent furniture, numerous paintings and a score of animal trophy heads on three walls. Deer, bear, antelope, and moose, all legal prey. And, yes, the illegally bagged elephant, tiger and rhino.

Behind the far wall were three sets of dual, glass French doors. Another servant was closing curtains in front of the doors. Anthony Montero sat behind a massive mahogany desk, Pamela in a Barcelona chair in front of the desk. Russell sat next to her. Rey stood with the trunk, beside the open door.

Montero smoked a very long cigar. Russell hid his disgust at Montero's desk ashtray: a human skull, with a pancake size hole in the cranium. The drug lord tapped an ash from his cigar into the eye of the skull cavity. He saw Russell note the action. "A unique accessory for a smoker, si? It is the head of an American DEA agent."

"Your ashtray is missing all its teeth," Russell said.

Montero replied, "That is to hide the ashtray's previous life. Mr. Rush, do you have identification?"

"No, Senor Montero. We are not permitted to carry IDs for this type of meeting." Passports and wallets were in the Rover, at the bottom of the cooler.

"How do I know you are who you say you are, Mr. Rush? Uh, would you like a cigar?"

"Gracious of you, but no thank you. And to answer your first question, allow me to quote a colleague, Mr. Krieg. 'You must have faith'."

"Are you religious, Mr. Rush?"

"No."

"Do you believe in God?"

"No."

"What do you think will happen after you die?"

"I will probably turn into dust." Russell paused then added, "Or, if I'm lucky, perhaps I'll be reincarnated. Maybe as an ashtray."

Montero froze, in mid puff. Then he tilted back his head and roared with laughter. "Ha! Ashes to ashes! Dust to dust! Man into ashtray!"

Pamela resisted an urge to cross her heart that God not strike the two men dead. She had forgotten that religion was also an issue about which Russell and she often disagreed.

Russell's mind was racing. He wanted to move the game forward. He turned, looked over his shoulder and said to Simon Rey, "Please leave the trunk there, near the door, and wait outside."

Rey nodded, walked out of the room and shut the door.

Over his shoulder, Montero said to the sole male servant, "Kindly bring in my Jewels, then leave Mr. Rush, his wife and myself alone." The servant left, shutting the doors.

Russell thought, Jewels, plural? Yes, the presenter had said he purchased two.

Montero asked, "Are you sure you would not like a cigar? A drink, perhaps?"

"No, thank you, we must conclude our visit." He looked at Pamela who managed a weak smile.

Montero took a deep drag, slowly exhaled and watched a pale blue plume waft up toward the 30-foot ceiling. Russell lightly drummed his fingers on the ankle of a crossed leg. A long silent three minutes passed. Then footsteps from outside and a door opened.

Montero broke into a wide smile and said, "Ahh, muy bonita! Ladies, please sit down. Senor and Senora, please meet Lois and Lana. I call them that, because they think I am a Superman! And, sometimes, when the moon is full, I am." Montero chuckled.

As Pamela turned to her right, two attractive young girls quietly walked over to the red leather sofa and sat down. They were so young. Pamela ached with sympathy. The blonde looked at Montero, blank faced waiting for a command from her master. The redheaded girl was staring curiously at Russell. Something about her looked familiar to Pamela. She would think about that later. The girls were identically dressed; white, long cotton skirts adorned with ruffles, pale blue Izod shirts, black crocodile belts, expensive-looking, lemon-yellow, leather sandals.

Russell knew the blonde was Lisa Collins. Adrenaline coursed into his system. She was only twenty feet away but 2,000 miles from home. He closed his eyes for one second and then forced himself to appear dispassionate as he studied the two girls. What was Pam's reaction? He dare not look at his companion. His heart had begun to race. His throat became dry. He crossed his arms so he could secretly ball up his fists to help release the tension. He had found her. Now to get her out!

Montero pointed his cigar hand at the girls. "I guess you know these two exquisite Jewels are from that catalog of yours?" Montero sucked loudly on the long cigar. The desk phone rang and he ignored it.

With a nod toward the girls, Russell began his act, every word of which had been carefully rehearsed. Pamela sat in docile silence.

"Mr. Montero, De Blauwe Organisation would like to express appreciation of your patronage. The two Jewels you purchased were among the finest in our inventory. Should any of your close friends or business partners express admiration of these matching gems, we ask that you refer them to us. Now, a few extra, stimulating gifts that we believe you shall find most thrilling."

Russell paused, smiled, slowly stood up and held out his left hand toward the trunk. "Now, what could be inside this magnificent, vintage portmanteau?"

He opened the trunk, briefly put his body between it and Montero to remove a black object, slipped it in his right front trouser pocket and turned.

"Many wonderful new toys. And very special pleasure aids. The Hitachi Magic Wand, " Russell held up the device, "the Rolls-Royce of vibrators." He proceeded to display a succession of sexual accoutrements. "The Naughty Nurse Harness…The BoiFriend…The

BoiToy…Goliath…The Twisted Hemp Rope Kit…Alligator Cuffs…The Slotted Paddle…Bliss Lube…ToyFluid…The Pony Bridle…Heather's Tethers. Last and not least: the latest edition of our catalog, De Blauwe Biblio."

Montero's face had slackened, and his mouth was slightly open in sexual arousal. Pamela watched in disgust, trying to control the vomit rising in her throat.

"Mr. Montero, I would like to demonstrate the newest sexual stimulators and then leave you with your Jewels. Yes?" Russell smiled and raised an eyebrow. He slid the trunk a few inches so the track lights in the ceiling better illuminated the contents of the tray. The colorful assortment of devices, restraints, gels, clothing and apparatus sparkled and glistened in the halogen glow. He removed a black leather case the size of a bible and opened it.

"I have refills of Viagra for you. And our pharmacists have now created an amazing elixir for the female gender. We call it Nectar from Heaven. It is instant, sexual, ecstasy. May I serve some to the young ladies?"

In a hoarse whisper, Montero answered, "That would be perfect. Absolutely perfect."

Russell winked at Montero, whose eyes were darting between the two detectives and the Jewels. Russell took clear liquid Rohypnol from a small bottle and poured several drops of the odorous, tasteless hypnotic into a cup of water. Within minutes the two pre-teens would become unconscious. He only hoped there was no harm due to cross

388

medications. Both were acquiescent and drank deeply from the cup.

Russell walked toward Montero, zipped the case closed and placed it upon the man's desk. "Please keep this, and if you like the ménage à trois you are about to enjoy, just repeat the recipe. Five cc's per Jewel is the perfect amount to be dropped in any liquid."

Montero rose and extended his hand, "You are too kind, Mr. Rush. I cannot tell you how hap... " His thought abruptly ended with Russell's whiplash slap of the leather covered lead blackjack to the man's skull, an inch above the left ear.

The drug lord instantly dropped to his knees, then all fours. Small droplets of blood began to spot the Turkish rug. Russell, very angry yet controlled, whisper-hissed in the man's ear, "They're not jewels, you sick fuck. They're little girls." He snapped the blackjack again, hard, onto the back of Montero's head. The man collapsed onto the rug and lay motionless. Russell confirmed he was breathing and resisted an impulse to end the criminal's life.

The girls were already showing signs of instability. Both were slumped on the sofa, Lisa asleep and the redhead not far behind. He had not planned on fitting two children into the trunk but was reluctant to leave the mystery girl behind. Pamela helped him remove the tray from the trunk. It was empty, except for an oxygen tank with mask, and a large tape recorder. Pamela lifted the tank and recorder, then Russell gently placed the girls inside, facing each other.

Pamela carefully pushed their mouths together as closely as possible. She pulled the mask off the oxygen tank, threw it aside and placed the tank on top of the redhead's legs. The 12-pound steel cylinder had enough air to sustain one person in the trunk for up to four hours. Pamela licked her finger, placed it next to the outflow valve and slowly twisted the plastic knob until he felt the tiny O_2 breathe cool on her fingertip. She worked the cylinder between the bodies of the girls, with the valve under their chins. The human cargo and cylinder completely filled the bottom of the trunk. They replaced the top tray. It was a tight fit. She closed the lid, locked it and glanced at her watch. That trunk must be opened within two hours.

Russell placed the Nagra 4.2 analogue audio recorder on the floor, next to the sofa, and turned it on. What an inspiration from Pamela! Two hours of a man and girl having long, relaxed sex. She had created the theatrical recording at an Atlanta studio. He adjusted the volume. The first five minutes of the recording were of a girl and man laughing. The two hours after that were a diverse series of sexual sounds: moans, sighs, rustle of clothing and laughter, interspersed with brief periods of silence. Then more of the previous with an occasional male orgasmic grunt and cry.

Russell and Pam worked the trunk onto the hand dolly. He picked up Montero's dropped cigar and took a

390

puff. He then began to wheel the dolly to the door. Rey was just outside. As he rolled the trunk through the doors, Russell said to Rey, loud enough for the two nearby male staff to hear, "Mr. Montero is examining our gifts and wishes privacy. Our visit is concluded."

As Rey began pushing the trunk, Russell shut the door, straightened his jacket, and took another puff from the cigar. Rey, Pamela and their cargo had walked about forty feet, when peripherally Russell saw a large figure walking briskly toward him. Russell pretended not to notice.

"Excuse me, Señor Rush?"

Russell turned to his left to see the approaching man suddenly halt. Large hands were balled into fists at his thighs. Attired in gym shorts, t-shirt and running shoes, he was covered with sweat. The complexion was very flushed in comparison with the rest of his hide. He was six-four, lean and finely tooled at wrists, knees and ankles, much like one of the anatomy drawings where only the muscles are seen. From the neck down, he was a masculine muscle machine, but from the neck up, by a striking contrast, were the features and countenance of an unearthly angel. Soft, purple, pouting lips that were slightly parted and trembling; long, silky black hair, with a contrived spit-curl on the forehead; light green cat's eyes framed by long, black lashes; two large, emerald-encrusted earrings that matched the eyes: and teeth that blazed so white they must have been cosmetically created.

391

"Yes," Russell replied. "I am Mr. Rush. And you are Señor…?"

"Saldariagga. How was your business with Señor Montero?"

Before Russell could respond, Pamela steeped forward and cooed. "Señor Montero is enjoying himself and wishes not to be disturbed."

"He did not answer his phone."

Russell slowly licked the cigar. He took a pull and politely blew the smoke aside. "Good sir, did you not understand what the lady said? Your boss does not want to be disturbed. I am not a prude, God knows, but I know when it is time to leave!"

Saldariagga's suspicions remained, but he knew Montero had sexual perversions that would, one day, condemn the man to Hell. He would tithe tonight at mass to atone for his sins and ask the priest for special forgiveness for continuing to work for such an animal. With disdain, Saldariagga said, "Yes, time to leave."

The strongman walked back to the door of Montero's study, listened and heard sounds of mild spanking, then a feminine voice in the throes of an extended orgasm. Disgusted, he turned away.

Pamela trotted toward the vehicle while Russell followed unhurriedly, enjoying his cigar. Simon Rey, with large beads of sweat on his forehead, was behind with the hand dolly, his face a shade paler.

Russell assisted in loading the trunk into the back of the Rover. Pamela, deep in thought about the second girl, was now certain of the young teen's identity: Julie Cantrell, a presumed runaway and the 13-year-old daughter and only child of Senator Thomas Cantrell, the senior U.S. senator from Louisiana! The Cantrell girl had also been blonde, but, Pamela was sure, this was the kid, only with hair dyed red.

She put her hand on the door handle and momentarily paused there, suddenly dizzy.

"Senora," Rey whispered. "Do you feel OK?"

"I'm fine," Pamela quietly replied. As they pulled out of the compound, Pamela whispered to Russell. "Clay, the other girl—do you realize who that is?"

"She seems American."

"Very much so. That's Senator Thomas Cantrell's missing daughter." Pamela looked out the back of the Rover. Nobody was following. Yet. "Simon, help me with this." She turned around, unlocked and opened the trunk and handed the tray to their assistant.

When the young man saw what was inside, he immediately realized their situation. "Oh no. I thought this was about drugs." He looked at Pamela. "If they catch us, they will kill us."

"Then they better not catch us. Clay, please hurry."

Russell glanced in the rearview mirror. He could still see Montero's estate in the distance. "Soon."

A few miles later they approached the sentries in the truck, still playing cards. Russell lowered the driver's side window, pulled out two Viper throwing knives and laid them on the console. Pamela knew what he was thinking. She reached out and squeezed his right hand. He squeezed back, pushed her hand away, picked up a Viper and rested it on his thigh. Pamela closed her eyes and began to pray. Simon Rey leaned forward and crossed himself. As they came abreast of the sentries, Russell hefted the Viper by its handle. The men just looked at them. Russell lifted his left hand and smiled. One of the men nodded. Russell put the knife back on the console.

Rey's face was extremely pale. He mopped his brow with a red bandana. Russell pulled away, checked the rearview again, and when the sentries disappeared, he sped up.

At Rancho Recito, Saldariagga stood by a huge window in the second floor foyer, gazing at the gray mountains twenty miles distant. He tapped his mouth, thinking. Then he went downstairs and returned to Montero's study room doors. A guard stepped in front of him.

"Señor Montero wants privacy. He is with his Jewels."

Saldariagga put his ear to one of the doors, "I have never heard them like *that*."

"Señor Rush brought gifts." The guard smiled. "I was told they are quite interesting."

Saldariagga gave him a hard look, and his smile faded. He went to his quarters and showered. He opened the refrigerator, removed a Frescolita cola and as he sipped the beverage, thought about the recent visitors. Something did not seem right. He suddenly had a gut feeling and ran back to the study. With a guard watching, he put an ear to the door and held his breath. He heard what sounded like light slaps and feminine laughter. He briskly knocked four times on the door and said, "Señor Montero." He heard a girl laugh, then stepped back and said to the guard, "Open it."

"Señor, I was told ..."

Saldariagga balled-up his fist in front of the guard's face and quietly commanded, "Open it, now."

The guard tried both doors, which had automatically locked. "Kick it in."

The guard stepped back, raised a foot and smashed it next to the right doorknob. He kicked it again, with more force. The third kick blew the door open. Saldariagga calmly walked into the room. He immediately saw the Nagra recorder and a smeared trail of blood leading to the body. Anthony Montero lay on his right side. Saldariagga knelt and placed two fingers on the man's neck. There was a slight pulse.

Sending the guard from the room to call the doctor, Saldariagga took a pillow from the couch and placed it over his boss' face. Then, gripping Montero's jaw and the back of his head through the pillow, he used both hands to give a sharp clockwise twist to the head. Two cervical bones snapped, their fractures muffled by the pillow. Saldariagga quickly crossed himself. He was truly thankful to God for providing this convenient advancement in position. Montero had no legitimate heirs. And any illegitimate ones, along with competitors, would not dare challenge the established machine. Many people feared Saldariagga more than Montero.

Within minutes the doctor and three guards appeared in the doorway. He yelled, "The visitors have killed Señor Montero! Get the helicopter and pick me up on the front lawn! Now!"

The guard ran away, as the tuxedo servant appeared in the doorway.

"The Jewels," Saldariagga yelled, "where are they?"

"I do not know," the servant replied, quaking.

"The trunk they brought here—did you look inside it?"

"Si, I checked it when they arrived."

"Did you check it as they left?"

"No," said the man, fearfully.

Saldariagga, disgusted, ran to his quarters, quickly washed his face, changed into a khaki jumpsuit, laced on black leather work boots, snapped on a new Breitling Airwolf wristwatch and tightly buckled a black leather web utility belt that carried handcuffs, pepper spray, a 9.5-inch Trail Master Bowie knife and an aluminum Ruger .45 Auto pistol. He checked the pistol loads, holstered the weapon and ran to the foyer. He was finally rid of Montero, and the soon-to-be dead Americans would take the blame. The girls, he would remove from the compound. Perhaps send them to a convent.

Four minutes later, the black and white Bell 429 helicopter landed on the front lawn, fifty yards from the main house. Carrying a large duffel bag, Saldariagga ran to the copter. A door opened from inside, he tossed in the bag, boarded, strapped the shoulder belts, donned headphones and yelled to Jorge the pilot, "Go west. Look for a black Range Rover. Hurry!"

The helicopter instantly lifted, banked left, and within moments the twin Pratt & Whitney engines were pushing the craft over the jungle at 150 miles per hour.

Flying 1000 feet above the Bolivariana Highway that leads to Maracaibo, the forest on each side was mostly thorn shrubs and cacti. Saldariagga raised a pair of Bushnell 8x32 Instant Replay Digital Binoculars. Anything he saw through the Bushnells could be digitally photographed. Traffic was moderate on the four-lane artery, and he knew it would thicken the closer they got to Maracaibo.

The traffic passed in both directions. They spotted a dark SUV, a Range Rover, but in British Racing Green, wrong color.

Suddenly he saw the black Range Rover, coming from behind, traveling at a high rate of speed. It pulled in behind the green SUV and slowed to the flow of the traffic. He tapped Jorge's shoulder. "See that black Rover? Get in front of them and land, fast!"

The pilot angled the copter down, accelerated and quickly passed ahead. At a quarter mile in front of the vehicle, the copter descended like a hungry hawk. The green Rover suddenly pulled ahead of the slower traffic and accelerated. One hundred yards ahead, the copter quickly landed in the middle of the road.

Saldariagga jumped out of the craft and raised a Heckler & Koch G36 Kaliber 5.56 x 45 mm. modern assault rifle. It fires single shot, continuous or semi-automatic. He switched to semi-automatic.

The Rover was now 200 feet away. The driver hit the brakes and straight-skidded to a stop. The vehicle changed into reverse, smoked all four tires as it accelerated backwards, executed a textbook 180° turn and blistered the tires again, roaring away. Saldariagga braced the Heckler against his right hip and sprayed the vehicle with six short, continuous bursts. The third burst blew the right rear tire. The Rover jerked to the left, fell onto the driver side and slid to a sparking, screeching stop.

Saldariagga ran toward the wreck. He could see no movement, only smoke from the tires. Crouching by the underside of the Rover, his head near the driver's side, he silently listened and heard nothing. After a few moments, he slowly lifted his head and peered inside the broken driver's window.

He studied the inert passengers: two gray-haired men in hunters' clothes and their quarry, a 400+ lb. wild boar.

At dusk the green Rover pulled up to the rendezvous point on a secluded beach 15 miles north of Maracaibo.

Rey created the tactics which allowed them to easily elude Saldariagga and colleagues. Having a twin black Rover act as a clone initiated the diversion. Rey had even insisted the two hired men pose as hunters and included payment for a large pig. He told the men nothing except they were to avoid capture. He paid half up front and would leave the balance at the hotel front desk.

Fifteen minutes from Montero's estate, they had pulled off the road just inside the forest. Rey quickly taped the paper templates that covered windshield and windows. Using a vegetable-based watercolor paint that could be easily washed off, they spray painted the black Rover a dark forest green.

The three individuals now sat on a log at the beach, looking across the ocean. The girls were asleep in the Rover. Simon Rey broke the silence.

"Mr. Russell, back there, what were you going to do with that knife? They had guns."

Russell rose, went to the vehicle, walked back and stood three feet from Rey. He pointed to a tall tree about 25 feet away, roughly the same distance the Rover had been from the sentries. He hefted three Vipers, and in 2.2 seconds his arm flashed out at the tree. The trio of blades, virtually invisible to the eye, each traveled at 72 mph, rotated 3.5 times and sank into the wood within two inches of each other. He retrieved the knives and sat back on the log, next to Rey. Russell, expressionless, looked at the young man, who slowly shook his head and whispered, "Holy-fucking-shit." Pamela smiled and covered her mouth.

Half an hour later, they heard the seaplane. Dempsey saw the Rover headlights blinking, altered the plane's position and in minutes had the Seawind nosed into the wet sand just a few feet from shore. Dempsey stayed at the controls and kept the engine running. Pamela and Rey helped the two girls out of the Rover. Both were awake but extremely drowsy. They were carried to the plane, followed by Pamela's antique trunk.

Back at the Rover, Russell gave Rey a small black velvet sack.

"Thanks Simon. You did an excellent job. And please thank your hunter friends."

Rey looked into the bag and saw the beautiful sight of Canadian Gold Maple Leafs. One of the world's purest gold coins, each was worth $2,599. There were twenty.

"Mr. Russell, Clayton, this is too much."

"Be generous with your cousin and the other two friends. Lay low, and maybe take a vacation abroad. Return to the states as soon as practical. It's safer for you there."

Eager to get airborne, Russell rocked the nose of the Seawind up and down until it dislodged from the sand. He pushed the craft hard, and as it edged away, waded in chest-deep water and hauled himself up into the plane. Within 90 seconds they were aloft.

Soon they would be home with not one but two kidnapped girls. The story of the Senator's daughter would rapidly become sensationalized by the news media.

Russell and Pam discussed a feature piece she had read in TIME, speculating about the Senator's presidential plans. Thomas A. Cantrell, the senior senator from Louisiana, was a third generation blueblood from The Pelican State. His grandfather started out in oil, and the family had kept the fortune intact. A profile of the wife and only child had reported Julie Cantrell as rebellious, who most likely ran away. The young girl was certainly beautiful. She probably had been photographed and placed into the DBO catalogue without the group realizing her father was a U.S. Senator.

"Eddie, got a phone?"

Russell took the cell from Dempsey, flipped it open and called Sidney Bressler's office number.

He closed his eyes to better concentrate. Darkness and the rhythmic hum of the Seawind were calming.

"Hello."

"Russell here."

"Clay! Where are you?"

"We're somewhere near Jamaica."

"Who are 'we'?"

"The pilot, Pam and Lisa Collins. We found her, Sid, and she seems healthy, at least physically. We also brought out another girl. The other child is, I am almost certain, Senator Thomas Cantrell's daughter. Fortunately, we got them both out."

"Hot-fucking-tamale! Cantrell! A big gun! This blows a gasket! What do you propose doing?"

"Just get the girl to her family. Can you set that up?"

"I'm sure I can. Goddam, this is hot stuff! Then what?"

"Blow a big fucking whistle. I want to blast the lid off of De Blauwe Organisation as quickly as possible. And I want to do so through a live press conference. Will you be the primary face? Do you know anyone at CNN?"

"No. But I occasionally bend an elbow with the guy who started CNN."

"Turner?"

"Robert Edward Turner III. Ted."

"Do you think you can set up a live press conference with CNN?"

"I would be damned surprised if I couldn't."

Saldariagga sat under an umbrella at the Montero compound's main pool. Señor Montero was dead, and he was now in control. Someone would have to pay. And it had to look good. Saldariagga smiled and began to mentally select the members of the new team he would assemble and the competition to eliminate to seal his power base.

Chapter 27

The Return Home

After quickly refueling in Jamaica, the Seawind began the last leg of its air journey. Ten minutes from Florida a soft voice asked, "Where am I?"

Pamela handed Lisa the family photos received from her mom. The child looked at the pictures, then toward Pam. "You will be home very soon, Lisa." The Senator's daughter sat silently and stared.

Over his shoulder, Dempsey yelled, "We'll touchdown at the Shalimar Yacht basin in just a few minutes."

Russell suddenly decided to change the agenda: "Eddie, I had planned to drive back, but would you take us to a smaller strip?"

Eddie tapped his thumb on the yoke, thinking. "Sure. I could probably get you into Dekalb-Peachtree Airport."

"Let's do it." Russell called Bressler's mobile number. "Sid, can you arrange for Sally Collins to meet us at the airport? Dekalb-Peachtree. Also, contact Senator Cantrell and remind him to please keep it quiet until the press conference. Call me back, and let me know the details once you've got them confirmed."

After convincing Ted Turner the story was not a hoax, Turner promised Bressler to have Alexandra Christian available. Bressler then notified the parents. The Senator's voice cracked as he heard the news and assured Bressler he and his wife would take a private jet from Washington D.C. to meet their child upon arrival.

When Bressler and Russell spoke again, the attorney inquired whether anyone else should be at the conference.

"Trent. Get Det. Trent at Atlanta PD. It is about time a good honest cop got some credit. Pam and I have decided it's too risky for us. We want to remain anonymous. This is a powder keg that's about to blow."

Two hours later the plane taxied on the runway at Peachtree-Dekalb Airport.

Pamela watched the group anxiously waiting outside on the tarmac. Tears streamed down Pamela's face as her gaze moved between the children and the three parents. The door opened, children were lifted down and the adults ran toward their daughters. There was not a dry eye in the group.

Brushing aside tears, Russell called his predecessor on the case.

"Trent here."

"This is Russell. Parents and children are reunited."

"I heard you found Lisa. Son of a bitch, Russell! And you picked up another stray, as well. How did you…?"

"I'll tell you everything. For now, though, I thought it might be nice to give the Collins family some protection while they are here. After this press conference, hell will break loose."

"You've got that right, partner. Russell, we've got to talk."

"In a few hours. Catch you later."

"Well, the department ..."

Russell hung up, cutting him off. Fatigue was setting in, quickly. He called Bressler.

"Clay, where are you?"

"I'm leaving the airport with Pam. We just left the kids with their parents. And you?"

"I'm at home, soon headed for the hotel. Are you sure you don't want to go? Tell the world how you two did it?"

"Nope. We're going to watch from a cool, dark place and make contingency plans for retaliation."

At 11:04 a.m. CNN broke away from its regular news feed, announced a Live Breaking News Conference and showed an establishing shot of the ballroom meeting wing at the Four Seasons Hotel in Atlanta. Seven people were seated at a long table. In the center was the chief international correspondent for Cable News Network.

"This is Alexandra Christian, from CNN, live in Atlanta. We are here to announce the discovery of a highly unusual organization, revealed through the recovery of two missing children. On my immediate right are attorney Sidney Bressler and Sally Collins. On my left are United States Senator and Mrs. Thomas A. Cantrell, Atlanta Police Chief David Remington and Atlanta Police detective Robert Trent. The Senator and Mrs. Cantrell's child disappeared some eighteen months ago from Baton Rouge, Louisiana. Another child disappeared just under five months prior from a residential neighborhood in Atlanta. Attempts to locate the girls by law enforcement agencies, local and federal, proved futile until joined with a private agency that prefers to remain anonymous."

The CNN technical crew had been provided a transcript of Christian's briefing and were adroitly synching faces and appropriate supers to close-up shots of the individuals seated at the dais. A tight shot of the CNN newscaster now appeared on home screens. In the background could be seen a duplicate image of Christian on a large TV monitor directly behind the group.

Alexandra Christian had won seven Emmys, two Peabody awards and was a Commander of the Order of the British Empire. She had long been noted for her skill in reporting from dangerous, international places. In her 50's, she was CNN's prime international reporter and rumored to be the highest paid television journalist in the world, universally acknowledged to be at the top of her game.

"This story involves the human trafficking of children for sex. Unlike the usual child prostitution and pornography rings, this one *sells* the kidnapped victim into sexual slavery after suffering from drug induced indoctrination. We believe that the group, De Blauwe Organisation, which is Dutch for The Blue Company, operates from Switzerland. The Cayman Islands is its financial center. This, apparently, is their chief marketing tool." Christian held up the latest copy of De Blauwe Biblio. "I am holding an absolutely incredible publication. It is an ordering catalog which we believe is also available on line, if one possesses the password." Christian opened the magazine, and a camera immediately picked up an extreme close-up, over the shoulder shot of her slowly turning through the pages. Her slim, manicured fingers pointed to the reporter's verbal references. Faces were electronically blurred to protect identities.

For the next half hour, Christian moderated questions directed toward everyone on the dais. Bressler declared that the United States Senate would be encouraged to seek assistance through the International Criminal Tribunal to open an investigation in order to identify, locate and extradite these criminals to the United States for prosecution and for a contemporaneous trial in the International Court in The Hague.

Several questions were directed to Senator Cantrell. One query from an NBC reporter was whether Cantrell would honor the personal $1 million reward for his daughter that was posted on the FBI's website under Kidnapped and Missing Persons Investigation.

"I certainly will, Mr. Williams. My people are making arrangements with Sidney Bressler's office to ensure that proper parties receive the reward."

The reporter continued. "Mr. Bressler, how were these girls found, then returned, and who are your clients?"

Bressler was prepared. "Because it may jeopardize their safety, my clients do not want to reveal themselves at the moment, nor explain how the girls were returned."

From the center of the audience, a thin reporter with a lean face and high forehead stood up. "Mr. Bressler: were these girls 'extradited' legally?"

All eyes were on the attorney. He pushed away his Scotch-filled tea glass and avoided the question, as any respectable lawyer would do. "No comment about that, yet."

Christian knew this was an excellent time to conclude and adjourn. She posted the CNN reward of $1,000,000 to anyone who provided information that lead to the identity and/or capture of the Head of De Blauwe Organisation. "Call this toll-free number we have established at CNN: 1-800-FIND-DBO-NOW. 1-800-346-332-6669."

Pamela and Russell sat alone at the bar of The Highland Tap, and he used the remote to lower the volume of the sole TV in the grotto-like pub. When the reward of a million dollars was revealed, Pamela thought Russell would be pleased to recover the money he had invested. Russell appreciated compensation, but his mind was on the repercussions. He speared the last of his escargot appetizer and chewed in an agitated manner as Pamela ate in silence.

Suddenly, Russell asked to be excused to call Bressler.

"Hey, who's this!" The attorney sounded high, in more ways than one.

"It's Clay. I just saw the show. Quite a display."

"Hot-dam! You've got that right! It's a zoo here! Hang on, let me get to a quieter place." During the muted silence, Russell thought about what he would do next.

"Hey, Clay, I'm in a private phone nook at the Four Seasons. Jesus, I've seen shit hit fans, but nothing like this! And you guys get a million from the good Senator Cantrell with the world as a witness! What now?"

"I'm not sure. You do realize that De Blauwe Organisation will be extremely unhappy?"

"I know that. So what? I'm not scared. What can they do? Fucking A, my man, they'll be *hiding*, not *hunting!*"

"You should be cautious, Sidney. They may come to you looking for Pam and me. Oh, they're going to hide alright. But they'll also be hunting."

Chapter 28

First, A Splash... Then, The Ripples

The live CNN broadcast made an impact that initially stung, momentarily immobilized and then sparked the government into unprecedented action.

The United States Attorney General, a personal friend of Senator Cantrell, made a prime time television announcement, vowing that the Justice Department would prosecute all individuals affiliated with the group known as De Blauwe Organisation.

Piers Morgan ran a 2-hour special on CNN that boasted former directors and lesser officers of the FBI, CIA, United States Secret Service and the four branches of the U.S. military. Morgan's primary theme was how to find the nexus of DBO, root it out and destroy the group. Fascinating suggestions were presented.

The CNN 800 number that Alexandra Christian introduced rang constantly. Every consenting caller was recorded. Those callers who did not identify themselves or grant permission were dropped. Sidney Bressler's office phones were so tied up that he obtained a new unpublished number which he promptly provided to select clients and friends.

411

Three days after the CNN broadcast, Sen. Cantrell's office reached Bressler via phone, at his home, shortly after seven p.m.

"Mr. Sidney Bressler?"

"Yes."

"It's Tom Cantrell. My wife and I want to again thank you for your role in returning our daughter. It's an absolute miracle. We wish to finalize transfer of the reward money. Please provide a wire number, so we can transfer the funds to your trust account on behalf of your clients. To whom do you want to make it payable?"

"My clients wish to remain anonymous, but for tax reporting purposes, please make the check payable to R & W Investigative Services."

"Mr. Bressler, I would like to meet the people who found our daughter."

The attorney suddenly had a flash. "Someday, sir. But in the meantime, perhaps there is a small favor you can do. For a good friend of mine."

––––––––––––––

Russell had prophesized "ripples."

More like waves, Pamela soon concluded.

Two weeks later, she called Sally Collins to inquire how mother and daughter were doing. "Just fine, the doctors said her health appears perfect, but she continues to

412

have nightmares and sees a pediatric clinical psychologist twice a week."

Sally told her Det. Trent, accompanied by a video technician, interviewed Lisa at length about every stage of her disappearance. The child related some details with exceptional clarity, while others had been spotty, which was consistent with all the hypnotic drugs she had been given. Trent left his card with instructions to contact him anytime should Lisa recall anything further. "Funny thing, though," Sally said, "this morning Lisa called him, and the station said he had not reported to work. They haven't been able to locate him for the past day and a half."

Pamela hung up, suddenly very anxious. She called Russell, could not reach him, so then called Bressler and got an earful.

The previous Saturday morning he awoke to find his two boxer dogs dead. Broken necks. The bodies were in his courtyard fountain. Nothing in the house or on the grounds was stolen or disturbed. Written in blood, on the Spanish tiles between the fountain and kitchen doors, was the single word: WHO?

Investigators initially assumed the blood was from one of the dogs, both of whom had shed modest amounts. Upon analysis, however, the blood was determined to be human, O-positive, male. Bressler had immediately hired two security guards from Toronto to live at his residence, indefinitely. He also informed Pamela he had checked with Alexandra Christian. Bressler was told a young female drama student from a nearby college had been hired to deliver a singing telegram to Christian's office and have it videotaped. The girl danced and sang an unidentifiable tune whose lyrics consisted of the word "who" in English and French, the languages in which Christian was fluent. When questioned, the performer produced the e-mail, but it was impossible to trace a source, and the wired funds were from a blind account in the Cayman Islands. The Eastern Onion personnel from the local office did not know who placed the order. When Christian saw a copy of the tape the following day in London, she had no comment.

And then it happened: Pamela came home from work for a lunch break and found the single word painted on her door: WHO?

That day she put her house and office into vacation mode. Her mail from both was forwarded to Bressler's office. She moved into a suite at the Sheraton Midtown, paid cash in advance and used a fictitious name. Neighbors and her office building's security were told she was going on an extended vacation. Russell had insisted that she stay at his place for a month, but she was reluctant to give up her independence. Plus, she preferred the city.

Pamela altered her appearance by dying the blonde hair brunette and wore layered clothing to give the illusion of being 50 pounds heavier. She was thankful it was late October and the weather cooler. She also took a refresher

414

course at the Atlanta Police Department shooting range and started carrying her Smith & Wesson snub nose 38, loaded with hollow points.

In the space of twelve hours, Sidney Bressler received three calls with the identity 'public caller'. The first two calls had simply asked, "Who?" Bressler had hung up without answering. When the third query rang, after hearing the soft, indeterminate gender voice ask "Who?" Bressler replied, "Who, me, the Jew, that's who. Who, may I inquire, the mother-fuck are you? And, if you elaborate a bit more on 'who,' perhaps I can tell you more."

"Who located the girls in Venezuela, and who brought them back? We know the female, but there were at least two men."

Bressler froze for a moment, his mind racing. He swallowed, his throat suddenly dry, and said, "I do not know. Try Christian. Or maybe Cantrell or Trent. I'm just an attorney, and my client, Ms. Collins, does not know. Smart money would bet on Senator Cantrell. He has the financial resources and government contacts to pull it off. By the way, killing my pets and painting signs on my door will accomplish little."

Bressler heard what sounded like downtown traffic. Then the sounds were slightly muffled. Perhaps the caller was conversing with a third person, then a click. The attorney looked at his watch, spoke the time and date into the receiver, tapped off the record button and thought in silence for a few minutes. He needed a safe line, se he drove to a pay phone in the Peachtree Battle shopping center, called CNN, left a message for Alexandra Christian and then he called Russell. Technology had become so sophisticated that it was easy to purchase the equipment to eavesdrop on conversations by cell phone, and he was convinced his house was bugged.

Russell and he agreed the anonymous 'who' messages had probably originated from DBO, with Montero an alternative but less likely source. DBO apparently had enough levels of intelligence, money and international reach to search for Trent and Waters. Russell, presumably, was still unknown to them or as yet, had not been located.

"What are you going to do, Clay?" Bressler asked, "Take a vacation? And what about Pamela? The fucks just found her. I think the only reason they did not just take her out is because they expect her to lead them to you."

"I need to go. I've got a lot of thinking to do."

Bressler hung up, depressed. And ashamed. He had been more worried about himself, especially after what had happened to his dogs.

Suddenly the pay phone rang, which made the attorney jump.

"Hello?"

"Mr. Sidney Bressler, please, this is Alexandra."

"Speaking."

416

"I heard about your dogs, Sidney. I am so sorry. And I am also sorry to give you some other bad news. Detective Trent is dead. His body was found several hours ago in a dumpster located near the Atlanta Police Department."

Before Bressler could reply, she continued. "Sidney, they don't know who killed him, but the body was found in three large plastic trash bags."

"Goddam!"

Christian sighed. "The body was vivisected into twelve pieces, packed four to a bag. An autopsy is being performed. According to the police, Trent was tortured, probably interrogated, before he died. His, uh, tongue was missing. Was he a friend?"

"No." Bressler poured a double Glenmorangie.

"Listen, can you do me a favor? The man and woman who brought the girls back—can you put me in touch with one or both of them?"

"Just a second; what makes you think it was a male and female?"

"The girls told me. I was alone with both of them for several minutes. Well, will you arrange for me to speak with them, preferably in person? You know that I can protect a source. I will go to jail first. Just tell me a number to call, or I'll give you a number for them to call me. I will communicate from a safe phone."

Bressler was hesitant, but it was not his decision. It was for Russell and Pam to choose. He was just the messenger. "What's the number, Alexandra?"

Christian gave him an international number, and added, "That is entirely safe. Please get back to me soon."

The following evening Russell was in the hammock, hands laced behind his head, staring in mid-space as the sun set and streaks of orange, yellow and red crossed the sky. He was worried about Pamela's safety. He also wondered when and how he might be discovered. He believed that anybody living can be found if the motivation is there.

His phone chirped. "Yes?"

"Am I speaking to the friend of a very smart attorney?"

Russell froze for a moment, then slowly sat up. "You are."

The woman's voice said, "Do you know who I am?"

"Yes." Russell had given his number to Bressler, gambling that Christian could be trusted.

The woman continued, "You know about Trent?"

"It's all over the media. He was a straight up guy." Russell jumped at the sound of a limb falling.

"Yes, such a shame. But here's some good news. I have a physical description for you. Of an individual. And an address. You may want to write this down."

Russell began walking to his house. "Go ahead."

Alexandra Christian spoke slowly and without emotion. "Our 800 number has been flooded. Thousands upon thousands. I asked to only be presented with the recorded calls that made 'the short list,' that is, calls that my head producer thought were definitely worthy of action. She selected seven. Six were certainly intriguing, but one was, to me, head and shoulders above all.

"It was from a man who spoke with a German accent. He said he was calling from a ship. He is apparently a disgruntled employee; said he had recently been dismissed from a job he held for three years where he was a valet to the man he claims ran the De Blauwe Organisation. He rambled somewhat and called his employer 'hedonistic pig' for firing him because his bath water was too warm. Although unlikely, this informant claims he did not know his employer's name. However, he swore the man we are searching for is about 65, short in stature and corpulent. He provided his employer's height and weight in metric terms. If true, Clayton, you are looking for someone who lives in an isolated home in the Swiss Alps. Piz Bernina, in the Eastern Alps on the Italian Swiss border. It is on the northern slope. The highest large residence, with a maroon colored roof."

"Why do you think this guy is the true bill?" Russell asked.

"Because he began to cry and wanted assurance that the reward would go to his family. The operator asked why

419

and was told: 'Because they will find me and kill me.' I've been a reporter for a long time, and my gut tells me he is the real thing."

Russell closed his eyes. He too felt that the tip was golden. This was the head of the snake that is De Blauwe Organisation. "I cannot thank you enough for that information. What do I owe you?"

Alexandra Christian laughed. "Oh, I don't know. I would like an interview someday in the not too distant future."

"That can be arranged. Someday."

"Good luck."

Russell hung up and called Manny Ruez. "I have another job for you. Weather's a bit different than that of the jungle. Are you open?"

"Sure."

"You'll need your passport again."

At dawn the following morning, Bressler called Russell. He, too, was worried about Pamela. Neither man had heard from her. Bressler had received a packet of mail, so he knew she had filed a forwarding address with the post office to his place of business.

"Clayton, do you think Trent talked before he died?"

"Sid, I believe he certainly said something, until they removed his tongue. The autopsy revealed his body was mutilated post-mortem. He died of a gunshot wound to the head."

"Are you going to stay at home?"

"Yes. And if you hear from Pam, tell her to get her ass out here, pronto. We can protect each other. There is no reason for her to be so independently stupid."

"Aren't you afraid someone might come up there? Someone who got information from Trent?"

"I'm concerned, but not going anywhere. I'm as safe here as anywhere."

"Clay, Senator Cantrell called me this morning. He wants to know if you would like some protection, gratis, from our government." Bressler was not about to tell his friend that he had suggested the senator offer Russell bodyguards.

After a few seconds of silence, Russell said, "That offer is appreciated and accepted. Can he send one person, currently working or recently in retirement?"

"From?" Bressler asked.

"The United States Secret Service."

Six hours later, Bressler followed up.

"Senator Cantrell is sending Special Agent Kevin Youngblood. I was told he is 29, with great credentials and flattering recommendations. Kevin will be arriving in Atlanta four hours from now. I'll drive him up. I also heard from Pam. She said to tell you she would call."

421

"That's it? She will call?"

"Yes, Clay. She'll call. I cannot reason with her any more than I can convince you when you both make foolish decisions. I'll see you tonight with Agent Youngblood." Before his friend could respond, Bressler hung up.

Three days later, Russell was finishing an early morning swim, floating on his back, when he saw the plane overhead. As he flipped over, he could see Pamela pacing impatiently on the dock. He'd convinced her to hide out at his place, but he knew she wouldn't stay much longer. Too restless!

The small, bright yellow airplane slowly flew above about two hundred yards. This was the third time in as many days that Pam had seen the plane fly around Russell's part of Lake Rayton. Today, the craft circled several times. The plane was too far up to distinguish any human silhouettes. After a third circle, the plane disappeared over the mountains.

Pamela Waters looked over at Agent Youngblood. He'd commented on the aircraft before and nodded at it. A lone figure flew the plane. He appeared to be holding a camera.

Winston beat Russell to the dock and vigorously shook water over Pam as his master stepped into a pair of worn black moccasins. Man and dog walked up the thin trail to home, with Pamela a few steps behind and Special

Agent Youngblood slowly following as he watched the sky.

Russell and Youngblood sat in the two Adirondack chairs while Pam went inside for coffee. The agent's attire was an interesting camouflage jumpsuit that blended in very well with the browns, greens and black shadows of the woods. Winston became intrigued with the young agent from the Secret Service as he had positioned himself in trees, behind logs and in one amazing nest he had quickly made: a pile of dead deciduous leaves and pine straw, with only his eyes and nose visible, making him virtually unseen. Russell had commented that these precautions seemed a bit overboard, but Youngblood disagreed. While hidden he was becoming accustomed to the natural sights, sounds and animals of the area. Youngblood also slept outdoors each night with his weapon and Winston accompanying him. Youngblood was 6' 3" and very fit, with lean muscle. He had light red hair cut short, bright green eyes and very white freckled skin. He either did not like sunshine or did not take it well. He spoke softly, although he seldom talked at all, yet was always extremely polite. In the few conversations they had, Russell concluded he was also an extremely intellectual young man.

"I appreciate what you are doing, Kevin, but after thinking about this, I do not see how your being here would make a difference if someone, or a group, was determined to kill Pam and me."

Youngblood replied, "You may be surprised, sir."

423

"Yeah, maybe, but this cannot go on indefinitely. Let's give it a few more days, and end your tour here. OK?"

"Certainly. I have been told to do what you say, sir."

Russell was getting weary of being called sir. "Good. Three days it's over and you'll receive very high references from me to whomever you wish. Done?"

"Yes. Done in three days, sir." Youngblood raised the binoculars and began to pan across, up and down the lake and distant mountains. Pam sat nearly silently sipping her coffee. Now what? The waiting was unbearable.

At 1:00 p.m. Pamela was seated at a corner inside table at South City Kitchen restaurant in midtown. She ordered, then rose and made her way to the pay phone just inside the entrance. The photographer answered.

"This is Pamela Waters. Are you packed and ready?"

"Good to go."

"There's a small package of Omaha Steaks in your kitchen freezer."

"Uh, no there's not."

"Yes there is. Believe me."

"Hold on." Pam heard a few seconds of the man walking, some minor clatter, then, "What the fuck! How in the hell did you … "

"No meat there. Check it out."

Manny Ruez quickly tore open the fruitcake-size package, studied the contents for half a minute and asked, "So, go to that coordinate, lay low in the snow, and get some long lens photos of the person described. Right?"

"Correct."

"I can do that. With white snow camouflage. I've been to that country, too, you know."

That afternoon, Pamela asked Russell if she could see his copy of De Blauwe Biblio. Tomorrow Bressler was coming to pick up the catalog and personally hand it over to a duo from the State Department who were flying in from Washington. They were scheduled to meet the attorney at his office, secure the publication and take it back to D.C. for analysis. When Russell asked why she wished to see the catalog another time, she replied she just wanted to check it out. She would probably never see anything like that again.

Russell complied, retrieving the catalog from his safe.

Pamela was honored that he allowed her to watch him open the most amazing safe she had ever seen. Smiling, he told her exactly where to sit on the large, deep blue leather sofa. She crossed her legs and was impatiently drumming fingers on a knee, when she saw him pick up the kitchen phone and dial a very long number.

She was just about to ask what he was doing when the 4 by 6 foot, gray and white block of marble that served as a coffee table made a strange noise. She froze and stared at the table. Though the top of the marble boulder was flat and highly polished, the four sides were rough and unfinished. On the side closest to her, a section of marble the size of a medium, flat desk drawer slowly opened one foot and stopped. Inside were various documents. On the top left was Russell's passport. On the right was De Blauwe Biblio. She gingerly picked it up, Russell tapped three phone numbers, and the drawer slowly closed. Pretty fancy, she had to admit. And she could not fault his logic. It was definitely something someone could not easily remove, assuming a thief knew what it was. He informed her that there were two other drawers beside the document compartment.

Two hours later, after studying the catalog over and over in great detail, she remained fascinated. All of those people, most photographed secretly, but all, certainly, did not know where their likenesses were destined. Pamela came to the last page. She studied the address:

De Blauwe Organisation
P.O. Box 32216
Zurich, Switzerland
DBO@merchandise.com

She had been to the Internet site multiple times. She'd opened the blog and knew it was useless. She could not penetrate the blind address. Those scams were used routinely to steal identities and money. *But every company has a 'net home.*

Pamela went to the large guest bedroom, opened her purse and removed the ten power triplet loupe, a professional jeweler's magnifying tool. She flopped back on the sofa, picked up the catalog and put the compact magnifier over the face of Jewel #79947. The powerful lens, one inch from the image, showed amazing detail on the face of Lisa Collins.

Pamela tapped the loupe on the magazine. A bright sun ray suddenly lit up the large teak deck. She walked outside to get a look in the better light. Squinting, she sat down on the wide deck rail bench, placed the catalog on her knees and positioned the loupe over the address:

De Blauwe Organisation
P.O. Box 32216
Zurich, Switzerland
DBO@merchandise.com

She held the magazine up so that it blocked the sun. She put the loupe back over the address, moved it down below and saw, very faintly, the pale, almost invisible watermark:

www.newblueheaven.org

Pamela stared at the watermark as the sun blazed on the web address. She closed her eyes and dropped the loupe and catalog on the deck. She would never forget those words. Goose bumps crept along her neck and arms. She stiffly walked back inside the great room and to the corner desk by Russell's immense bookcase and sat in the black mesh office chair. He had been reading newspapers online, and the computer was hibernating. She wiggled the cordless mouse, the screen came alive and she immediately went to the MetaCrawler home page. She typed in the watermark: www.newblueheaven.org. She hit *Enter*, and within seconds the first image, a man's hands on a catalog, appeared with the opening words.

"Welcome to the new cyber world of De Blauwe Biblio. My name is Phillip, and you will soon be in a new, blue heaven."

Pamela, shocked and excited, shouted over her shoulder, "Clay, there's something here you should see! Now, please!"

As Henri Bergmann strode into the plush boardroom of De Blauwe Organisation, all eyes were focused on their chairman. They scrutinized his face and body for any clues that would reflect his mood, but the countenance, as usual, was unrevealing.

"As you can see," he began, "one of our colleagues is not present. Several days ago, he informed me of his reluctance to gather here so soon after our much trumpeted introduction to the public. He wished to retire from the board and used the hackneyed cliché 'waiting until the dust settles.' Well, this Board member will have to wait no more, because the dust has settled—the dust of his human remains. Alas, poor Phillip, we knew his wonderful mind so well. He died yesterday morning in an automobile accident

428

and was cremated last night. His cremains are in the sugar bowl at the sideboard in this room. Feel free to add a spoonful of Phillip to your coffee or pocket."

Remarkably, the entire board remained poker faced about the morbid news of their colleague.

Avoiding eye contact Bergmann trained his gaze to a point very high on the opposite wall. "Now that our group is planetary news, we will need to disband and reassemble in the future. We have indentified the two primary individuals involved in the capture of our Jewels and murder of a valued customer. Once they are punished and all connections to us severed, I will contact you."

It had taken a long time, but Mr. Krieg had identified the detective. Krieg sent copies of the photos he took of Russell to police departments in the sixty most populous U.S. cities. A St. Louis, Missouri city cop provided the name. Phone calls to the various Sheriff's departments throughout the State of Georgia finally revealed someone that could provide Russell's home address. A deputy in Rabun County knew him and provided the information after receiving $1,000 in cash, delivered overnight in a lead lined Bible. Krieg verified Russell's presence after he took photos of the man sitting on his dock. The female described by Montero's guard was photographed with him.

The minimal movements of the DBO board members immediately ceased. The room was completely silent, waiting for Bergmann to reveal more.

"It is a man and his female companion. Both are Americans. Currently, we have confirmed where they are hiding." Bergmann said. "The couple is in the mountains in the northern portion of the State of Georgia." Bergmann slowly took another drink from his goblet. He was furious by the audacity and luck of the two American detectives, yet determined not to display his anger. He wished to project an air of calm.

"Some of our enemies must be eradicated," Bergmann continued. "I will erase this man and woman. But not yet. They may be under surveillance and/or protection, so while we know where they are, we must ensure that they are not bait to lure us in. We must be patient and wait until these two interlopers are the most vulnerable to strike. In order to protect ourselves, I have decided that all Catchers we have employed within the past two years must be erased. It is a pity but necessary. This task has already been assigned and is in progress.

"Let me tell you my opinion of what has happened. When I created De Blauwe Organisation, I assembled the machine with as few parts as possible. There was a dual reason for that: profitability and stealth".

"Profitability. We all want the highest return on investment for our time. And we have achieved that. What is the inventory of DBO? It is in this room. The entire inventory. No warehouses, no trucks, no factories, not even a postal box. You are the inventory. Your brains. When we leave here, the inventory of DBO goes down in the elevator. Now, how many business organizations can boast that? The industry that most resembles ours, in first-world countries, are drug cartels. They have to transport drugs, in various pipelines. Drug cartels have to deal with extremely dangerous people. Drug cartels are known entities, whose makeup and movements are, basically, familiar to law enforcement agencies. The two main things we have in common with drug cartels are the fact that we ship an item…which we don't have to manufacture, I might add…and we need people to transport our product. In the drug trade, such people are called Mules. In our trade, they are called Catchers. If a Mule gets caught with, say, heroin, that Mule is in serious trouble. If a Catcher gets caught with a child, they can talk their way out of it. We have a 100% success rate in that area—the area of being caught. How many drug cartels come close to that?"

"Stealth. We, the Board, convene on no set schedule, in a variety of places. We, the Board, do not socialize with each other. Ever. I know this for a fact. Our Catchers are freelance, who I hire via blind communications. The same goes for our Presenters, along with Mr. Krieg, whose real name even I am not sure."

"Profitability and stealth. We have both, in spades. The only Achilles Heel we have is a temporary one, this blast of publicity. CNN. Fuck. Sensational news that is like a snowman: it shall melt. DBO is front page news. It

431

will soon be page two. Then it will be footnotes in minor media. Other sensational news will outshine ours. A young motion picture celebrity will die."

With a nod to the servant standing nearby, envelopes were handed to each member. "Pardon the oxymoron, but in those envelopes, are your 'temporary final honorarium.' They are temporary in the sense that I intend not to disband De Blauwe Organisation, not to maim it, but to give DBO a brief and luxurious vacation. In those envelopes you will find your largest dividend to date. De Blauwe Organisation shall regroup, re-commence operations and, undoubtedly, be more successful than ever. Think of De Blauwe Organisation as a phoenix that has merely been scorched. This blue bird—Blau bird, if you will—shall quietly heal and soon fly very high indeed. It has been a unique and extraordinary experience to have worked with you." Bergmann rose to leave.

Two of the DBO board members began to applaud. The remainder quickly joined in, clapping politely. Without comment, gesture or looking back, Henri Bergmann slowly walked toward his private door. As the king left his peasants, he began softly cursing to himself. Among Bergmann's many foibles, the one he least liked and most tried to hide, was coprolalia, the most aberrant type of Tourette syndrome.

Chapter 29

Retiring the Catchers

Within five weeks of the press conference, five of the six Catchers died, all differently: struck by an automobile with a driver that left the scene, a freakish fall down a short flight of stairs, drowning in a bathtub, cardiac arrest from a Taser and suicide from a handgun. One Catcher eliminated per week. Fionna Marceau was the last to remain.

She had suspected that pig Bergmann would want to eliminate any dispensable person who may lead back to him. Such a coward! She'd heard Phillip was also on the chopping block. Jealousy must be the motive for his killing. Bergmann would regret that decision. Lousy in bed, but Phillip was brilliant and creative. Such a loss.

Fionna had moved. Her residence was now the River Street Inn, 124 E. Bay Street in Savannah, Georgia. She selected the Inn because it was discreet, in an eclectic part of a city neither too large nor small and overlooked the Savannah River. Within walking distance of many things that could keep her body, mind and emotions satiated, it was also afflicted by boring, obese, loud tourists that abound everywhere in America where there is a nearby body of water and a McDonald's. But, like Charleston, New Orleans and other Southern seaport cities, Savannah had enough healthy, salacious locals and tourists to keep her mind and body filled as much as she wished. The Inn took up an entire city block and was built in 1817 as part of the city's Cotton Exchange. None of the Inn's 86 rooms are alike, and Fionna's second floor quarters had a king four poster bed, thick, cool brick walls and tall ceilings.

For two evenings she had amused herself with a 20-year-old restaurant server named Beau who adequately serviced the Catcher in her room. But tonight she wished to be alone. She walked onto her balcony and observed the charcoal grey Camry that had been parked along the wharf earlier this morning. She noticed when she was on a morning work-out, running. Fionna lit a cigar and continued to watch the river traffic but focused on that car. She spent a few minutes preparing her bed and then tied her hair into a ponytail, twisted it into a bun and pulled a black shower cap tightly onto her head. She wore black: a sweat suit, running shoes and leather gloves. Then she turned off the light to sleep.

At 2:14 a.m., a man in the hall removed the purchased pass key, which was coated with DuPont TFL 50 Dry Teflon lubricant, slipped it into the lock and soundlessly began to open the door. He had experimented earlier in the day to ensure a silent entry. Dressed in expensive slacks and long sleeve turtleneck shirt, he had splashed George Dickel bourbon on his clothes should someone question him as he entered the wrong room. He would pretend intoxication. As he slowly pushed the door open, he could hear the sounds of the street and the river. The balcony door was open, which was good. It would help mask the sounds.

He slowly closed the door behind him and waited for two full minutes, to let his eyes and other senses adjust to the room. His quarry was softly snoring. He began to distinguish the light blue and gray shapes. The chair and table beside the balcony. The TV. The large four-poster bed with a lone figure under the covers. The room smelled of cigar smoke, a trademark of his target. A passing convertible of laughing people began to recede in the distance.

He went to the bed and could now make out her long hair fanned across the pillow. The man removed a four inch Swiss army knife from his pocket, opened the large blade and as he slowly pulled back the sheet, the rhythmic snoring continued. Suddenly he froze, and adrenalin raced into his bloodstream.

The hair covered a very large cantaloupe and small audio recorder.

He felt movement behind him which galvanized the man into a spasmodic rush toward the balcony. As he raced across the oak wood floor, Fionna quickly grabbed him in a headlock and twisted in an expert maneuver that propelled both bodies out onto the balcony. She directed his head toward the cast iron railing and smashed it into the top, instantly putting him into a stunned level of semiconsciousness. She had the advantage of surprise against the powerful and stout man. Just seconds after the intruder entered the room, a strong, black, cotton thread, attached to the inner door handle and looped over Fionna's left ear had instantly roused her from the makeshift bed in the nearby closet.

Both bodies dropped four feet to the concrete balcony floor. She instantly stood to grasp his legs and drag the man back inside. Holding a knife at his neck, she smiled down on the moaning man and recognized the identity of her would be assassin. Fionna pulled a 21″ black, high carbon steel ASP baton from the bedside drawer and began to pelt the intruder with a series of blows. Four to the left thigh, stopping only as she saw bone protrude from the skin. Then a series to the left shoulder, pausing after she heard the sound of the upper scapula cracking. Wait for a few seconds. Good, he is rolling over, NOW, smash the right foot. Only one blow to hear metatarsal bones break. In excruciating pain and "softened up," as she liked to think of the pre-interrogation drill, Fionna pulled the groaning, semi-conscious man to her bathroom and placed him in the tub, closed the bathroom door, soundproofed the base with wet towels and flipped on the lights.

"What the hell!" Fionna hiss-whispered. "If it isn't Luke! So Bergmann sends his own board member to do dirty work. Well, before you pass out, limp dick Luke, you will tell me where I can find that fat bastard."

Fionna resisted the impulse to put Luke out of his pain, permanently, as it would be extremely difficult to dispose of the body. Better to grab her things and leave, calling 911 on the way out. Luke would have difficulty explaining why he was in her room in such condition. His main goal would be to check himself out of any medical facility at the first opportunity, leaving the police with an unsolved criminal investigation.

In the meantime she needed to locate Luke's accomplice. It took very little persuasion to convince Luke to identify the other man she had seen him with in the automobile. Not surprisingly, it was that attorney, Cogburn, No. 8. After Luke lost consciousness, she went to the balcony, but the Camry was not in sight. A cursory search of the Inn parking lot proved unsuccessful.

Cowards! All of them are loathsome cowards! And so they hire female Catchers to perform tasks they deem too risky.

Chapter 30

Dark Waters

Henri Bergmann did not sit alone in his spacious great room.

He had hired armed professional guards to provide twenty-four hour security around the exterior of the mountain home, and another guard was to be stationed in his presence at all times. Bergmann even required a man to stand in the bathroom while shaving, showering and eliminating, much to the guard's disgust.

Any new visitor to the room would initially look at the spectacular view: three sides of the two-tiered centerpiece in his alpine home were glass, from floor to ceiling. Support at the three corners of the 15-foot high walls was provided by 18-inch diameter acrylic columns. Automatic shutters closed in sequence, as needed, to keep out the cold. Bergmann's wait staff kept the glass and columns meticulously clean, inside and out, which provided the illusion of an open-air patio and not merely a glassed room. Sunlight brilliantly illuminated the nearby Alps with fresh snow from the previous three days. But the view no longer interested Bergmann. He was leaving, permanently. What did interest him was his new body.

Bergmann looked at his short stubby fingers and the backs of his hands. They were unscarred and unremarkable. Then he turned them over. The appearance here, too, was commonplace, but ten features were particularly uncommon. Over a period of three months, his fingerprints had been expertly altered and, according to the Viennese surgeons, were unlike those of anyone else to date archived in the world's fingerprint databases. The technology utilized was micro lasers to retool the friction ridges on each fingertip. Bergmann was proud of his new "touch." And he was even more proud of his fresh, astounding countenance.

He walked over to the large bar at the refreshment and entertainment island in the center of the room, careful to avoid sight of his face in the mirror. Selecting a heavy crystal highball glass, he filled it half way with grape-size ice cubes custom carved from glaciers. He reached for a bottle of Xellent Swiss vodka, poured three fingers into the glass and topped it off with an equal measure of Blue Curacao. Raising the glass, Bergmann stirred it with a thin, gold bar spoon and paused for a few seconds, staring at the cocktail. As the pudgy man drank deeply, consuming half the glass, he slowly turned and stared in the mirror at his new face.

Before, Henri Bergman had jet black hair with a receding hairline, combed straight back, flat pale face, a bit too fat, and very dark eyes. Through cosmetic surgery, most of the fatty tissue had been removed, along with facial lines.

439

In addition to the slimmer face, his nose had been entirely reconstructed. No longer was it small and plump. When he admired his profile from the side, his nose was prominent with a slight hook at the tip; Greek would be a stranger's first impression. He was most pleased with the expertly-dyed platinum hair with darker lowlights. Implants had filled the hairline, and he sported a full head of beautiful bright silver hair. Vainly, he had a jejunectomy to reduce weight, and in a mere few weeks was already thirty pounds lighter.

Bergmann spent his recuperative time on the French Riviera and was tanned a deep bronze. With the aid of contact lens, his eyes were now bright blue. He smiled at the new image. It hurt his facial muscles to do so, both from the newly tightened skin and because he had rarely smiled.

In a few days, the helicopter would ferry him to Geneva, then the private jet to his new home on a small Grecian Island he had recently purchased. The remaining funds had been transferred from Switzerland to another Cayman account. Despite the fact that his vocation was temporarily in abeyance, he would enjoy the hiatus with fleshy diversions in the nighttime and ponder his future by day.

Those possessions Bergmann considered most precious had been shipped ahead. He was leaving much of his furniture. He walked over to the sofa, sat where he could easily see himself in the mirror and smiled again, feeling immensely proud of himself, as he was about to embark on a new chapter in his life.

Glancing at the mail on his coffee table, the only piece of mild interest on the stack of letters was a rather large, flat, DHL express package. Bergmann set aside the drink, picked up the package and cut it open. He pulled out a number of large color photographs and used a large, brass magnifying glass to study the photo sheets more closely.

There's that Clayton Russell, swimming, and the woman, Pamela Waters, on the dock. Bergmann used a small penknife to jab Russell's body in each of the shots, cursing him with each thrust.

Two hundred fifty yards away, on the nearest Alp, several climbers were scaling the snow-covered mountain. Three of the figures wore bright, neon colored clothes. The fourth figure, dressed in white, was several yards away from the trio and had stopped climbing. He raised a Nikon 35mm SLR camera, also shrouded in white, focused on his subject seated in the large armchair and, balancing the long lens on a knee, began to take a series of shots. The subject was perfectly positioned, and the shooter could clearly see the photo sheet the man was poking with the point of some tool.

The photographer panned the residence and located two guards positioned near the house. He could not confirm who may be accompanying the subject inside but would surmise that the odd, somewhat squat man was not alone. For almost an hour the photographer chronicled his subject

441

and the residence. Then he packed his photo gear, opened a large flap pocket on his parka, removed a silver hip flask with *MR* engraved on the side and took a deep drink of brandy.

"Sir, would you still like me to leave in two days?"

"Yes Kevin. I'm sure Treasury has some much more interesting assignments than this bird-watching."

Youngblood lowered his binoculars and quietly said, "I doubt it, sir." The agent continued in an unemotional whisper, "By the way, across your cove there are two men, probably foreign, in a fishing boat. They have been in and around the cove since just after dawn. One man is fishing. The other man is pretending to fish."

Russell stood and walked toward the glass doors. Youngblood handed him the binoculars.

He quickly spotted the modest fishing boat, about 18 feet long. It was anchored at the far end of the cove, 300 yards from Russell's dock. Two men sat on the twin, elevated swivel chairs. One man wore khaki, the other camouflage and both had on hats and sunglasses that hid most of their faces.

"You said one man is pretending to fish. Yet they're both holding poles?"

"The bow man occasionally casts. Stern man has not casted once but looks around with his binoculars. He has also taken photographs, 360 degrees."

Russell focused in tighter on the men, looking for clues. "What makes you think they're foreign?"

"Have you ever seen anyone around here wear a ski cap on the water, especially in this weather, fishing?"

"So, what do you recommend Kevin?"

"I've had a Department of Natural Resources law enforcement boat patrolling this section of the lake since I arrived. They're a mile away, and I can request they check out these anglers."

Russell looked at Youngblood with new respect. "Do it."

The agent pulled out a cell phone, scrolled down to a number, pressed it and within seconds was talking. He closed his phone. "In the week I've been here, sir, this is the only suspicious thing I have seen. It may be nothing, but..."

Russell interrupted, "Kevin, please cruise out to meet the DNR people."

Russell handed him keys to the runabout, and the younger man jumped off the deck and began trotting down to the lake. Minutes before, Russell had been bored. Now the day was more interesting. Pam should be here for this. She's missing the action.

From the dock, Russell heard the healthy rumble as Youngblood started the Larson runabout. He also heard peaceful sounds of the morning woods, and, in the distance, the quiet drone of the rangers' 22-foot Cobalt with its 300 hp Mercruiser, now approaching the two strange fishermen.

Russell focused the binoculars on the two rangers—they wore baseball caps, sunglasses and serious expressions. Both appeared to be thirty-something, slim, with dark hair showing under the caps. The Cobalt stopped in the water about 50 feet from the fishing boat. The ranger riding shotgun, left front seat, spoke through a small bullhorn. The two fishermen slowly laid down the poles, put hands behind their heads and stood up in the boat. The driving officer heard Youngblood approaching from about 90 yards away and turned his head toward the Larson.

Too many people and guns were converging, so Russell decided to get closer. He set aside the binoculars, jumped off the four deck steps and hit the ground running. Winston leapt off the porch, scratched twice in the dirt and soon began to tear ahead. Russell jogged through the woods and slowed to a walk when he emerged from the shadows near the gangplank of his dock. Winston sat behind, just inside the tree line, observing. Russell drew the Glock but held it behind his back.

Suddenly, in unison, the two fishermen whipped their caps toward the faces of the officers, and three guns roared. The ranger with the megaphone was knocked up, off his feet, as his head exploded. The officer at the wheel dropped down out of sight, between the seats, either ducking or felled. The third gun was from Kevin Youngblood, now about 40 yards from the two boats. The agent had pulled back the speed of the Larson, stood up, both elbows braced on the windshield frame and shot like Hawkeye. The fisherman on the left caught a bullet in the sternum, which made him drop down in the seat and slump forward. The fisherman on the right still had his weapon trained on the rangers. He must have suddenly realized what happened to his companion. He turned and saw Russell's boat but was too late: Youngblood's SIG-Sauer roared three times, and the man's torso was rocked twice, then his lower jaw erupted in a crimson spray. The body turned 90° to the right, exposing his back, and two more Youngblood shots hit the thoracic and lumbar areas of the man's spine. The man spun in a half forward flip over the side and into the lake. It was classic, law enforcement shooting: two to the torso, then one to the head. The last two in the back came from Youngblood's adrenaline.

Russell kept both hands on the Glock. Had the dead fishermen been a point team? Were others in the woods? Damn good shooting from Youngblood! Echoes faded off the blue-green mountains. Russell gave a sharp wolf whistle, which turned Youngblood's head. Russell waved, and the agent lifted a hand. He could see Youngblood yelling something to the surviving ranger, who had risen, then slowly sat onto a seat and held his face in both hands. Youngblood appeared to be talking on his cell phone. Soon, three other Cobalts filled with rangers came to the scene.

Photographs were taken, bodies were covered with small yellow tarps and the fishing boat secured behind one of the Cobalts. Two rangers boarded the boat with their dead colleague and the surviving one. Three law enforcement boats slowly motored away. Youngblood drove Russell's boat at a no wake speed back to the dock. The fourth Cobalt with two rangers followed close behind.

Russell helped Youngblood tie up the boat. The rangers' boat was a half minute from the dock when Russell advised Youngblood, "I'm going to the house." Russell walked up the bank, to just inside the woods. He looked through the trees, at the house. He closed his eyes and listened. He smelled the air. He detected nothing out of the ordinary. The agent talked briefly to the DNR men, who then fired up their boat and sped away.

Youngblood began to walk up the trail. He was poker-faced. The two men looked at each other for a few seconds and said nothing. Russell continued walking to the house, keeping his senses fine-tuned. Winston raced ahead. Halfway up the hill, Russell looked back over his shoulder at Youngblood. The agent was 20 feet behind, his gun out, held in both hands. The man was nimbly walking up the trail backwards, covering their rear. He was feeling the way along the rough trail with his toes, staying well-balanced in a slight crouch. He walked indian-style, toe-heel. What other talents did the agent have?

"Sir, I'm going to spend a few minutes to scope the perimeter of the dwelling. Why don't Winston and you do the same inside? Other visitors could be close."

"Good idea."

Thirty minutes later, both men were sitting on the deck when Pamela arrived. She knew something serious had occurred in her absence by the strained greeting followed with pregnant silence. Once Russell briefed her, she knew they could no longer rely on seclusion for protection.

Russell suggested, "Tomorrow, let's all leave. Kevin, you take off around noon, Pamela and I will follow soon after."

"That's fine with me, sir, but I would prefer to leave with you two. That way, I would consider my assignment completed."

"Very well. Let's all leave at noon. Kevin, can you throw a knife?"

"No. Why? Can you?"

"Ha!" Pamela barked, not able to resist comment. "Is the sky blue?"

Russell ignored her remark. "Yes Kevin." He wanted to show this Treasury Agent he could do a couple of things well. "Would you like to learn the basics?"

Youngblood pondered for a moment. "Sure. Why not?"

Russell rose, went into the house and returned with eight Viper I Black Bevel 14-ounce knives and eight of the smaller Viper IIIs, half the weight.

"This way." Russell led Youngblood out to the practicing tree. He handed the Vipers to the agent, went under the deck, rolled out the large, round wooden target board, leaned it against the tree, picked up four big Vipers and walked fifteen paces away. "Wound, wound, fatal, fatal."

Russell flipped four overhand, no-spin throws in just over three seconds. The blades hit the painted man's left thigh, left bicep, socket of the throat and heart.

Chapter 31

Crimson Waves

At dawn, Winston woke and began his usual morning patrol. The Airedale silently moved toward the steps. In a corner of the deck, Kevin Youngblood sat motionless on a chair. He wore the camouflage suit and had the SIG-Sauer on his lap. The agent called Winston and gave a wave. The Airedale's answer was a double tail wag without breaking stride.

Winston padded around the immediate perimeter of the house. He stopped frequently, in a point, to listen and smell. He would freeze for several seconds until he could identify the sounds and odors. Sometimes birds. Sometimes squirrels. Occasionally deer. Satisfied with the usual sounds and scents around the house, the dog circled back to the lake side of the large A-frame. As he passed the deck, he looked and saw that the visitor was now standing, focused on Lake Rayton.

Winston slowly worked his way down to the lake. A half mile distant he could see a lone boat. Usually anything that far away would not disturb the Airedale. But the boat came closer.

Winston kept his gaze on the boat, which was getting bigger. Then, gradually, he moved backwards, across the grass, keeping his eyes locked on the vessel. Now in the trees, out of sight, he turned and ran. In half a minute, he was at the house. Youngblood quickly stood up. Winston ignored him and buried his large snout into the ivy on the north side of the large A-frame, found the tennis ball on a wire and yanked it twice.

Russell had been asleep but fully dressed. He reached over to wake Pam, but her side of the bed was empty. He filled his pockets from the drawer in the bedside table and tightened the shoelaces of the black British Knights. He attached two of the custom leather sheathes to his body, one in sight and one hidden.

Russell walked out onto the deck to Pam, standing with a hot mug of coffee. On the railing in front of her was the .38 Smith revolver. Youngblood sighted through the large binoculars. "This place is on a roll: another odd boat. Six people, probably all men, pretending to fish. Coming this way, slowly. Trolling motor."

Russell took the binoculars and zeroed in. Half a dozen silhouettes, with faces not yet discernable. He lowered the glasses, took a sip of Pam's coffee, then focused again on the boat, faces now visible. At the stern, one hand on the trolling motor, was Mr. Krieg, mysterious delivery man of the DBO catalog. Krieg looked quite calm. Russell looked at the other five faces. All men, all very serious, none overweight, very thick necks. Krieg was quite thin. He was the conductor of this muscle orchestra. Russell lowered the binoculars. "What do you think, Kevin?"

"We can leave and call the authorities on the way out or stay and fight. I'll back your decision."

Russell again trained the binoculars on the boat. These men were pros, mercenaries. Yesterday's duo was probably freelance talent; local yokels hired by DBO, who did not know Russell's capabilities and were not aware that an ace from The United States Secret Service was here as backup. Yesterday was the B team, so this most certainly was an A team. It struck Russell curious that they would approach the same way? Perhaps they thought that nobody would dare repeat the prior day's fiasco. Plus, the lake may not be their only avenue of attack. They could also have talent in the woods. DBO could be here to kill or to extricate, to take one or all out, for interrogation. Bergmann and company like to use helicopters. Whatever the scenario, yesterday was softball and now it's hardball.

Russell looked at Pam. She was poker faced but gripping the mug with both hands. Her knuckles were white. Agent Youngblood stood focused and relaxed, confident of his abilities. Winston was a statue, frozen, total attention on the boat. Pam still had a gunshot wound, but regardless of that, she was inexperienced with serious physical encounters. Were it just Youngblood, Winston, and he, Russell would opt to stay and dance. He had some

451

very nasty items, indeed, cached in his home and throughout the woods that could wreak havoc on several boatloads of assholes, especially with a pro like Youngblood assisting. But Pam was here and Winston was getting older. Maybe it was just he who was getting older? Russell made up his mind. "Let's go, guys. We'll call the sheriff from my car."

Within a minute they were in the big convertible, top down, slowly pulling away from the house. In the rear seat, agent and animal kept their eyes on the lake until it shrank from view.

Bergmann clapped shut his cell phone and threw it across the room. "Scheisse!"

The CEO of De Blauwe Organisation stepped outside on his balcony, comforted by the newly hired guards. He could not reach Cogburn or Paluzzia, nor had they called. The first cloud of doubt formed on Bergmann's mind. True, he was now being hunted, courtesy of that pathetic passion play on CNN. However, that was not a problem, merely a challenge. He would just take an extended vacation, and this too shall pass.

But that woman, Marceau! Contemptible, Catcher cunt! He warned them not to underestimate the bitch. She had more lives than a charmed cat. There were many reasons that gash had been his finest Catcher: beautiful, fearless, ruthless, heartless, genius. Absolutely stunning in the field, which was why he paid her double than the next best Catcher. Had Bergmann believed in the supernatural, he would also label her sorceress. A living, breathing witch incarnate.

Krieg was after Russell, and Bergmann knew the kraut was relentless, unstoppable. He would, inevitably, catch the lucky meddler and kill him. Then he could unleash the hun on Marceau.

Russell, Youngblood and Winston flew first class, Delta.

The Airedale was allowed to fly with the humans, since Youngblood presented Winston as a service dog. The dog sat at the feet of Russell, who wore sunglasses the entire flight. Russell tried to sleep but rested fitfully. The agent and animal slept like babies.

Pam could never remember such a bitter argument with Clay, but he was emphatic she not accompany him. She finally relented when Youngblood received authorization to accompany Russell "on his own time," without approval from the Secret Service. (Plus compensation from Russell, along with a generous bonus should they get Bergmann.) Her lover admitted he would be preoccupied with her safety, and that could result in a fatal mistake. She had already taken a bullet in Bermuda, so she relented. Winston was not prepared for snow, Pam thought, so she went to a local pet store and bought the animal an extra large sweater in a camouflage pattern. Still too small, she took the garment to a local shop for alterations, modifying the sweater further to fit the large dog.

Russell laughed when he saw Winston dressed in the tailored garment but agreed since the Airedale would be in snowy mountains. "Thanks Pam."

Russell would remove the clothing later when she was not present to protest. Airedales have a natural, double coat of fur and love frigid weather.

Fionna booked the first flight from Savannah that would eventually connect to Zurich.

She had to layover in London, so she took the opportunity to shower and sleep a few hours. Awakening refreshed, Fionna packed the gear and reflected on her current status.

Her career with De Blauwe Organisation had been stellar. From the first assignment with DBO, she was the acknowledged top Catcher in the motley stable of freelance kidnappers. Krieg had immediately known it, then Bergmann, then the various Presenters and other Catchers. Fionna's reputation soon spread in that small circle. Her compensation per Jewel was increased significantly, and bonuses were frequent and large. Every remuneration had been in cash, and she had saved wisely. She converted part of her cash into gold coins, and kept her life savings evenly split between safe deposit boxes in New York City and Brussels, Belgium. She had modest apartments in both cities and had chosen those two locations for homes because of the international amenities, combined with convenient, efficient airport hubs. She traveled frequently, for personal and professional reasons, and LGA and BRU were superb, no-nonsense facilities. She saw no reason to change either domicile, despite the fact that her professional status was currently in limbo and that even more people may, very soon, be hunting her most seriously. Fionna took great pains to keep her personal life separate from her professional one. Disguises, a variety of routes home and other efforts made her quite confident that nobody from DBO knew where she lived. And of course none of the Jewels' families, along with law enforcement groups, knew of her identity, much less her residences. Otherwise, there would have been the big knock at her door. She wasn't concerned with what lay ahead professionally; she was sure to find work. Trafficking in human beings, THB as the law often refers to it, was certainly something to consider. God knows she can do it well. But she was somewhat weary of the drill. Fuck, she would think about the next career on her upcoming vacation, which should start within 48 hours. First, get to the slug Bergmann, kill him quickly and quietly, then vanish. She had it all mapped out. Fionna had met with Henri U. Bergmann only once, after her third Catch. She had stolen twins, flawlessly, and the DBO Chairman personally congratulated her in the boardroom several hours prior to a meeting. A servant had handed her the Catcher's first bonus, then the big cheese told her she had a very bright future with the organisation. Her impression of the man was one of personal disgust but professional admiration. Despite his bland appearance and lacking any morsel of charisma, Fionna admired his mind. He was a very shrewd troll.

Though a challenge to reach, he would be simple to kill, once she got in the same room.

She brushed aside the nagging thought that the meddling female at Vogel's auction, and her male sidekick, may know too much.

Shortly after dawn, snow began falling again as Fionna Marceau began the five hour drive to Bergmann's residence.

The Catcher had obtained a map of the property and studied the terrain. She would park her car a safe distance from the address, proceed on foot through the woods and then climb. She planned to maneuver in the shadows so dressed in black: leather gloves, fur lined snow boots, skin-tight water repelling pants, leather jacket filled with down. The cashmere scarf was wrapped tightly around her neck for warmth, and a ski mask would cover her head and face. She had a compound bow and custom-made back quiver with twelve arrows. Her right front pocket would hold a .45 caliber Glock with sound suppressor and on her belt was a

Swiss knife with serrated edge in a leather case. A bow, bullets, blade, Bergmann. Slip in and out quietly.

As she drove, Fionna's only concern was her final approach to Bergmann's home. She knew it was unique; her only question was could she do it?

The trio arrived in Zurich just after 5:00 a.m. They checked into a local hotel, rested for a few hours, then set off in the rented Volvo, up through the Italian Alps.

Russell was extremely nervous, a rare state. He was away from home, out of America, in the most intelligently operated nation on the continent—if not the world—and he was about to commit some dubious, probably felonious, actions. His uneasiness contrasted with the calm of his companions. Winston loved car travel and new places. Kevin Youngblood had traveled the globe with the Service and knew the ins and outs of airports, customs and law enforcement agencies. At Atlanta's Hartsfield, LaGuardia in New York and Zurich Airport, his 5-star, United States Secret Service badge and much-used passport had sped them through, weapons included. The agent insisted on driving, as he had done so many times in Europe. Russell navigated, using printed directions provided by Youngblood. They should arrive at Bergmann's residence sometime in mid-afternoon. An hour from their destination, Russell wanted reassurance from the agent.

"Kevin, you're comfortable with this?"

Youngblood had great patience. "From the book, and I quote, 'The United States Secret Service can make arrests without warrants for any offense against the United States committed in their presence, or for any felony recognizable under the laws of the United States if they have reasonable grounds to believe that the person to be arrested has committed such felony.' Bergmann certainly qualifies, and I have approval from Mark Sullivan, Director of the Service, for this task. If needed, we can tap the Swiss militia."

Russell took a deep breath. "We're just a few kilometers from chez Bergmann."

Youngblood spotted it first. He stopped the car. "There, look up. That's Piz Bernina, and, it appears, the only home on this face."

Russell got out and trained the high power binoculars. It was Bergmann's home, undoubtedly. The exterior was what Manny had captured in his photos. Frank Lloyd Wright goes Alpine. Magnificent wood and stone, dramatic deck extending over the steep mountain slope and the astonishing, enormous, glass-walled great room. As Russell panned across the drive, snow-covered grounds and then again to the home, it suddenly hit him: the house was a more lavish version of the villain's lair from the Hitchcock film North by Northwest. What a sanctuary, in the perfect country, where money, over all, ensures privacy. Russell nodded to Youngblood.

The agent popped the hood of the Volvo, and Russell raised it. Youngblood placed a large note on the dash, which read OUT OF GAS, BACK SOON. The agent and Winston got out and the three began walking along the side of the highway. At Bergmann's driveway they kept going, twenty yards past, then turned left, up into the woods.

It was probably a third of a mile to the home, and their macro plan was simple: infiltrate, subdue, phone Interpol. Their micro plan included multiple variables. Youngblood's arctic white hunter attire was filled with as many tricks as a magician's coat.

Fortunately, the snow was fresh powder and soft, not icy. Large fir trees with long green arms were beautifully dusted with the clean Alpine snow. They trod silently through the pristine forest. The climb became steeper.

Winston, per command, walked thirty feet ahead, the point man.

Two minutes into the trek, the Airedale froze, leg muscles twitching, the dog's head aimed at ten o'clock. The men looked in that direction and saw, about fifty yards distant, sitting in the snow, his back against a huge tree, their first obstacle: a guard with an Uzi slung over the left shoulder. He wore a smart ski outfit; black on the torso and broad, white stripes on the shoulders, arms and outside the legs…a snow tuxedo. Possibly, the man was one of the B-team security, hence his post so far from the dwelling. The fact was immediately confirmed as he pulled a very long silver flask from his coat, tilted it up and began to drink deeply. This was not his first quaff. The man's cheeks and nose were Rudolph red. Russell pulled out a Viper and held it cocked, as backup, while he watched Youngblood go to work.

The agent used a tree in between to mask his approach. He crouched and moved toward the sentry. From twenty feet away he fired the Taser. A small click, twin barbs flew and the tiny electric fangs bit into the flesh of the man's exposed left neck. His reaction would have been comic had it not been for the mission: he jacked legs straight out and spasmodically tossed the flask high into the air. Youngblood gave an extra jolt from the gun as he approached, then the agent injected chloral hydrate into the stunned guard's wrist. Youngblood' extra safety measure was heavy duty PlastiCuffs. He put two each of the cable ties on the man's wrist and ankles. Russell and Youngblood did not speak. They had verbally rehearsed and would practice silence as long as possible. Russell dragged the man off into the forest, well away from the winding stone driveway. Youngblood snapped off a small fir limb and used it to sweep flat the drag marks in the snow.

One down and no blood, Russell thought. Good so far.

They resumed the trek. A third of a mile is 586 yards, and they had encountered the first guard about 150 yards into the forest, Russell figured. He looked around at the silent forest: a smooth white carpet of clean snow, tall straight fir trees and no sounds except for their footsteps. It seemed almost a crime for these three Americans to soon disrupt the peace, but their quarry up ahead had committed atrocities for years. Russell gritted his teeth and imagined what was to come. The home should be in view any second. Russell swung his arms back and forth to warm up.

Suddenly they were there. The route had put them in a position where two giant firs framed the home of Henri U. Bergmann. Russell had not appreciated the quality and aesthetics of the structure from afar. But now, up close, everything he could see bespoke the finest quality, taste and expense—attributes he would have thought far from the grasp of that squat man he saw on Vogel's ship.

Men and animal got down prone and slowly crawled ahead through the snow a few feet, stopping just inside the shadows.

Thousands of palomino colored fieldstones formed a tremendous, pyramid-like base on the steep side of the house, the stones supporting a huge deck and the glassed great room. The view must be breathtaking. Bergmann's great room and deck must be the focal points of the home. Russell counted four large, stone chimneys. The black brick driveway curved up and around the left side of the home. Garages would be there. Trees had been removed for about 50 yards all around the home. Exposed to sunlight, snow on the treeless perimeter was ankle deep, which would make for easier running. Russell spent all of three seconds studying the structure—he now studied the next obstacles between them and Bergmann.

One guard was positioned on the immense overhanging deck, in the same black and white ski suit uniform, sitting at the end of the long balcony rail. At a picnic table grouping to the left of the house sat two guards drinking coffee. Steam arose from one mug; he had recently been in the home. How many were inside? Russell gave it two minutes. Nothing changed. He whispered, "Kevin, ready?"

"Yes."

"First the picnic table, then the front? You?"

"Copy."

The agent crawled backwards and disappeared into the trees.

The plan was to take it as close to Bergmann as possible, silently. Then play it by ear. Russell reached out and petted Winston. The minutes ticked by. The only sounds were a peaceful wind, here and there chattering squirrels, the occasional bird. Russell looked at his watch. Youngblood had been gone five minutes. What was he doing? The guard on the deck walked inside. Now was a good time to strike. Come on Kevin...

Suddenly, commotion erupted at the picnic area. One of the guards bucked off his chair, in a spasm. The second guard jumped up, instantly had an epileptic fit and then fell.

Youngblood had tased both. The agent ran in a crouch and quickly put PlastiCuffs on the two sentries. He injected both with the chloral hydrate. Then he ran up the drive on the left side of the house.

Russell had to admit, the agent was a pistol; he had not fired his, and three guards were down.

When Youngblood had been out of sight for 90 seconds, Russell began to walk casually toward the back of the home, Winston at his side. He carried a five-foot stick he'd picked up. A hiker with his dog. They would box Bergmann in and then blow the whistle.

As he got closer, Russell saw sliding glass doors in the stone wall underneath the massive deck. Fifty feet from the door, a guard inside saw the man and dog, said something over his shoulder and then jerked open one of the doors.

"Halt! Stop! Private Property!" The guard waved them back with his right hand, his left now grasping the Uzi on his shoulder. Another guard appeared at his side. Both guards stepped out. The second guard cocked his Uzi.

Russell smiled, held up one hand and removed a map from inside his coat. He unfolded the map, reached down and put his thumb across the hilts of two Vipers, keeping the knives hidden from the men. "Down, boy." Winston sat. Russell pretended to study the map and moved forward, slowly.

Inside, muffled but still extremely loud, Youngblood ignited one of the stun grenades.

Fionna had almost completed her climb of the steep side of Bergmann's property, an approach she correctly assumed would be unwatched.

It had been fortunate that Luke was assigned to kill her, as he knew where Bergmann lived. When she had thrashed that information out of him, she soon concluded the smartest way to gain access to the slug's home. The north side of the residence was a sheer rock wall, 250 meters high and would surely be unguarded. Outfitted with rope, pitons, a hammer and vicious determination, she had muscled her way up the rough, jagged wall. It was a Herculean feat, an effort that tore as her arms and shoulders, which only made the Catcher smile. Her appearance should surprise any and all at the top. She looked up at the thick, wooden balcony rail, now just twenty feet above. She no longer needed the pitons, thanks to the large foundation stones of the balcony. Six inches below the balcony rail, she quietly tapped in one long, knifeblade piton, looped the long Kernmantle, nylon rope through the hole and secured it. She untied the rope from her waist, let the long end drop, grasped the wooden rail and pulled her body slowly up. Sixty feet away, at the other end of the deck, a guard with his shoulder weapon, an Uzi, slid open a glass door and went inside.

Fionna slithered over the rail and crawled to the near corner. She knelt behind a massive marble planter which held a ten-foot fir tree. She took the Browning compound bow from her shoulder, notched a broadhead fiberglass arrow and peeked around the base of the planter. A few minutes later, the guard walked out onto the balcony. He took a sip from his coffee mug, rested an elbow on the rail and gazed into the distance. His back was at a three-quarter angle; the man's peripheral vision would not include the marble planter.

Fionna slowly stood up, keeping her eyes on the man and her ears tuned to the home. It was silent. The only sound was a peaceful wind whisper from the slopes of Piz Bernina, the fifth highest Alp. She braced her left hip on the planter and drew back the arrow, only halfway, so the broadhead would not totally exit the torso. The guard raised his mug, and the instant it touched his lips, Fionna released. The tiny twang of the bow was almost simultaneous with the small thunking sound as the spinning, razor-sharp tri-blade pierced the ski jacket. The man's upper body was punched forward slightly, much like someone had jostled him in an elevator. He dropped the mug, the left hand weakly grabbed the deck rail, and his knees began to bend. Fionna was at him in six long, light steps. She looped her right arm around his neck to stifle any shout or groan, then swiftly dragged the dying man back toward the corner. She glanced down at his chest. Half a foot of the arrow protruded from just below the sternum. At the rail, she gripped the fabric at his right thigh and pitched the man over the top, careful to avoid her tethered rope. The body spun a half turn, chunked into the rock cliff, ricocheted out a few feet, crashed into the top of a big fir tree and disappeared.

Fionna returned to the stone planter and looked at the deck. It was empty, save the dropped coffee mug. She saw no blood. The deck was so large that the mug would not stand out. Anyone looking for the guard would initially assume he was elsewhere in the home. After a few moments, she moved across the deck, hugging the fieldstone wall. At the edge of the panoramic glass wall, she knelt, leaned forward and peered inside. Three feet away was the back of a giant leather sofa. She raised her head. Bergmann's massive, opulently furnished great room was brilliantly illuminated from the afternoon sun. The ceiling was at least forty feet high, made of broad cedar beams. Oriental rugs, white leather sofas and brown wing chairs, a black telescope on tripod at the far glass wall. No humans. At the far end of the room, in what appeared to be a portion of an adjoining kitchen, a figure walked by the arched doorway. The fleeting silhouette looked too tall to be Bergmann. Another guard? How many more inside?

Suddenly, an explosion in the home shook the glass and deck. Was it the Royal Marines? Fionna notched the compound bow. From below a man shouted in German.

When the stun grenade blew, the two guards ducked their heads and looked back at the home. Russell gripped a Viper by the handle and hurled the stainless steel blade in a half spin. He could hit a dollar bill at twice the distance, and this time the knife flew true: the half-pound, bevel blade shot through the cold air at 62 miles per hour, 90 feet per second. The butt of the blade hit the first guard in his left temple, as intended, and the man crumpled. Russell rushed the second guard as he yelled, "Heel!" Winston bolted ahead, kicking up snow. The Airedale was a blur as he leapt; the guard turned and had begun to raise the Uzi when Winston hit him in the chest. The man fell back on the concrete porch apron, his head popping the floor once. Winston tore the Uzi from his grip, flung it aside and locked powerful jaws on the man's right boot. The dog violently ground the man's ankle, jerking the entire leg back and forth. The guard bellowed and tried to grab the dog's head with his left hand. He immediately gave up, pulled a pistol from his belt and snapped back the slide. Russell was on him and lashed out with his right foot. The steel tipped Timberland boot hit the man under the chin, smashing the hyoid bone and ruining several teeth. The man collapsed, unconscious and perhaps dead. "Winston, stop." The dog released, stood next to the body and looked at Russell. He ran to the sliding glass door and opened it as a second stun grenade exploded, from somewhere upstairs.

Holding a Viper at waist level, Russell quickly began to go through the downstairs floor. In a few seconds, he heard the drumming of feet above. He ran to the spiral, carpeted stairway and was halfway up when he met two more guards racing down, panicked. As the first man crashed into him, Russell grabbed the front of his coat and yanked him left, into the rail, and kicked back. They rolled down the bottom steps and onto the floor. Both sprang up, and before the taller, bigger guard could punch, Russell struck up, fast, with the Viper, into the man's diaphragm. The shallow stab is a commando tactic for taking out a sentry, and the man at once went slack, like a marionette with cut strings, and puddled on the floor. The second guard, still descending the stairs, but now at a controlled walk, lifted his Uzi and cocked it. Russell had no choice and acted instantly: he snapped an underhand toss, and the Viper bit into the socket below his Adam's apple, sinking to the hilt. The man fell, crashed onto the steps and rail, then tumbled in a ragged, clanging roll. His trigger finger must have contracted and froze—the Uzi began to chatter and blaze, firing everywhere. It blew chunks of carpet from the stairs, sprayed a line of holes on the closest wall and kept going. Russell sprang aside, but not before one of the .22 long rifle slugs stung his right calf. The guard ended his tumble at the base of the stairs, the Uzi empty and silent.

Russell leaned against a sofa and snapped up the pants leg. The bullet had entered and exited muscle in the largest part of the calf, mercifully missing the tibia and fibula. Both holes appeared the same size and wept a small trickle of crimson.

He retrieved his Viper from the corpse, wiped the blade on the body's jacket and moved cautiously up the stairs, Winston close behind. The dead man had meant to kill. The hell with being humane! He hefted the Viper in his right hand and pulled another from the back sheath with his left.

Near the top of the stairs, he could smell burnt magnesium from the grenades. The head and back of a man was slowly revealed—Russell tip-toed and saw it was a guard. The man was in a T-stance, lifting another damn Uzi to his cheek, aiming. Russell could not see the man's target but assumed it was Youngblood and instantly struck: the coat looked unusually thick so the knife bit into the back of the left knee.

"Ahhcchh!" the man yelled and turned 90-degrees clockwise, just as Russell's second Viper sank into the right side of his neck. The man folded onto the floor. Russell put a boot on the man's head, withdrew the knife and moved right, hugging the wall, Winston a silent shadow. He gritted his teeth and wiggled the injured leg, which was holding up extremely well. Russell was furious. He breathed deeply, containing the fury, focusing it. He tightly gripped both Vipers, his fingers itching. These fucking child merchants! Insolent, impudent, arrogant bastards! By God he would kill them all and then get his hands on Bergmann! He would beat the living shit…

"Russell!" Youngblood was close. "Russell, are you…"

"In here." Russell moved down behind a sofa and raised a Viper. A guard could have a gun to the agent's head, leading him…

Kevin Youngblood walked into the room, moving slowly. His right arm hung straight down, the hand wet, crimson and dripping. He held the pistol in his left. The agent's face was very pale and covered with sweat. He saw Russell and then leaned against a marble column. He managed a smile. "I think you got the last one. I pegged two, in the foyer. I think that's all. That last one, Jesus, he had the drop on me. Didn't see him. Thanks." Youngblood dropped the pistol, gripped his shoulder and closed his eyes.

Russell gently lifted Youngblood's right arm.

"I'm OK. It's muscle and nerve. Mostly shock."

Russell led the agent to the sofa and helped him sit down. "Kevin…Bergmann—did you shoot…?"

"No. Got two sentries. No sign of Bergmann. He's probably in the house, hiding. Maybe ready to pounce."

Russell doubted the latter. Bergmann was a thinker, a schemer. Not a fighter. They should probably call the Swiss authorities and let them sort it out. Russell posed the question to Youngblood.

"Yes, but let's report via the Service. We have field offices in Germany and Italy…maybe they'll coordinate. I'll contact Washington, the Director." Youngblood used his good hand to fish a cell phone from inside the snow jacket and began tapping numbers.

Russell petted Winston. "I'm going to fast-comb the house. C'mon boy."

They started in the foyer. Russell commanded, "Search," and the Airedale switched to bloodhound mode. He began sniffing anything and everything, beginning with the two dead guards near the front door that Youngblood had shot. Winston moved quickly, snuffing everything, briefly. If there were anything else alive in the structure, the dog would detect it and point. Within ten minutes, they had covered all rooms on the three levels. Nothing. Had the chicken flown the coop? Certainly this was the right place; the exterior matched the earlier photos, and though there were no visible photographs, the initials "**HB** " adorned a silk bathrobe, humidor, luggage and several other items.

Russell returned to Youngblood, whose complexion had improved a level. "The Director's office is unleashed. Swiss Police and Interpol have been contacted. Top emergency. Blue lights should be here within 20, including a med team. Two agents from the Rome Secret Service office are hopping aboard a military jet, ETA four hours. Those are the prime members of the cavalry. Is the house clean? Any sign of Bergmann?"

471

"There's no Bergmann, and no other live human in this mansion. Perhaps he wasn't here when we approached, but I doubt that, based on the resistance…"

Winston had bolted to a window near the deck, assumed the classic point stance and stood frozen, except for one haunch that trembled slightly. Russell went to the window and immediately saw the discouraging sight: emerging from the forest was a cadre of the uniformed guards, each staggered a dozen feet, successively, behind the leader. They were clones of the others. Same attire, all men, all with Uzis. There must be a barracks or cabin nearby, and this unit was just now responding to the skirmish. Russell counted six, moving unhurriedly, their heads and weapons scanning the property.

Youngblood joined Russell, took one look and said, "Let's see how they break up, then defend accordingly."

Russell, very tired, nodded. He was running out of steam, physically and emotionally. Then both men saw something abnormal: the last guard, number six, just a few feet out of the forest, dropped to his knees, bowed his head and joined hands in front of his chest…praying?

Hans Mueller was permanent tail man on forest patrol, and today was no different, except this was no drill. As he emerged from the trees, he began to study his employer's chateau when he was violently kicked from behind. He looked down, slowly. Half a foot of the 20-inch arrow was visible standing out of his midsection. The colors were striking: dove gray shaft and a steady flow of crimson blood coursing off the end of the razor-honed, tri-blade tip. He dropped to his knees, slowly reached for the arrow, managed to put his hands on it...then he closed his eyes, blacked out and fell forward in the shallow snow.

Youngblood whispered, "Hunting arrow, from behind. What in the hell?"

Before Russell could reply, the fifth man in the group, now last, put both hands out, carefully sat down, then keeled over on his right, the arrow shaft with yellow feathers in the center of the corpse's back.

The four guards were now halfway between the forest and Bergmann's home. They all continued to press forward, cautiously. Suddenly, something made the last man halt and slowly turn around. A brief silver flash in the sun, and the third broadhead struck its target, the man's chest. He, too, sat down, for a second, then flopped forward.

Russell was entranced. Brilliant strategy, and superb shooting. Just picking them off from behind, like strolling turkeys. Surely this could not go on?

As if to answer him, a black figure swiftly emerged from the forest. The man held a compound bow out front, aimed, arrow notched and string fully drawn. He walked at top speed, just this side of a trot. He stepped over the first body, then around the second. The third man turned his head, then spun his body, aimed the Uzi and the archer nailed him in the neck. Arterial spray was instantaneous,

473

pulsing. His spasms in the snow alerted the remaining three men. They also spun around, but the archer stood poised, ready: his left foot was on the chest of the new kill, the body on its back, arterial spurts growing weaker.

Momentarily shocked, the three guards did not move. The archer yelled something in German. Two of the guards raised their arms. The other guard put hands on his hips and began yelling back at the archer. He was shot in the chest, and as he slowly turned, the archer put a second arrow in the back of his skull. The fourth guard folded in the snow.

Instantly re-notched, the archer jerked left and right with the drawn bow. The two guards carefully tossed aside the Uzis. They put hands on their heads, simultaneously, evidently following an order. For half a minute, the figures remained basically still. Russell assumed they were talking. If there was a conversation, it abruptly ended: the archer shot both in the chest, in about two seconds. They sank and fell, one two, the second atop the first. The archer shouldered his bow and began to walk toward the deck side of the home.

Russell and Youngblood were stunned, both trying to fathom what they had just seen. It was almost as if the thing had been a violent video game, something so wild and preposterous that it could not happen in real life. Except that it just had. The extraordinary archer looked like he knew precisely where he was going.

"Let's cover the stairs," Youngblood said, "and see where he appears. We've got ten minutes until backup."

Russell nodded and took a position behind a marble column. Youngblood crouched behind a sofa. Both kept their eyes glued on the top of the circular stairs, where the archer should appear. Except he did not show. A good five minutes ticked by. Nothing. Youngblood stood and moved to the stairs. Russell followed, covering the agent's back. Youngblood peeked over the rail. Russell, ten feet behind, began to wiggle the Viper in his right hand. He was nervous, anxious and, above all, very curious.

Suddenly, they heard a man whistle from behind.

Russell jerked around, and his heart sank. In a crouch, he stood up and tossed the Viper onto the closest sofa. Youngblood did the same with his Sig Sauer.

Russell did not believe in ghosts, but it seemed he was looking at one. The archer was cloaked head to toe in black, with a ski mask covering hair and face. The compound bow—notched, drawn and aimed at a space between the two men—was painted camouflage. Where the eyes should have been on the ski mask were black, apple sized mesh circles. The man was six feet tall, and Russell immediately downgraded the magical phantom to mere mortal, albeit a very talented one: twenty feet to the left of the archer, a section of stones on the raised hearth fireplace hung open. It was a hidden door. Silent hinges. Smart, secret and sinister; in keeping with the home's owner.

475

"Who are you?" Russell asked.

"Pull up those pants. Let me see your ankles. If you are stupid, you die."

A woman! Youngblood looked at Russell, who nodded for the agent to comply. They raised their cuffs. Youngblood had a small Glock in an ankle holster. He removed the pistol, with thumb and forefinger, and tossed it onto the sofa.

Satisfied there were no other weapons, Fionna raised the bow, keeping aim, and used her bowstring hand to pull off the ski mask. She lowered the bow to chest level.

"Christ, what a circus! While you were playing Cowboys and Indians, you let the prey drive out of here, in his silent electric car! A fucking Tesla roadster! The chickenshit ran and left impotent servants to throw rocks at us. Isn't that why we are all here, to get that pig Bergmann?"

Russell was speechless. She had medium long, red hair, pulled back and bound in a tight ponytail to the side and back, at five o'clock. She was very beautiful. Perspiring. A sizeable cut was on her left cheek, an inch from the corner of her mouth. Probably a stray bullet. .22 long rifle slugs ricochet like hell. "My name is Fionna."

"But who, what are you?" Youngblood asked. It suddenly clicked for Russell. She was the fake cop. Lisa. Timmy. Nudus Bleu. "What do you do, Fionna?"

Youngblood continued. "Why are you here? Are you from DBO?

Fionna Marceau shifted her weight from foot to foot. The compound bow did not waver. "DBO. Pseudo. I'm freelance. I am, or, rather was, a Catcher for De Blauwe Organisation. But now, thanks to you Clayton Russell, I am going to change professions, but not until I finish some business. What do you Americans say? Tie up some loose ends? Bergmann. The biggest loose end."

Russell stared at her and wondered what to do next.

Fionna smiled, showing brilliant white teeth. Russell thought her amazingly beautiful. He noted how she held the bow and arrow: *She's right-handed. Move to my left, her aim will be more difficult.* He slid one pace to his left. The woman's bow instantly corrected aim, keeping the arrow centered on his torso.

"Don't move, either of you. Are you stupid? I could have killed both of you and Lassie, too, if I had wanted."

Russell looked at the agent. Blood was dripping off his hand, dappling the floor. The wound must have expanded. Russell's leg ached, but he could move. It immediately occurred to him that Winston was absent. Where in the hell? Then he saw the Airedale, across the room, frozen in a point, camouflaged next to a wing chair that was about the same color as the dog's brown fur on his head, chest and legs.

Winston stared at his master's face, waiting for a command. Russell could say, "Heel," and the animal would be on the woman in an instant. Fast enough to avoid the arrow? Maybe. Maybe not. Surely fast enough for Russell to pull a Viper from behind his neck, in the back sheath under his coat, and put it into the Catcher.

Risk Winston and kill her?

She may miss. He would not. She said she could have killed them both, along with Winston. She certainly could have, yet this strange woman had refrained.

Russell crooked his right forefinger down, and Winston immediately sat.

Fionna spat a bloody phlegm boll onto the Oriental rug. "Consider this act of saving your life a favor; a favor that I intend to collect upon, sometime when convenient, in the future."

She walked backwards toward the panoramic glass wall. Without looking, bow still trained on them, she extended her right leg and slid open one of the doors. She continued to walk backwards, out onto the deck, and across it, out of sight.

Youngblood, weak, stiffly walked towards the sofa and weapons.

Russell went outside. The deck was empty.

He limped slightly on his way to the steep side of the deck. The sting in his calf had started to bite. Soon, the bite would turn into chewing. He reached the rail and looked over.

Already a hundred feet distant, or more, Fionna slid down the nylon rope, rappelling off the sheer, jagged rock cliff. Her energy was astounding, barely feasible, in light of what she had done today.

Youngblood appeared at his side, gazed down and used both hands to aim the Sig Sauer. The agent zeroed in on the top of her head. He closed one eye and began to squeeze the trigger. Russell put a hand on the pistol and gently pushed it aside.

When she reached the bottom of the cliff, the Catcher looked up at them. Russell lifted his left hand and kept it raised.

Fionna Marceau nodded, once.

Then she turned, adjusted the bow on her shoulder and vanished into the forest.

Made in the USA
Charleston, SC
27 March 2014